THIS IS WHERE *the* FUTURE BLEEDS

MIKE BROOKS

TITAN BOOKS

This is Where the Future Bleeds
Print edition ISBN: 9781835417614
E-book edition ISBN: 9781835417621

Published by Titan Books
A division of Titan Publishing Group Ltd
144 Southwark Street, London SE1 0UP
www.titanbooks.com

First edition: June 2026
10 9 8 7 6 5 4 3 2 1

A CIP catalogue record for this title is available from the British Library.

EU RP (For authorities only)
eucomply OÜ, Pärnu mnt. 139b-14, 11317 Tallinn, Estonia
hello@eucompliancepartner.com, +3375690241

Designed and typeset in Goudy Oldstyle by Richard Mason.

Printed and bound in Great Britain by CPI Group (UK) Ltd, Croydon, CR0 4YY.

*This book is for anyone who's ever felt like they're no good
at being a person. Derna knows how you feel.*

Maybe don't stab as many people as her, though.

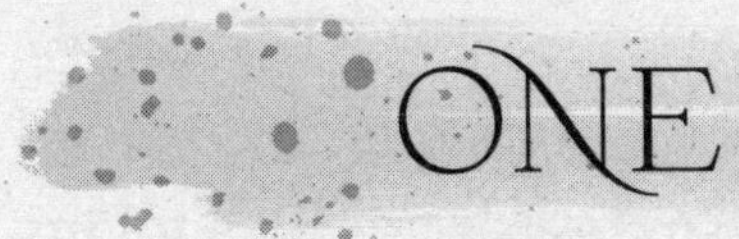

ONE

This is where the future bleeds.

On the high moors, the sky is frozen in time. It is not the flat black of the deepest night, but holds the faintest tint of colour if you look at it sideways. It is a permanent pre-dawn, the first hint that the sun has not been swallowed forever, and that light greater than those of the stationary, non-twinkling stars may soon return. That is a lie, because the sun no longer kisses these moors. The heather flowers may be purple in truth, but in this place they are always a deep grey, and the sandy soil nothing but pale patches. A particularly sane god tried to kill the future here, with a star forged from the embers of a dying sword.

Not even a god can kill the future, but it can be wounded. So it bleeds, and what used to flow into the world invisibly and naturally now crystallises out of nothing, forming like pearls or amber: a protective response to an intrusion or attack. They are futures; individual destinies, which would once have either sought out their intended subject or fallen by the dictates of chance, depending on which god, if any, you believe. Now they lie here and there under a frozen sky, in the deeper darkness beneath the stems of the colourless heather.

The high moors are a coldly beautiful place, and utterly silent, for even the wind is—

'Kitt?'

Even the wind is froz—

'Kitt!'

And utterly silent, for—

'KITT, IT'S COMING!'

For fuck's sake.

People cannot live here, because people cannot live where time does not flow, but people rarely pay attention to what they can and cannot do. Where common sense or even reality itself throws up obstacles, people will find solutions through ingenuity and sheer bloody-mindedness. In a world where the future is wounded, time is a little more… *malleable*. A good chronomancer can do amazing things, so long as you can afford their price. A bubble of portable time for you to use when the need arises – such as when you have ventured into the high moors north of Mereport – is certainly within the realms of possibility. Although of course, you do need to be sure that you have engaged a *good* chronomancer, since those frozen in time can rarely come back to demand a refund.

Overall, braving the timeless spaces of the high moors should really be more trouble than it's worth, but it can be worth a great deal. There is always a market for destinies, and they are free for the taking up here, assuming you can get around the time problem.

And the slydewasps.

Kitt Carver held the two thin rods of moonstruck iron out in front of her again, arms bent at the elbows, and tried to clear her thoughts. This was not an easy thing to do, even for a five-year veteran of the moors like her, mainly because one of her crew was already screaming his head off. The prospect of impending death had a tendency to concentrate the mind, but usually on the death itself rather than anything useful.

Breathe in. Breathe out. *Focus.* Don't look up. Don't try

to listen, because slydewasps didn't make any noise, despite their immense size. They *should* make noise; there should be a thundering, their wings should tear the air up and leave it shredded, but they were silent all the same. No one knew exactly what sense they used to home in on their prey, but shouting didn't seem to make them find you any faster. It just put your diviner off.

Focus.

Kitt said a quick prayer; not to a god she believed in, or indeed to any god in particular. It was just a prayer, because the structure of syllables helped her mind to get a grip on things, and she was far too practical to ignore a decent tool once she'd found it.

There. The rods began to twitch again, and she had the trail once more. She stepped forward cautiously, fighting the urge to rush. Moonstruck iron was sensitive, which made excellent divining tools for those with a gift like hers, but it was easy to stumble on a dark moor where the deep shadows of the heather hid hazards as effectively as a politician's smile.

Three steps forward. One to the right as the iron started to swing in her hands, a subtle shift of pressure on her skin. Then the rods split, moving apart from each other.

'Godsdamn it!' Kitt spat. 'Solly! Rods out, now! Help me get a bearing!'

Solly Doonam pulled his own rods of moonstruck iron from their sheath on his thigh, although Kitt could practically smell the sweat coming off him. Solly was a good diviner, but he got shaken easily, which effectively bumped him back down to mediocre when there was any pressure involved.

'C'mon, boss, you can do this,' Mizzik said nervously, from just above and behind Kitt's left shoulder. Mizzik was often nervous, but then the world was exponentially more dangerous for wellyn, who were approximately two feet tall, winged, and blue: a vivid cobalt, in Mizzik's case. His nervousness was an improvement on usual. Normally, Mizzik would already be wanting to abandon the job and flee.

Kitt tried to put Mizzik out of her mind. The problem was not that the pull was weak. If anything, it was too strong, and swamping her. She was half-tempted to abandon her moonstrikers altogether and go hunting by hand, but there was a reason skilled diviners could make a good living from the high moors. There were plenty of fortunes up here, to be sure, but there were many more stems of heather, thick and close-set, and almost malicious in the way they obscured the ground beneath.

Solly's moonstrikers were tuned in now, and were swaying back and forth. Kitt retuned herself, and they both started to move haltingly, converging on the same patch of ground from different directions. The slydewasp was still coming, but crews that ran as soon as things got dangerous might as well not venture up onto the moors at all. It was all about knowing how fine to cut it.

'KI—'

That half-scream was abruptly truncated. Kitt didn't look around. Chase Farson was a newbie, fresh out of the poorholes down Tannock's Lane in Mereport, desperate enough for coin that he signed up to a trip onto the high moors in search of a fortune, in more ways than one. He knew the risks. Well, he didn't, but he'd had them explained to him, and it wasn't Kitt's fault if he was unable to square the equation between 'high mortality rates' and 'Chase Farson'. If the work was safe, it wouldn't pay so well.

The time to cut and run despite the potential rewards was fast approaching, but Kitt was so close now, *so* close, she could practically taste that destiny…

'Boss?' Solly asked urgently.

'Hold still!' Kitt snapped. He stopped moving and she pressed on, triangulating between her own moonstrikers and the direction of his, until she finally felt an insistent tug downwards. *Now* she crouched, fingers groping frantically through the woody stems, searching with touch when sight would be useless. Her skin scraped across scratchy bark, and skimmed over soft earth.

Then her fingertips brushed something small, and cold, and hard. The slydewasp was close, so there was no time for reverent gazing at her treasure, no time to hold it up in front of her eyes and marvel at its strange, asymmetric perfection while the rest of her crew looked on in awe.

Kitt did it anyway.

It was a small, irregularly shaped lump of colourless… something. The future, Kitt supposed. It looked a bit like rock, it looked a bit like metal, it looked a bit like water, if water was somehow solid without being ice. It was weightier than it looked, and smaller than it felt. Now, wakened by the life of Kitt's fingers, it began to glow softly: a warm light, the colour of honey, and utterly alien to this landscape. Kitt was no soothsayer, to caress a destiny between her hands and get a read on the nature of it, but she could feel the not-heat of it on her skin, and she knew it was a big one. This was the one they'd come to find: this was the one the Swallowmage had seen in her vision, falling from the sky like a single flake of particularly heavy snow.

Even when entranced by the destiny's strange, heavy beauty, Kitt didn't completely lose her sense of her surroundings. She studied her find for two breaths, eyes locked on its amber glow, then stuffed it into her belt pouch and straightened up. A big score was useless if they got eaten by the wasps.

'Mizzik!' she snapped. The wellyn's eyes went white for a moment while he looked through time. It was a strange ability, at least to Kitt, but it was crucial up here. From the vantage point of the timeless lands, the rest of the world was frozen too, so you couldn't see what was waiting for you when you left. Mizzik could find a way down that avoided unpleasant surprises.

It was always the way. Some people made a living by working hard, and others made a living by hanging around to take the proceeds off them. Pirates, bandits, landlords; call them what you would, the outcome was the same.

'That way!' Mizzik yelped, pointing as his eyes shivered back into normality. He flapped away, leathery wings beating frantically, his job done. Mizzik might have been able to see through time, but he couldn't see the future, and he didn't want to play 'dodge the slydewasp'.

No one wanted to play 'dodge the slydewasp'.

'Go!' Kitt yelled. She took off after Mizzik, sprinting as best she could across the moorland, and the rest of her crew went with her. Aside from Solly, there was the muscle: Gallows Jayne, the Hamley brothers – Dick Hamley and Definitely Human Dirk Hamley, whose nickname tended to prompt questions already answered by his nickname – and Falzine Halfshade, who always walked in shadow no matter how bright the lights were, which was what happened when you tangled with a draksnipe and were lucky enough to live. Those four didn't do anything up on the moors, unless another crew started a fight beneath the frozen sky, which would be reckless indeed, because it was all too easy for a chronocharm to be damaged in a scuffle, and then you were a living statue. There were a few such unfortunates dotted here and there across the moors, victims of violence or shoddy chronomancy, but the muscle were mainly there to protect the crew's score from anyone waiting below.

Finally, there were the spotters: Tamyll Nevers, Pigtail Vem – the source of whose name rested at the base of his spine, not at the back of his bald head – and Sorra Marsh, all of whom were old hands, and either lucky or skilled enough to avoid death so far. The two remaining newbies were Olukan… something, and… well, quite frankly, Kitt couldn't remember the other girl's name right now. Gallows had hired them both. If they made it off the moor alive and wanted to come back for a second run, she'd make the effort.

A scream behind her, abruptly truncated, as the slydewasp

claimed another victim. Learning the mystery girl's name wasn't going to be an issue after all.

Kitt cut right, heading for a narrow clough carved by water long ago, back when rain still fell on these moors, which stood out as a slightly darker rent in the landscape. Altitude was the key: she had to get *lower*, back to where time flowed more naturally and the sun illuminated the land, and – most importantly – where the slydewasps didn't follow. They were creatures of frozen time, predators that hunted in the gaps between seconds, and they couldn't survive away from the moors. Kitt had never been cornered by one before, and she had no intention of starting now. She pushed herself harder, each footfall a desperate, fleeting gamble as she trusted to her balance and her instincts against the wiles of the heather and the uneven ground beneath it.

No one could gamble and win forever. Kitt's left foot came down and kept going down, finding a hollow in the ground that she never saw. The impact jarred her hip and threw her stride off, her right foot tangled on something, and she faceplanted into the foliage. It was a relatively soft and springy landing, as such tumbles go, but it slowed her drastically, perhaps fatally. She pushed herself up again, spitting out tiny leaves and curses in equal measure.

The slydewasp shimmered out of the frozen seconds and descended in front of her. Its massive, segmented, blue-and-black striped body sizzled slightly as the ooze it excreted to allow it to slither between the moments was eaten away by temporal friction. There was no way something that big should stay airborne, let alone hover in place as it did, but slydewasps paid as little attention to gravity and air resistance as they did to time.

It was the first time Kitt had seen one up close. The head bulged with muscle, sufficient to power the two sets of serrated jaws which snagged prey and stuffed it, still quivering, down the thing's throat. Its sting was short and rapier-thin compared to its abdomen, but easily long enough to pierce Kitt's body and reach her heart, and still smeared in blood from its last victim. It had no eyes, but the twitching antennae were clearly sufficient for it to locate prey. After all, it had located her.

Kitt was suddenly aware of the chronocharm around her neck. If she ripped it off then, to the best of her knowledge, the slydewasp would ignore her. She would become another statue on the high moors, forever frozen unless one of her crew returned with more time to free her. Except they were all running for the moor edge, and they wouldn't stop to see what happened to her, any more than she would stop for them. They would probably assume she got eaten, and curse her name for taking the destiny down with her.

The destiny.

What if Kitt claimed it as her own? Even she could tell it was something that would shake the world, and potentially worth a fortune. All the religions were in the market for destinies to feed to their gods and avatars, although they tended to use middlemen rather than sully themselves by dealing directly with the moorhands. Then there were the rich families who wanted glory for their children, not to mention the royals seeking to ensure that destinies of ruling stayed firmly where they belonged, thank you *very* much. If Kitt claimed the destiny, surely that meant the slydewasp *couldn't* eat her?

But reading the details of a destiny was a fine art, and Kitt had no idea what this one was. Cautious moorhands sold their destinies on to brokers cheap, before they were read, and let the buyers gamble on what they bought for a bargain price. A great destiny did not mean a *good* destiny, and Kitt had no desire to lead armies in conquest, reddening her hands with the blood of thousands, or gain martyrdom that led to the overthrow of a nation. That could very well be what was in her grasp right now, and it was possibly better to let the slydewasp eat its fill than take the chance of ending up as some power-drunk overlord.

Besides, destinies weren't fireproof, as the saying went. They might give you an edge in staying alive, but they wouldn't do all the work for you. Thammeus Scalebane famously paid a small fortune for a twice-verified dragon-slaying fortune, only to find out – briefly – that he was merely a choking hazard.

The slydewasp drew back its sting. Kitt's indecision melted into desperate adrenaline, and she threw herself to one side into the heather as the creature thrust its abdomen towards her. The displaced air carried with it the salty smell of its last victim's blood and the acrid stink of the venom itself. The slydewasp swung around, wings beating frantically; a chitinous leg brushed over Kitt's back, but it failed to grasp her as she scrambled away.

This wasn't going to work. She couldn't just flee, not unless she wanted to feel the slydewasp's sting in her spine as it pounced on her from behind, but she hardly had the capacity to fight the thing and kill it. Nor could she dodge it from here to the moor's edge. She had options, true enough, they just all *sucked*.

By rights, Kitt should have drawn her short sword as she turned: maybe tried to fence with the beast's sting, parry it, even cut it off; slice at its grasping legs, hack through the chitin, at least make it think there were easier meals elsewhere. That would be the sensible thing to do.

Instead, she found herself slipping one of her rods of moonstruck iron into her hands. It wasn't even the length of her forearm, and slenderer than her smallest finger. Not a weapon, by any stretch of the imagination. Nonetheless, that was what she had, and that was what she threw at the slydewasp's head.

The wasp's jaws, wide open, easily accommodated the rod as it sailed between them. However, when the iron hit the back of its throat, the massive predator came to a halt in midair and started making distressed wheezing noises, its mandibles opening and closing futilely. The rod had lodged somewhere in its gullet; not enough to choke or kill the beast, but sufficient to distract it.

Kitt ran for the clough. Never look a gift miracle in the mouth.

Sometimes, when coming down off the moors, it was hard to tell at exactly what point time started to behave more normally again. Warning posts were erected centuries ago to make sure people didn't stray unknowingly into endless stillness, but they were old and sparse now. If you were returning from on high at night, there might not be a sufficient change in the light levels to make it obvious. You had to rely on more subtle clues, like the sound of wind, the chitter or chirrup of a bird disturbed by your passing, or the fact that the stars were suddenly in a different position.

Sometimes, of course, you emerged into blustery afternoon sunshine and caught a wet leaf in the eye, which was what happened to Kitt. She stumbled slightly and swore again, but there was no real force behind it.

She scrambled down the clough, her feet skidding on loose pebbles, until the sides of the little ravine became less pronounced. Then she clambered up out of it, pushing stems of bracken aside, and looked around for the rest of her crew. They had made it out – most of them, anyway – and were now picking their way down the steep ground, finding purchase for their boots in the little runnels where water flowed when it rained, or where generations of small animals had criss-crossed the slope. Kitt hurried towards them, absent-mindedly patting her belt pouch to make sure the destiny was still there. They wouldn't make it back to Mereport before nightfall, judging by the sun, but once there it would be a case of hauling Sulian the Swallowmage out of whatever tavern in which she was numbing her brain this time and getting her to verify that this was *the* future, the one about which she'd babbled broken-rhyme poetry on the mezzanine of the Golden Anchor, before spinning around three times and vomiting. That last part might have been part of the foretelling, or just a reaction to how much alcohol the Swallowmage had consumed prior: the sparkling threads of fate burned strange and painful pathways through the mind, and the afflicted tried many methods of dampening the sensation.

Kitt skirted a lumpy gorse bush and headed for Gallows Jayne, but paused between one step and the next. Did that gorse bush look a bit… odd?

Time was a strange thing, even here. Kitt's mind snagged on the sensation that something was wrong and clung to it, exploring the uneasy feeling and spreading it through her body like sewer water through her veins, all in the space between one breath and the next. However, her reactions occurred at nowhere near the same speed, so despite the fact that every part of herself was already tensed and prickling, she wasn't able to actually *do* anything before the concealing spell dropped away. A dozen figures at least, all rising into view from where they had been crouching or laying with bits of undergrowth affixed. The camouflage would be very unlikely to deceive on its own, but it provided just enough to anchor a spell which led the eye to believe it saw nothing out of place.

Jayne's hand went to her axe, but it was a useless reflex. Kitt's party had four professional fighters, and good ones at that, which would be enough to warn off other crews or desperate bandits on the road between here and Mereport. They couldn't take a dozen mercenaries, which was surely what these were. Kitt turned and found that the gorse bush was in fact a tall, stern-faced man aiming a wrist-mounted spine thrower at her face. The branches of his disguise should have made him look ridiculous, but instead they simply concentrated the mind on how unlikely it was that a man who had spent hours pretending to be a bush would be willing to let all that effort and discomfort be for nothing.

But how had they even known where to hide? A hideous suspicion crystallised in Kitt's chest, and she turned her head.

'*Mizzik?*'

The wellyn cringed away from her, despite already being well out of her reach, and able to fly to boot; as good an admission of guilt as if he'd thrown himself to the ground begging her forgiveness. He fluttered a bit higher before any of the others could take their anger or frustration out on him, and Kitt tasted bile in her throat. You do everything right, you hire someone to get you down off the moors away from where anyone might be waiting in ambush, and the little shit leads you right into one when you've just managed to claim your biggest payday in years?

'Don't blame him, Kitt,' a voice said, interrupting her thoughts of rage and revenge. 'Not too much, anyway. I threatened him.'

Kitt swallowed. She knew that voice.

'Hello, Derna.'

Two Tongue Derna Towbright sauntered into view from behind one of her hirelings – probably the gutter-mage who'd cast the concealment spell, judging by his lack of notable weapons and the way Derna patted him on the shoulder in a congratulatory manner, but Kitt wasn't looking at him.

Two Tongue Derna was Queen of the Streets and the Duchess of Death; pretty like a knife was pretty, in that she was aesthetically pleasing and seemed perfectly formed for her place in the world, but you wouldn't want her approaching your face at high speed. Derna had made her reputation as a street duellist in Mereport, if you stretched the word 'reputation' upwards, downwards, and sideways to accommodate her. She was a legend in other people's lifetimes, often involving them coming to an abrupt end.

She poked the two halves of her tongue out at Kitt, playfully. She'd split it with a knife for a bet when she was thirteen, which was coincidentally the moment Kitt learned never to make a bet with Derna. She always found a way to win, *always*, regardless of the cost or consequences.

'You don't tend to follow through on threats like that,' Kitt said, trying to keep her tone light. The bile hadn't gone, its nature had just changed slightly. Being ambushed by heavily armed strangers? Terrifying, but always a risk. Being ambushed by Derna? Who in all the planes of the world knew how *that* was going to go? Derna had saved Kitt's life before. She'd also endangered it, many times.

'No one's ever given me cause to,' Derna replied cheerily. 'Can't think why.'

Her warm, dark brown eyes were the same colour as her skin, and unblinkingly steady. Kitt couldn't find it in herself to hate Mizzik for what he'd done. Two Tongue Derna might have harmed him if Mizzik hadn't done what she wanted, or she might not, but no one, including – in Kitt's very private opinion – Derna herself, knew which way that would go until the moment in question.

'Hand it over, please,' Derna said. It actually sounded like a request. 'And don't pretend you didn't find anything. You weren't the only one who heard the Swallowmage, but you *were* the only diviner anyone saw within earshot. I knew you'd be up here as soon as you could gather your crew, and I know you're too good and too bloody stubborn not to succeed. It's why I like you.'

Kitt's stomach twisted. Derna didn't bother with flattery, she just said what was on her mind.

'Is that the only reason you like me?' she asked, shifting her weight onto one hip and raising an eyebrow.

'Nope.' Derna grinned at her. 'But I really do want that destiny, Kitt, so I'd suggest you give it to me.'

'What the hell use do you have for it?' Kitt demanded. 'You've got money. You'd have power and influence, if you ever paid attention to anything for long enough to use them.'

Something ugly lurked in the back of Kitt's mind. Two

Tongue Derna had carved – quite literally – a space out for herself in the world. The thought of what she might do if she got her hands on a destiny, a powerful destiny like this one… A destiny was not completely immutable: it took energy and shape from the person who held it. If person and destiny were poor fits for each other then you got unlikely heroes, or people raised up far beyond their ability to function. If they were compatible, you got people who said things like 'This is what I was born to do'; although of course, plenty of people also said that about themselves even when it was not at all true.

Derna was great already, in her own special, sharp way. It was hard to imagine a great destiny at which she would not excel, but it was also hard to imagine a way in which that greatness would manifest that would not involve a lot of blood.

'Come on, Kitt,' Derna said. 'It's me. You can trust *me*.'

Kitt sighed. Was it better to be complicit in changing the fortune of the world, potentially for the worse, or was it better to get yourself and your crew killed and have the world changed anyway when a mercenary pulled the destiny from your corpse? Symbolic gestures had limited appeal under such circumstances.

She removed the destiny from her belt pouch. A small spark of rebellion made her throw it casually underarm, instead of placing it carefully into Derna's hand. Kitt wanted the petty victory of seeing the Duchess of Death scramble to catch the precious thing she was stealing.

Derna didn't move. She waited until the destiny hit the ground, bounced once in the sandy soil, and came to rest. Then she stamped on it, the impact sending her black curls wavering as though caught in the aftershock of an earthquake.

Kitt's jaw dropped.

'What did you just—'

'I don't hold with it,' Derna said firmly. 'Great futures going to those with money, bought and sold on demand? It's not how the world should work. Let that future find the person it should have always found, not be presented to some spoiled rich kid as a coming-of-age gift, or fed to a god to shore up a temple.'

'But that's *literally* how the world works!' Kitt found herself shouting. 'The future is damaged, it doesn't work properly! You can't change that!'

'*Fucking watch me!*'

Kitt stared at that face. She'd known it since they were both kids. It had been the source of some of her greatest joys, and also some of her basest terror.

If Two Tongue Derna decided she was going to change the world, you had limited options. You could get out of her way, you could help her, or you could die. Or, admittedly, you could wait and hope she lost interest, but that was more of a long-term plan.

'Okay, Derna,' Kitt said. 'If anyone can, I guess it's you.'

Derna's face split into a grin again. 'Thanks, Kitt. That means a lot.' The Queen of the Streets untied a purse from her belt and threw it to Kitt, who caught it. It jingled with coins.

Kitt looked up. 'You could have just offered me this for it. I might've haggled, but—'

'No buying the big destinies!' Derna snapped. 'Not me, not anyone.'

Kitt shrugged. Derna's logic sometimes gave the exact same outcome very different weightings depending on how things unfolded to get there, and Kitt had never been sure if that was admirable or aggravating. This wasn't the big score she'd hoped for, but it was more than nothing, and considerably more than death.

'We're done here,' Derna announced, and the mercenaries relaxed. Derna looked back over her shoulder as they moved away, and stuck her tongues out again. 'See you later, Kitt!'

Kitt stared after her, feeling the familiar sense of loss tinged with anger. Derna was infuriating, and undoubtedly dangerous, but she was also like a campfire that attracted you with brightness and warmth, even though it might burn you if you got too close. She wasn't malicious, any more than fire was malicious, but she also had fire's pitilessness. Kitt had been burned before, but every new absence made her feel a little colder again, and she resented that.

Fine, let Derna go off on her wrong-brained quest to change the future, or whatever she'd set her sights on now. Kitt wished her good luck, but it wasn't like she was going to start following her, or—

'Hey, isn't that the way we're going?' Pigtail Vem asked, looking at the receding mercenaries. Well-armed and well-equipped mercenaries, so numerous that your average band of robbers wouldn't even *think* of trying their luck, and although being held at the wrong end of assorted pointed items wasn't pleasant, that was over and done with now. No hard feelings, unless anyone was foolish enough to hold onto them.

Kitt gritted her teeth, but pride could get you killed.

'Hoi, Derna!'

'Yeah?'

Kitt sighed. 'Which way are you going?'

'Mereport! Why?'

Kitt closed her eyes and groaned, but…

'Wait up.'

TWO

Official city legend had it that Mereport was founded when Merevast, an ancient god of the sea, was slain by his children and cast upon the shore. The impact of his mighty body shattered the ground and created Mereport Bay, and his flesh was scavenged by the local beasts, which in turn led to the great variety of overlarge and strangely-formed wildlife that populated the area. Indeed, his bones could still be found in the depths of the city, forming the structure of ancient buildings and the foundations of new ones built atop them.

(Another legend, popular with Mereporters themselves, was that Merevast vomited up the contents of his stomach onto the shore after a particularly heavy night of drinking, before sinking back into the depths in a hungover stupor from which he'd still not yet emerged. The mighty bones were, in this version, the remnants of whatever he'd eaten before the event, which was why the local phrase of 'you look like a god's supper' was not the compliment some outsiders assume it to be.)

Regardless of its true origin, the city had grown and expanded both back up the valley of the Great Song, the mighty river which the city straddled, and out into the bay itself on pilings and pontoons. Kitt was now sitting on a stool at one end of the bar in the Dubious Gecko – a tavern of moderate respectability and higher-than-average cleanliness that sat above the waves in the New Docks quarter – idly swilling her drink around its earthenware mug and thinking about nothing in particular, when her reverie was interrupted by the appearance of two hairy-knuckled hands on the counter. She looked up, and then further up, until her gaze met that of Timony Picknett, owner and proprietor not only of the tavern, but also a shock of coarse, curly blond hair that breezed through such adjectives as 'sizeable', ricocheted off 'impressive', and landed firmly in 'downright threatening'.

'Evening, Kitt.'

'Tim,' Kitt replied in greeting, raising her mug in a half-salute.

'How goes the divining business?' Timony asked, wiping half-heartedly at the bar top with a cloth from which any good pestilentia would have been able to pluck the sources for at least half a dozen plagues.

'Currently?' Kitt said. She raised her mug again. 'I'm trying to find the alcohol in this piss.'

Kitt heard a cautious intake of breath on either side of her, as other patrons became aware of what she'd said in the same way your hair standing on end gave you an early indication of a forthcoming lightning strike. There was a subtle shuffling of feet and scraping of stool legs on the wooden floor, as people cleared out of the blast area. It was generally unwise to speak to Timony Picknett in such a manner, for he was a large man, and not inclined to humour those who frivolously impugned his business.

Timony snorted a laugh, reached behind him to seize a dark green bottle, pulled the cork out with his teeth, then poured a generous slug into Kitt's mug. 'There you go.'

'Cheers, Tim,' Kitt said. She took a sip of her revitalised beverage and nodded approvingly as her eyes began to water. 'So, what gives?'

'Don't follow you,' Timony said cheerfully. The other patrons, having concluded that violence was apparently not in the offing, began to drift casually back into whatever they'd been doing before.

'Oh, come on,' Kitt said wearily. 'You gave me a free shot. Do I really look that bad?'

'Kitt!' Timony protested. He leant a little lower. 'It was a genuine question, is all. You used to be running up to the moors every few weeks with a crew in tow, and bring most of 'em back along with whatever fortune you found while you were up there. Haven't heard about anything like that for what, four months now? And the Swallowmage hasn't stopped her foretelling, I know that much. They say a fight started in the Anchor two nights ago over people trying to get close enough to hear her.'

'Sulian does tend to mumble,' Kitt muttered, scrubbing a hand through her hair. It was getting long again; she'd have to take a knife to it.

'So what happened?' Timony asked. 'Slydewasp get too close? Never seen one of the bastards, but I've heard tell, and they sound pretty terrifying. Couldn't blame someone for knocking the moors on the head after a close encounter.'

'No,' Kitt said, shaking her head, then paused. 'Well, actually, yes, one *did* get too close, but that's not why I've stopped going up there.'

'So?' Timony prompted. 'Come on, girl, don't leave me hanging.'

Kitt sighed and downed the rest of her drink in one aggressive movement, then replaced the mug on the bar. 'It's Derna.'

Timony's eyebrows raised in surprise, then lowered again in brief understanding, before diverging in confusion. 'Okay. So, are you two dating again, or…?'

Kitt stared at him, aghast. '*Dating?* Gods, no! She threatened to kill me!'

'That was my second guess.'

'And what do you mean, "again"?' Kitt demanded, as her brain caught up with her ears.

Timony frowned. 'Weren't you two together when you were younger?'

'No! We were friends! We were *best* friends! And then she got obsessed with *swords*, and *duelling*, and suddenly she didn't have time for me anymore!'

Kitt became aware that she'd been speaking slightly louder than she'd intended. She cast a foul glance at her mug, and composed herself a little.

'Look, the last time I went up we got a big score, but Derna was waiting for us when we came down,' she confided more quietly, rubbing at her temple. 'She took it off us – paid us for it after, but that's not the point – and just crushed it. She's got it into her head that selling futures is wrong, and it's kind of hard to psych yourself up to go onto the moors when you know there's every possibility Derna's just going to ambush you again afterwards. It's been easier to take different types of divining jobs. Well, sort of easier.' Some weirdos thought diviners could find anything. Kitt grimaced in memory of the last contract she'd tried to take, for someone who'd ended up instructing her to find him *love*, of all things. She'd scribbled down the address of Laeron's Singleton's Paradise Lovematch Emporium – often misconstrued as a brothel by those who only heard the name, but in actuality a well-stocked bookshop and coffee shop with an emphasis on conversation and reading groups – and charged him ten keshels for wasting her time, which at least helped cover the cost of replacing the moonstriker she'd thrown at the slydewasp.

'She might not be wrong, at that,' Timony said, causing Kitt to look up in surprise. 'Not the ambushing, the other thing. There was a break-in over at the Combined Futures auction house last week. A big destiny got swiped the night before it was due to go up for the toffs to bid on, and three guards got killed. Some people will do anything to get their hands on one. Can't be healthy.'

Kitt eyed him, but he didn't seem to have made the immediate connection that she had, so she kept quiet. Timony heard a lot of gossip, and if he hadn't learned of anything that linked the robbery to Two Tongue Derna then far be it from Kitt Carver to suggest it.

'You talking about the break-in?' a new voice said from beside Kitt. It was warm and male, with a slight upriver accent. 'Heard about that. The bastards'll cut their payouts and blame it on additional security requirements, just you wait.'

Kitt glanced sideways, then straightened and swivelled on her stool with as much insouciant grace as she could manage, although she took care to keep her short sword clear for a draw. 'A fair face can hide a hollow heart', as her mother always said, a phrase inevitably followed by Kitt's father's tired joke of how that must mean his heart was as fine and full as any in the land.

Said fair face in this instance was situated above simple but clean clothes: brown jerkin, loose-sleeved shirt of undyed cotton, and dark leg wraps tucked into calf-high boots. Not exactly fancy duds, but then divining often took you to – or at least through – places that would make a mockery of silk or fine linen.

'You're in the trade?' she said casually.

'Donal Klae.' He was perhaps a few years older than her, enough to have a couple of lines on his face to give it character. His shaggy hair was ash-grey – too smooth and solid a colour to be the result of anything other than a sorcerous comb – and reached to his jawline, or thereabouts.

'Kitt Carver.'

He smiled ruefully. 'I keep hoping someone will recognise my name, but they never do. Pretty sure I've heard of you, though.'

'Whatever they say I've done, I didn't,' Kitt blurted, then

winced internally as Donal flinched. Hot people approaching her in bars was not something she wanted to be discouraging with flippant self-deprecation. 'You been in Mereport long?' she asked, trying to angle the conversation back on track.

'A few moons.' He took a sip of his drink. 'I was trying my luck in the future mines out in the mountains past Uppersong, but it got really cutthroat. It used to be everyone for themselves, you took a lightstone and your divining rods and found what you could, but now the cartels have claimed entire branches. They take your finds off you when you come back up, and you're lucky if they pay you a tenth of the worth.' He shrugged. 'The moors are no picnic, but at least you can shop around for a buyer afterwards. Besides, everyone knows it's the motherlode for destinies.'

'You didn't fancy trying other sorts of work?' Kitt asked, trying not to be too obvious about her perusal of him. He had a solid build, muscle with a bit of fat over it, and she considered it a crying shame that his shirtsleeves were, in fact, quite so loose.

'The gods gave me divining magic. It seems a waste not to use it. Besides,' he continued, eyeing her slyly. 'It's sort of addictive, isn't it?'

'Yeah,' Kitt agreed. It wasn't a *problem*, but she certainly got a small rush of satisfaction when she coaxed her magic into successfully guiding her to something.

'What are you drinking?' she asked Donal, who peered into his mug dubiously.

'That's… I honestly don't know. I told the big guy to give me whatever was – excuse me?'

Kitt had snatched the mug off him, peered into it, and sniffed. A familiar sour, malty smell met her nose, and she wrinkled it in response.

'Wrack's Tapjuice?' She looked up at Timony. 'Seriously?'

'He wanted cheap, he got cheap,' Timony replied, unabashed, from farther down the bar. 'If you want to upgrade, you know better than most how much everything costs.'

'He is *not* implying that I have a drinking problem,' Kitt told Donal firmly. 'Tim's an old friend of my parents, and I used to help him load the barrels in before I was old enough to go up onto the moors.'

'That's true,' Timony agreed. '*And* you have—'

'We'll have a flagon of Old Barley's,' Kitt snapped, putting two keshels down on the bar. She'd caught sight of an unoccupied nook in the corner of the Gecko and had decided it needed company in the form of two diviners, one with a shirt that was a little tight around the shoulders. 'C'mon,' she said to Donal. 'Let's get you something decent to drink.'

'Seriously?!' Kitt spluttered, only narrowly managing to avoid spraying ale across the table. 'The whole thing?'

'Down in one!' Donal replied gleefully, waving his mug for emphasis. 'I swear to you, I thought he was going to die!' He wiped tears from his eyes at the memory. 'Oh man, that was a good time, but we never went there again.'

'Sounds like Uppersong wasn't quite as bad as you made out,' Kitt said, nudging him. She was feeling pleasantly warm and fuzzy, which was partly down to the flagons of Old Barley that Timony had been providing, and also definitely partly down to the fact that she had a funny and attractive guy jammed in next to her.

'Uppersong wasn't a problem, it was the work,' Donal said. 'Well, it wasn't even the work, it was the fact I couldn't get a fair price for it.' He took another swig. 'Who do you go to around here, anyway? I've sold to Marrowright since I got here, but I don't think I like him much.'

'Old Marrowbone? He's not the stingiest, but he's got a face like a slapped arse, and he doesn't smell much better. I go to Mazen Rauk, up on Dendryn's Holloway. He's a bit odd, but so's every broker I've ever met, and he gives a decent price.'

'Can you imagine what it would be like, surrounded by all

those destinies?' Donal said, staring off into space with the disconnection of the slightly drunk. 'No wonder they're all odd. You'd think they'd just take the best for themselves.'

'Most brokers are destiny-proof,' Kitt said. 'That's what Mazen told me, anyway. You know, a destiny just doesn't take, whether you want it to or not. Must be sort of nice, knowing your life can't get twisted out of shape, good *or* bad. Besides,' she added, 'why haven't *you* taken the best destiny you've found?'

'Because I don't know what they are when I find them,' Donal said with a laugh, 'and I can't afford to get them sooth-sayered myself in case they turn out to be bad and then I can't sell them! Hey, how do you experience them?' he added, taking another swig. 'I get, like, a smell. Big ones usually have a really strong lemon scent, but I've had cherry blossom before. Fresh-cut grass a few times, too.'

'It's heat, for me,' Kitt said. 'Little ones are barely warm, right, but the big ones... They don't *actually* burn me, but they *feel* like they could burn me, know what I mean?'

'Oh wow,' Donal said, looking at her with wide eyes. 'That's *wild*. Never heard that one before. So is that an actual corre... corral... thing, y'know, where the hotter it is, the bigger it is?'

'Seems to be, based on what Mazen pays,' Kitt said smugly.

'What's the biggest one you've ever had?'

Kitt smirked. 'Destiny?'

'Obviously.'

'Obviously,' Kitt echoed. 'No, go on, you go first.'

'Since I got here?' Donal scratched his slightly stubbled jaw. 'Uh, I got seventy keshels out of Marrowright for one about three weeks ago, but I've not, y'know, got my eye in on the moors yet. Haven't worked out the good places, still need to find another decent spotter, that sort of thing.' He waved his mug again as he gesticulated, spilling a little as he did so. 'Whoops! Come on then, what about you? What's your biggest score?'

Kitt grinned. 'Are you ready?'

'I dunno,' Donal said, raising his eyebrows. '*Am* I ready?'

Kitt leant forward, until her face was mere inches away from his. 'Ten gold crowns.'

'You're shitting me!' Donal spluttered, a wide and goofily incredulous smile spreading over his face. 'Ten golds? What the hell did you find?'

'Damned if I know!' Kitt said cheerily, leaning back again and taking a slug of her ale. 'And that was for it unsoothed, too. Mazen didn't know what he was buying, but he still put ten golds down for it. I think his palms were prickling!'

'*Unsoothed?* Honestly, I dunno if that's encouraging or depressing,' Donal said with a laugh. 'I mean, it's something to aim for, but... How long ago was that? Have you, like, cleaned the moors out now?' He adopted a mournful expression and clutched one hand to his chest as though to nurse a broken heart. 'Am I wasting my time here?'

'That was a couple years back,' Kitt said. 'Just as summer was starting. Pretty much made my reputation. Y'know how it is: once you've had a big score you get better crew wanting to sign on with you for a cut, so the next jobs get easier, and so on. The old hands say fewer and fewer destinies are coming through these days, but that's old people for you; the world is never as good as it was when they were young.' She shrugged. 'Still, strange stuff is happening. They say some city out east just got completely swallowed by an earthquake, nothing left. And I've heard some sailors say they couldn't get through the Straits of Damarkus anymore, they just sailed into mist and then sailed back out again going the opposite direction, without moving the tiller. Maybe the old folks are right, and the world *is* getting worse.'

'Unless we're complaining about something,' Donal said, with a mischievous smile. 'Then we don't know how good we've got it.'

'Hah! True!' Kitt laughed. She was already feeling more

upbeat about divining again, after swapping anecdotes with Donal. Perhaps she *should* get back up there, and to all the hells with Two Tongue Derna and her strange beliefs.

Still, she reflected, those were thoughts for the morning. Right now, she'd already quietly slipped Timony enough to reserve one of his rooms for the night should she need it, and she intended to need it. She wasn't in the habit of taking strays back to her own place – that was just asking to get burgled – but a night of fun under Timony's roof might be just what the apothecary ordered.

'So,' she said, leaning back. 'What are your plans for later?'

His eyes went to the ties of her shirt, and she grinned.

Struggling out of breeches

Balancing on one foot to get out of breeches

'Oh shiiiiiit—'

thump

Giggles

One leg still in the damned breeches

'This bloody belt…!'

'C'mere.'

Lips on lips

Fingernails

Sweat on a collarbone

'mmph…'

gluk

More fingernails

'C'mon then…'

Rumpled bedsheets

Laughter

Lips everywhere

*No seriously, there's no way these bedsheets are ever going
to be flat again*

'fUcK…!'

And…

sleep

THREE

Donal wasn't in the room when Kitt woke up, and that was fine by her. He hadn't stolen what money was left in her purse, her short sword, or the piece of shell her mother had carved for her on the cord that habitually went around her neck, and it meant she had more bed to stretch out into. Mornings tended to be awkward, certainly more awkward than the nights that led up to them. Donal was welcome to his share of the memories, and if she bumped into him again then maybe they'd make some new ones.

The Dubious Gecko was already alive and bustling by the time Kitt emerged, partly since Timony appeared to need virtually no sleep and Flix the wellyn had opened up the kitchen, and partly because Kitt had allowed herself a generous lie-in. She paid three bits for a breakfast – possibly more like brunch – of two small silverfins, fresh from the Gecko's overnight tide nets, and a piece of bread fried so hard that it shattered most satisfactorily when she bit into it. Thus fortified, she set out into the morning with a spring in her step, albeit with a bruise on her forearm from when she'd accidentally whacked the bedside table while in the throes of passion.

It was a bright day with a high blue sky, and the world looked crisp and sharp enough to draw blood with a glint of reflected sunlight; or, alternately, that the right knock in the right place might shatter the entire thing into shards. Kitt wended her way up from the docks through Old Rivergate, made a stop at Tall Alice's in Ferryside for a swift cup of Morning-After Tea, and then on through the narrow alleys of Crafton, where Mereport's artificers plied their trade amongst an atmosphere of permanent slight haze, the clicking and ticking of clockwork and cogs, the frequent tang of smoke, and more tiny screws than you could shake a reasonably sized stick at. In New Rivergate she eased her way past a swearing city official trying to reason with a morass of infinite shadow that had taken up residence at a crossroads, swallowed at least one carriage so far, and was stubbornly refusing to move on despite the traffic backlog it was causing. A puffing mage response team hurried past her towards the same problem a few moments later, their expressions suggesting that negotiations were about to get a little more forceful.

It was all just another day in Mereport. The city's position straddling the Great Song, where the mighty river emptied into the sea, would have made it a hub for regular commerce in any case. Add in its location close enough to the high moors to be the natural staging post for the destinies trade, and it had become one of the largest and most thriving metropolises in the known world, complete with garish painted signs over the main gates reading *FIND YOUR FUTURE IN MEREPORT*. However, that kind of size and status did not come without certain side effects. Many strange things in the world had decided that civilisation had tasty byproducts, and not all of them were happy to stick to the food stalls, or even the garbage heaps.

As such, the appearance in the mid-afternoon of a plume of smoke somewhat thicker than that which would normally emerge from a chimney was not particularly unusual.

Sometimes a fire got out of control, sometimes someone really pissed off a smoke sprite or found out that yes, demons *did* exist and yes, they *were* bad news; these things happened. However, the first wisps of concern began to congeal in Kitt's chest as her feet took her away from the river and towards Dendryn's Holloway. She'd spent the day leaving messages for her old crew to see if they'd be up for another run into the moors, and had intended to drop by Mazen's place to make sure he hadn't placed her on a boycott list for not bringing him any goods for a few months. Unfortunately, she got closer and closer to the smoke pillar as her route twisted and turned, and by the time she stepped onto Dendryn's Holloway itself, she had already accepted what she was going to see.

Destiny Calling, Mazen Rauk's shop was, by necessity, something of a many-natured beast. It had to be ostentatious enough to appeal to the really big-name clients who would send a servant rather than come to his premises themselves, but would balk at having said servant seen entering somewhere that looked *disreputable*. That was what the hanging lanterns of guilder fire on either side of the shop's frontage were for, since only the rich could afford the sorcerous flame that provided constant light, but would self-extinguish as soon as it escaped its confines. However, the shop also had to be welcoming to the bulk of his customers: the merchants, traders, and local politicians whose desires for an edge over their rivals drove the majority of Mazen's day-to-day custom. A steady stream of small destinies heading out of the door kept him solvent and allowed him to purchase the big destinies for when the nobles, royalty, and temples came calling. Too swanky a premises risked making his wares look too pricey, and the majority of his customers hesitant to step inside.

Even with all *that* said, you still couldn't put a destinies parlour like Mazen's in the middle of one of the fanciest areas, like Highmarket or Temple Cross, due to people like Kitt herself. Destiny hunters were rough and ready types, and rarely of good breeding, as the Highmarket set would view it. If Kitt walked onto a street in Highmarket then she would quickly find herself escorted off it again by private guards. Dendryn's Holloway, on the other hand, sat in just about the right place; not the sort of area where they polished the flagstones overnight, but also not where the shadows carried knives for protection.

Unfortunately, Destiny Calling was bringing the tone of the street down somewhat now, due to being on fire.

It wasn't a full-throated blaze, of the sort that ends plagues and has historians and architects alike reaching for pen and paper with sorrowful smiles. Instead it was sullen and workmanlike, steadfastly attempting to get on with the job of carbonisation while its more glamorous cousins flickered prettily but uselessly in their hanging lanterns. However, Mereporters had their own opinions about fire, and work was already underway to quench it. Buckets were being filled at the corner pump and passed from hand to hand, and Kitt could hear people shouting for a waterworker. She pushed closer through the gathering crowd, keeping a careful hand on her purse as she did so – pickpockets and cutpurses loved a good bit of street drama – expecting to see the tall, thin shape of Mazen clasping his hands together in horror, exhorting the bucket chain to greater efforts with his reedy voice, or possibly even throwing water into his burning premises himself.

She wasn't prepared to see him on his back on the cobbles with one arm outstretched as though about to deliver a dramatic soliloquy, except he'd have needed someone else's vocal cords since his throat had been well and truly slit.

Kitt had lived in Mereport all her life, and had spent the last few years of it heading up onto the high moors where danger lurked on giant wings, ready to eat the unwary. She'd seen her share of dead bodies – more than a few. She'd never killed anyone that she knew for sure, but she'd been involved in a couple of fights where blades had been drawn, and when you were trying to hack your way clear of something like that you rarely had a good idea of exactly what damage you'd done on the way out. It was a shock to see life ended in such a violent form here on Dendryn's Holloway, though, where the upper limit of hostility was to nod politely at someone as you passed them and then comment witheringly on their attire in a low voice to your companion. Besides, Kitt had liked Mazen well enough, and even though she'd seen death before, it wasn't as though she was as inured to it as someone like Derna—

Like Derna.

Two Tongue Derna, who had destroyed the last big find Kitt had made on the moors, because she'd got it into her head that the buying and selling of destinies was wrong. Two Tongue Derna, banned from all destiny shops in the city for attempting to smash the merchandise. Two Tongue Derna, whom Kitt privately suspected might have had something to do with the killings and theft from the Combined Futures auction house. Could Two Tongue Derna have sauntered into Destiny Calling, slit Mazen's throat – and that of whichever of his guards had been working today; there was another, larger body over there – and set a fire?

Yes. Yes, she could have.

Kitt swallowed the bile that was rising and grabbed at the sleeve of Makema Ottemia, the old woman who ran a bakery three doors down. She looked around, and her already tear-stained lined face crumpled further.

'Oh, bless you my dear!' she sobbed, and collapsed onto Kitt's shoulder.

This was not exactly what Kitt had expected. She always treated herself to one of Makema's ridiculous sweet creations after she made a sale to Mazen, and Makema had eyed her suspiciously at first, but in time had come to greet Kitt cheerily whenever she walked in. Still, this seemed a bit... more.

'What happened?' Kitt asked, patting Makema on the back somewhat tentatively. 'Did anyone see?'

'I don't know!' Makema wailed. 'Poor Mr Rauk! I didn't hear a thing until people started shouting about the fire, but Serry from across the way went in with my Akini, and they found the bodies and pulled them out, and they said his strongbox had been smashed open!'

Kitt looked around and saw Akini, Makema's middle granddaughter and senior shop assistant, sat on the ground and coughing heartily between swigs of water from a pitcher. She didn't look like someone who could haul bodies out of a burning building, until you saw the muscles of her forearms and remembered exactly how hard kneading dough was.

'You'll find who did this, won't you?' Makema asked tearfully, pulling back and gripping Kitt's shoulders with hands that had clearly not forgotten their own dough-kneading past.

'Me?' Kitt said, shocked. 'I was just—'

'You're a diviner, aren't you?' Makema cut her off with a shake of her head that sent her greying locs swaying. 'You find things! You can find who did this!'

Kitt's first and instinctive response was *No I can't, because that's not how divination works*. Finding *things* was a matter of practice, and was drastically helped by knowing where to focus your search to begin with. Not everyone had the same sensitivities: some diviners would never get the knack of tracking down destinies, while Kitt herself could not reliably get her irons to point to water even if she was standing on the bank of the Great Song.

Finding *people* was another matter entirely, and most diviners didn't even bother with it. To find a person you needed some sort of connection to them. Being related was the best way, but unless you had a massive and exceptionally forgetful family, that was of limited use as an income source. Otherwise, you needed something like a lock of hair, a treasured belonging, or a relative who didn't mind trailing around with you. Even then, it was hardly reliable, and could be thrown off if the subject actively did not want to be found.

On the other hand, given Kitt had an idea of where, or at least with whom, she might start…

'I'll do my best,' she said, giving Makema a smile and trying to think where in the all the hells she was likely to find Two Tongue Derna.

FOUR

Derna was easy to find if you didn't want to – such as on a hillside waiting for you to come down from the high moors with a destiny in your pocket, or just out of sight behind a pillar in a tavern when you drunkenly proclaimed yourself the best street duellist in all of Mereport – but difficult to track down if you did. That was partly because telling someone her location was the sort of thing that could lead to a rapid shortening of one's lifespan – if nothing else, from the backflips your heart went into when Derna appeared unexpectedly in your field of view, demanding to know how the person whose blood was currently adorning her blade had found her. She existed in a strange binary state where if you knew *who* she was then you wouldn't admit to knowing *where* she was, sort of like the cat Kitt was dimly aware a mage had stuffed into a box for some reason that presumably made sense to mages.

Kitt had a bit of an advantage on this front. Her divining abilities were fairly meaningless without an appropriate focus, but she *knew* Derna. If you'd hung around with someone on and off since you were kids, you had an idea of where they'd be, even in a city the size of Mereport. Also, although Kitt wasn't famous herself – certainly not as famous as Derna – people had seen her *with* Derna. Someone who would deny all knowledge of the Queen of the Streets whether approached by well-dressed fellows with coin aplenty or scarred ruffians wielding notched blades might cautiously avow that they thought Derna was down near the docks today if asked by whatshername, you know, that diviner girl, some say the two of 'em were *involved* when they were younger, don't know if it's true, best not let Derna hear you speculating on that; anyway, *her*.

It was the singing that tipped Kitt off finally, as she made her way down a narrow alley that had been blessed with the twin smells of fish from the harbour and piss from last night's drunks. It came from ahead of her, a godsawful racket of two competing melodies – to use a kind term – being bellowed at the top of several pairs of lungs. They were duellist songs, and if two were taking place at the same time then a standoff was occurring, which meant that Derna would likely be gravitating towards it if she was anywhere nearby.

Mereport's layout hadn't been planned in much more detail than someone making a split-second choice of whether to throw up out of the window or into a bucket, but it was still littered with little squares and plazas. Some had once been areas of common land, or an old village green swallowed up and paved over. The docklands were the ancient heart of the city, though, and the open spaces here were where the little fish markets had been held before arguments over theology about which gods they should be dedicated to caused them all to be grouped into the same place, known locally as The Stinkhole.

It was here, in Mereport's old heart, that the sashes came to fight.

You could tell a duellist's allegiance by the colour of the sash of soft cloth they wore crossways, offhand shoulder to the other hip. Most duellists in the city ran with a sash; it wasn't a gang – Mereport's gangs were a far murkier world, with less bravado in public and more kneecapping in private, although that was not to say that there wasn't some overlap – but it was still a group of likeminded souls who'd have your back if someone you'd defeated decided to take their loss a bit personal. You had to earn your cloth by showing promise, and any sash of merit had a rabble that tagged around after them hoping to get noticed by running messages, acting as lookout or interference when the watch came by, or as was the case here, by providing extra noise for the fight chorus.

The sashes had long histories, with some going back a century or more. Kitt identified the two groups facing off in front of the statue of Cadmia, a god of coin and commerce, as about a dozen members each of the Flowers of Iron and the Bleak Sisters. Both were bellowing their fight songs as loudly as they could, stamping on the ground or slapping their chests to keep the beat, while one chosen representative danced their sash's dance in front of the other group. The thing was, of course, that each sash's song and dance had a different speed and a different beat, and the trick was to drown out your opponents so their dancer fumbled their steps, at which point they would be roundly and raucously mocked.

Kitt wasn't really sure what the point of the whole thing was, since it usually led to a duel one way or another. Either one side wanted to regain their honour for messing up, or neither side fumbled and so they had to find another way to settle their dispute. Still, if traditions were abandoned just because they weren't logical then the world would be a very different place.

A small crowd was gathering to watch, since the sashes were essentially violent street theatre. It wasn't all deaths and stabbings, though, or the city would have clamped down on the sashes far more rigorously. First blood drawn from anywhere except the hands was the standard winning condition, and while that *could* involve being run through, more usually it was a nick to the cheek or a slash on the arm. Cutting through your opponent's cloth was another manner of winning, and the one involving the greatest level of skill, as well as considerable personal insult: a duellist so defeated would have to earn their cloth back in the eyes of their sash. Duels of no regard, which finished either through death or verbal withdrawal, were far rarer and considered somewhat less suitable for small children to witness.

Two Tongue Derna did not belong to a sash, and it was even money whether that was because she didn't want to, or because even her undeniable skills were outweighed by her sheer unpredictability. However, even an unaligned duellist like Derna would make all speed when they heard fight songs being belted out, because the rattle of blades was what they all lived for, in one manner or another.

Kitt saw Derna's familiar dark, curly hair arrive on the far corner of the square, just as the representative of the Bleak Sisters – a gangling, red-haired lad who had managed to be surprisingly nimble in his dance steps so far despite his lanky limbs – finally placed a foot off-beat and stumbled over his own ankle. A mocking roar went up from the Flowers of Iron at his failure, the crowd responded with one more akin to that of a pub joyously reacting to the sound of a smashing mug, and the Flowers' dancer pirouetted on the spot before coming to a rest with her head cocked to one side, her tongue protruding, and both middle fingers extended.

Her tongue was split down the middle. Kitt sighed and shook her head as she began to push her way through the thickening crowd towards Derna. Why did people not only choose the most foolish heroes to worship, but then almost always chose the most foolish thing about that hero to emulate?

The Bleak Sister, his already pale cheeks whitening further with rage, drew his blade. His opponent responded in kind – her weapon had a flash of silver on the hilt – and that was it. As anyone with half a brain could have predicted from the moment the two groups came face to face, an honour duel was about to take place. The assembled sashes now began a far more generalised yelling, alternating between enthusiastic support for their own fighter and epithets directed at their opponent, as the two sized each other up.

The Bleak Sister stepped forward first, thrusting with his slender blade. It was little more than a rangefinder, and one which the Iron Flower parried easily, but they had crossed swords now. The noise of the crowd rose accordingly, and Kitt swore under her breath as her going became more difficult. Late arrivals were piling in, eager to see what was going on, but those at the front of the crowd were well aware of what a safe distance was from duelling sashes, and were holding their ground so as not to get pushed closer than was comfortable. Kitt paused for a moment to go up onto her toes, trying to make sure Derna hadn't moved, and was rewarded with a sight of Derna still where she had been and cheering along with everyone else.

The upwards bob of her head must have caught Derna's eye, because the Duchess of Death turned towards her and waved cheerily. Kitt ground her teeth at such carefree mannerisms from someone she strongly suspected had just killed two people, but at least Derna wasn't avoiding her. Also, Kitt reckoned she was one of the few people who could straight up ask Derna whether she'd murdered someone and set a fire without getting stabbed for it. Knowing Derna since childhood had *some* advantages.

Kitt raised a hand as she pushed forwards, clearly indicating that she wasn't here by accident and was actually trying to reach the person who might, in some senses, be termed as her friend. Derna cast a glance at the duel, then began to make her own way through the crowd towards Kitt – with considerably more success, Kitt couldn't help but note, although she was unsure whether that was down to people not wanting to be in Derna's way, or Derna not being bothered about where or how hard she deployed her elbows.

They were only a couple of yards apart when Derna drew her sword.

Kitt froze. Had she misjudged things? Had she placed too much trust in whatever passed for their friendship, mainly rooted as it was in bonds forged when they were younger? Had she underestimated Derna's ruthlessness? Had she—

OW

...had she just been stabbed?

Kitt looked down as she felt herself begin to crumple. Yes, that was the hilt of a blade sticking out of her left side, just below the ribs. Her mind fixed on it with a curious detachment. There was a hand holding it, a calloused hand that was probably the mate of the one she could now feel gripping her other shoulder. She looked up at her attacker's face, just as a furious scream and a flash of steel announced the arrival of Two Tongue Derna and the loosing of blood from the knife man's throat.

He staggered backwards, clutching desperately at his neck. Kitt hissed as the departure of his hand from the hilt in her side introduced her to new, interesting, and thoroughly unwelcome flashes of pain, but she wasn't alone. Derna's blade dipped to take her assailant in the groin for good measure, and drew forth a disgustingly bubbly howl of agony.

Had his three mates simply backed away in fear at seeing someone cut down in front of them, they might have passed for innocent bystanders. Indeed, Kitt wouldn't have even known they were with him had they not simultaneously and instinctively drawn their own weapons, and in so doing merely focused Derna's rage onto them as well.

The uninvolved members of the crowd around them were desperately fleeing. Derna took the thumb off one man's knife hand, batted away the panicked thrust of a dagger by the dark-haired woman next to him, put her sword in the eye socket of the first one, then whipped it out and across the woman's face. The last man clearly decided that he had no interest in taking on Mereport's premier street duellist while armed with nothing but a knife, and turned to run.

Unfortunately for him, he chose to do so across the open space in which the actual duel was being fought.

'*Sashes!*' Derna screamed, taking a moment to point at his fleeing back with her dripping blade while the dark-haired woman staggered away with her hands over her eyes. '*Take him!*'

Two Tongue Derna might not belong to a sash, but they listened when she spoke. The collection of youthful bravos drew their swords and spread out to encircle the fugitive while Derna casually stabbed the dark-haired women in the back, twisted her blade, and pulled it out. The man who'd put a knife in Kitt was on his knees now, and judging by the amount of blood he was losing from the two holes Derna had made in him, he wasn't going to be getting up again. His colleague was flat on his back, staring sightlessly at the sky with one whole eye and one ruined one.

'Kitt!' Derna said, turning back to her with concern written across her face. She grimaced at the sight of the knife. 'Oh, Kitt. Who've you been making enemies with?'

'Didn't know I'd made enemies with anyone,' Kitt managed weakly. Breathing was just about possible, but it was a long way from pleasant, as was any sort of movement. The knife blade felt like a sliver of ice in her side, but Kitt Carver knew better than to pull it out. It was keeping her blood inside her, and blood staying inside was definitely better than it all leaking out like the bastard Derna had just done for.

'Someone get me a barrow!' Derna yelled. 'One with some straw in! Now!' she added forcefully, and Kitt, now on her knees and looking down with an increasingly heavy head, was dimly aware of a few pairs of feet rushing off.

'What do you want us to do with him?' one of the duellists called, gesturing uncertainly at the last knife man. He was also on his knees, although he knelt in the middle of a gleaming circle of swords.

'Bring him!' Derna shouted. 'I'll want to ask him questions later!'

The sashes noticeably relaxed, which struck Kitt as odd for a moment, until she realised they'd been worried Derna was going to tell them to kill him. Duellists didn't kill unless it was a duel of no regard, and they certainly didn't execute a disarmed man on his knees.

Well. Not unless they were Two Tongue Derna.

'Hurry up with that barrow!'

'What are you doing?' Kitt mumbled, squinting through the pain.

'Taking you to help.' Derna absent-mindedly wiped her blade clean on the shoulder of the man who'd stabbed Kitt – and who had now collapsed onto his side – and sheathed it again. 'Sulian shouldn't be *that* drunk yet.'

Kitt let out a low groan. 'Does it have to be her?'

'She's the only one I'd trust with you,' Derna said earnestly, squatting down. 'Especially since we don't know who these bastards were, or why they were after you.'

Kitt wanted to argue, but arguing with Derna was generally a futile endeavour even when you *didn't* have a knife in your side.

'Fine. Let's go see the fucking Swallowmage. How much worse can she make it?'

'Well—'

'That was a rhetorical question, damn it.'

FIVE

TOMMAS UNDERWYNE WAS an assassin, although that had never been his intention. However, given he'd been cursed from a young age with a destiny that doomed him to have blood-soaked hands, his original aim of becoming a baker had never really been viable. It would have played merry hell with the flour, for one thing. All in all, becoming an assassin had seemed the safer, or at least more controlled option. If his hands were going to be stained by the blood of *someone*, he might as well get paid for it. What was more, if his destiny was fulfilled by killing strangers, then hopefully it wouldn't latch on to his friends and family. Such was the way with destinies. If you tried to ignore them, they had a way of twisting things just enough to make your life really difficult without bestowing any of the benefits, dubious though they might be, that you could potentially get if you'd leant into them in the first place.

However, there were also plenty of things that could make one's life difficult which had nothing whatsoever to do with destinies, and the most obvious example of that for Tommas Underwyne, right at this moment, went by the name of Carl Whyteaves.

'I thought we had agreed,' Tommas said, with the deliberate patience of one trying to subtly draw attention to the fact that he had several edged weapons at his immediate disposal and would appreciate recognition of the fact that he was not resorting to them, 'that I would handle anything in this engagement which required the termination of life.'

'Did you think we had agreed that?' Carl replied casually. He inspected the nails of his right hand as he leant on the railing of their ship, which was being borne across the waves on the back of a sea spirit that had been called and cajoled as soon as they had left Mereport harbour by the tideweaver sitting on the bow. 'I cannot imagine why you would.'

Carl Whyteaves was not an assassin. He was a factor, which to Tommas's understanding was the term for someone hired by rich people to make events unfold according to their wishes without them ever having to know the details or, if it came to it, be implicated. After all, how could an upstanding pillar of society have known that their employee would do something so callous and crude as *breaking the law*? Obviously, they had never intended for anything untoward to happen, and all activities which might reflect badly on the employer in the eyes of the law – or of deities whose creeds espoused inconvenient principles – were entirely the factor's responsibility, and so on, and so forth. Being a factor was a position requiring ingenuity, discretion, and a greater capability for arse-covering than even the most enthusiastic censor at a burlesque hall.

Tommas didn't hold with factors, personally. Hiring someone else to get their hands dirty for you was one thing – it was how he made a living, after all – but you might at least have the decency to look a killer in the eyes yourself and let the name of the person whose life you wanted ended drop from your own lips. There was recognition that you needed something done that you could not achieve yourself, for whatever reason, and then there was cowardice.

Unfortunately, cowards not only paid well, but also tended to have other leverage in place to ensure it was difficult to refuse their commissions. Tommas was still not quite sure exactly for whom Carl was working – cowards, again – but it had been made abundantly clear to him that while his presence on the venture would lead to great reward, refusing would lead to unspecified but still very definite misfortune both to him and those to whom he was attached. If there was one thing that assassins knew not to do, it was to trigger an obvious trap, and so here he was.

That did not mean that he had to like *unprofessionalism.*

'If you want someone dead, and you have an assassin on retainer, then why in the name of the Pantheon of Death would you not use him?'

'Would you have killed the diviners?' Carl asked, then held one hand up to forestall Tommas's answer, the morning sunlight glistening on his rings. 'Allow me to rephrase that question. Would you have killed the diviners without *complaint*? Would you have killed the merchant, and set the fire? Or would you have forced me to listen to your opinions about whether such deaths were *necessary*?'

'They were *not* necessary,' Tommas said, with some distaste.

'And there is where we differ, you and I.' Carl fixed Tommas with a stare from beneath the curtains of his dark brown hair. Whyteaves was somewhere in his twenties, probably more towards the rear than the front, around the point that the hunger of youth met the pragmatism of experience and passed it a bag of cash under the table. 'It is vitally important that our venture is not interrupted, and that means ensuring no one realises what we are doing.'

'Had you asked me, I would have told you that a spate of killings is more likely to provoke interest than dissuade it,' Tommas said bluntly. 'A single death can occur for any reason, especially if it's made to look like an accident, such as a *professional* would be able to achieve. A trail of bodies with stab wounds invites people to make connections and find links between the victims, if only to assure themselves that they are not at risk of being next.' Precision, that was the key. An assassin never wanted to be *messy*, unless that was in the contract.

'You worry too much,' Carl said dismissively. 'You're not even being *paid* to worry. Never fear, you will get your chance to exercise your skills once we reach our destination. We will have neither room nor use for local amateurs then.'

Tommas should have left it there. Deadly though he was, individual deadliness was of little use when set against the sort of far-reaching influence that a factor like Carl represented. In some ways, factors were to be feared more than their masters, since the whole point of them was that their shoulders were not overlooked every step of the way. Carl Whyteaves could undoubtedly leverage his position into taking care of any number of small personal grudges, or greasing his preferred wheels, so long as he delivered what he was expected to deliver and could come up with a reasonable excuse for his indulgences should he ever be challenged on them. The sensible thing to do would be for Tommas to bite his tongue and just enjoy the view over the waves.

'Have you told him?' he asked instead.

'Told him what?'

Carl had hesitated only for a moment, but hesitated he had, and although assassins might avoid obvious traps, discerning weaknesses was also second nature.

'About your improvisation,' Tommas said. 'It feels like the sort of thing of which he should be kept informed.'

'Nonsense,' Carl said with a snort. 'It's not important.'

'Not important?' Tommas echoed. 'Multiple murders and the setting of a fire in Mereport is not *important?* You're not even going to let him decide that for himself?'

'I am perfectly capable of taking responsibility for what needs to be done.'

'Then take responsibility,' Tommas said. 'Tell him what you did, if you're so certain that you made the right call.'

For the first time, a flicker of irritation broke though Whyteaves' expression of languid superiority. The corner of his lip twitched, like a man trying to shoo away a fly. 'Do not try to bring him into this.'

'Why not?' Tommas thought he knew very well why not – which was absolutely not the same thing as *actually* knowing why not – but Carl's superciliousness had irritated him to the point where puncturing the factor's smugness a little was worth a minor piece of imprudence. 'Is he not your superior?'

'No!' Carl snapped. 'He is not.' He looked away, fiddling with the ring on his right forefinger. 'He is present as an additional asset. One we should take all pains not to require.'

Tommas stared at him for a moment, then barked a brief, humourless laugh. 'You don't know who he is, do you?'

'I know enough,' Carl said, looking down into the waves, 'and I know more than you. I suggest you remain content with that state of affairs.'

Tommas snorted. 'What sort of a name is 'Plainsong', anywa—'

Carl Whyteaves rounded on him, eyes wide and furious, and grabbed Tommas by his forearm. Normally such an imposition would have been greeted with a blade held pointedly to the offender's throat, no matter their relative position, but Tommas's hand was stayed by naked fear. Not his own, though; it was the fear visible on Carl's face that held him still, the silent plea from one prey animal to another not to do anything that would draw the attention of their predator.

'Don't say the name!' Carl hissed through his teeth, as though the syllables were treacherous and reluctantly released. 'Don't say the name! He comes when called!'

Tommas nodded hesitantly. He was abruptly aware that his ploy to discomfort his companion had succeeded rather more comprehensively than he had foreseen, and now he tried to readjust his mental footing in the light of this unexpected reaction, and what it might mean.

He did not get long in which to do so.

'*Gentlemen.*'

Carl's grip disappeared from Tommas's arm as quickly as it had manifested, and the factor turned away as though the contact of skin on cloth had been burning him. A shape in a hooded robe was emerging from the hatchway that led below. Tommas had seen the occupant of that robe only once, a brief introduction on the deck before they had got underway. Now two long-fingered hands threw the hood back, and Tommas got his first proper look at the head beneath.

Plainsong was not that unusual to look upon, as things went. He was human in appearance, for starters. It was not until Tommas looked closer – he was proud of his eye for detail – that he noticed the lack of any hair. Not just a lack of hair itself, but of any sign that hair had ever existed. The skin over Plainsong's skull was not marred by any hint of another colour, no matter how slight. His brows were hairless, his cheeks and chin and upper lip were hairless, and even his eyes, lined with kohl though they were, lacked lashes. His was a handsome face, in fact, once one's eyes had adjusted to the missing elements.

There were markings visible on his neck, Tommas observed. A tattoo of a chain, apparently unbroken, wound completely around his throat and disappeared down on each side towards his collarbone.

'I heard what sounded like an argument,' Plainsong continued mildly. 'I do hope we are all getting along.'

He walked from the deck hatch to the rail, and Tommas noticed that he was not inconvenienced in any way by the pitch and roll of the deck. An experienced sailor, then? No, even sailors made adjustments: a momentary halt in their step, a brief readjustment of weight to counter the sea's movements, things that had become second nature over time. Plainsong just *moved*, as though the deck under his feet was as stable and motionless as a ballroom floor.

'Of course,' Carl said, with a smile that Tommas could hear even if he couldn't see it properly, given that the factor was facing away from him. 'We were just—'

'I was telling Carl that I felt it was unprofessional for him to have hired amateur footpads to kill the diviners and the merchant in Mereport,' Tommas said. 'He disagreed.'

Some people could literally smell lies. Tommas Underwyne knew that for a fact. He had no idea if Plainsong was one of them, but he suddenly felt it unwise to go along with any attempted deception.

'Is that so?' Plainsong said. He turned those eyes of deep, dark brown onto Carl. 'To cover your trail, I presume? No loose ends?'

Such a calm reaction to discussion of murder would unnerve many a person, but to Tommas it simply counted as talking shop. What unnerved him was the intangible yet very definite impression he got that Plainsong had intended to say something else entirely, and yet those were the words which had emerged.

It may or may not have been for the same reason, but Carl clearly wasn't comfortable either; Tommas saw the muscles in the factor's throat move as he swallowed. 'Exactly that.'

Plainsong pursed his lips and nodded once. 'Very thorough. What price is a little more blood? After all, we are trying to save the world, are we not?'

'Yes,' Carl managed. 'Yes, we are.'

Plainsong nodded again. Then he blinked, and when he opened his eyes, they were locked onto Tommas.

'I am sure you gentlemen have everything under control, and there is no need for arguments.' He smiled, without showing his teeth. It was a smooth, fluid motion, yet as artificial as a marionette's dance. Tommas had heard of a smile not reaching someone's eyes, but he'd never before seen a smile which barely reached someone's mouth.

'I will leave you to your discussions,' Plainsong declared. He replaced his hood and walked back to the hatch, through which he disappeared, all without ever giving any indication that he had noticed they were at sea.

As soon as he disappeared from sight, Carl rounded on Tommas again. Fury had crowded out fear from his face, although it had obviously been a ferocious struggle.

'Are you out of your *mind?*' the factor demanded.

Tommas bit his lip and took a hasty recount of his presence on this ship, and who else was sharing it with him.

'Possibly.'

SIX

THE JOURNEY TO the Swallowmage was one of the least pleasant experiences of Kitt's life. Actually *being* stabbed had been no picnic, but the aftermath was even worse: a drawn-out fog of grey pain interspersed with all-too-frequent jangles of silver agony, of caught breaths and whimperings, of the futility of trying to find a way of sitting or lying or just generally *being* in a barrow full of straw that didn't knock, jar, or otherwise interact with the fucking knife still sticking out of her fucking side. They said the unknown god who tried to kill the future up on the high moors had done so because they had known what the future held, and right now, Kitt could empathise. Given a choice between her current experience and forging an immensely powerful weapon to rip a hole in reality, she'd reach for the hammer and tongs without hesitation.

But of course, people like Kitt Carver didn't get to change the world based on their own preferences. They just had to make the best of what the world gave them, and right now that was a fucking knife sticking out of her fucking side.

'Hang in there,' Derna urged, from somewhere behind Kitt. Say what you like about her, the Queen of the Streets was pushing the damned barrow herself. 'Not far now.'

'Shut the hell up, Derna,' Kitt managed to wheeze, biting down on a yelp as they hit yet another cobblestone.

There was a moment's silence.

Then: 'Kitt, are you blaming *me* for this?!'

'Yes,' Kitt snapped. She was in too much pain for anything other than honesty, albeit honesty somewhat tainted by the pain in question.

'I've been responsible for a lot of things,' Derna said, in a considering tone of voice. 'The treacle riots. That business with the one-legged wyvern. The explosion at the Lucky Shrimp Bar—'

'Wait, that was *you?*'

'They lied about their ingredients, and three people died. Food allergies are serious business, Kitt.' Derna took a deep breath. 'But I'm really not sure how you can lay this one on me.'

'I'll explain once we get this bloody thing out.'

Kitt looked up at the sky, which was visible as a jagged, pale blue line between the outlines of rooftops hunched together above her. Damn it all, she'd intended today to be a fresh start; to ease her way back into Rauk's good books and get the wheels moving on her career as one of Mereport's top diviners. Now she was in a bloody veg barrow – it was becoming literally bloodier by the moment, since the knife did not entirely plug her wound – and being wheeled towards a mage who was either drunken or hungover, possibly both, with the notion that this was somehow better than her current state of affairs.

It probably *was*, but that didn't mean she had to like it.

'We're here,' Derna announced, bringing the barrow to rest. She appeared in Kitt's view and pounded on a door. 'Sulian! Get your arse out here!'

'Are there going to be stairs?' Kitt asked weakly, eying the building. You would have expected the Swallowmage to live in a small mansion given her power, but they had arrived at a narrow and somewhat rickety-looking townhouse of dark timber and pale plaster, little different to that in which Kitt's parents lived.

'As if Sulian would want to deal with stairs,' Derna said with a snort. 'She's on the ground floor.' She switched to hammering on the window shutters. 'Sulian! I'm coming in one way or another, so choose whether you want to keep your door!'

'What if she's not here?' Kitt suggested. She really *wanted* the Swallowmage to be at home, since travelling anywhere else in the damned barrow with a knife in her side was very low down on the list of things she ever wanted to do, but the notion of just lying here in pain while Derna uselessly threatened an empty set of rooms was even lower.

'She wouldn't dare,' Derna muttered, which was a statement as emphatic as it was nonsensical, and thumped on the shutters once more. '*Sulian!*'

Between one strike of her fist and the next the shutters flew open to reveal a figure radiant with power, its long hair standing on end and with eyes as incandescent as miniature stars. Derna was knocked backwards by a blast of unseen force and disappeared from Kitt's view with a startled squawk. The apparition raised something that could only be called a hand because the noon sun rarely formed itself into the shape of four fingers and a thumb, and spake thusly in a voice akin to thunder:

'*WHO DARES INTRUDE UPON MY* – oh, it's you.'

The blaze of power faded, leaving Sulian the Swallowmage leaning on her windowframe and blinking owlishly. Briefly standing on end apparently hadn't done anything for the condition of her hair, because it collapsed back into the greying, lank tresses that always seemed to have gone one too many days without a wash. The swallow tattoo on her right cheek from which her name originated glowed for a moment longer, then settled back into its usual blue-black shades.

'Shitting griblets, Derna, what time do you call this?' Sulian demanded in a far more normal tone of voice. Normal for her, anyway, which meant trying not to speak too loud in case her own head fell off. She was clothed, at least, although the shapeless fabric draped over her upper body was a far cry from the ornate robes donned by those mages who moved in higher levels of society. It wasn't that Sulian was notably less powerful than many of the high and mighty, it was just that her magical gifts – numerous and diverse, which was what set actual mages apart from people like Kitt or Mizzik, who were good at one thing and one thing only – were tempered by the curse of her foretellings. What great noble wanted a mage with a tendency to stagger sideways and babble nonsense every now and then, not to mention who kept herself in a state of near-constant inebriation in an attempt to numb the impact of the future on her tortured brain? The Swallowmage of Mereport could manage most things that most mages could do, she just couldn't necessarily do it *now*. Or completely correctly. Or again.

All of which was why instead of dwelling in a beautiful tower, or a suite within a governor's palace, Sulian lived in a single room at street level within staggering distance of the nearest tavern, and instead of wearing the finest dragonsilk patterned with constellations or the sigils of a patron god, she was wrapped in a sturdy-looking but decidedly handed-down shawl on which she had almost certainly thrown up since it was last washed.

'It's nearly evening,' Derna said, picking herself up. 'And more to the point, it's time you helped Kitt.'

'Hi,' Kitt said, weakly. Sulian looked down at her and started in surprise.

'What in the – Kittreous Carver, have you been *stabbed?*'

'That's not my full name,' Kitt said, glaring at her. 'Also no, this is an elaborate prank and the hilt of the knife in my side is just a prop, *of course I've been fucking stabbed!*'

'Well, bring her in!' Sulian waved hurriedly at Derna. 'I'll unlock the door. Uh, Derna?' she added, her eyes narrowing unevenly as she squinted back down the road. 'Is there a reason why four duellists from two different sashes are following you with a rather unhappy-looking man at swordpoint between them?'

'Yes,' Derna said, taking up the handles of the barrow again.

'Oh. Well, good. I think. I'll file that under "problems to deal with later", shall I?'

Derna wheeled Kitt straight into Sulian's room, where the Swallowmage fiddled and fussed with various glass bottles on a table which also held a small mirror, a wooden carving of a crow that looked so lifelike Kitt was half-expecting it to fly away at any moment, and an actual stuffed crow that looked like someone had tried to assemble it out of rubbish they'd found in a gutter and with only a loose grasp of ornithology – or, indeed, of the materials they were using.

'Are you sure this is going to work?' Kitt asked through gritted teeth, as Sulian sniffed something, pulled a face, and replaced it.

'Of course I'm not sure, it's magic. If we were ever *sure* about magic, it wouldn't be magic.' She cast a glance over her shoulder that was almost fond. 'On the other hand, I *am* sure that this is your best option for a wound like that. Standard apothecary herbs would be practically useless.'

'Sooner's still better than later,' Derna put in impatiently.

'And not letting her get stabbed in the first place would be best of all,' Sulian replied, without looking around.

'I don't believe this!' Derna fumed. 'How come *everyone* is blaming me?'

'Most injuries that take place anywhere near you are your fault,' Sulian said. 'Ah! Here we are!' She pulled an unlabelled bottle out from amongst its fellows, uncorked it, and then turned around to look at Kitt. She pursed her lips, sucked her teeth, bent down to inspect the knife hilt with narrowed eyes, then straightened up again. 'Yes, this should do.'

She put the bottle to her lips, tilted her head back, and drained it.

'Er… Wasn't that meant to go onto the wound, or something?' Kitt asked, as the last drops disappeared.

'Eh? No, that was gin.' Sulian threw the bottle over her shoulder, where it shattered against the wall. She blinked rapidly three times, rolled up her sleeves to expose forearms covered with tattoos in sufficient quantity to make a sailor envious and of sufficient crudity to make one blush, and smiled widely, slightly higher on the right side of her face than the left. 'Now hold still, this is going to hurt. A lot.'

'Wait!' Kitt said desperately. 'I really don't like pain! I've had quite enough of it already!'

'Do you like dying?' Sulian asked. 'Because that's your alternative.'

'Honestly, I don't know,' Kitt wheezed. 'Never tried it.'

Sulian grimaced. 'That should have been an easy question. Let me put it like this: do you want a short period of extreme pain, and then probably continued life; or do you want a longer period of increasingly extreme pain, and then definitely death?'

'Well, when you put it like that,' Kitt managed. 'The first one.'

'Good. Hold on to that thought,' Sulian said. 'I mean that literally. Healing magic usually only works if the person being healed is conscious and wants to live. So, sorry about this, but you've got to sit through it. Derna, knife.'

Kitt yelped as Derna's fingers closed around the knife hilt, and then there was the hideous, slithering pain of the blade being pulled from her side.

'What are you doing?' Sulian yelled.

'You said "knife"!' Derna protested.

'I meant for you to be ready to take it out, not take it out right then!'

'Well how was I supposed to—'

'Help?' Kitt suggested, since no one else seemed to be focusing on what was, to her, the most pressing issue. 'Starting to lose blood here.'

'Right. Right right right,' Sulian said, shooing the sullen-faced Derna and her bloodied knife away. She placed her palms together pointing upwards and began to whisper under her breath, then twisted her hands so they were at right angles, the fingers of her right hand pointing towards Kitt while those of the left remained aimed at the ceiling. Then, just as Kitt was starting to wonder if the Swallowmage was going to be whispering sweet nothings to her own fingertips until Kitt Carver bled out into a barrow in the middle of her room, Sulian opened her eyes again and the room was once more filled with the glow of power. The Swallowmage's right hand caught light too, like fire spreading from one patch of dry grass to another through sparks carried on the wind, and then she slammed her glowing fingers over Kitt's wound.

Kitt screamed. Not from the lungs; it started lower than that. The scream began where the white-hot tendrils of Sulian's magic were crawling into her body, then forced its way upwards and outwards, locking her muscles rigid and compressing her lungs until the air was squeezed out through her mouth, activating her vocal cords on the way past before her throat closed up completely, like intruders discovered in a house pulling the back door shut behind them with a bang as they fled.

'eeeeeaaaarrrrrrrrrgggGGGGHHHHKKKKkkkkk…!'

Kitt floated in a tight golden world of her own pain, eyes squeezed shut so hard that non-existent colours flashed in front of her. Gods above, below, and all the bastards in between, she could *feel* her flesh knitting back together! It was a disgusting sensation, just as painful as being stabbed in the first place, and all the worse because at some deep level her body knew that what was happening to it was unnatural. She wanted to squirm, to crawl, to *get away* from her own side where this awful thing was happening—

'Kitt!'

It took her a moment to register that the voice was shouting her name, and another moment to recognise that it was in her ear and not in her mind. It wasn't until it shouted again that she remembered that the name that went with that voice was Two Tongue Derna, and the dim pressure across her chest was probably Derna's arm.

'Kitt, hold still!' Derna shouted from a thousand miles away, or possibly a few inches. 'And hold on! She says you've got to hold on!'

It works better if you want to live.

Kitt tried to focus on that; to block out the pain, and block out the nagging feeling that there was a very easy way to escape that pain and the disgusting, wriggling *wrongness* that was taking place in her flesh. The dark void wasn't calling to her as such, but that was the appeal of it: it was silent and still, a place where all sensation ceased.

'Kitt!'

Kitt fumbled blindly for Derna's forearm with what were probably her fingers, and gripped it as hard as she could to remind herself that there was at least *something* on this side of the void that wasn't just the agony in her flesh – and also, probably, to try to pass on just a bit of what she was going through to someone else.

The crawling fire in her side began to pull outwards, and time abruptly began to have some meaning again. Things had changed since before the painful *now*, and while the before had also consisted of pain, the notion of a before also indicated the presence of an after, and the after might exist in a place where things changed so much that the pain stopped. Kitt took what felt like her first breath in a century, and tried to resist the temptation to thrash. She could feel Sulian's magic withdrawing, but the agonising slowness of it made her want to wrench herself free, unable to tolerate it any longer now that the concept of it being over was on the horizon. She forced herself to remain still for another second… and another second… and another second…

Until quite suddenly, there were no more seconds.

Every muscle in Kitt's body turned to water, and she slumped further into the barrow with her arms and legs dangling over the side like boiled noodles. Her head fell back into the straw and gave her a good view of the Swallowmage's ceiling, and also Derna's upside-down face, looking at her in concern.

'Well,' Sulian said breathlessly. 'That could have gone worse. I need a drink.'

'You just *had* a drink!' Derna snapped.

'Accurate, but irrelevant,' the Swallowmage said cheerily. There was a glugging sound. 'Right. Why *is* there an unhappy man being held at swordpoint in my room, Derna?'

Kitt managed to turn her head to one side. The knife man was indeed with them, still flanked by two Iron Flowers and two Bleak Sisters, who had apparently decided that whatever Derna had got caught up in was interesting enough to ignore their sashes' rivalry for now.

'He's one of the ones who tried to kill Kitt,' Derna said. She removed her arm from across Kitt's chest and pulled a knife of her own, since apparently there weren't enough edged weapons already drawn inside the room. 'I want to know why, and who hired him.'

'Dunno,' the man said instantly. He looked positively desperate to be questioned, so long as the questions were delivered in a manner that didn't involve torture. 'Didn't know who she was, didn't know she was a friend of yours! We just got a name and a description.'

'Was the hiring linked to the scrying someone did on her?' Sulian put in. Kitt laboriously heaved her head around to look at the Swallowmage, who paused in the process of putting another bottle down. 'What? Sorry dear, I noticed it when I was doing the healing. Didn't realise it was a secret.'

'What scrying?' Kitt managed to ask, in a voice that might have belonged to a pair of punctured bellows.

'Oh!' Sulian looked at the bottle she had been about to put down, shrugged, and took another mouthful. 'Well, someone's scried you. I could feel the residue. You've done something that *someone* was very interested in finding out more about, and you got caught up in their scrying net.'

'Can you tell who it was?' Derna demanded. 'Or what they were scrying for?'

'Sorry, that's, *pfft*.' Sulian wiggled her fingers off into the air. 'I mean, I'm not saying it's *impossible*, but basically, yes, it's impossible. I don't know if Kitt was the person being scried or she just ended up being relevant in some way, but someone somewhere did a scrying spell recently in which she came up. You can always tell, it tastes…' She made a face. 'Chalky.'

'I don't know anything about that,' the knife man said instantly.

'All right,' Derna said, in a considering tone of voice. 'What *do* you know about?'

The thug's brow wrinkled. 'Excuse me?'

'You tried to kill my friend,' Derna said matter-of-factly, and something jumped a little in Kitt's chest. Derna considering you to be her friend was a dubious honour, but it was a hell of a lot better than being considered her enemy.

'Really,' Derna continued. 'I should kill you.'

'Not in my bloody room, if you *please*,' Sulian interrupted, exasperated.

'I'm prepared to believe you're not going to be foolish enough to try to kill Kitt again if I let you go,' Derna said, ignoring the Swallowmage. 'So give me a reason to let you go. Tell me something useful that's going to help me find out who wants my friend dead. Did whoever hired you for this give you any other jobs to do?'

'Uh, yeah,' the thug admitted. 'But you've gotta promise not to tell anyone!'

'I can promise to slice your nose off if you don't tell me *right now*.'

'Fine!' The thug grimaced. 'There was a destinies parlour up on Mazen's Holloway. We killed the owner and set fire to it, after the geezer had found out whatever he needed to find.'

'Wait, that was *you?*' Kitt demanded. 'I thought…' She blinked blearily at Derna. 'Never mind.'

Derna said nothing, but the look she cast at Kitt indicated that she had caught wind of Kitt's thoughts, and would be interrogating them further in the future. However, for now she turned back to the thug and twirled her knife in the air to encourage further loquaciousness. 'What *geezer?* What did he look like? What did he want to know?'

'Dunno,' the thug said instantly. 'He had some sort of charm going that made his face all wobbly and his voice weird. He found something in some big book, then burned it. We set fire to the rest of the place, and then we all legged it.'

'Anything else?' Derna demanded.

'There was another diviner,' the man said grudgingly. 'Two diviners and a destinies parlour, those were the jobs. Paid well, half up front. We were to pick the other half up from a ship called the *Spirit of Freedom* down at the docks when it was done.'

Kitt gasped as a possibility occurred to her. 'The other diviner. Was it Donal Klae?'

'Well?' Derna demanded into the resulting silence. 'Answer her!'

'Yeah,' the thug admitted. 'That's the name we got. Never got to him, though,' he added hastily, seeing Kitt's expression. 'He was going to be next.'

'Anything else?' Derna pushed. 'Any other names, any descriptions, any places, anything?'

'No, swear to all the gods,' the thug said desperately. 'That's all I know!'

Derna hummed to herself for a moment and tapped the tip of her knife on her teeth.

'*Not* in my room,' Sulian repeated sternly. 'If you're going to kill him, do it somewhere else. And not just outside the front door, either,' she added hotly after a second. 'I know what you're like!'

'Yes, mother,' Derna said sarcastically, sticking both halves of her tongue out.

'Oh, please. If I was *your* mother, I'd have turned to drink long ago,' the Swallowmage muttered, and took another swig of whatever it was she was holding. Then she blinked fast, winced, and clutched the side of her head. 'Damn it... *three times they turn* oh for crying out *on five golden leaves they rise and* shitting griblets, will you please *a face of bone turned to the sky with pools for eyes, hunger drawn down into the earth* I have had just about enough of *DEATH! DEATH! DEATH! DEATH!*'

That last was screamed so loudly and so strenuously that on the final syllable Sulian lost her balance and ended up flat on her arse, her left hand carefully outstretched to avoid her clutched bottle spilling even a drop of its contents. She grimaced and rubbed furiously at her forehead, then looked up and met Kitt's eyes.

'It's getting worse,' the Swallowmage said wearily. 'Not just for me. *It* is just getting worse. It's like all the futures are jumbled up and nonsensical. I honestly don't know how much longer the world has got, but that might just be the alcohol talking.' She sighed, and peered past the barrow in which Kitt still lay. 'Just get him out of my house, will you?'

'You heard her,' Derna said to the thug. 'Piss off. If I see you again, I'll kill you.'

She leered a smile, then jerked her head at the duellists, who lowered their blades. The thug didn't wait for a second invitation, and scrambled off his knees and out of the door with the urgency of a man who'd decided that city living was no longer for him.

'And you lot!' the Swallowmage snapped. 'Everyone out, and no duelling on my street! I've had enough damned disturbance for one day, thank you very much!'

The Iron Flowers and Bleak Sisters ducked their heads and muttered meek words of assent, then hastily made their own exits. Duellists were proud, but that pride was very much based around their reputation within the sashes. No one in their right mind was going to draw their blade on a mage over a grumpy word – even a drunken mage who sometimes fell over because she was shouting a garbled prophecy too hard.

'I'm thinking we should find the *Spirit of Freedom*, then,' Derna said.

Kitt groaned. 'Do we have to? I'm literally only just whole again.'

'Fine, I'll go and take a look myself. Sulian, can you—'

'Nope,' the Swallowmage said firmly. 'You're not leaving her here. Everyone out means *everyone*, including you two.'

'How much do I owe you for the healing?' Kitt asked, heaving herself out of the barrow. Her limbs were wobbly but apparently prepared to reluctantly bear her weight so long as she didn't make any sudden changes of direction.

'Your parents were very kind to me when I moved here, even though at that point they didn't know me as anything other than a grumpy woman with a hangover. We'll say that you can find something for me sometime,' Sulian said. She waved a hand to shoo them out, then lay back on the floor. 'Fuck, my head.'

Kitt looked at Derna. Then they each took hold of one of the barrow's handles and began to tug it back out of the door.

SEVEN

THE SPIRIT OF *Freedom*, it turned out, had departed with the tide just after noon, but beyond that not even Derna's reputation could shake much loose in terms of information. It had been a fair-sized ship that looked built for speed, had unloaded no cargo, and had only taken on a few provisions. Otherwise, the dock hands had ignored it.

'What kind of person pays for people to be killed, then doesn't even hang around to find out if it's been done?' Kitt said irritably, between mouthfuls of fried squid. Being magically healed had left her with a ferocious appetite, and if there was one thing Mereport was good at, it was sating hunger.

'The same sort that travels in a ship and pays a bunch of knives half up front, then pisses off,' Derna said. 'Someone who doesn't think they'll be tracked down afterwards.'

'So a toff, then. Which means anyone in authority might be mates with him.'

'Yeah, pretty much.' Derna snagged a squid ring and tossed it into her mouth without asking, but Kitt could hardly begrudge her that. Derna had got her to the Swallowmage in the first place and, even more surprisingly, had not been at fault in any way for the stabbing.

'So,' Derna said, after they'd walked a few more steps. 'You had me pegged for some destinies parlour being burned down?'

'Can you blame me?' Kitt asked, trying not to sound too defensive. 'Don't try to tell me that the Combined Futures break-in wasn't you. That had your fingerprints all over it.'

'What, really?' Derna frowned at her hands. 'I was *sure* I'd worn gloves.'

'No, not literally!' Kitt snapped. 'But you broke in, murdered three guards, and stole a big destiny, yes?'

'I wouldn't say "murdered". It was self-defence. They tried to kill me.'

'Because you broke into the place they were guarding, and that's a guard's job,' Kitt said, with strained patience.

'Then they shouldn't have taken a job that involves trying to kill someone because they didn't like where she was walking,' Derna said, somewhat haughtily. 'If you value a stranger's life less than her destroying something you were never going to see the benefit of anyway, don't be surprised if she doesn't value your life either.'

Kitt sighed. Conversations usually went like this with Derna. There was logic in there somewhere, but it was a very strange shape, and if you tried too hard to follow it you could never be entirely sure where you'd end up.

'It's not like I broke into someone's *home*,' Derna was saying. 'I could understand someone being angry about that—'

'I need to find Donal,' Kitt said. She'd been mulling this over ever since the thug mentioned his name. It wasn't a hugely appealing prospect – it smacked of jilted lover, which Kitt definitely wasn't – but there was no way of knowing if their mysterious enemy was going to take action against them both at some point in the future. 'He deserves to be warned, and he might know something.'

'And who is Donal?' Derna asked, in a tone of voice that was entirely too innocent.

Kitt sighed, but there wasn't any way around it. 'I spent last night with him, if you must know.'

A knife appeared in Derna's hand. 'Ah, so he sold you out. Got it.'

'No! He's a diviner. We got chatting at the Gecko, and then we got to… other stuff. You heard Sulian, this scrying picked *me* up. He's probably just collateral damage. I've probably endangered *him*.'

'We'll see,' Derna muttered ominously. 'How are we going to find him, anyway?'

Kitt pulled her divining rods out from their pouch. Finding a person was usually far harder than this, but when you'd slept with that person the previous night…

'He's over that way,' she said, as the moonstruck iron swung to the right. 'Still in the city too, I think.'

'If you find him before sundown, I'll buy you a beer,' Derna said, tucking her knife away. 'Lead on.'

THE SUN WAS just dipping below the rooftops, but was still technically in the sky when Kitt's rods stopped giving steady directions and started to move around rather more erratically.

'We're close,' she said to Derna, turning on the spot to get a better fix.

'He's a diviner too, you said?' Derna asked.

'Yeah, why?'

'Grey hair?'

'Yeah, how—' Kitt looked up and, through the bodies moving back and forth down Shander Street, made out the shape of Donal Klae poring over his own divining rods. 'Oh.'

'You know, he seems to be moving this way,' Derna said, in a tone of voice so studiously neutral it was practically begging to store a totalitarian regime's gold reserves.

'Shut up, Derna.'

'Just saying, but—'

'Shut *up*, Derna.'

'—his rod's pointing towards you.'

Kitt shut her eyes for a moment. It was nice, in a weird way, to be hanging around with Derna like they were kids again, regardless of the circumstances. However: 'You are awful, and I hate you.'

'Eyes open, princess.' Derna nudged her. 'Here he comes.'

Kitt sighed, opened her eyes, and shoved her moonstruck iron back into its pouch. Donal looked up a moment later. He met her eyes instantly, and stopped in apparent confusion about ten feet away.

'Uh.' He attempted a smile and was only about halfway successful. 'Hi.'

'Hi,' Kitt said back. They looked at each other in silence for a moment. Meanwhile, Kitt could feel the amusement radiating off Derna in waves.

'So I was—' Kitt began.

'I heard about—' Donal said, at exactly the same moment.

Kitt stopped, biting her lip. Donal's cheeks flushed, but then his eyes widened. 'Gods' blood, Kitt, have you been *stabbed?*'

Kitt looked down at her side, where her shirt was indeed sporting a narrow hole and bloodstains. She hadn't had time to change it yet, and things had seemed a bit too urgent to run back home. 'Uh, yeah, but I got fixed up.'

'Oh shit,' Donal said, his face falling.

'He's guilty,' Derna said instantly, and her knife reappeared.

'Guilty?' Donal protested. 'Guilty of what?'

'That's what we'll have to find out,' Derna said, with considerable menace.

'Kitt, who's your friend?'

'We're asking the questions, bucko!' Derna snapped. Kitt elbowed her.

'Derna, knock it off.' She eyed Donal. Much as she hated to admit it, he *did* have a slightly guilty look to him. 'Donal, someone tried to kill me earlier, and apparently they were also after you until Derna… dealt with them. I was coming to warn you. Why were *you* divining for *me?*'

'Derna?' Donal repeated, his eyes widening. 'As in, Two Tongue Derna?'

'If you've heard of me, you know I don't mind stabbing people,' Derna said flatly. 'Talk.'

'I… heard about the fire and the deaths at Mazen Rauk's place,' Donal said slowly, speaking to Kitt but not taking his eyes off Derna. 'I figured you might be in trouble.'

'And why,' Kitt asked suspiciously, 'did you figure that? I told you last night that I hadn't dealt with Rauk in months.'

'Yeah, but the thing *is*,' Donal said glumly, 'I was hired to find out what the biggest destiny you'd ever found was, and who you sold it to. You're a diviner too, they said, get her talking shop, swap tales. And you told me you sold it to Rauk, and then he shows up dead, so I was thinking—'

'Wait, someone *hired* you to sleep with me?' Kitt demanded, her gorge rising.

'No!' Donal protested, throwing out a splayed hand as Derna took a meaningful step forward. 'I was hired to find out about the biggest score you'd ever made, that was all. I didn't know you were going to be *hot*, or into me. That was, y'know, separate. You'd already told me about the destiny before that, remember? By rights, I probably should have left then, but things seemed to be going… well.'

'Can I stab him yet?' Derna asked.

'No!' Kitt snapped, then pointed at Donal. 'You. Who hired you?'

'Was it a man with a wobbly face and a strange voice?' Derna put in.

'…Yes?' Donal admitted, his face creasing into worried anticipation.

'And you went to a ship called *Spirit of Freedom* to give him the information?' Kitt asked wearily.

'Er, yes?'

'Well, congratulations!' Kitt said, raising her arms. 'That's who burned down Destiny Calling and hired people to kill both of us! Well done, you absolute *prick!*'

'Look, I needed the money, okay?' Donal whined. 'I figured he was just some business rival of Rauk's who wanted some inside information! I didn't know anyone was going to get hurt!'

'Tell me truly,' Derna said to Kitt. 'What did you see in him?'

'I am honestly disappointed in my own self,' Kitt admitted. She glared at Donal; good arms had a lot to answer for. 'I didn't want anything more from you than a night of good-natured fun and hopefully a lack of awkward follow-up, so "selling on conversation details and nearly getting me killed" is a pretty *spectacular* way to shit all over even those *very modest* expectations.'

'You're right,' Donal said, looking thoroughly miserable. He brightened a little. 'Let me try to make it up to you. Are you trying to find this guy? I'll help. I owe him nothing, especially if he wanted me dead!'

'He's *gone*,' Derna said in disgust. 'His ship left earlier. Unless you managed to steal something from him you could use as a focus – or you slept with him as well – how are you going to track him?'

'You'd also need a ship,' Kitt put in, with a glare at Derna for her joke. 'Because we certainly don't have a way to follow him over the sea.'

'Do you actually want to find him?' Derna asked, turning to Kitt. Passersby were giving them a wide berth now, probably because Derna was gesticulating without apparently remembering that she was holding a knife in one hand. 'He tried to have you killed, he failed, he disappeared before finding out if he was successful. If we manage to find him, he'll know you're still alive, and he might try again. You could just hide and pretend it never happened.'

'I can't believe *you* are suggesting that I hide.'

Derna grimaced. 'Trust me, it doesn't feel good. But I know you're not me, and I'm trying to look out for you. You've already nearly died once today,' she continued, resting her hand on Kitt's shoulder. 'I sort of think I should try to prevent it happening again.'

Kitt thought about it. The cold terror of her near-death experience had been replaced by hot fury – and ravening hunger – when they were heading towards the docks, but now… What *did* she want? Did she want to find this mysterious man and take revenge? Slip a knife between *his* ribs? It wasn't something she could easily envisage herself doing. In the heat of the moment, yes; if it came down to her or someone else who was waving a blade at her, then she'd be doing her best to make it someone else. But tracking someone down with the intention of killing them? It didn't sit right in her stomach.

On the other hand, nor did letting it lie. This man had not only tried to kill her – and Donal, but she was rather less bothered about that now than she had been five minutes ago – but he *had* killed Mazen Rauk, who'd never harmed anyone to the best of Kitt's knowledge, plus Mazen's guard, and set fire to the shop, endangering the whole street. How did someone feel they just had the right to do that?

'This probably isn't the first time he's done this,' she said slowly. 'Which means he's probably going to end up killing more people.'

'True,' Derna agreed.

Kitt opened her mouth to continue her train of thought, then stopped. 'Okay, but you've killed a *lot* of people. It sort of feels dishonest not to address that.'

'I've only really killed people who've been trying to kill me,' Derna protested. 'Or trying to kill my friends. Or have been doing things that *might* kill my friends—'

'The Lucky Shrimp Bar?'

'The Lucky Shrimp Bar.'

'Anyway, fine, I don't know if I want to *kill* him,' Kitt said, waving that away. 'But I want to ruin whatever it is he's trying to do. He's certainly got that coming to him. The problem is, we don't know what that is, except that it might be linked to the big destiny I found.' She glanced at Donal, who was eyeing Derna with even more trepidation than before. 'He didn't say anything about the destiny at all? Nothing about why he was interested in it?'

'No, just that he wanted to know what had happened to the biggest one you'd ever found,' Donal said. 'If you sold it to Rauk, then he'd know, right? He'd know who he sold it to, so we could get an idea of what this guy found out, and where he's going next.'

'Yes, but Mazen's dead!' Kitt snapped.

'He'd have kept records?' Derna asked.

'There was a *fire!* Come on, think about this!' Kitt bit her lip, as what she'd just said started ringing a bell in the back of her mind. 'There was a fire. That had to be deliberate. They didn't want anyone else having access to Mazen's records. They were trying to cover their tracks, so they *must* be heading for whoever bought that destiny.'

'And given their track record so far, they're probably going to kill whoever it is,' Derna said.

'I don't mean to repeat myself,' Donal said tentatively, 'but… Rauk would know.' He looked from Kitt to Derna, and back again. 'He'd still know.'

Kitt looked at him, then looked at Derna, and found Derna looking back at her.

'Is he—'

'He's talking about necromancy,' Derna said. 'You're talking about necromancy, aren't you?'

'Yeah.' Donal smiled weakly. 'I know it's not the *best* idea, but if it worked, it would tell us what we need to know.'

'I hate to admit it,' Derna said to Kitt in a low voice, 'but the prick is right. It would work. *If* it works.'

Kitt bit her lip. 'And Mazen's only just dead, which would make it easier. I think.'

'So I guess the question is,' Derna said, 'how much do you want to stop this guy from killing again?'

THERE WERE A large number of ways to dispose of a dead body in a city like Mereport. Most were dependent on which religion, if any, the deceased followed – or perhaps more accurately, which religion their next of kin thought or wished they had followed (the rest, of course, were dependent on which crime boss you'd pissed off).

Followers of Salita the moon goddess were placed in a small craft and sent downriver on fire, much to the annoyance of local fishermen. Adherents of the Seven Scriptures were winched up to high platforms in a demarcated area of parkland and left for the birds. No one really knew what happened to the disciples of Tornuous the Horned, but their funeral rites were quiet and didn't lead to you having to keep an eye out in case a dismembered leg fell on you from above after a raven had severed a crucial bit of gristle, so people took care not to ask exactly what it meant when their wakes were described as 'self-catered'.

However, the majority of people living within Mereport would be either buried or burned, and it was to one of these denominations that Mazen Rauk had belonged. Not for him the communal coffin to take him to an unmarked pauper's grave; he had been a man of some means, and so his body was moved to one of the city's three morgues while a ceremony was organised.

'You're sure it's this one?' Derna asked quietly, as the four of them clustered at the end of Spinetucket Road.

'No,' Kitt admitted. She'd gone back to Destiny Calling, but there was nothing left within the shop's burned-out shell to use as a focus from which to find Mazen's corpse. Makema hadn't been certain which morgue her neighbour had been taken to, but she'd thought it was Spinetucket Road, so here they were lurking in the dark: a street duellist, two diviners (one of whom was very definitely only being allowed to tag along), and a half-drunk mage.

'Why didn't we bring an actual necromancer?' Donal asked quietly, looking pointedly at Sulian.

'No ethical necromancer would agree to set foot in a morgue under false pretences,' Sulian said with a sniff. 'It would ruin their reputation if they were found out.'

'So why not find an *unethical* necromancer?'

'Why would you take an unethical necromancer into a morgue?!' the Swallowmage demanded incredulously. 'Kitt, where did you find this guy?'

'Don't ask,' Kitt muttered, checking her hastily assembled outfit once more. Sulian's presence wasn't ideal, but she was the only possible choice. Necromancers were a bit of a strange breed, but that was just the way that some people's natural magic ran. A good necromancer could summon the spirits of the dead for conversation or advice; an ethical necromancer respected the wishes of the dead as much as they did those of the living, and would not compel a spirit to do anything, unless the spirit was restless, destructive, and needed quieting.

Not all obeyed those unwritten rules, of course. Entire armies of rotting corpses were stories from legend, but even a few unquestioningly obedient undead thugs could be a force to be reckoned with. That was why unethical necromancers could expect nothing more than very swift and extremely thorough execution, which was usually deterrent enough, and why ethical necromancers were very eager not to have their actions misinterpreted. Spirits were unable to speak of whatever awaited after death, but general consensus amongst the living was that magical ability did not carry over. As a result, it was considered that those who enslaved the dead in body or spirit could expect, after they passed on themselves, the supernatural equivalent of a line of shapes at the end of a narrow alley, meaningfully tapping cudgels into their palms.

'Are you *sure* you're up to this?' Kitt said, looking back at the Swallowmage.

'I'm not going to be able to get him to stand up and dance,' Sulian said. 'A conversation? That should be fine, so long as you stick to the rules.'

'The rules?' Donal asked.

'You don't ask the spirit a question until I tell you to,' Sulian said. 'You don't keep addressing it if I tell you to stop. You do not ask about the death of its body, where it is now, or what it's experiencing. And you never, ever, lie to it.'

Donal nodded. 'And, er, what happens if we do one of those?'

'Very bad things,' Sulian said ominously.

'Also, I stab you,' Derna added.

'That counts as a very bad thing,' Donal pointed out.

Derna shrugged. 'That depends on your point of view.' She nudged Kitt. 'Are you ready?'

Kitt fingered the glass bulbs in her belt pouch. 'Yes. Let's do this.'

For reasons that everyone understood, although could not necessarily immediately verbalise, the city of Mereport had not placed its morgues in residential areas. Despite the fact that the dead were very rarely rowdy, raucous, or likely to let themselves into your house via the backdoor and help themselves to the pie you'd just cooked, most people preferred neighbours who were alive, even though they were statistically more likely to do any or all of those things. Spinetucket Road was not, therefore, alive with the noise of family homes, nor lit by the flickering light of candles or fires from behind window shutters. Instead, it was a dark street of looming warehouses and factory buildings around which darkness lurked like spilled molasses.

The thing about a morgue was, of course, that it was never truly closed. People died at all times of the day, and the dead could not be trusted to form a queue.

'Are you sure that's the right place?' Donal asked in a whisper as they approached the smallest building on the street, only two storeys and about the size of a modest tavern. 'It doesn't look big enough.'

'It doesn't need to be that big,' Kitt told him quietly. 'Most bodies don't stay here for long. Besides, the vault's below ground.'

'The dead don't need windows, see?' Derna said, with a throaty chuckle.

'There should be two guards on the main door,' Kitt said in a low voice. 'Possibly two more at the entrance to the vaults. There'll be a clerk, and a couple of porters.'

'How do you know so much about morgues?' Derna asked.

Kitt shrugged. 'I have tracked down *some* missing people in my time, and you'd be surprised how many of them have turned up dead.' She eyed Derna. 'Then again, maybe you wouldn't be. Just remember, we're not here to leave more corpses than there were when we arrived.'

'We'd best hope those sleep spells are worth what you paid for them, then,' Derna muttered. 'My reputation's colourful enough without people thinking I'm getting into grave-robbing.'

Kitt grimaced. There were many rumoured uses for parts of dead bodies for which the undermarket reportedly paid top coin – which was what the guards were for, since morgues were not normally concerned about the occupants trying to leave of their own accord – but that was a commerce of which Kitt had always steered well clear. The dead might *technically* not have any use for their departed flesh, but one could never be sure. The whole notion made Kitt feel a little queasy, and she tried to refocus.

'The sleep spells *should* work for about half an hour,' she said, 'but as the Swallowmage reminds us, you can never be sure with magic, so we want to be in there for a lot less than that. Ready?' Everyone nodded. 'Right. Here we go!'

She walked up to the main door and knocked. The impact of her knuckles on the wood sounded shockingly loud, but she did her best to swallow her nerves. Looking unsettled was entirely to be expected, but panicking would help no one.

The watch-slot in the door slid open, and a pair of eyes peered out at her. 'Yes?'

'My name is Meyla Rauk,' Kitt said, her heart fluttering. 'I believe you have my father here.'

'We are very sorry to hear of your loss,' the clerk said, and she almost sounded as though she meant it. It was a practised condolence, undoubtedly delivered by rote so many times that the meaning of the words had got lost long ago.

'Thank you,' Kitt said neutrally. She hoped this wasn't going to cause too many problems down the line for the real Meyla Rauk, whose existence she only knew of because Mazen had liked to talk about his children when they were discussing prices for Kitt's finds, perhaps in hope that she would take a lower price simply in order to escape the inanity. Kitt had always held out, however, and as a result had sat through interminable details of the eldest Rauk child's life as a merchant. She fancied she could play Meyla better than the woman herself, at least to anyone whose only knowledge of her was Mazen's stories.

'You have an address in Mereport?' the clerk said, opening her book. She was an elderly wellyn woman with a pair of half-moon spectacles on her nose, over which she looked at Kitt expectantly.

'No, I only arrived back in the city today,' Kitt said promptly. 'I was to be staying with my father. If you need an address, then it's Farsign Street in High Ashknocking.' Mazen had been so proud: High Ashknocking was nowhere near as large as Mereport, but Farsign Street was one of its finest, according to him.

The clerk marked this down dutifully, then looked up with every sign of sympathy. 'You understand, Ms Rauk, that your father's death was a violent one? And that his body has not yet been prepared in any way?'

'I do,' Kitt said, biting her lip and nodding.

'Very well. In which case, you may proceed to the vaults. Toray will see you down.'

She gestured, and a porter walked over. He was a solid-looking man whom Kitt would have placed at somewhere in his forties, with patches of white stubble standing out on his cheeks against his deep brown skin. He nodded to her and turned to lead the way, but the clerk cleared her throat as Kitt and her companions made to follow.

'My apologies, Ms Rauk, but unless anyone else in your group is related to the deceased, they must stay here.' She smiled humourlessly. 'We can't have whole parties traipsing about below ground, you see.'

Kitt nodded, and invented desperately. 'Of course, but Jeela here needs to come with me.' She motioned to Sulian, whose fixed expression gave away nothing other than the fact that she wasn't quite sure what was going on. 'She's a priest of our faith, and she needs to pray over my father.'

'Hmm. And what faith is that?' the clerk asked. She didn't appear overly suspicious, but her pen was poised, and it was a question to which Kitt had no answer.

'That of Great Kensha,' Sulian said immediately. 'The prayers must be said before the dawn after death.'

'Of course,' the clerk said, looking down and making a note in her book. 'Carry on.'

Kitt breathed again as she and Sulian followed the porter to the vault entrance, but her heart rate rose once more when the door was pulled back. One of the guards within was human, with the bored expression of one who had little imagination and was therefore excellently suited to a job guarding corpses. The other, however, was a kyn.

The gobel-kyn were, on average, a little shorter than humans, and covered with short dense fur that varied in shade just as much as that on a human's head; an ash-blond, in this case. Most of the features were similar – two eyes, a nose, a mouth, two ears, two arms, and two legs – but were subtly different. A kyn's eyes were always golden, their noses were flatter and pushed back into their heads so they seemed to be looking at you with their nostrils, their ears were larger, pointed, and twitched this way and that, their mouths tended to be slightly wider, their arms were proportionately a little longer and their legs perhaps a touch shorter, and their posture not quite as upright.

Kyn had their own great catacomb cities, but they were not uncommon in Mereport and tended to live and work in enclosed spaces or underground where their keener vision and sharper hearing benefited them. By the same token, they stayed away from areas like the dock front, where they found the stink of fish overwhelming, and the bright glows and ringing hammering of smithies were positively painful for most. However, their main difference from humans was that they had very little, if any, magic.

There were no gobel-kyn mages and precious few who exhibited even minor talents like Kitt's own. Perhaps as a result, they were also very *resistant* to magic. Kitt would find things *for* a kyn, but she would never waste her time trying to divine the whereabouts of an *actual* kyn, no matter if she had samples of their hair, their blood, and all their nearest relatives to hand. Spells cast at or onto a kyn might work, but they very likely would not.

Like, for example, the sleeping spells Kitt had ready, just in case their ruse was rumbled.

Well, there was nothing for it. Kitt wasn't sure what the penalties were for impersonating a deceased person's relative in order to gain access to their body – that sounded a lot worse than she felt it should – and nor, now she came to think about it, was she certain what the consequences would be for performing unauthorised necromancy in a morgue, but it was too late to back out now.

She and Sulian followed Toray past the guards and down the stone steps into the cold, still air of the vaults.

NINE

The air smelled of cold stone, and slightly of damp, and of linen. There were other scents as well, mixed in and under those dominant ones: the chemical tang of preservatives, and the faint rancid sweetness of decay from those bodies for which such processes had not begun in time. It was not wholly unpleasant, but neither was it air that Kitt had any desire to breathe for longer than she had to.

Toray held up a lightstone as they descended, and the enchanted rock began to illuminate their surroundings. There were three archways at the bottom of the steps, one leading off ahead, another to the left, and the third to the right.

'There's room for a lot of bodies down here?' Kitt asked, curious despite herself.

'Mereport's a big city,' Toray replied. He had a voice like a creaky cupboard door. 'That's a lot of people dying every day.' He turned to the right and led them through a passage that was too long to be merely an archway but too short to properly be called a tunnel, and into the vault beyond. 'Your father should be… Ah, here we are.'

He came to a halt beside a sturdy wooden trolley, on

which lay a linen-shrouded form. The cloth was stained dark around the throat.

'Thank you,' Kitt said, not needing any acting to make her voice small and shaky. 'Do you… Do you have a spare stone? The rite is a private one,' she added by way of explanation when Toray looked at her questioningly. 'Jeela and I should perform it alone.'

'A Kenshan rite?' Toray asked, and Kitt nodded. His brow creased. 'Well, I'm Kenshan myself, and I don't know of any—'

Kitt's fingers were already on one of the sleep spells, and she whipped one out to smash the thin glass in her gloved hand against Toray's chest. The porter staggered backwards with a startled grunt, but he took a breath of the greenish smoke that burst out of the vial and his eyes immediately began to droop. Kitt managed to catch him as his knees folded, and lowered him to the ground gently.

'Wow,' Sulian said. 'That stuff's good. Maybe I should get some.'

'I'm told it leaves a blinding headache when you wake up,' Kitt panted. Her heart was racing fit to burst, and she was uncomfortably aware that they were now well into the 'crimes' section of her plan, with two guards between them and the surface, and another two between that and the morgue's main door.

'You mean you wake up *without* a blinding headache?' the Swallowmage asked. Kitt snatched up the lightstone and held it over the body of Mazen Rauk.

'Just get on with it,' she hissed.

'Just remember the rules,' Sulian countered, moving around until she reached Rauk's head. She pulled down the shroud to expose his face – although to Kitt's relief she left the throat wound covered – and revealed waxy features with a slightly yellow tinge that had not been there in life. Mazen's mouth was open, as were his eyes, which were clouded over.

It was unmistakably a dead body. There was nothing about it which gave any suggestion that a person's spirit still inhabited it, but it was as much a focus for necromancy as a lock of hair would be for Kitt to track someone down. The greatest necromancers were able to call upon the spirits of the dead without needing access to the deceased's bodies, just like Kitt could find destinies up on the high moors without any focus other than her moonstruck iron, but Sulian wasn't a necromancer. She was a mage, and she needed all the help she could get.

The Swallowmage extended her hands so they framed Rauk's head without quite touching it, and began to chant softly under her breath. Kitt couldn't follow the words – indeed, she didn't *want* to follow the words – but images rose up unbidden in her mind as Sulian droned quietly on: doors opening, curtains being pulled back, a search for something that lay just *beyond* and inviting it to step back for a brief while.

A faint sparkle appeared between the Swallowmage's fingers and Mazen Rauk's head – hard to see under the illumination from the lightstone, but the palest blue, and somehow greasy-looking. It began to crawl across the corpse's cheeks, diving into its ears, slipping into its nostrils, and delving down into the dark cavern of its mouth. Kitt held her breath and watched, waiting for Sulian to nod her head to say that yes, she had succeeded.

Mazen Rauk's body didn't move. There was no visible change. However, Kitt *felt* the moment that something else was in the vault with them. She opened her mouth, glanced up at the Swallowmage, and closed it again. Sulian was sweating.

A few more seconds crawled past, thick and charged. Sulian opened her eyes and nodded tersely, at the same time as – still without moving – a noise emerged from the corpse's mouth as though it had taken a sharp breath.

'*Who is there? What is this?*'

It wasn't a voice, in the sense that the sounds were not

being formed by air moving over flesh, or shaped by lips and tongue. It was dry, and whispery. Nonetheless, it was still recognisably the clipped, precise tone of Mazen Rauk, destinies merchant.

'Mazen?' Kitt said, barely able to get the word out of a throat constricted by nerves.

'*Who is there?*' the voice repeated. It sounded less agitated this time, but angrier.

'Mazen, it's Kitt,' Kitt said quickly. 'Kitt Carver. I'm sorry to… disturb you. But I need your help.'

'*Kitt,*' Mazen's voice said musingly, then with more conviction. '*Kitt. Yes. I haven't seen you for a while.*'

'No, I've been busy,' Kitt said. She glanced up at the Swallowmage, who managed to convey with nothing more than a meaningful waggle of her eyebrows that Kitt should get the hells on with it. 'Mazen, do you remember the biggest destiny I ever sold you? Two years ago, in the summer. You paid me ten gold crowns for it, unsoothed.'

'*Yes,*' Mazen said distantly. '*Yes, I do.*'

Kitt took a deep breath. 'I need to know who you sold it to.'

'*I… Miss Carver, you know that confidentiality is the cornerstone of my business.*'

'Mazen, this is *important,*' Kitt said urgently. 'People are dead.' Her heart jumped into her mouth and she looked up at Sulian again, who widened her eyes warningly. Talking about other deaths was fine. Talking about the death of the spirit being interrogated… that was definitely not fine. 'Someone seems to be after whoever bought that destiny. They tried to have me killed just for selling it to you. I need to warn whoever bought it!'

'*Well, that's very unpleasant,*' Mazen said, as though Kitt had told him about stepping in dung. '*But I suppose if it's that important… I'd have to check my records. Where is my ledger…?*'

Sulian's shake of the head was minute, more of a spasm than anything else. If Mazen began to look for his ledger, he would start to become aware of his surroundings, and that was something else which they could not afford to happen.

'Mazen, you're the most organised person I know,' Kitt said, with total honesty. 'You don't *need* your ledger. You've told me that yourself any number of times. You only have it because you're obligated to record your takings. I know you can remember who you sold that destiny to.'

'"*To whom you sold that destiny*",' Mazen corrected her primly. '*Honestly, Miss Carver, you are an excellent diviner, but somewhat lacking in matters of grammar.*' The spirit tutted with an invisible tongue against invisible lips. '*You are correct, however: I can indeed recall to whom that destiny was sold, since it was not purchased until quite recently. But… you are certain that this is a matter of utmost importance?*'

Sulian was sweating again, and her hands were shaking. In any other situation Kitt would have assumed the Swallowmage needed a drink, but here and now there seemed to be a more obvious and less benign explanation. There were walls between the worlds for a reason, was how it had been explained to her. If a body expired and its soul drifted off to wherever souls drift off to, that was all fine and natural, and rarely would it give rise to any issues. If someone started poking holes in those walls, however – such as to ask questions of a spirit that no longer belonged in this world – then something else might come through with it.

That was why you didn't ask the spirit about their death, or where they were. To do so was a fairly surefire way to ensure you joined them before long.

However, magic was never a sure thing. You could obey all the rules and avoid all the proscribed topics, but necromancy still wasn't *safe*. If the necromancer in question lost their grip on the spell without properly ending it, the ends could fly loose and shatter the walls between the worlds on their own, and then you'd be neck-deep in shit faster than a bungee-jumper over an open sewer.

'Yes, Mazen,' Kitt said, keeping her eyes on the Swallowmage. 'It really is vital.'

'*Well, in that case… It was to the Grike family of Derringsmoot, or more accurately their factor. A nice chap named Marquin, with a fondness for chamomile tea. I hadn't seen him for some years, although he bought another big destiny from me, many years before. Not one of yours, of course – you'd have barely been born back then, I'd wager! – but that was a large one as well, although I hadn't had time to get it soothsayered, so perhaps it didn't meet their needs—*'

'It's been lovely talking to you, Mazen,' Kitt said, fighting through a lump in her throat. 'But I need to be off, and I should really let you go.'

'*Really? But we haven't chatted in a while! And it's been so good to see you… although I say "see", but for some reason…*'

Kitt looked up at Sulian and, with considerable urgency and a certain lack of propriety that she did not register until somewhat later, made a slashing motion across her throat with her hand.

'*Kitt…? Where are you? I can't…*'

Sulian was wavering, her legs barely supporting her, but she was muttering the incantation that would end the connection. Greasy light crawled over Mazen Rauk's face again, but it looked different now.

Hungry.

'Mazen, your daughter,' Kitt said quickly, trying to deflect the merchant's mind. 'How is she? Has she been well?'

'*Kitt, you never ask about Meyla,*' Mazen said crossly. '*Don't try to distract me. Why can't I see you? Where…?*'

Kitt pulled out another sleep spell. She had absolutely no faith that it would work on anything that might break through, but it felt marginally better than standing around helplessly.

'*Where am I?*' Mazen Rauk asked, and the horror in his tone was underlaid by a deeper noise, as though his voice was echoed by one comprised of splintering granite. The light spiderwebbing across his face flared brighter—

And winked out.

'Shit,' Sulian said weakly, sitting down heavily on the stone floor.

'Shit? Is that good? Bad?' Kitt asked, looking around in case the air started trying to eat her.

'Spell's ended properly,' the Swallowmage said. She lay backwards, looking up at the ceiling. 'I just need to die for a while.'

Kitt replaced the sleep spell under her cloak, hastily drew the shroud back over Mazen's face – no point in tempting fate, or disrespecting the dead any further than they already had – and heaved the Swallowmage back up with her hands under the older woman's armpits.

'Are you actually okay? And don't say that you need a drink.'

'I *do* need a drink,' Sulian said breathlessly, and delved into a pouch to pull out a small flask, from which she took a quick swig. 'Right. What are we doing about *him?*'

In all of the stress involving Mazen Rauk, Kitt had quite forgotten about the gently snoozing form of Toray, who was still stretched out on the vault floor.

'If we have to fight our way out of here,' she said quietly, 'how much use will you be?'

'Right now?' Sulian grimaced. 'I could probably fall over on someone. If they stayed still.'

Kitt bit back a curse. She wasn't much of a fighter, which was why she'd taken people like Gallows Jayne and Falzine Halfshade up onto the moors with her. Derna was a fighter, *obviously*, but if she got into the mix then people were probably going to die. Donal was a well-built man of reasonable size, but Kitt knew nothing about how he'd handle himself, if he'd even get involved at all.

'I'm going to call the guards,' she said quietly. 'We'll pretend he's just collapsed. Maybe we can get out while they see to him.'

Sulian raised her eyebrows, but shrugged and knelt heavily down next to Toray's prone form. 'Ready when you are, I guess.'

Kitt huffed a breath, squared her shoulders, and then ran back through the archway. 'Hello? Hello! Help!'

A head had already appeared around the doorway at the top of the steps by the time Kitt reached the bottom of them, and she waved urgently at it. 'Help! It's Toray! We'd just finished saying the prayers and he collapsed, I don't know what's wrong with him!'

The two guards clattered into action, hastening down the steps with thudding boots. Kitt stepped back to let them pass then cautiously followed, her fingers once more reaching for the sleeping spells. It wasn't her preferred course of action by any means, but if her improvisation failed…

The human guard cursed when he saw Toray on the floor with Sulian bent over him, gently slapping his face like a distraught maid in a novel whose lady had just swooned. Kitt hauled her up and away as the kyn knelt down and placed his fingers – dark on the underside with bare, padded skin – to the porter's throat.

'His heart's still going,' the kyn said, 'and he's breathing.'

'He's not back on the juice, is he?' the human groaned.

The kyn sniffed. 'I can smell alcohol.' He looked up at Kitt and Sulian with bright, golden eyes. 'Did he drink anything while you were down here?'

Kitt swallowed, thinking of the Swallowmage's flask. 'We were busy praying, sir, I honestly couldn't say.' She held out the lightstone. 'I'll leave you with this, and go and tell the clerk.'

'Bloody fool,' the human muttered, taking the lightstone without really looking at her. 'The physician *told* him, "if you keep on that stuff then they'll be putting you in the vaults next", but did he listen…?'

Kitt grabbed Sulian by the elbow and pulled her away. The Swallowmage said nothing as they hurried through the archway and up the steps. Nor, indeed, did she say much once Kitt had hastily spun her tale to the clerk, and had somehow managed to get them all outside without anyone picking up on exactly how much of a hurry she was in.

TEN

'You're sure he said Derringsmoot?' Donal asked, as the four of them sat around a table in the Dubious Gecko.

'I was listening to the voice of a dead man,' Kitt told him sourly. 'I was concentrating pretty damned hard.'

'Well, that's not even in the Song valley,' Donal said. 'That's on the other side of the high moors.' He unrolled a map, weighing one end down with his tankard and pinning the other in place with his elbow, and jabbed his finger at a dot on the thick paper. 'See?'

'Where did you get a map?' Kitt peered with interest at the part of the world it claimed to show. It wasn't that she'd never left Mereport, but her excursions had taken her no farther than a couple of days' travel up the valley, or into the timeless lands to the north. She wasn't well-travelled and wasn't embarrassed about it, but it took her a few moments to puzzle out what she was looking at.

Mereport sat in a giant bay on the west coast of the mainland, with bumpy arms of land stretching out into the sea to the north and south. The area of the high moors in which time stood still was depicted as a great dark blob without any details, since the representatives from the Mereport Guild of Cartographers had only succeeded in charting the gullets of slydewasps, after which they'd decided that diviners could probably get around fine on their own. However, there were other places listed of which Kitt had only heard rumours; the sullen mass of the Drakwoods to the east, the high peaks of the Farsight Mountains to the south, the shining northern city of Kir-Lu where every building was supposed to be carved from crystal – and which, entirely unrelated, had the highest concentration of curtain shops anywhere in the known world – and others.

'Well, shit,' Derna said, sitting back on her stool. 'So much for that idea.'

Kitt looked at her in surprise. 'What do you mean?'

'Look where it is,' Derna said, drawing her finger across the map, to Donal's obvious discomfort. 'There's no way we'd reach it before our mystery man and whoever he has with him. They just need to nip around here,' she pointed at the peninsula to Mereport's north, 'and then head up whatever river that is, the… Solwynd?' She squinted in the poor light. 'Sulian, pass the candle over.'

'No,' Donal said instantly. 'No fire near the map! Or hot wax.'

'Anyway, we don't have a ship, and if we could get one then it almost certainly wouldn't be as good or as fast, *and* they have a head start on us,' Derna continued. 'They'll be there in a week, maybe ten days? We'd be lucky to get there in less than a month.' She traced her finger around the narrow strip of land between the western edge of the high moors and the coast. 'Most of that is thick forest. Not many people live there now, and the roads are bad. The travelling's better if you go up the valley and head north from Songsbridge, but that's a lot farther, and probably wouldn't get us there any quicker.'

Kitt bit her lip and stared at the map, as though a stern glare would cause it to rearrange its features into a configuration that would make what she was trying to do possible. The paper, unsurprisingly, refused to comply with her unspoken demands.

'Before anyone says anything,' Sulian said wearily, 'no, I can't turn people into birds, or anything like that.' The Swallowmage was resting her chin in one hand, and looked like she was about to fall asleep.

'Maybe we could send a message?' Donal asked. 'Messengers travel fast, right?'

'Saying what?' Derna demanded. She shifted her voice into a singsong. ' "Greetings your excellencies, we think that someone we know neither the name nor appearance of might be trying to kill you because of a destiny you bought, which we learned from a dead man".' She snorted. 'Who'd listen to that? Anyway, messengers can move fast, but I still don't think one would get there in time, no matter how much you paid.'

Kitt took a swig of her beer, still staring at the map.

'Why does this mean so much to you, anyway?' Donal asked her, somewhat hesitantly.

'Why *doesn't* it mean so much to you?' Kitt demanded in reply. Donal had been tiptoeing around her ever since he'd admitted how he'd deceived her, and it was starting to gall. On the one hand, yes, he should be ashamed of what he'd done. Even if he'd genuinely thought he was simply passing on information to one of Mazen's competitors, he'd potentially been hurting Kitt in the process. As for them sleeping together, then sure, *technically* that hadn't been anything more than what she'd taken it to be at the time, but it felt very different knowing that his initial conversation hadn't been the casual chat she'd assumed it to be.

On the other hand, this lily-livered sop was a far cry from the charming, confident man she'd met in this very tavern only one day before. She'd taken him at his word that he wanted to make amends, and she was content to let his actions prove that, so why keep up the cringing?

Derna elbowed Donal. 'If *you're* not bothered about people trying to have you killed, then…' she said mockingly, drawing a knife.

'You know what?' Kitt said, verbalising something for the first time, even to herself. 'It's not that he tried to have me killed. It's that he didn't stick around to see if it happened or not.' She looked around the table, trying to see from their faces whether they understood. 'It's the casualness of it. If it doesn't actually matter to you if my life ends, why try to end it in the first place?'

'What?' the Swallowmage said muzzily. 'You're insulted because whoever this was didn't try *harder* to kill you?' She shook her head, insofar as she could do that while it was still resting in her hand. 'You kids've got some messed-up values.'

'No, she's right,' Derna said, with a fierce grin. 'If someone's worth killing, they're worth killing well.'

'Derna,' Sulian sighed. 'You're somewhere near the bottom of the list of people whose support counts for anything when it comes to "messed-up values".'

'It's not my fault we live in a messed-up world,' Derna said with a shrug. 'Killing someone is a serious business. If you try it, it should be because you really want to succeed.' She threw a few nuts into her mouth and crunched them. 'I'm confident that no one I've killed can say I did it just because I could.'

'No, Derna, they can't say *anything*,' Sulian said wearily. 'Because they're *dead*.'

'I'm glad Derna understands,' Kitt said firmly, prompting a look of surprise from Donal and the Swallowmage, and a delighted beam from Derna herself. 'I know it sounds strange, but yes, I'm angry he tried to kill me, but I'm even more angry that it didn't matter enough to him to see it through. The sort of person who thinks like that,' she continued, sounding the thoughts out loud, 'is dangerous, and I don't want him to achieve whatever it is he wants to achieve.'

She grimaced, trying to get a grip on her swirling head. She was tired, and stressed, had nearly died today, and then talked to the spirit of someone who had, so it was entirely possible that she wasn't thinking straight. Even so…

'I think this is something I should be doing,' she said slowly. 'I can't really explain why. It just feels like...' She tailed off, staring at the infuriatingly obstinate map.

'Destiny?' Donal offered quietly.

'I don't know!' Kitt said, to their stares. 'Maybe!' she added, somewhat defensively.

Sulian frowned. 'You never—'

'No, I never took a destiny for myself!' Kitt snapped. 'I couldn't tell what they were up on the moors, and I couldn't afford one once it had been soothsayered. Wouldn't want one anyway,' she added, and although it was an honest statement, she found herself slightly resenting the approving nod Derna gave.

'Some destines can still find a subject naturally,' Donal said. 'Maybe it *is* destiny.'

'Or maybe it's *revenge* that our Kitt is after,' Sulian said dryly. The Swallowmage took a deep draught of her drink. 'Confusing the two can lead to an awful lot of trouble, I'll foretell you that for nothing.'

'Destiny or revenge, neither one is likely to get anyone to Derringsmoot faster than the *Spirit of Freedom*,' Donal said, in a tone Kitt interpreted as relieved resignation. 'I'm honestly not sure if we've got any better ideas than just sending a messenger and hoping for the best.'

Kitt stared at the map one last time, and suddenly everything clicked into place. It was simple. It was also foolhardy and dangerous, but that didn't necessarily stop something from being simple.

'So we don't go around,' she said, tracing a straight line from Mereport to Derringsmoot with her finger, right through the dark blob of the timeless lands. 'We go across.'

There was a moment's silence.

'Are you serious?' Sulian asked. 'Has anyone ever done that? Gone right through?'

'Not so far as I know,' Kitt admitted. 'But I also don't know that anyone's ever tried. Diviners go up onto the moors to collect destinies, not go adventuring. No one else really goes up there at all.'

'Yes, because it's so damned dangerous!' Donal said.

'No one knows the territory,' Sulian said, clearly trying to sound reasonable. 'There aren't any maps, there aren't any paths—'

'There *are* paths!' Kitt interrupted her. 'People went up onto the moors before the future broke! Nothing changes up there, which means the paths are still there, and they've never been overgrown.'

'Where do the paths go, though?' Donal asked, and Kitt shrugged.

'Okay, not sure about that, but *nothing* changes up there. The stars don't move. If you pick one and walk towards it, you'll go in a straight line. You should be able to get clean across.'

'Moorland is well-known for being easy to navigate in straight lines,' the Swallowmage said with a snort. 'I can't see any problems there at all.'

'And what about the slydewasps?' Donal asked. 'They always turn up. *Always*. It's just a case of when. How far would we get before we're overrun by them?'

'I don't know,' Kitt admitted, trying not to think about the monstrosity that had hung impossibly silently in the air in front of her, its sting still slicked in blood. 'But when we're divining, we're going back and forth over the same small area. If we were travelling straight, maybe they wouldn't notice us so much.'

'That's a very weak "maybe",' Donal muttered, and Kitt's urge to slap him grew even stronger.

'We *can* do this,' she said forcefully. 'We'd need chrono-charms, and some supplies, but this isn't a case of it being too far, or taking too long. We could make it over the moors in...' She hesitated, looking at the map. It was large-scale, with cities as little more than dots.

'Three days, perhaps?' Derna said, chewing noisily. 'Whatever "days" means up there, anyway.'

Kitt's heart sank. No matter what she might have said about avoiding slydewasps, three days was an awfully long time to be under that unchanging sky, waiting for silent wings to bring death down upon you. She'd been up there for most of a day, once – the long hunt which had led to her finally locating the destiny she'd sold to Mazen Rauk for ten gold, and which was apparently at the heart of all this trouble – and that had been exhausting in a way which went beyond the simple act of staying awake for that long.

'Plus most of a day to get to the moors in the first place,' Derna was saying. 'If we get what we need tomorrow, we should be able to make a start the day after. Allow a couple more days to get to Derringsmoot once we get out the other side, and we should still be there before Mr Bastard. What? That's what I'm calling him until we have a proper name,' she added, seeing Kitt looking at her.

'It wasn't the name that surprised me,' Kitt said slowly. 'You're actually intending to do this?'

'Of course,' Derna said, looking puzzled. 'You think I'm going to let you walk over the high moors by yourself? And what about if Mr Bastard and whoever he has with him turns up earlier than we expect, or you get delayed or something?' She shook her head firmly. 'No. You need someone to watch your back. I'm coming.'

Kitt fought back a foolish grin. Knowing Derna had never been a simple thing. Sometimes it was dangerous. It was certainly often alarming, confusing, or both. When it came down to it, though, Two Tongue Derna was the most person Kitt had ever known. Not really the most anything in particular, just the *most*. There didn't seem to be enough of Derna to contain all of who she was. When she was opposed to you, she was your enemy in fire and blood; or more accurately, she would allow you to make yourself *her* enemy, and treated the fire and blood as the price you'd already accepted for your choice. When she was with you, however, she was with you body and soul.

'Okay then,' Kitt said, excitement and unease warring in her stomach. 'It looks like we need to make some preparations. We've not got much time.'

ELEVEN

'ONCE AGAIN IF you please, Master Arkony.'

Arkony Grike sighed, and raised his sword. It was a narrow and nimble practice blade, blunted for safety – which was not to say that the point or the edge could not leave a bruise, even through padded fencing gear. Arkony had received enough over the years to testify to that.

His opponent was Master Gerone Plynn, whose thin limbs, thinning hair, and definitely not-thin pot belly belied his past as one of the land's most prominent blademasters. Plynn's glory days of high-profile displays of skill at royal courts and tournaments might have been behind him, along with the rich and varied romantic liaisons such prowess had apparently commanded, but that didn't mean he couldn't still best 'young whippersnappers', as he referred to his students. Arkony was on the cusp of turning twenty-three, and simultaneously uncertain whether he still wished to be classed as 'young', and worried that if he made too much of an issue out of it then people would start to say 'Well, go on; *do* something then'.

For now, what he needed to do was to go another round with the old weasel, who was bouncing up and down on the balls of his feet as though he were a barely tethered balloon on a gusty day. Arkony raised his blade to guard position and waited.

'No, that won't do,' Plynn tutted. 'You're too passive, young man. You need to take the initiative!' He readied his own blade, then flicked it a couple of times to beckon with the tip. 'Come, strike at me!'

Arkony groaned inwardly. He had undoubtedly improved over his years under Plynn's tuition, but he detested attacking. For one thing, he found it hard to envisage a situation in which he would ever *want* to attack someone else, even in the context of a duel. More to the point, he always felt that being struck while defending yourself was considerably less embarrassing than taking the same hit while pressing the action. It was the difference between not being as good as your opponent and looking like an overconfident fool.

Still, Plynn had been hired by Arkony's parents to improve his fencing, since it was a skill young nobles were supposed to possess, and although the Grike coffers were not short of money, Arkony felt it was disrespectful to everyone involved not to engage fully with the services that had been purchased on his behalf. Besides, his tutor reported Arkony's progress to his parents, and feeling like a fool for being struck by a former blademaster was far preferable to the cheek-burning embarrassment of his father's steady stare once he had been informed that his son was *not trying*.

Arkony approached in the light-footed hop he had been taught, and twitched his wrist as though feinting a cut. However, the feint itself was a feint, and he restarted the attack immediately, attempting to disguise it behind not only his own actions but also his tutor's expectations. He whipped his blade in towards Plynn's torso—

—and got soundly jabbed on his left pectoral a split second before Plynn hopped athletically backwards, leaving Arkony's thrust dangling tantalisingly short in mid-air.

'Good!' Plynn said cheerfully. 'Excellent speed. You still need to work a little on disguising your intended attack but, and I say this without arrogance, you will face few opponents with my years of experience, or my finely honed reflexes. You would have hit home against many an adversary, I am sure.'

'And what about not getting hit back?' Arkony asked glumly, rubbing his chest.

'Well, you don't have the greatest reach, it's true,' Plynn acknowledged. 'Hence why I am encouraging you to get on the offensive more! If you sit back and allow a taller, longer opponent to pick at you from their favoured range then you'll be at a true disadvantage. You need to get forward and get into their face, into a position where you can at least land a strike as well. You're quick enough for that, at any rate.'

Arkony shook his head. He was a little sensitive about his height, being a few inches shorter than most men. 'Honestly, if my best-case scenario is that I might be able to stab someone at the same time as they're stabbing me, I fail to see why I would ever resort to a duel.'

Plynn sighed. 'No one is so ridiculed as the one who wears a blade but never uses it, no matter the provocation, but *not* wearing a blade marks you out as an easy target for the worst type of oafs and braggarts in society, whether they be noble *or* common. Although at least you only have to worry about one of those.' He clapped Arkony on the shoulder with a bony-knuckled hand. 'People who walk with a blade on their hip as though it is part of them benefit from notably politer strangers. I'm teaching you the blade so you can wear one with the confidence that should you find yourself needing to use it, you will not embarrass yourself; I'm not teaching you so you can kill anyone. Duels of no regard are for the worst insults only, where it's that or start a small war. Well, and for the street rats,' he added, with a sniff.

'How do the street duellists compare?' Arkony asked, intrigued despite himself. 'I've heard tales—'

'Oh, *tales*, I'm sure,' Plynn said, not bothering to keep the scorn from his voice. 'Tales grow in the telling, as everyone knows, and what starts out as a lucky hit against an inebriated opponent, or someone losing their footing by tripping over a, a *turnip* that has rolled loose from a market stall, is transformed into a breathtaking display of skill in which the nominal hero has suddenly bested half a dozen adversaries!' He shook his head. 'The sashes of Mereport, the marks of Kir-Lu, and all the rest are simply ruffians, possessed of a certain amount of raw courage but little skill except in comparison to each other.' He squeezed Arkony's shoulder. 'You could best any of them, I have no doubt. No, what we need to focus on is how you will measure up against others who have been trained in the same manner as yourself.'

'A few inches shorter, is my bet,' Arkony muttered.

'No excuses!' Plynn snapped, withdrawing his hand and shaking his finger. 'I've known women whose heads wouldn't reach your nose, who'd have had it off your face with their blade before you could blink! You can't be so scared of your opponent's sword that you dare not attempt to land a touch. You'll just have to use your quickness instead, and you have plenty of that.' He raised his blade. 'Now, come at me again.'

Arkony sighed once more. 'I can't help but feel that there should be more to life than learning how to stab people.'

'And there is,' Plynn agreed. 'However, my job is to teach you how to stab people, Master Arkony. So blade up, and *come at me again.*'

Arkony obliged. This time he didn't bother with feints, and attacked Plynn's blade instead. Steel rattled as Arkony tried to bat his teacher's weapon aside long enough for him to land a strike, but Plynn was slippery, with just enough strength in his guard to keep Arkony at bay but never committing sufficiently to anything to be thrown off-balance. Their exchange paused after a few breathless seconds, with Arkony still not having come close to landing a touch.

'Good!' Plynn declared. 'That's the sort of aggression I was talking about!'

'I didn't hit you,' Arkony said, trying and failing not to sound sullen.

'No, but you kept me from hitting *you*,' Plynn pointed out. 'You controlled the exchange. Now, show me your defence.' He raised his blade in a momentary warning, then came forward in a metallic flicker. Arkony tried not to give too much ground, but his attempted riposte was awkward, and Plynn slid past it to land a thrust on his shoulder.

'Your instincts are good,' his teacher insisted, putting his blade up. 'You just need to practice those movements, so they become smoother.'

'Will any of this do me any good in an actual fight, though?' Arkony asked, rubbing at what would shortly become his newest bruise. 'We won't be taking turns attacking and defending.'

'We practice under idealised conditions to hone our skills as best we may,' Plynn said seriously. 'I hope you never need to defend yourself with a blade, Master Grike, but if you do then knowing the balance of your weapon and how to turn it to your will is the best possible starting point. There may of course be other factors that render it difficult or impossible to fight as you have been taught.' He shrugged. 'You learn the fundamentals, then adapt to your surroundings as best you can. Now—'

'You've travelled the world, haven't you?' Arkony cut in, eager to put off the next painful lesson for a few more moments.

'More than many, although the world is a big place, and I can't claim to have seen anywhere near all of it.' A twinkle in Plynn's eye suggested that he knew what Arkony was doing, but that the play to his ego was sufficient for him to go along with it for now.

'Are our "surroundings" changing?' Arkony asked, gesturing vaguely around them. 'I hear people talking about how the world is dying—'

'Who says that?' Plynn snapped, his expression shuttering immediately. Arkony gaped, wrong-footed for a moment by the vehemence of his fencing tutor's reaction. His mind raced while he tried to work out how to avoid dropping the servants in it.

'It's something I've heard more than once,' he managed after a moment. 'It sounds like a reasonably prevalent theory.'

'Nonsense commoner superstition,' Plynn sniffed, with the assurance of a man whose birth had left him barely above commoner in the eyes of the nobility, and had only risen further through exceptional talent. Arkony had never worked out whether that meant Plynn's disdain for those who shared his former station was more or less repellent than the sort of sneering comments he'd occasionally been regaled with by some of his own peers.

'But logically, if the same account comes from multiple different sources—' he began, but Plynn tutted and cut him off.

'This isn't your logic class, Master Grike, and you would do well not to pay attention to such talk. There are many strange things in the world, it's true, but to say that it's *ending* is melodramatic in the extreme. Natural disasters happen, tales from other lands are distorted in the telling, and so on.' Plynn attempted a smile. 'I am sure it has always been thus.'

Plynn's demeanour suggested he was done with talking, and had he been a little less stern in his initial reply then Arkony might have gone along with it. However, he strongly suspected that he'd brushed up against one of the topics that the tutors and staff were Not Supposed To Talk To Arkony About, and he had no intention of letting Plynn off lightly. After all, he *was* the heir to Derringsdale.

'What about the hills to the south-west?' he said. 'Towards the timeless lands? There are rumours that they're practically impassable in late summer, but no one says *why*, and I'm sure that wasn't the case when I was a child.'

Plynn shook his head irritably, as though trying to dislodge a wasp that had settled on his ear. 'There are rumours of all sorts of things, Master Grike. Now, unless you want one of those rumours to be that you spent my lesson doom-mongering instead of honing your skills, I suggest you raise your blade again.'

TWELVE

Kitt's parents lived in Duke's End, a neighbourhood that supposedly took its name from when a nobleman did what noblemen do best – take part in a rebellion against their liege lord and die on a battlefield while bitterly regretting their life choices – back before Mereport had swelled into such a sizeable city. To an outsider, it was a veritable maze; the narrow, cobbled streets all looked much alike, and ran back, forth, and around in a layout that appeared to have been designed as a deliberate affront to straight lines. For Kitt, navigating them was second nature, even when the blanket of summer evening gloom was pressed up against the walls of the houses, making every edge softer and indistinct.

She rapped on the door, and waited. She was not expecting the eagerness with which it was thrown open.

'Auntie Kitt!'

A small hurricane of ginger hair and dirt tackled her at waist height, headbutting her in the stomach in the process. Kitt winced – even a magically healed stab wound was not without some remaining tenderness – and pried the child off her, then hoisted her up crossways.

'Has someone lost this?' she shouted, crossing the

threshold sideways and backheeling the door shut behind her. 'How did you know it was me?' she asked her niece in her arms.

'You always knock like that,' Faere said, giggling.

A similarly ginger head to Faere's peered out from the doorway to the back room. Annity Carver – no, not Carver any more, Kitt reminded herself, it was Sauvers since they'd got married, and hadn't *that* been a barrel of laughs – looked like both of their parents at once: more like their mum from the side, with the chin and snub nose in profile; more like their dad from the front, with the brown eyes and thick eyebrows.

Kitt, by contrast, had managed to somehow inherit a mix of features that combined to make her look like neither of her parents. Her hair was a rich mid-brown with only the faintest hint of auburn, not quite as curly as her mum's nor as straight as her dad's, and her nose was neither snub nor sharp. Her eyes weren't her mum's deep blue or her dad's brown, veering more towards the blue-grey of her nana's. She had a chin strong enough that she'd been self-conscious about it in her teenage years, a smattering of freckles across her nose and cheeks, and cheekbones about which the most that could be said was that they were in there somewhere.

Annity clucked their tongue disapprovingly, as Faere thrashed around in her usual game of 'make Auntie Kitt drop me'. 'Faere, stop kicking! I didn't know you were coming over tonight,' they continued, addressing Kitt.

'And I didn't know you were going to be here,' Kitt said, placing Faere back on the ground before she lost her grip and her niece ate floorboard. It wasn't a *problem* to have her sibling here as such, but it potentially made for a slightly more awkward conversation later. 'How's Tavid?'

'You can ask him yourself,' Annity said, jerking their head towards the room in which they were standing, and Kitt's heart sank a little more. Still, it wasn't like she could turn around and leave now, so she smiled instead, and entered the back room.

If there was one thing you could say for Farren and Lavine Carver, Kitt's parents, it was that they knew how to make the most of the space they had available. Kitt wasn't sure exactly how they'd managed to organise things to make sufficient space for half a dozen adults to sit, but organise it they had, even if it did depend on most of those involved having negotiable knees.

'Hi Dad!' she shouted in the general direction of the small, one-storey kitchen annex.

'Kitt? Is that you?'

'You know anyone else who'd wander in like this?' Kitt called back cheerily, making her way over to the rocking chair in which Nana Carver sat, busily clacking her knitting needles. It might be Kitt's parents' house, but everyone knew to whom respects were first paid upon entering.

'Evening, Nana,' Kitt said, leaning down to hug the old woman.

'Kitt,' Nana Carver said happily. Her old lips brushed close to Kitt's ear. 'What's this I hear about you getting stabbed yesterday?'

Kitt shouldn't have been surprised; Nana Carver sat in a web of gossip like a spider god.

'What's this I hear about you sharking the army widows at three-card pike when Mum thinks you're at the temple?' Kitt whispered back, and felt her nana stiffen in response.

'Fair play,' the old woman murmured. 'Silence for silence?'

'You taught me well,' Kitt replied, and kissed her on the cheek.

'What are you two whispering about?' Farren asked, emerging from the kitchen. Kitt's dad was in his fifties now, and the mid-brown of his hair was increasingly being swallowed by the grey advancing down the sides of his head, but his fingers were still nimble enough to work as a seamster.

'Secrets,' Nana Carver said, happily and openly enough to make it seem as though their whispers had been nothing of any import at all. 'She's a sharp one, is our Kitt. Are you sure she's yours?'

'Mother!' Farren said crossly. 'That's not a thing you should be saying!'

'Yeah, Nana,' Annity said, folding their arms as they leant against the doorframe. 'You've never called *me* sharp.'

'You're sharp in your own way, dear,' Nana Carver said, so pleasantly that it almost didn't sound like an insult. 'After all, you managed to bag yourself this handsome young man, didn't you?' She nodded in the direction of Tavid, who was sitting in the other corner with Kitt's baby nephew Jallon – Faere's half-brother – on his lap. 'Which is more than Kitt's managed.'

Kitt groaned. 'And on that exceedingly awkward note: Hi, Tavid, how are you?'

'I'm good,' Tavid said, smiling in the slightly glazed way that Kitt understood to be quite common when around grandparents-in-law. Nana was right about one thing, in that Tavid Sauvers certainly was handsome, in a square-jawed sort of manner. Kitt had no problem with him: he was a nice enough guy, and the problems at his wedding had very much been caused by his family, with whom he had stopped being on speaking terms shortly afterwards. They were paper merchants from uptown, and hadn't approved of their eldest son marrying the child of a seamster and a dockhand, let alone one who'd already had a daughter with a different man. However, despite his estrangement, Tavid still moved in different social circles, and Kitt was always wary that her exploits would become the subject of tales he would tell of his wild young sister-in-law.

It was going to make the conversation she intended to have later more difficult, but there was no way around it. She'd just have to trust that Annity had married him for more than just his jawline.

...

'So,' Lavine Carver said. 'What brings you to see us this evening, Kitt?'

The bowls of fish stew had long been finished, and everyone had praised Farren for his cooking and seasoning. Jallon was asleep, and Faere was playing on the stairs with a regular light thunder of feet going upwards, then a *bump-bump-bump* as she came back down again on her backside.

Nana Carver's brown-stained fingers didn't pause in their work of stuffing her horrible old pipe with foul-smelling sailor's tobacco, but she did look up with renewed interest.

'I'm going away from the city for a while,' Kitt said.

'I thought you were done with the moors,' Farren said. It was delivered in a neutral tone of voice, and anyone outside of the family might have taken it as such, but Kitt knew how to speak Carver. There was disappointment and disapproval in there, but buried so deep that to challenge them would involve a mining operation strenuous enough to make her the villain.

'I said I was done with the moors for *a bit*,' Kitt said, hating how defensive she sounded. 'But yes, I'll be heading that way.'

'You've never told us specially about going to the moors before,' Lavine said carefully. 'Not since the first couple of times.'

'Which means she's not just going onto the moors as one of her regular jobs,' Nana Carver said, tamping down her tobacco and reaching for her matches. 'It's something else. Right?' she added, looking pointedly at Kitt.

'I'll be away for longer this time,' Kitt said, trying not to glare at her nana. 'Maybe a couple of weeks.'

'A couple of *weeks?*' Farren echoed incredulously. 'Kitt, that's ridiculous! Why would you go up there for weeks? *How* would you go up there for weeks?'

'I won't be on the moors for that long,' Kitt said testily. 'But we need to go *over* the moors.' She sighed, and settled into the semi-lie she had pre-prepared. 'Someone needs to deliver a really urgent message to the other side, faster than you could manage by going around. I've got experience on the moors, so…' She spread her hands.

'I've never heard of anyone going all the way over the moors,' Annity said, looking at Kitt with concern. 'Is that even possible?'

Kitt shrugged. 'We'll find out.'

'You're taking people with you?' Farren said. 'You're not going alone?'

'No, Dad, I'm not going alone,' Kitt reassured him, and he nodded in what seemed to be some level of mollification, although he still looked uncertain. Lavine, on the other hand, narrowed her eyes.

'*Who* is going with you? And please don't say that awful Towbright girl.'

'Okay,' Kitt said with a smile. It took her mother a moment to catch on to her meaning, at which point she groaned.

'Kitt, I know you think she's harmless, but—'

'I do *not* think she's harmless!' Kitt protested. 'Mum, I've known Derna for years, and I know she's as dangerous as they come, but gods help her, at least she's honest! If she says she's going to help me get to the other side and back in one piece, then that's what she's going to do.'

Lavine simply shook her head sadly. 'Who else is going with you? Other criminals?'

'No, Mum,' Kitt said with a sigh. That old saying of it being easier to ask forgiveness than permission probably applied here. She loved her family, and she was confident that they loved her, but sometimes the gap between *love* and *understanding* was more like a yawning gulf. 'Look, I didn't come here for a discussion, or to ask your opinions, because I'm doing it. I came to let you know that I won't be around for a couple of weeks. That's all.' She looked around at them. 'So take care of yourselves, and I'll see you when I get back.'

'And what if you don't *come* back?' Lavine demanded.

'Then I guess you'll get to say that you were right,' Kitt said, and walked out.

THIRTEEN

Kitt's crew were waiting for her the next morning at Mereport's northern gate.

It wasn't her full crew, of course. Not like the old days, as Kitt now thought of that time only a few months back. Some had gravitated to other jobs with other people, and most of the rest had no interest in a trek all the way across the high moors to no real reward. Kitt hadn't even been able to entice them with the prospect of picking up any destinies they found along the way to sell upon their return, because she couldn't guarantee Derna wouldn't just crush them.

In the end, she'd only been able to convince two to join her. Pigtail Vem was a stout, red-faced man somewhere beyond his fiftieth year with a moustache that looked like he'd glued a small dog to his upper lip. He apparently felt some sort of paternal affection for Kitt despite the fact she'd only ever interacted with him as his employer, but he was one of the best slydewasp spotters in the game, since his innate magic granted him stupendous eyesight. He could sometimes be a little condescending, in the way of older men who assumed that them liking you meant they had the right to offer approval of your actions that was in some way definitive, but he was never overfamiliar.

Falzine Halfshade was very different. He didn't say much, and what he did say was to the point. Kitt thought he was in his thirties, but she'd never asked, and it was difficult to tell given that his face – and indeed every part of his body that she'd ever seen – was always in deep shadow. The draksnipe of which he'd run afoul at some point in his youth hadn't killed him, but it had sucked the light from him, so he tended to wear his hood up and drawn well past his face, simply because it made his condition less obvious. He carried a long, heavy-bladed spear, and had a dagger at his belt that wasn't much smaller than Kitt's short sword. Falzine had no particular affection for Kitt so far as she was aware, but when she'd mentioned crossing the moors completely he'd looked up with what would have been a glint in his eye, had he been someone for whom such things were still possible. It seemed that the heart of an adventurer lurked beneath his laconic exterior.

Donal was there when Kitt arrived, trying to make conversation with Vem and keeping the other two men between him and Derna, who was watching him with her arms folded. Donal had been insistent that he come as well, apparently being serious about making amends, and Kitt really hoped this wasn't some misguided attempt to charm his way into her heart or back into her bed. He'd made a bad decision, but it had been the sort of bad decision that many people made from day to day in Mereport: you needed money, someone offered you a job, and you didn't look too closely at what the job was. Donal couldn't realistically have been expected to foresee all the consequences of his actions, but just because Kitt wasn't prepared to let Derna stab him didn't mean she'd forgiven him, either. *Fool me twice, shame on me*, she thought ruefully.

They all had packs, but no beasts of burden to carry them, because pack animals were a liability on the moors. Animals needed chronocharms too, and that was money which could better be spent on other things when you were just going up, finding a destiny, and coming back again. Besides, animals were unnerved by the stillness of the never-changing pre-dawn up there, which made them skittish. If a slydewasp appeared then your animal would probably have the sense to run, but it wouldn't know to run for the nearest way off the moors, which meant anything important it carried was likely to disappear off in the opposite direction to you.

Kitt came to a halt and swung her packs off her shoulders. 'Right, has everyone got everything? Spare chronocharms, food, water, all that?'

Her crew made affirmative noises, although Donal didn't look quite confident. Kitt sighed, and looked at him.

'You worried about something?'

'Well, I haven't been up there as often as you,' he said. 'How do you know if a chronocharm is about to run out?'

'You don't!' Pigtail Vem said with a jovial laugh, and clapped Donal across the shoulders in a manner that earned him a glare.

'The glow fades over time, but it's never particularly reliable because, you know, magic,' Kitt said patiently. 'They're reckoned to last for about a day, we just have no way of measuring that up there. We'll try to replace them in good time, but if someone's runs out or doesn't work then we won't have to leave them behind. We just might have to move more quickly.'

'I'm not intending to dawdle,' Donal said, rearranging his packs from where Vem's slap had knocked them loose. Then he squinted past Kitt, back down the street. 'Hey, is that—'

'It's the Swallowmage!' Vem said, shading his eyes against the sun, and definitely not showing off his superior eyesight. 'All laden up, too. Kitt, you didn't say she was coming with us!'

'I didn't know she was,' Kitt admitted, turning around. Sure enough, Sulian was headed up the Northway with a bulky satchel slung over each shoulder and Jandi, her semi-sentient staff of knotted knowood in her hand. She looked more like an actual mage than Kitt had seen for some time, and possibly ever.

'Is this good?' Falzine said quietly behind her. 'Or bad?'

It took long enough for Sulian to reach them for it to be slightly awkward, as they all stood around waiting for her without really having anything else to do. It gave Kitt time to think of half a dozen greetings, only to discard one after another. The Swallowmage had wished them well, but had been quite adamant that she didn't see Kitt's quest – as she insisted on calling it – as anything to do with her. This was an unexpected development, and Kitt wasn't entirely sure how to react to it.

'Good to see you,' she said, as Sulian approached to within a comfortable earshot, then clammed up as her brain refused to let her go any further. *I didn't think you were coming* sounded accusatory. *What are you doing here?* was downright hostile. *Thanks for coming* sounded sarcastic, at least in her head. *Did you change your mind?* implied that Kitt was unable to interpret the context of the Swallowmage turning up at the time and place that she, Donal, and Derna had agreed upon for departure, while clothed and equipped for a journey.

'What gives?' Derna asked, which was not necessarily better than any of Kitt's options in and of itself, but was superior from Kitt's point of view because a) it was coming from Derna, from whom no one really expected social grace, and b) it was coming from Derna, and therefore not from Kitt.

'Had a vision last night,' the Swallowmage said. She was chewing something, and staring off past them into the distance towards where the high moors lay, where the land rose out of the greens of fields and the burgeoning gold of ripening crops into the bumpy darkness of heather, and then further up to where the timeless lands began. It looked like nothing unusual, from here. No one Kitt had ever spoken to could explain why the timeless lands were only in permanent gloom on the inside. Magic was a strange thing.

'A vision?' Donal echoed, sounding decidedly uncomfortable.

'Yep. Not like usual, of some destiny or another.' The

Swallowmage pulled a hip flask from her belt, uncorked it, and took a small swig. 'This was the real thing. Haven't had one of those in a while. I don't know exactly how or why,' she continued, finally tearing her eyes away from the north and looking at Kitt, 'but I think it's very important that you get that message to Derringsmoot. So I'm coming with you to make sure it happens.'

'Ah,' Falzine Halfshade said, as the Swallowmage set off without another word, her staff clicking on the road. 'Bad, then.'

FOURTEEN

LATE AFTERNOON WAS sliding lazily into early evening in the world outside the timeless lands when Kitt reached the post that marked its boundary, although the party had all put their chronocharms on before leaving the dry gulch at the bottom of the valley, just in case. The charms were an enchanted bubble of time captured in a silver lattice, usually worn around the neck. So long as a part of it was in contact with your skin then – assuming the charm had been correctly fashioned, and retained some power – you would continue to experience time flowing at the normal speed, even if the world around you was frozen.

'How did anyone find out they could do this, anyway?' Donal asked, looking down. 'I've never heard of chrono-mancers doing any other time magic, just this.'

'You've never heard of it because it's illegal,' Sulian said grimly. 'And I don't mean illegal as in you spend a few nights in the town cells somewhere, I mean it's illegal in the sense of they cut your head off.'

Donal grimaced. 'Wow. That bad?'

'Oh yes,' the Swallowmage said, staring up the slope. 'Chronomancy is a rare gift, thank all the gods. There's always someone who wants to push something too far, and time is one of those things that you really shouldn't try to unravel.' She sucked her teeth. 'You can imagine how it was when the so-called Lords of Time decided they wanted to rule and were just going to accelerate into old age anyone who got in their way, or thought they could avoid assassination by diving backwards in time to before the danger appeared. Enough people banded together to stop them, and chronomancy became punishable by death.'

'But not in Mereport?' Kitt asked. She'd never really thought about chronomancers before. They were just from whom you got the chronocharms to go up on the moors, and she'd assumed that was all there was to it.

'Oh, it was illegal in Mereport too, until the timeless lands came into being,' Sulian said with a humourless laugh. 'The first idea was that they would try to undo the whole thing, but that didn't work out. The histories suggest the chronomancers reduced the size of it a bit on the north side, but it didn't end up with a clean border like we have on this side, and things got a bit... weird. Then the Guild Council realised the sheer amount of money the destiny trade would bring into the city. So in Mereport, and Mereport *only*, chronomancers can use their magic so long as they only use it for the one purpose the city has decided is profitable, which is why Mereport is the world's centre for the destiny trade. Everywhere else thinks we're playing with fire, but not so much that they don't come to buy the goods.' She shrugged. 'I'm not saying that chronomancers here and there don't use their powers a little bit, every now and then. It's just that if they get caught doing it...' She drew one finger across her throat with an accompanying gurgling sound effect.

'On the other hand,' Pigtail Vem said cheerily, 'since chronocharms are all they're allowed to do, chronomancers are really good at them! So we shouldn't have anything to worry about!' He beamed at them all, then marched past Kitt and disappeared into the timeless lands.

One moment he was there, and then he was gone. The illusion of the timeless lands hadn't changed – the land and sky beyond the marker post looked exactly like you might expect it to, bearing in mind the light and weather outside – but he apparently blinked out of existence between one step and the next.

Kitt took a deep breath – an instinctive reaction even after all this time, as though a little bit of extra air in her lungs could help her if her chronocharm was faulty – and took the next step.

The gloom of the timeless lands enfolded her immediately, and she was once more back on the still, silent, and dark heath. When she turned around to look back, she could see nothing other than the same dark hillside leading down to a deep, shadowed version of the valley out of which she'd just climbed. There was no sign of the rest of her party, until the Swallowmage stepped into existence right in front of her.

'Ugh,' Sulian said immediately, and shivered. She looked around and took a swig from her flask. 'This place feels weird. The magic's all off.'

Donal came through next, and he shivered too. Falzine Halfshade was no stranger to the high moors, of course, and he carried on past Kitt without a second glance. Last through was Derna, who blinked in apparent surprise as she emerged into darkness.

'Well,' she said, fidgeting with her cloak to settle it more comfortably across her shoulders. 'I'm glad that worked.'

'Were you *nervous?*' Kitt asked incredulously. The notion of Two Tongue Derna being apprehensive about anything was one she was going to struggle to get her head around.

'Look, stepping into a place where time doesn't work might be second nature to you, but it's not something I've ever done before,' Derna said, a little testily. 'It's only natural.'

'Well, yes, but...' *But you're not natural.* Kitt didn't

complete the sentence. It wasn't that Derna was unnatural in the same way as Mazen Rauk's disembodied voice during Sulian's seance, but you only had to spend a few minutes in her company to realise that she wasn't like most other people, no matter the species. Most people took the world as they found it and tried to make their way through it as best they could. Derna knew how she wanted the world to be, and set about making it conform with such unshakeable certainty that it sometimes sort of worked, or at least didn't fail in a way that meant she died. It wouldn't be natural to have too many Dernas; civilisation probably wouldn't survive.

Derna's expression suggested that she'd heard the unspoken words, and Kitt hastened to replace them with something else. 'I just assumed you'd been up here at some point.'

'Why would I have?' Derna asked. 'This is your world, not mine.'

'It's not really mine anymore, either,' Kitt said. 'I haven't been up here in months.' They both knew why that was, of course, so she didn't elaborate any further. Instead she cast around for a suitable landmark, and settled for a bright, slightly orange star just above the horizon in the opposite direction from where they'd just arrived.

'Okay everyone,' she said, pointing. 'You see that? That's what we're going to make for. If we keep heading in that direction, we should come out the other side.'

'Should,' the Swallowmage muttered.

'For someone who thinks we really need to succeed, you're not being very positive about this,' Kitt told her. She pointed towards a path that led in the right direction, the sand paler than the surrounding heather even under the dim light of the high moors. 'Come on, let's get moving. And no picking up destinies, even if you happen to see one,' she added, looking mainly at Falzine and Vem, but remembering to include Donal at the last moment. 'There's no point tempting fate.'

'I don't know why people make a big issue of tempting fate,'

Derna commented as their party started walking. 'If you're doing the tempting then you're the one in control, right?'

'You're mixing up "tempting" and "seducing",' Kitt said. 'Seducing fate sounds a lot better, to be honest.'

'Maybe you should give it a try,' Derna said with a laugh. 'Find yourself a couch somewhere, recline seductively in a nightdress next to a bunch of prophecies, see what happens.'

'What probably happens is that someone starts a religion,' the Swallowmage grunted, from Kitt's other side. 'Do you fancy being a priestess, Kitt?'

'Yikes, no.' Kitt shuddered. Her family worshipped at the Temple of All Gods, a handy catch-all for people who wished to honour the general pantheon of deities that existed in the world – or, alternatively, those subject to decision paralysis. The priesthood there were more like caretakers, ensuring that the myriad shrines were kept clean and no one started any fights. Kitt had never experienced the iron-hard sense of *belief* embodied by the priests of the individual temples and churches, and she couldn't really imagine what that would feel like.

Would it feel like trekking right across the high moors to warn people you've never met about a threat you know very little about, simply because you're convinced that it's the right thing to do?

Kitt decided to ignore that thought. The Swallowmage had, after all, experienced a vision which suggested that it was important that they succeeded, so that meant there was something behind her compulsion.

On the other hand, that placed rather greater pressure on her for this to actually *work*, and that would require this family Kitt had never met before to believe what she was telling them. Kitt did a hasty reassessment of herself and her companions: one diviner, twenty-two years of age and recently stabbed; another diviner, a few years older; a man whose face you could never clearly see; another man who had a pig's tail, for reasons Kitt had never discovered and, quite honestly, didn't want to; an alcoholic mage afflicted with prophecy; and a street duellist who was notorious for all the wrong reasons.

'Oh yes,' she muttered to herself. 'What a trustworthy bunch.'

MEASURING TIME ACCURATELY was impossible on the high moors. The gobel-kyn created the finest timepieces in the world, making up for their overall lack of magic through innovation, but even their ingenious devices of intermeshed toothed wheels became nothing more than frozen boxes in the timeless lands. The sky didn't change, and the light didn't change, so the only way to have any idea of how long had passed was a person's own internal sense of time. Diviners and their crews worked until they either found what they were after, or they got too tired to keep their eyes open for slydewasps any longer.

As a result, Kitt couldn't say exactly how long they had been walking across the moors towards the orange star. She suspected it had been several hours, judging by the tiredness of her legs and the rumbling in her stomach, but she'd already determined not to call a stop for food until someone else asked first. Such considerations fell away, however, when Vem raised the alarm.

'Wasp!' the spotter called, raising one hand. Everyone crouched instinctively, even though Kitt had never heard of it making the slightest bit of difference.

'Where?' she said in a low voice, making her way forward to join him. He pointed ahead of them and to the right.

'Down there, in that little dip.' He squinted. Kitt followed the line of his finger, but could barely make out a dark shape moving against an equally dark background. She'd never have seen it if he hadn't drawn her attention to it.

'How much sharper *are* your eyes than mine?' she asked, curious.

'Don't know,' Vem replied. 'Lend me yours, and I'll tell

you! Ha!' He snorted a laugh at his own joke, then sobered up. 'Hmm. Looks like there's a party over there, just beyond. They must be what it's after.'

Kitt couldn't really see what happened next. It was like trying to follow the progress of flakes of ash in a darkened room. The other group were far enough away that sound didn't carry well, either, even in the deathly silent air of the high moors. She heard a few distant shouts, so quiet that they were nearly drowned out by the breathing of her companions. The wasps made no noise, of course. It was only Vem's running commentary of 'Oh dear,' and 'No you fool, the *other* way!', and 'Well, at least that one's made it out,' that gave her any indication what was happening.

'Is it over?' Falzine asked, after Vem hadn't said anything for half a minute.

'The wasp's still there,' Vem replied. 'Wait, there's another one coming in. Looks like... Yes, they're picking up a body each. Flying off. Not towards us.'

'Do they normally take people?' Donal asked, his voice dripping with a revulsion with which Kitt heartily empathised.

'Couldn't say,' Vem replied. 'I've never hung around long enough to watch.'

'Which way *did* they go?' the Swallowmage asked.

'I'd say, roughly the same direction as we're going,' Vem admitted. 'Which is not, I'll grant you, the best omen.'

'Should we change our plans?' Donal asked nervously.

'No,' Kitt said immediately. 'Who knows where we'll end up if we change course? We *might* run into slydewasps, but if we start wandering in different directions and get lost then we'll *definitely* be stuck up here when our chronocharms run out.' She pointed. 'Besides, the path's been heading in more or less the right direction so far. Maybe it was a route all the way across the moors before time stopped! I'd rather not leave it and try to cut across the heather. Trust me, that gets exhausting very quickly.'

'Kitt's right,' Derna said firmly. 'We can fight slydewasps if we have to, but we can't fight time.'

'No surprise that it comes down to fighting with you,' Sulian muttered.

'What can I say?' Derna replied. 'When all you have is a hammer, everything looks like a nail.'

FIFTEEN

TIME MIGHT NOT pass as such on the high moors, but those who brought their own time with them still had to obey its requirements. No one felt comfortable remaining near where the slydewasps had attacked the prospecting party, but it wasn't more than another hour or so – at Kitt's best guess, anyway – before she called a halt for them to get some sleep while someone was still awake enough to keep watch. The Swallowmage and Donal were up first, with Kitt and Derna due to take the swing shift, and then Vem and Falzine being woken to see the others through until whatever might be defined as a morning.

Kitt hadn't slept in the timeless lands before, and it was a decidedly strange experience. The quietness of the place was odd at the best of times, but it was usually drowned out by the scuff of footsteps, the huff of breathing, the voices of diviners comparing notes, or calls from lookouts. As a city girl, trying to get to sleep with no background noise at all other than the faint rustlings from her companions was unnerving. The silence was just *too loud*. Her eyes were grainy by the time she managed to drop off, and when Sulian shook her awake again it felt as though her chronocharm must have failed and she hadn't actually slept at all.

She and Derna sat back to back on one of the quartzy boulders that dotted the moors, facing opposite directions. Kitt was glad for the feeling of warmth that transmitted through her clothes from the back pressed up against hers, even though it wasn't cold up here. It wasn't really *anything*, in all honesty. With no sun and no clouds, the body expected the bitter bite of a chilly night, but it seemed that temperature, like time, was something that had ceased to exist on the high moors unless you brought it with you. You couldn't even light a fire, since nothing would burn up here, so the presence and body heat of another person was a reassuring anchor in an environment so persistently strange that it could wear down even those accustomed to it.

'Why do you hate the destiny business so much now?' Kitt asked quietly, after the faint wheeze of rhythmic breathing allowed her to be reasonably sure Sulian and Donal had fallen asleep, and she wouldn't be keeping either of them awake. 'You never used to.'

'Didn't really think about it when I was younger,' Derna said. Her voice was a murmur on the edge of Kitt's hearing, but Kitt could feel the faint vibration of it through her back. 'But then someone said something to me. A girl in the Silver Hind said "I just feel like I should be doing something more with my life". And it struck me that maybe if the future wasn't broken, she might do. Maybe she's *meant* to, it's just that whatever destiny would have found her got picked up off the ground up here by someone like you, and then got sold on to a broker, who then sold it on to someone rich.' Derna shifted position slightly, and the curls of her hair tickled the back of Kitt's neck.

'And the thing is,' Derna continued, 'that rich person gets a good destiny, which makes it easier for them to be successful and get even richer, which means they can buy good destinies for their children, and so on. The whole damn system just keeps repeating itself, and there's people like you coming up here and risking slydewasps to make rich people richer, and taking bits off the keshel when you sell them on because you either can't afford a soothsayer yourself to find out how valuable they really are, or you don't dare in case they turn out to be worth nothing and no one wants to buy them.'

'It's how the world works,' Kitt said. 'I don't particularly like it, but… It's how the world works.'

'It doesn't have to be, though,' Derna replied. There wasn't any aggression or challenge in her tone. In fact, it was the closest to resigned that Kitt had ever heard her.

They sat in silence for a few minutes more, until Kitt broke it again.

'So. The Silver Hind, huh?'

'You know it?'

'Know of it,' Kitt said. 'It's still a joyhouse?'

'Yup.'

'I didn't know you liked girls,' Kitt said, picking at the rough surface of the boulder beneath her with a fingernail.

'You never asked.'

'True.' Kitt snorted. 'To be honest, I didn't know you liked *anyone*. You always seemed more interested in knives. And then swords, and duelling.'

'People are confusing,' Derna said softly. 'Blades are easy. It's why I tend to go to joyhouses. Everything's agreed beforehand, you pay for a service and you get what you pay for. It saves all the…' Kitt's peripheral vision picked up Derna's hand waving vaguely in the air. 'Awkwardness.'

Kitt stifled a laugh. 'You'll fight anyone who challenges you, no questions asked, but you find it awkward to chat someone up?' Although that made sense, to an extent. Even when they were kids, Derna had been largely fearless of actual danger, but very wary of talking to most people other than Kitt.

'Like I said,' Derna repeated. 'People are confusing.' She shifted her shoulders. 'Anyway, it's not like your recent adventures on that front worked out particularly well.'

'Okay, that's harsh,' Kitt said stiffly. She lowered her voice even further. 'You don't get to offer to shank him for me *and* drag me for sleeping with him.'

Derna snorted gently. 'I think I just did.'

Kitt said nothing for a while, straining tired eyes to make sure that there were no slydewasps approaching. On the one hand, the lack of any sort of change in the landscape in front of her should at least make it easy to pick up on movement, dark though it was. On the other hand, her eyes weren't used to staring at something that remained so utterly still for so long, without even the faintest breath of air to move a heather stalk, or the looping flight of a bird through the sky. Her mind began imagining tiny movements here and there, forcing her to focus and check on them to ensure she wasn't missing something that could end up killing them all.

'What did you mean about the hammer?' she asked, when she couldn't take the stillness any longer without having some sort of distraction to prevent her mind from spiralling off into the distance.

'What hammer?' Derna asked.

'That thing you said to Sulian. Something about only having a hammer and everything looking like nails.'

'Oh, that.' Derna shifted her shoulders again. 'It's just something I heard once. I guess it means that if you have a good solution to one problem then you look for a way to apply it to others.'

'Yes,' Kitt said with forced patience. 'But what did *you* mean by it?'

'It can't have escaped your notice that I tend to approach most things with a sword,' Derna said levelly. 'Result of my magic, I guess.'

Kitt twisted around. 'You always told me you didn't have any magic.' That was far from unheard of: gifts ranged from the powerful mages who could master many different forms of magic, down through those whose magic was attuned to one thing in particular, like Kitt, and then those whose magic was either so weak or specific that it was essentially useless. However, there were plenty of people who appeared to have no magic whatsoever.

'I didn't think I did,' Derna said. 'I only figured it out a while ago. I guess it's like your friend Vem, and his eyes; I didn't realise what my magic was, until I realised other people couldn't do it too.'

'What is it, then?' Kitt asked, intrigued. This was the longest conversation she'd had with Derna just about *them* in years. It was almost like they were kids again, sitting next to each other with their legs hanging over the edge of a bridge that spanned one of the Great Song's side channels, and tossing pebbles into the water below. Then Derna had split her tongue at thirteen to win that ridiculous bet Kitt had made with her, and then she'd got into fights with other kids who'd mocked her for it, and *then* at fourteen she'd become fascinated with the sashes and had picked up a rusted, cast-off blade from somewhere or another. She tried to get Kitt interested as well, but Kitt had never seen the appeal of placing herself in the way of sharp pieces of metal, and they began to spend less and less time together. That was when Derna's parents gave her an ultimatum: give up any idea of becoming a street duellist, or be kicked out of their home.

Kitt could have told them how that was going to go. They'd never really known their daughter as she had.

At fifteen, Derna killed her first opponent with that rusted blade. A cruel older lad baited her into a duel of no regard with the intention of cutting her repeatedly to make her concede, simply in order to show off. He bloodied her up nicely at first, but he got cocky, and Derna was never going to give up. The cocky lad ended up with Derna's blade buried in his chest, and his own rather better one in her hand. That was the beginning of the legend of Two Tongue Derna, the girl who'd mutilated herself to win a bet and would kill without compunction.

'I know what people are going to do, I guess,' Derna said, after a few moments' thought. 'It's why I'm such a good duellist.'

'Wait, you can read minds?!' Kitt asked, incredulity warring with trepidation.

Derna snorted a humourless laugh. 'Hah! No, the opposite. I can read *bodies*. It's like my reactions get a head start. I still need to know what I'm doing with a sword if I'm going to win, of course,' she added, 'but I don't even need to be able to see, sometimes. I've practiced against someone with a sack over my head, and it turns out I'm still pretty good. I couldn't see the knife, before you got stabbed, but I just *knew* what the man coming up beside you was shaping up for.'

'You're going to have to explain to me again how that's not mind-reading,' Kitt said shakily.

'You're not getting it,' Derna said, and Kitt was shocked to hear a catch in her voice. 'I'm a brilliant duellist, Kitt, but I'm really bad at being a person. I'm just a hammer. Because I know *what* people are going to do. I just hardly ever know *why*.'

SIXTEEN

KITT COULDN'T REALLY find many words after that, even with the stillness of the moors staring her down, and Derna didn't seem to have conversation on her mind either, so they sat in silence for some time instead. Derna might think people were complicated, Kitt reflected, but she was not uncomplicated herself. Or perhaps she was, and that was the point: Derna moved through the world in straight lines, without seeing the curves and corners that everyone else navigated unthinkingly, and took chunks out of everything on her way.

After a while, by largely unspoken agreement, Kitt and Derna woke Vem and Falzine to take their turns, and settled down into the heather once more, a little farther away from each other than they had been the first time. Kitt stared up at the stars, both incredibly weary and not tired at all, until she was shaken awake once more from the sleep that had crept up on her without warning.

'Ugh,' she groaned, sitting up. 'What time is it? Never mind,' she added immediately. Gods, it was so disconcerting to wake up beneath exactly the same sky as that under which she'd fallen asleep! It had never been too bad when she'd been up here for a single stretch. Her brain could process that as a unit of time, one part of a very strange day. She'd now slept twice and woken up to near-darkness both times, and her body absolutely and instinctively hated it.

With no fire, there was no cheery breakfast, or even boiled water for a tin mug of tea. Not that they could afford to waste the water for boiling in any case, given they were in a place effectively as parched as the most scorched desert. Kitt's mouth was already a little drier than she would have liked, but she had no intention of emptying her canteens within the first day and then being forced to beg drinks off her companions for the rest of their journey.

Of course, not everyone in her party had the same restraint.

'You shouldn't drink so much, you know,' Donal offered tentatively, as the Swallowmage took another swig from a flask of something that was certainly water-based, but with a sharp scent that punched right up the nostrils and made the eyes leak. It smelled fruity, in the sense that it was possibly what a blackthorn would point to and warn their sloes that *that* was how they would end up if they didn't behave.

'Young man,' Sulian simply said, fixing him with a stare. 'Stop assuming you know how to be me better than I do. I've had a lifetime of practice at it.' Which made no real sense, but had enough logic to it that no one said anything as they trudged on with the Swallowmage gradually depleting her supplies, mouthful by mouthful.

'We're still going in the right direction?' Vem asked, a while later. Kitt rolled her eyes, but she supposed it wasn't entirely unreasonable for him to want to check.

'Yes,' she said, pointing. 'We're still heading for the same star as before. It hasn't moved.'

'That's a big old hill coming up,' Falzine Halfshade said, pointing at a ridge of land that was starting to loom up and block out the stars as they approached it. It was not, in fact, massively higher than any of the other features they had passed, but this one lay directly across their path and was definitely going to hide their guide star from view. 'Should we climb it, or go around?'

Kitt sucked her teeth. The slope looked fairly steep, and the route so far had not exactly been a level one since they left the bottom of the valley to climb up into the timeless lands in the first place. However, she didn't like the idea of losing sight of the guide star for too long.

'If we start taking diversions, who knows where we'll end up,' she said. 'We'll go over it.'

She wondered whether that decision would prove to be unpopular, but it seemed her companions were of a similar mind that the climb wasn't ideal, but better than getting turned around, or taking another route only to encounter something impassable. Still, there was enough cursing and huffing as they made the ascent to put Kitt on edge, even if the cursing and huffing was not directly aimed at her. The journey across the moors was unsettling and dangerous anyway, and Kitt wouldn't have wanted to attempt it without company. The last thing she wanted was to get too dictatorial and drive away the people in whose hands she was placing her wellbeing.

It wasn't as though anyone else was particularly tied to this journey, either. The Swallowmage claimed she was here because of a vision, but she'd flaked out on stuff before. Falzine seemed to want to cross the moors, but that desire could easily flicker and die if it got too difficult. Vem was doing Kitt a favour, and that could be just as fickle if he decided she was taking advantage of his good nature. Donal was here out of guilt, which was one of the worst motivating factors going.

Oddly enough, it was probably Derna whom Kitt most trusted to stay with her. She was a woman of her word, even if her words were often unexpected and sometimes downright alarming.

And speaking of downright alarming...

'Oh *shit*,' Kitt muttered under her breath. She had scrambled over the last boulder and crested up onto the comparatively flat top of the hill, which stretched away into the distance in a plateau. However, off to the left, in the lower lands they would have passed through had they attempted to skirt the hill to that side, was something she had never seen before either within or without the timeless lands.

It was also something she could have done with never having seen at all, and certainly never wanted to see again, but that did not appear to be an option.

'Whatcha looking at?' Vem asked cheerily, coming up behind her. He came to an abrupt halt when he reached level with her, and she sensed rather than saw the colour draining from his cheeks in the dim light.

'Oh, mercy of the Mothers,' he whispered.

'Yeah,' Kitt said, gripping the hilt of her short sword as though it would do her the slightest bit of good. 'Something like that.'

It looked, at first glance, something like a large house of worship; not of a particular denomination, as such, but the long, bulky main structure and tall spires – three of them, in this case – were characteristics shared by several of the larger religions.

However, once you got past the initial impression, your eye began to register the differences. Most religions favoured clean and smooth lines, even if not necessarily straight ones. A temple might be circular, or oval, or rectangular, but it was rarely a jagged jumble of angles. This structure rambled along with lumps and bumps here and there, its footprint only a rough approximation of anything geometric, and although its spires were clearly able to support their own weight, they were definitely a bit wonky. All in all, it looked decidedly organic, and there was a very good reason for that.

'Well,' Kitt said, swallowing hard. 'I guess we've found where the slydewasps were going.'

It was a nest. A massive, dark nest that glistened faintly under the light of the unchanging stars. It was hard for Kitt to judge the scale of it at first, crouching as it did in a valley with nothing except the dark landscape against which to measure it. It wasn't until she managed to make out first one, then two, then more and more faint specks of darker darkness against its bulk that she realised those were slydewasps, and began to get some sense of the nest's immensity. She was fairly certain there was no building in Mereport that approached it in size except perhaps the Merefort, the old fortress in which the Grand Council met and where the city's treasury was guarded by soldiers, magical wards, and one small dragon – small as dragons went, anyway, so approximately the same size as a bull elephant – who had been hired as Hoard Administrator.

'Oh my,' Donal said in a small voice. The others had arrived, and each one of them looked just as horrified as Vem.

'I don't care what your star says,' Falzine said flatly. 'We're not going *that* way.'

'No, we're not,' Kitt hastily agreed. 'That's not our direction.'

'Still think you can fight them?' Sulian said sarcastically to Derna.

'Fight them? Sure,' Derna replied. 'Win? Probably not.'

Despite herself, Kitt turned to stare at Derna. '*Probably* not?'

Derna shrugged, as casually as if she'd been asked whether she thought it might rain tomorrow afternoon. 'You never know until you try.'

'What are they *doing* down there?' Pigtail Vem asked, his voice dripping with horrified fascination.

'Probably just trying to live, like anything else,' Kitt said. It made her decidedly uneasy, looking down at such a massive nest of already massive creatures – at least in terms of how big she felt wasps should be, which was 'no larger than my thumb' with a side order of 'a long way away from me' – but it wasn't as though she'd ever got the impression that slydewasps were *malicious*. They just… were. People such as Kitt insisted on coming up into the timeless lands where the wasps lived, and the wasps ate the ones that they caught. She had no desire to go down and see what the wasps were doing, even if she'd had a cast-iron guarantee that she'd be safe from them while she did so.

'Come on,' she said, suppressing a shudder. 'Let's get moving.'

They walked on, and by unspoken agreement didn't pause for lunch until the great nest was well out of sight behind them. Even then, everyone hastily chewed their food and was eager to be on their way once more, despite sore feet and weary legs. To be fair, it wasn't just the wasps causing the uneasiness. Kitt could see it in her companions, and feel it in herself. No normal life form could properly acclimatise to these timeless lands, and the constant near-dark and oppressive silence was a gentle but suffocating pressure on their spirit.

It was just after they'd set off again that the first chrono-charm failed. For a moment Kitt thought Donal had just paused between one step and the next, but when she stopped to ask him whether he'd seen something she realised that no living human could be as still as he was.

'Hold up!' she called to the others, and began digging through his pockets. It was strange how uncomfortable it made her feel, given a lot more of her had been in contact with him, and while wearing far fewer clothes. It wasn't even as though he would be able to sense what she was doing, since so far as he was concerned, time did not exist. Still, it felt like an invasion of his privacy.

'We could just leave him,' Derna offered casually, one hand resting insouciantly on the pommel of her sheathed sidesword.

'No,' Kitt snapped. 'We're not *just leaving* anyone.'

'Just give him one of your spares,' the Swallowmage said, leaning on Jandi, her staff. She wasn't looking good, and Kitt had already been wondering if the strangeness of the high moors was affecting her more than the rest of them for some mage-related reason.

'No chance,' Kitt said with a snort, rummaging in another belt pouch.

'Why not? He could just give you one of his spares in exchange once he unfreezes,' Sulian pointed out.

'Because,' Kitt said, as her fingers closed around something that felt right, 'I don't know where he got his charms from, and they might be a lot shittier than mine.' She pulled out another chronocharm and looped it around Donal's neck, then stepped back hurriedly.

As she expected, Donal continued with exactly the same momentum as he'd had before he came to a halt. He took another step before stopping and looking around in confusion, then pointing at her.

'How did you get—'

'Your chronocharm failed,' Kitt told him shortly, and turned away to address the rest of them. 'Everyone check your own!'

As ever, with magic, nothing was completely certain. The glow of a chronocharm indicated how fresh it was, but it wasn't unheard of for one to wink out without warning. Kitt's was dimmer than she'd ever seen one before, but it still seemed to have some juice in it. She swapped it out all the same, replacing it for one that glowed brightly, just in case. The others followed her lead, although they had to come to the rescue of Sulian when she tried to take her old charm off after having placed the new one around her neck, but the chains got tangled up and she inadvertently pulled the new one away as well. The Swallowmage grimaced as she blinked back into life, and strode onwards with barely a grunted thanks. As Kitt watched, Sulian's head twitched to one side.

'Is she okay?' Vem asked quietly, coming up alongside Kitt and nodding in the direction of the Swallowmage.

'She hasn't thrown up recently. Beyond that, who can tell?'

They slept again, after a few more probable hours of walking, with Donal and Sulian once more taking first watch. When Donal shook Kitt awake he glanced meaningfully in Sulian's direction and shook his head slightly, as though to indicate his doubts about her. Kitt wasn't prepared to trust his judgement on much, but the way the Swallowmage twisted and muttered even after apparently getting to sleep certainly suggested that he might have been on to something. Kitt and Derna sat back to back on a rock once more, and tapped each other's arm with their fingers periodically to confirm their charms hadn't failed and they were still keeping watch, rather than risk waking the Swallowmage with conversation.

SEVENTEEN

By the time Kitt had fallen into and then been roused once more from thoroughly unrestful sleep, she was about ready to scream. The timeless lands always felt oddly relaxing when she first stepped into them; even amidst the ever-present anxiety about slydewasps and faulty chronocharms, there was a sense that the worries of the outside world couldn't touch her while she remained under these stars. Now, however, she would have happily passed up a table groaning under the weight of her favourite foods for the feel of a breath of air on her cheek, a spot of rain on her forehead, or even catching the sun in her eyes, and would have embraced someone who bumped into her on a busy Mereport street just for the joy of hearing the bustle of a crowd around her once more. Had she the power to do so, she would have torn the sky open simply to get back into a world where things actually *happened*.

'I don't know if any religions have a hell like this,' Falzine Halfshade said as they trudged on, 'but if they exist, I vote we stamp them out just in case they're right.'

It was some time later, as they worked their way across a slight valley, that Kitt noticed the Swallowmage muttering under her breath. It was barely audible at first, despite the silence of the moors, but it gradually built up from scattered fragments of whispers into a steady stream of susurration. Then, as though dragged out of her without volition, Sulian's voice kindled into life and the whispers became mumblings, loose and soft-edged.

The rest of the party, without any words exchanged, drifted away from her a little. Mages were fine, in and of themselves; often useful to know, if unwise to antagonise. Their power was enough to make anyone wary, however, and a mage muttering under her breath and flinching for no apparent reason was not something that inspired confidence. What if she lashed out with mystical power at some unseen threat, or a particularly horrific vision, and one of them happened to be in the way? Kitt certainly didn't want to end up being flash-broiled, but she still ought to do something. She was the leader of this expedition, for some reason, and that probably came with certain expectations. One of which was 'check on the mage before she starts blowing stuff up'.

'You doing okay?' Kitt called, easing her way closer again. The Swallowmage was setting a furious pace now, striding forward with her staff thumping into the ground as she went, and she was even going in broadly the right direction.

No answer, other than the muttering. Kitt gritted her teeth and hurried up alongside Sulian, hoping she wasn't about to be blasted or frozen or something equally unpleasant but rather more unorthodox, and reached out to place her hand gently on the Swallowmage's shoulder.

'Hey. Everything okay?'

The Swallowmage turned a face towards her on which pain was writ large, in capital letters, and also underlined. 'Sorry,' she muttered, gesturing at her head. 'The futures are... loud, at the moment.'

Understanding dawned. 'It's worse up here than in Mereport?'

'It's like they're all in my head at once,' Sulian replied,

through gritted teeth. 'And they're arguing. Usually one comes through, and it knocks me sideways, and then it's done.' She grabbed Kitt's elbow, with rather more force than was strictly necessary. 'You know when you're about to sneeze?'

'I guess?' Kitt said, uncertain where this was going.

'Imagine that, but rather than that second or so, it just goes on and on and on, and it's not a sneeze, it's dozens or hundreds of voices shouting in your head, and every one of them is important, and every one of them wants you to *listen*.'

Kitt blinked. 'That certainly sounds unpleasant.'

'It's not actually anything like that,' the Swallowmage said, still not letting go of Kitt's elbow, 'but that's the closest I can manage.'

'Okay. Is there anything we can do to help? And do you think you could—'

She reached up to gently pry the other woman's grip loose from her arm, but the moment their fingers touched, the Swallowmage's eyes flared a bright green.

'Ah, nuts,' Kitt said, waiting for emerald-tinged obliteration, but after a single, frozen moment, the Swallowmage released her and began to run.

'What the hell did you say?' Derna called from behind Kitt, as Sulian pelted away through the heather at a faster pace than any of them had moved since leaving Mereport.

'I think a prophecy's got hold of her!' Kitt replied, once she'd managed to breathe again after staring down what had looked an awful lot like imminent death.

'She's not slowing down, is she?' Donal commented. Sure enough, the Swallowmage was still running, gradually receding into the gloom that surrounded them. She wasn't moving heedlessly – that would have seen her going over onto her face within the first few seconds, given the nature of the footing – but there was no indication that the woman herself was in charge of her own body.

'No, she's not.' Kitt sighed, and scrubbed her face with

her hands. 'Right, come on! I said we weren't leaving anyone behind, and that includes her.'

'But she's going in the wrong direction!' Vem protested, pointing towards the star they had been following, to which Sulian was heading off at something like a forty-degree diagonal to the right.

'Then we'd best catch up quickly!' Kitt snapped, and set off in pursuit.

She immediately remembered all the bad things about running over the moors. The treacherously uneven ground, the snaggling branches clutching at her ankles and trying to trip her up, and just how *hard* it was. You could pick your way across the moors at a steady pace without too much difficulty, although it became wearying after a while, but half a minute of running up here left Kitt feeling like she'd sprinted across half of Mereport.

Yet somehow, despite the Swallowmage having at least thirty years on Kitt, she was maintaining her lead.

'Where's she going?' Derna shouted, hurdling a small and unexpected gully.

'Beats me!' Kitt yelled back. Sulian was heading for the col at the valley's head, a lower area between the two slightly higher peaks on either side, but *why* was a question to which Kitt had no answers. The ground began to rise now, and all of them – the Swallowmage included – slowed to little more than a speedy stumble, but Sulian pressed on doggedly, using Jandi as a prop to lever herself up the incline that little bit faster than she could have managed otherwise. Kitt gritted her teeth and forced herself to keep up, not wanting to lose Sulian for too long once she got to the col and passed out of sight into whatever lay beyond. Kitt would feel awful if the Swallowmage of Mereport ran off and got herself killed by some as-yet-unknown peril of the high moors because her mind had been overtaken by prophecies on some fool quest of Kitt Carver's.

Sulian reached the col and scrambled through it with Kitt some thirty yards behind her, at the head of the pursuit. Derna was on her right and Donal on her left, with Falzine a little way back thanks to the added burden of carrying his long spear, and Pigtail Vem gamely bringing up the rear. Kitt followed the Swallowmage's footsteps, forcing her burning thighs to propel her up the last bit of ground and desperately hoping that whatever geas had overcome Sulian was going to loosen its grip on her before someone's heart exploded, possibly Kitt's…

…and came to a halt as the sky changed.

Well, the sky didn't exactly *change* so much as something new came into view in it. To be fair, it wasn't exactly the sky as such, either. To Kitt's mind, the sky was distant, overhead, out of reach. This was more like… the air. There was something hanging in the air which had previously been out of sight to them, and as Kitt reached the middle of the col she completely forgot the ache in her legs.

'Is that…?' Donal puffed, coming to a halt next to her.

'It's the rift,' Derna said in tones of awe, her face painted with shimmering, shifting colours because here, alone in all of the timeless lands, there was light.

The rift was a jagged rent in the air hanging just above the downwards slope before them, a long, diagonal split in reality where the unknown god had tried to kill the future but had only succeeded in wounding it, or splitting it into component parts, or however else people tried to describe what had happened up here centuries ago. It looked like someone had torn through fabric; narrow at the top left as Kitt looked at it, then spreading outwards to its widest point, with the stars and the sky beyond the edges of the rift looking sort of *bunched up* as though being viewed through distorting lenses, and then narrowing again to the bottom right where a brilliant light blazed.

'The Swordstar,' Kitt breathed. This wasn't a distant

pinprick of light like the unchanging stars of which she'd become so thoroughly sick since they'd crossed out of normal time and onto the moors. The Swordstar still wasn't exactly *large* – Kitt estimated it was certainly no bigger than she was, and probably somewhat smaller – but it seemed *alive*. Even now, all this time after it had been forged and used, its light blazed like a furnace and cast shadows, actual shadows, across the heather.

There was other light here as well, though, because the rift's interior glowed with all the hues of a rainbow that had drunk tea steeped with entirely the wrong sort of mushrooms. It was less bright than the clean, fierce illumination of the Swordstar, but there was far more of it; the rent in reality was perhaps as long as a tall tree, and something like thirty feet across at its widest point, and the radiance of whatever lay *beyond* spilled out from it like ribbons of luminescent taffeta. That was what glided across Derna's face, bringing her features to life for the first time in what had to be at least a couple of days by any normal measurement.

'Oh, wow,' Falzine said, as he crested the rise behind them, although the light did nothing to illuminate his face. 'That's certainly a sight.'

Kitt shook herself out of her brief reverie. This spectacle was something stupendous, something barely seen by anyone else alive, the sort of experience a person might get once in their lifetime. However, she had come up here with a different purpose in mind, and that purpose was a dark shape below, still stumbling towards the rift.

'Sulian!' Kitt shouted, setting off down the slope.

The Swallowmage was reaching out towards the great expanse of shimmering air as she ran, as though it was a long-lost lover whose embrace she could bear to be parted from no longer. Her hands opened, reaching for it…

…and as though deciding that this was all a very bad idea, her staff Jandi dropped from her grip, tangled between her legs, tripped her up, and finally brought her to a violent halt face down in the heather.

'Shit,' Kitt cursed, trying to put on an extra burst of speed. If she could just get to Sulian before she managed to rise again, Kitt might be able to stop her from actually reaching the rift, and although Kitt Carver was no expert on holes torn in the world by gods using arcane weaponry, she was fairly sure that nothing good would come from a human mage making contact with it.

Luckily, Sulian was not getting up very fast. She made it up to her hands and knees, and then began to vomit very loudly. Kitt slowed down, sensing that the immediate danger might be past and having vivid images of herself rushing to the Swallowmage's side and then going arse-over-tit on a patch of sick-slimed heather.

'Hey!' she shouted, just loud enough to be heard over more sounds of retching. 'You doing okay?'

The Swallowmage's right hand came up, but instead of forming an arcane symbol that would shoot a bolt of ravening lighting, Kitt simply found herself on the receiving end of a middle finger wielded with considerable intent.

'Understood,' Kitt acknowledged. 'I just wanted to check you weren't still, you know… possessed, or whatever.'

'It's actually a bit easier here,' Sulian said weakly, wiping her mouth. 'My head still feels like it's splitting open, but it's the eye of the storm, or something. This is where the future breaks into shards, over and over and over again.'

'Huh.' Kitt looked around at the ground. 'You're not kidding.'

There were destinies everywhere.

Kitt had brought her moonstruck irons along even though she'd had no intention of doing any divining while up on the high moors, simply because they were as much a part of her as her fingers. She would normally have to get her rods out, concentrate, and follow the faint tugs and dips of her moonstrikers to have any hope of finding a destiny. The notion of coming up onto the moors, looking around, and simply *finding* one was so far-fetched as to be ludicrous.

Yet here they were. Kitt could see three just from where she stood: two tucked away nearly but not quite out of sight under boughs of heather, and one sitting out in the open on a patch of pale sandy soil, where anyone passing by could pick it up without any need for actual *talent*. It was almost insulting. To think that Kitt had been spending her time hunting through the slim pickings of the south, when all she'd needed to do was walk for the equivalent of two or more days through the soul-crushing, never-changing timeless lands to get to the place where the future had nearly been killed…

Yeah, well. Maybe she hadn't been making bad decisions after all. Or at least, not notably *worse* decisions.

Oddly enough, Kitt realised as the Swallowmage groaned and rolled over onto her back, she had no desire to pick the destinies up. Given how hard she'd worked in the past to get her hands on any destiny of a reasonable size, she would have expected herself to be running around and groping under bushes, searching for the telltale warmth-that-wasn't-warmth in her hands that indicated she'd found something big and, therefore, profitable.

This wasn't why she was here this time, though. She hadn't come *to* the high moors, she was going *through* them to reach something that her gut, or her heart, or some other internal organ was insistent was more important than the prospect of trivial enrichment. If nothing else, at least she knew this place was here. Perhaps once everything was done – whatever that turned out to mean – she could come back and make her fortune. For now, however—

'Kitt, look at them all!'

For now, however, *she wasn't the only diviner up here.*

Donal was on his hands and knees, gleefully holding up a destiny. He brought it up to his face and inhaled, which confused Kitt until she remembered that was how he got a sense of whether a destiny was worth taking. Donal seemed to like whatever it was he smelled, because he shoved the destiny and its just-awakened light of warm honey into a pouch, and scrambled through the heather towards the next one.

'Donal!' Kitt snapped. 'That's not why we're here!'

'I know!' Donal protested. 'But we *are* here, and they're here, so what's the problem?' He pointed at the Swallowmage. 'This was her detour, not mine!'

'The lad's got a point, lass,' Pigtail Vem said, despite the look of slight distaste he directed at Donal. He was making his way towards her, breathing heavily after running, but Kitt didn't think his slightly wide eyes were just due to his exertions. 'We've spent hours up here searching for a single one of these before, and now they're just in front of us! Why not load up while we can?'

'Don't *lass* me,' Kitt told him sternly, waving a finger at him. 'As for why we shouldn't take them...'

She hesitated. She had a strong feeling that they shouldn't, but struggled to verbalise it in a way that appealed to someone who was, fairly understandably, being driven by a profit motive.

'What are we going to do with them?' she asked, as some sort of inspiration struck. 'We're going to be going down into places we don't know with a whole lot of potential wealth on us, and a long way from anywhere we can easily sell them. Not many people are willing to come up here to find a destiny, but lots would be prepared to take them off us when we're back in the normal world, and a fair few won't be too bothered about whether we're alive afterwards. I don't fancy walking around with that sort of target on my back.'

Vem huffed, and the light from the rift gave Kitt a clear view of the warring emotions crossing his face, but after a few seconds he blew his moustaches out and nodded reluctantly.

'Alright, fine. That's a good enough argument, I suppose,'

he conceded. He inched closer to Kitt and lowered his voice. 'And I guess *she* might kick up a fuss over it, too.'

He nodded in the direction of Derna, who was picking her way through the heather off at an angle to the rest of them – and straight toward the rift.

'Derna?' Kitt called, a sense of alarm creeping through her; a many-legged, skittering sensation, like woodlice in a logpile. 'What are you doing?'

'Look at it, Kitt,' Derna said. She was smiling gently, which was unnerving in its own way because Derna didn't really do *anything* gently. 'It's the most beautiful thing I've ever seen.'

'What, the rift?' Kitt asked, taking a few steps towards her. 'Yeah, I guess. In a weird sort of… end-of-the-world way.'

'Not the rift,' Derna said, with a throaty chuckle about which the hairs on the back of Kitt's neck had definite opinions. 'The Swordstar.'

'Okay, figures that you'd be interested in the weapon,' Kitt said, hurrying towards her. The blazing light upon which Derna was fixated hung at about chest height from the ground, and looked like it should be scorching everything within at least a hundred-yard radius, but even the heather directly beneath it was untouched. All the same, Kitt was far from convinced of the harmlessness of something that had been used to cut a giant tear in reality. 'Come *on*, Derna, a god used that, and it nearly destroyed everything!'

Derna came to a halt and looked at her with an odd expression.

'Kitt, do you think I'm going to destroy the world?'

'Honestly?' Kitt none-too-subtly interposed herself between Derna and the brilliant light of the Swordstar. 'I'm more worried about what's going to happen to *you* if you touch it. *Then* I'll start worrying about what you might do with it.' She looked around and hissed with frustration as she saw Donal reaching under another bush. 'Can everyone please just *stop touching stuff*? We literally haven't got time to be hanging around here, and it's starting to give me the creeps. Vem, can you get Sulian up?'

Pigtail Vem wasn't paying any attention to her. He was frowning up at the sky, back towards the south.

'Vem!' Kitt shouted. Vem breathed in, and for a moment Kitt thought he was going to yell at her. As it turned out, that would have been preferable.

'*Wasps!*' Vem bellowed. 'Run!'

He suited actions to words as soon as said words had left his mouth, pounding off as fast as he could without pausing to do anything about Sulian, who had managed to regain her grip on her staff and was beginning to lever herself upright again. Falzine Halfshade had his great spear in two hands and was moving crablike, trying not to turn his back on whatever was coming, even if he couldn't see it properly yet.

Derna squinted upwards. 'Is he pulling our legs?'

'No,' Kitt said, her stomach sinking. 'Look at the stars.'

The stars were unchanging here, without even the gentle twinkling that they exhibited in the lower lands. They certainly didn't blink in and out of visibility, like they were doing right now. There was only one explanation for that, which was that just like Kitt stood between Derna and the Swordstar, the light of the stars above them was being obscured, again and again, by something.

Well, somethings. *Lots* of somethings.

'Do they... normally come in a swarm?' Derna asked slowly.

'No,' Kitt said, fighting against her body's instincts. She knew she should run. She *wanted* to run. However, her body had its own beliefs, hardwired into it by ancestral memory all the way back to when fire was something scary that happened after lightning storms. Oh sure, you ran if something scary was actually coming *at* you. If it wasn't something you could see properly, however – if it was just barely glimpsed shapes somewhere in the sky above – then the body wanted to freeze, to remain still and avoid the attention that usually came from moving. It wasn't a perfect evolutionary strategy by any means, but it had worked often enough for long enough to remain lurking in the back of the skull, ready to reach out and envelop everything in a smothering blanket of inaction.

It was Derna that broke it.

'Right, sod this,' the Duchess of Death said, taking another step towards Kitt and reaching out for the Swordstar, while still looking up at the silent, flickering sky. 'I'm gonna need a better weapon.'

'No!' Kitt said, and without thinking, she stepped in and took hold of Derna's elbow to push her arm down to her side.

Derna's head whipped around, her curls bouncing, and Kitt found herself staring at very close range into the face of someone on whom you did not lay your hands unless you had a burning desire to suddenly reduce the number of digits under your control.

'Might need the help, Kitt,' Derna said softly, so close that her breath warmed Kitt's lips. Derna made no move, but Kitt could feel the tension in the arm beneath her fingers.

'I'd rather have you definitely alive,' Kitt replied. The power of the Swordstar was throbbing behind her, bright and cold and alien. She swallowed and tried to pretend that physically interposing herself been a deliberate decision. 'Now come *on*, and help me with Sulian, will you?'

Kitt saw the next few seconds playing out in her mind's eye. After all, this was Two Tongue Derna, possibly the world's greatest street duellist, reaching out for the weapon of a literal god. Kitt was just Kitt Carver, whose skills were moderately respected amongst the divining community of Mereport, but who was otherwise entirely unremarkable. If Kitt had a role in a story beyond that of 'woman in the market,' it was always going to be something like the helpful local who assisted the hero in their quest, or perhaps the loyal friend whose death galvanised the hero into taking drastic and decisive action. The world didn't *care* about people like Kitt Carver.

Derna would shove her aside and leave her sprawling in the heather, then take hold of the Swordstar, whereupon Derna would either burst into screaming flame, or would wield this terrifying weapon to fight off the slydewasps before setting off to conquer the world, or go on a quest, or…

Instead, much to Kitt's surprise, the corner of Derna's mouth crooked upwards into a wry smile, and she nodded.

'Okay.'

And so they ran.

EIGHTEEN

Tommas never intended to kill the man. It was just that sometimes he couldn't help it (equally, sometimes he *could* help it, which was called 'being an assassin').

They had put in at Solmouth, apparently for Carl to send a message to whomever his employers were. Tommas had taken the opportunity to stretch his legs on ground that didn't move beneath his feet, and also to get as far away from Plainsong as he reasonably could. He had barely seen the bald, robed man since their brief conversation on the deck after leaving Mereport two days before, but just knowing he was on the ship set Tommas on edge. There was nothing overtly threatening about him, but there was a subtle sense of *wrongness*, and Tommas had long ago learned to listen to his instincts.

His instincts also guided him to an upmarket tavern set a little way back from the docks, where he had enjoyed a tankard of quite pleasant ale and an engagingly spicy fish stew while listening to a perfectly competent harper perform the lesser-heard third movement of Avatoly's *Music from Other Lands*. With his meal done, and sweating slightly, he had stepped out into the salt-scented warmth of the early evening and begun to make his way back towards the docks; a route that took him, as it turned out, through some streets that were decidedly less upmarket.

Tommas's first impression that things weren't quite right came when voices were raised further along the alley down which he was making his way. He pressed on, secure in the knowledge that he was well able to protect himself if the need arose, but mainly that those caught up in an argument were likely to ignore someone passing by and minding his own business. Things got more heated as Tommas approached, but he kept his head down and stayed on the other side, away from where three men were arguing in increasingly agitated tones about… something.

The second impression that thing weren't quite right came just before he reached the fractious trio in question, when one of them made a sharp, sudden movement that Tommas's brain instantly interpreted. The closest man grunted and stumbled backwards away from the other two, who fled. Tommas instinctively reached out a hand to steady the struck individual as he turned, and his thrust-forward palm made contact not with the man's upper body, but with something small and hard that protruded from it.

The knife, which until this moment had only penetrated far enough between the victim's ribs to stick in place, slid all the way home with a wet whisper that became a faint, hollow *thud* as the hilt impacted against the man's chest. His eyes went wide as the blade punctured his heart, and he dropped to his knees. Tommas stepped back in horror, but what was done was done. Granted, there was no *actual* blood on his hands this time, but his curse had done its work once more.

'Bother,' Tommas Underwyne whispered to himself, and hurried away before anyone showed up and started to ask difficult questions.

...

He was standing at the stern of the *Spirit of Freedom*, looking back at the sunset as the ship made its way up the River Solwynd, when Carl Whyteaves came up alongside him.

'Where is he?' the factor demanded, his voice tight and clipped.

'Where is who?' Tommas asked, without looking around. He did not, in fact, have any clue what Carl was taking about, but a lack of reaction would suggest that he did, and would wind the other man up. He had been forced to endure Carl's company for several days now, and with the death of the stranger in the alley still weighing on his mind, Tommas was prepared to take his pleasures where he could.

'Don't joke with me,' Carl said. Tommas could practically feel him vibrating with fury. 'This is serious.'

'Don't tell me you've mislaid your "additional asset".' Tommas turned to face him. The mysterious Plainsong was the only thing Tommas had yet seen evoke a strong reaction from Whyteaves, who otherwise remained infuriatingly smug and superior, and the twitch at the corner of Carl's left eye gave Tommas all the information he needed. 'You *have?* Well, that's made my evening considerably better. What happened, did he get off when we put in at Solmouth, and didn't make it back on board in time?'

'This is not a laughing matter,' Carl bit out, despite Tommas's chuckle suggesting otherwise. 'Do you have any idea how dangerous this could be? Not to mention the fact that he can move a lot faster than you would think. He could be a great distance from us by now.'

'Can't you just say his name and call him back?'

'No!' the factor snapped. 'Don't you understand? He is *bound.* Or at least, he's supposed to be. The enchantments allow him a certain level of autonomy, since a mindless puppet is of little use, but he is not supposed to be able to just leave the ship if he feels like it. If he can do that, then attempting to call him back is one of the worst possible things we could do.'

'Enchantments? Compulsion enchantments?' Tommas shuddered. Killing people was not a pleasant business, but it still felt more *honest* than using magic to override someone's free will. That was a murky area, nearly as proscribed as chronomancy. 'Exactly how far are your employers prepared to go to achieve success?'

'As far as is necessary,' Carl said quietly. 'And believe me, so far as the asset is concerned, compulsion enchantments are the only way. Needless to say, were he to be in his original state of mind then he would be quite… *displeased*. If the magic loosens to the stage where he is no longer forbidden from using violence against us, things will get very unpleasant, very quickly.'

'Wait, "us"? I'm no less of an asset than him! This is your cause, not mine. I had nothing to do with whatever you did to ensnare him.'

'I honestly doubt he would care,' Carl said, with a smile that would have knifed its sister in the kidneys for loose change. 'He sees things very simplistically. If you are with us, but not with him – and no one is *with* him – then you are party to what has been done to him. So I will ask you one more time, Tommas: were you involved with his disappearance? Have you interfered with his body, his clothing, or his cabin in any way? Have you recited any spells without knowing their full meaning, or moved or destroyed any object the purpose of which you were unsure?'

'No,' Tommas said instantly. 'I've not been near him. Besides, I'm an assassin, Whyteaves; I know better than to interfere with anything that is not absolutely required for the successful completion of my work. It's not a profession that enjoys complication.'

'Then we have a problem,' Carl said. He was still angry, Tommas could tell, but he was scared as well. What was more, Carl Whyteaves was obviously not used to being scared. Tommas had encountered that before, mainly in the sort of rich person against whom his services might be engaged. The ideal, of course, was to eliminate the target without them ever being aware of your presence. Sometimes, however, things didn't go quite to plan. The first dart missed, the mark wasn't where they should be and had to be hunted down before they could reach help, or they stumbled across a guard or servant removed from the equation through a sleep spell or soporific venom. Then the mark realised that death had come for them, and they found themselves in a situation which, unlike most in their coddled lives, couldn't be solved by money, or bluster, or the threat of a father's name.

Panic wasn't always the result, of course. Tommas had always been mildly intrigued by those victims who were able to process a threat to their life and adapt in short order, despite their wealth. What experiences had they been through? What twists had their privileged lives thrown at them, where fear of death was familiar enough to be faced and overcome?

Carl did not fall into that category. He wasn't quite panicking, but in the very deliberate way of a man consciously holding himself together, and that was just at the notion that something *might* be wrong. Plainsong wasn't on the ship with them, threatening vengeance and doing whatever terrible things of which he was apparently capable. Were that to happen, Tommas was fairly sure Carl would be either cowering or leaping into the water in a desperate attempt to get away.

'If he was constrained once before, I imagine he can be constrained again?' Tommas asked. He wasn't familiar with compulsion magic, but he was relatively certain it was not a one-to-a-customer affair.

'One would presume so,' Carl said tightly. 'The enchantments have certainly been renewed several times in the past. Ours is far from the first purpose to which he has been attached. The question is why the enchantments failed in the first place, and whether they will work as intended if recast.'

'This is why I prefer using my own hands,' Tommas said. 'You can never properly rely on magic.'

It was at times like that he truly regretted not becoming a baker. If you got magic wrong with bread then maybe some dough didn't rise as quickly as you wanted, or maybe it rose too much and you had to start again. Tommas certainly couldn't imagine a circumstance where baking would require the use of magic which, if it failed, would see your kitchen destroyed by a vengeful yeast demon or similar.

'We were *intending* to rely on your hands,' Carl said impatiently. 'However, the people whom I represent were insistent that Pl—that *the asset* be brought as well, as a last resort.'

Tommas drummed his fingers on the taffrail. 'When you say "last resort"…?'

'I mean that for him to be of use in this situation, certain enchantments would have to be lifted. He would unquestionably be able to eliminate our target. The question is always whether he can be released to do *that* without allowing him free rein to kill as he sees fit.'

'He has been used before, then?' Tommas asked, as casually as he could.

'Once, of which I am aware,' Carl said. He was looking up at the sky now, as though the clouds coloured a rosy gold by the setting sun could offer him inspiration. 'There may have been other instances in records to which I do not have access. The primary goal was achieved on that occasion: a dangerous revolutionary was eliminated before he could plunge an entire country into chaos and anarchy.' He heaved a sigh. 'Unfortunately, the asset also butchered his own handlers, as well as half a village whose allegiance to the revolutionary in question was tangential at best, and once his task was completed he headed directly for the person who had ordered the mission. Fifteen guards died while delaying him sufficiently for the mages to recast the enchantments.'

'Wonderful,' Tommas said sourly. 'So your employers have placed a bridle on a being they cannot truly control, yet dare not release. And presumably, cannot kill?'

'I suspect there is a way,' Carl said. 'Not one of which I am aware, however, and I wouldn't have the authority to do such a thing.' He grimaced. 'If the enchantments *have* started to fray, perhaps he has learned from last time and knows that if he seeks vengeance then he will be brought to heel once more. Perhaps he simply seeks to get as far as possible from us, in the hope that this will prevent us from reforging his bonds.'

'Will that work?' Tommas asked, trying to disguise his hope. He was a master assassin, damn it, and he didn't need assistance to fulfil his contract from what was increasingly sounding like some archaic horror in the shape of a hairless man. Plainsong disappearing into the unknown and keeping out of sight in the interests of his own liberty would suit Tommas Underwyne down to the ground.

'No,' Carl said bluntly. 'If I don't have the authority to kill him, I certainly don't have the authority to *lose* him. The attempt will be made to reestablish control; it will just be made when I am as certain as I can be that it will succeed, rather than merely enrage him and provoke him to return from wherever he currently is and attack us.'

He turned to Tommas. 'In the meantime, do let me know if you see anything unusual, won't you? You know, a hooded figure lurking in the shadows, an eviscerated deckhand, or a blade coming for your throat...'

NINETEEN

'COME ON, YOU miserable old woman!' Derna raged at the Swallowmage, who was staggering along with one of their arms under each of her shoulders. 'You ran fast enough to get to the bloody rift, what's wrong with you now?'

It was a somewhat unfair characterisation in Kitt's view, but given they were currently stumbling down the slope of a moorland hill with a silent swarm of giant insectoid predators in aerial pursuit, she was prepared to accept anything that might get them moving faster. Even rousing Sulian's temper enough for her to start throwing magic around would be an improvement. Kitt had never seen a mage fight a slydewasp — most mages worth their salt had better things to do, not to mention too much pride, to sign on with divination parties to be something as crude and mundane as a bodyguard — but she was prepared to bet that it couldn't go *worse* than trying to take the entire swarm on armed only with the weapons that the rest of them had.

'Come on!' Donal shouted from farther down the slope, looking back and waving his arm as though it was a simple lack of enthusiasm which was causing the three women to lag behind. He'd managed to put enough distance between himself and them that he could afford to slow slightly and make it look like he cared, without actually being close enough to either offer assistance or be in any danger once the slydewasps caught up with them. Her grudging tolerance for him, which had built up like grease on a dish, was rapidly washed away by the detergent of her disgust.

'I'm gonna stab him,' Derna stated bluntly, from the other side of the Swallowmage.

'Later!' Kitt hissed. Something huge swooped down out of the sky, and she threw herself into the other two. 'Get down!'

They tumbled into the heather as the slydewasp scythed through the air, its sting slashing through the space they'd just vacated. Kitt rolled back up into a crouch, reluctant to get any closer to the sky than she had to, but terrified of being on the ground and seeing a giant abdomen descending towards her with no ability to get out of the way. At least with her feet under her she might be able to make a couple of clumsy dodges before she was impaled…

'Come on then, you stripy bastards!' Derna bellowed, springing back to her feet with her sidesword in hand. She flourished and spun the blade as though she was facing down an entire sash of street duellists, a fey smile on her lips.

Predictably enough, what might have intimidated even a moderately sized group of humans had no effect on slydewasps. Another of the giant insects dropped from the sky, with two more flanking it, and came for Derna.

She wasn't there.

It wasn't that she disappeared in a puff of magical smoke or flickered out of existence to reappear somewhere else. It was simply that the Queen of the Streets was one step ahead of anything that came her way, even if that was the razor-sharp sting tipping the abdomen of a slydewasp. Derna swayed backwards to avoid one blow, ducked under another, then lashed out with her sword. Chitin gave way before the blade's edge with a crunch, and a stinger tumbled to the ground, uselessly leaking venom.

'Watch it!' Kitt yelped, as the foot-long barb stabbed into the ground a mere hands-breadth from the Swallowmage's arm.

'Oh, I'm sorry!' Derna shouted back sarcastically, hacking off half of a leg that swung too close to her. 'Feel free to join in if you think you can do better!'

This was no time for throwing moonstruck iron; Kitt drew her short sword and tried to gather her courage. Farther down the slope she caught a glimpse of Falzine Halfshade skewering a wasp with his spear and driving it down into the ground, and Pigtail Vem desperately slashing with his axe at another one to keep it away from Falzine's back while he did so.

'Don't stab 'em!' Derna warned, parrying a slash aimed at her head. 'You'll lose your sword!'

'Got it!' Kitt shouted, more to convince herself than Derna, and swung upwards with a scream as a body passed over her head intent on attacking Derna from behind. The thing's armour turned her blade aside, but she had attracted its attention. That was, Kitt realised immediately, not such a good outcome for her; it swung towards her, hovering upright with head up and abdomen hanging down. This was the wasp whose sting Derna had managed to sever, but it still had six legs that each terminated in a single large claw, and mandible-flanked jaws wide enough to swallow Kitt whole.

Also, Kitt was very definitely not Two Tongue Derna. Where Derna evaded the wasps' lunges with a prescient grace almost balletic in nature – if ballet dancers had intimate familiarity with edged weapons and an infamous disregard for the safety of others – Kitt's reactions were more like panicked spasms punctuated by screams. Her vision narrowed until there were no stars, no Derna, and barely even any moor other than what her feet were standing on at any given moment. All the slydewasp needed to do was bear her to the ground and clamp its massive jaws around her head, and there would be no more Kitt Carver. However, the wasp had already tasted steel and had no desire to feel it again, so it feinted and jerked with hideous quickness, seeming to taunt her while it waited for her to tire and provide it with the opening it needed for guaranteed success.

It waited too long. Something long and thin and sharp emerged from the front of the wasp's thorax, and it fell to the ground like a puppet with its strings cut. The slydewasp thudded down onto its front and Derna withdrew her blade, then used it to strike off the creature's head.

'You said not to stab them!' was all Kitt could manage, as the world faded back in.

'I said *you* shouldn't stab them,' Derna replied, glancing around with her sword held ready. 'Are you hurt?'

'No,' Kitt said, checking herself over hurriedly and finding no bleeding wounds she hadn't noticed receiving while in the grip of the dual cocktail of terror and adrenaline. She looked up, but striped death did not seem to be in a hurry to drop out of the stars at her again. 'Where are the rest?'

'That's a good question,' Derna said, moving smoothly from stance to stance, ready to fend off attacks that weren't coming. She was breathing heavily, but otherwise seemed unharmed, although her clothes and hair were spattered with slydewasp ichor. 'Vem! You see anything?'

'They've gone!' Pigtail Vem was bent double and gasping for breath with his hands on his knees, but he managed to raise one to point upwards. 'They're heading back towards the nest!'

'That feels suspiciously too easy,' Derna commented, still not sheathing her sword. 'But you know what? I'll take it.'

Falzine Halfshade removed his spear's head from the body of another wasp, and looked around.

'Where's Donal?'

As one, their collective gaze went skywards. Kitt squinted, but she could barely even see the silhouettes of the receding slydewasp swarm against the stars, let alone whether any of them carried a captive.

'Did he get eaten?' Derna demanded. She didn't sound entirely displeased at the notion.

'I didn't *see* him get eaten,' Falzine said. 'I was busy, though.'

'What if they carried him off?' Kitt asked. The image of being borne aloft by thick claws and buzzing wings and taken into the glistening interior of a nest the size of a castle swam up in her mind, and she shuddered so hard she nearly dropped her sword.

'What if they did?' Derna said. 'I'm not going back to get him, bugger that for a game of soldiers.'

'You'd think we'd have heard him screaming,' the Swallowmage offered, picking herself up.

'Thanks for joining us,' Derna said sarcastically. 'You would have been really useful thirty seconds ago.'

'I can assure you, I would not have been,' Sulian replied sourly, leaving heavily on Jandi. 'And for reference, I'm also not offering to go back and get Donal if he's been taken. So what now?'

Vem raised a hand. 'I vote we get the hell out of here. I never want to see that many wasps in one place at the same time again.'

Kitt swallowed uncomfortably, but it was hardly different to how she'd always run her crews on the high moors before. Occasional losses were expected, and people – especially lookouts – were expendable. Granted, she'd never slept with any of her crew before, but any emotional attachment she might have formed with Donal had been thoroughly outweighed by his dishonesty and his lack of help when the wasps had been bearing down on them.

'Do a quick search,' she said wearily. 'Make sure he's not lying in the heather somewhere.'

The heather of the high moors was perfectly capable of concealing destinies, but less good at hiding human bodies. It only took a couple of minutes of fruitlessly quartering the ground before Kitt was prepared to accept that wherever Donal was, it wasn't here.

'Okay, let's get moving!' she called, fighting down the scrabbling claws of guilt. Donal had made his own decision to come on this journey, and she wasn't responsible for him. 'If we keep heading—hey, where's Vem?'

'He was right here,' Falzine said, peering around with his spear held ready. 'Vem?'

'I was looking at the ground,' Derna said with a shrug.

Kitt went cold. Losing someone in a slydewasp attack was unfortunate, but hardly unsurprising. Losing a member of her party to no visible threat, as though he'd just winked out of existence...

She laughed.

'Wait a second,' she said, cautious relief washing over her. 'Give it a moment.'

Pigtail Vem reappeared before she'd finished her sentence, emerging as if from thin air just down the slope from Falzine, and waving eagerly.

'It's here! I've found the northern border!'

'What about Donal?' Kitt called.

'Yeah, found him too,' Vem said, blowing out his moustaches and glaring back over his shoulder towards where Donal presumably stood, just out of sight on the outside of the gigantic bubble of frozen time.

'Well,' Derna said, wiping her sword blade clean of goo, 'at least that means I still get to stab him.'

TWENTY

IT WAS KITT'S first experience of emerging out of the timeless lands anywhere other than north of Mereport. The landscape was similar, of course – no one wanted to get too close and be trapped by mistake, so farmland didn't start until farther down the slopes – but it was the strangest sensation to come out with the sun at her back and on her left. It was a couple of hours until sundown, their shadows stretched away across the moors, and the air was thick and warm; with the coast many miles to the west, the refreshing sea breeze she was used to in Mereport simply wasn't present.

Donal *was* present, however, grinning up at them from a few yards away.

'Guys!' he said happily, spreading his hands. 'I'm so glad y—*aaaargh!*'

'Derna!' Kitt called, as the Queen of the Streets advanced towards Donal with the point of her blade extended towards his chest.

'I said I was going to stab him!' Derna said crossly.

'I know!' Kitt replied. 'And I'm asking you not to!'

'Why not?' Sulian asked. 'He's the one who drew the slydewasps down on us.'

Everyone turned to look at her. Even Derna paused in her advance.

'Okay,' Donal said, raising his hand and peering somewhat apprehensively past Derna. 'First of all, that's not true. Secondly, even if it *was* true, don't pretend that you were with it enough to notice what was going on.'

Kitt grimaced. 'He has a point.'

'We hike for however damned long that was, and there are no wasps?' the Swallowmage said. 'We see other people being attacked by wasps, but none come for us? Not until *he* starts picking destinies up when we're next to the rift, and suddenly the bastards are everywhere! You disappear, taking the destinies with you, and they fly away again.' She folded her arms and glowered at Donal. 'You don't have to be the Enlightened Scholars of Ul-Mar to work out the connection there.'

'You think the wasps are guarding the destinies?' Kitt asked, confused. It didn't make any sense… unless it sort of did. No one went onto the high moors except to hunt for destinies, so if that was indeed what drew the wasps, they would always attack. People would assume that wasps always attacked, so no one would go onto the high moors unless they had a very good reason – such as to hunt for destinies for profit – and so on, and so on.

'Dunno about "guarding". Maybe they want them for themselves,' Sulian said with a shrug. 'Either way, it's his fault.'

'I'm not seeing any compelling reasons not to stab him,' Derna said, looking over her shoulder at Kitt.

'Just stop talking about stabbing people!' Kitt shouted, storming down the slope to stand between them. 'Put it *away*, Derna!' She stared furiously into the other woman's face, and for a wonder, Derna grunted and sheathed her sword. Donal huffed a sigh of relief, but Kitt rounded on him. 'And you! You're bloody useless, you ran off when we were being attacked!'

'Right, but if what *she* says is true,' Donal countered,

pointing at the Swallowmage, who frowned at him while making some comment about a cat's mother, 'then me running off actually meant the wasps stopped attacking. Right?'

Kitt spent a couple of seconds trying to work out whether accidentally being helpful through cowardice was better than being brave and inconvenient, then decided that the whole thing was foolish.

'Forget it. No one is stabbing anyone, and we are *all* going to head down to whatever that village is down there, and find out where the hell we are.'

THE VILLAGE WAS called Hobden Bridge, named for the old stone bridge that spanned a watercourse that had been dry since the arrival of the timeless lands starved it of rain runoff from above. It was also no village, but most of the homes were out of sight, since it was a town of the gobel-kyn.

Not exclusively the kyn, of course; most settlements had been founded by one species or another, and bore the characteristics with which the original occupants had been most comfortable, but places of any size would usually have some diversity of occupancy. Even wellyn colonies, which mainly resembled giant, sprawling treehouse complexes strung through stands of massive, mature gnarloak or ironbeam, would often have a few residents from other species, so long as those residents had a head for heights. Hobden Bridge was no different, and although most was underground there were some twenty buildings above the surface, including an inn that delighted in the name of the Hanging Rock.

'Well, that's not at all ominous,' Kitt commented, as they approached the sign.

'It's probably just a precarious local geological formation,' Pigtail Vem said cheerily, pushing past her and heading for the door.

'I'm just saying, it could be that *and* where they execute

people,' Kitt pointed out to the rest of them, but her concerns fell on deaf ears.

'I want hot food, and a bed that's not made out of bushes and dirt,' Derna said flatly. 'The countryside sucks.'

'And I want a drink,' the Swallowmage added, following them.

'You *always* want a drink,' Kitt reminded her.

'Just means I'm consistent,' Sulian said, without turning around.

'Being consistent isn't admirable in and of itself,' Kitt protested. 'You could be consistently awful, and… Oh, never mind.'

Falzine and Donal were heading for the inn as well, and Kitt realised that actually she'd be prepared to risk quite a bit in the interests of a good meal and a bed, so she heaved a sigh that she hoped would adequately communicate that if they were all summarily executed by locals for imagined crimes then it wouldn't be *her* fault, and tailed in behind them.

The interior of the Hanging Rock certainly had no nooses or similar items nailed to its beams, just the usual collection of plank tables stained with years of spilled drinks, and stools worn smooth by an endless succession of buttocks. The apparent owner was a stout human man in an apron so stiff with grease and dirt it could probably be used as armour, who was already eyeing Kitt's companions with the expression of someone whose livelihood hung on being able to smell trouble and had just got two nostrils full of it.

'I want a beer, hot food, a bath, and a bed. Preferably in that order, but I'm open to negotiation,' Derna said without preamble.

'You got money?' the barkeep asked, tackling the thorny issue of implying that armed strangers might be dishonest with what Kitt considered to be admirable bravery. On the other hand, who knew what form his magic might take, if he had any? Not everyone who could fight wanted to become a sellsword.

'Sure.' Derna pulled out a pouch that jingled, which seemed to ease the barkeep's nerves some, and before long Kitt found herself parting with a few bits in exchange for half a small loaf of sourdough bread, a lump of cheese, and a bowl of surprisingly thick stew in which scraps of meat lurked between glistening, pale lumps of parsnip. Another bit got her a mug of malty beer which, loyalty to Timony and the Dubious Gecko aside, she had to admit was one of the nicest that she'd tasted in a while.

'So, did you folks come from downriver?' the barkeep asked, now his worries had been eased by the revelation that the armed strangers were also, and far more importantly, paying customers.

'No,' Falzine said, around a mouthful of bread.

'We came over the moors,' Kitt said, taking pity on the barkeep's blank expression. She probably needn't have bothered, since it immediately morphed into one of alarmed confusion instead.

'Over the moors?!' he repeated. 'But that's the timeless lands!'

'Chronocharms,' Derna said, pulling one out of her pocket and waving it at him for moment, before replacing it and returning to her food. 'Although I'll admit, the wasps are a bitch.' She looked down at her shirt, still sticky with patches of ichor, and grimaced. 'Actually, I'm going to need something to wash my clothes in. Or maybe just get in the tub with them on, that might work too.'

'We're heading to Derringsmoot,' Kitt said. 'What's the best way from here?'

'Derringsmoot?' The barkeep picked up a mug and began wiping it with a cloth, although it seemed to be more of a nervous reaction than anything that was actually required. 'You don't want to be going that way, not from here. Not right now.'

Kitt frowned at him. 'Why, what's going on right now?'

'Well, it's long summer, isn't it?'

Kitt looked around the table at her companions and, upon finding no hint of understanding there, looked back at him.

'Long summer?'

'Long summer!' the barkeep repeated, as though adding emphasis to his words would make her understand. When this didn't do the trick, he sighed and set the mug down somewhat more forcefully that he needed to. 'Look, there's no clouds in the sky, we've not had rain for near on a month, crops are going yellow in the fields, and not just because it's wheat, neither. It's the sort of weather that sees wells run dry; we'd be in trouble here, if it weren't for the kyn and the water they find underground. You don't go travelling in long summer. There's things out there what are...' He scrubbed his hands together uncomfortably. 'Thirsty.'

Donal paused, a spoonful of stew halfway to his lips. 'That somehow sounds very unpleasant.'

'Unpleasant's not the half of it,' the barkeep said miserably. 'There's whole farms what's untouched now, because *something* took the people what lived there, and no one wants to move in and see if they're going to have better luck. We're alright in the towns, I guess there's too much light and people here for anything to take a chance on us, but there's a few folk what's decided that no windows feels safer, so they live down with the kyn now.' He nodded towards the floor. 'Three buildings or less together, though, and the next time someone comes to visit you there might only be a splintered front door to say as what's happened to you. Travellers, outside with no walls and no roof, just... disappear. Or something might be found, but it ain't exactly recognisable.'

Kitt chewed that over for a second. It felt like a ghost story, but you ignored local wisdom at your peril. Slydewasps probably sounded pretty far-fetched if you hadn't grown up in a city that made a substantial chunk of its money off the destinies trade, and in which knowledge of the timeless lands was therefore commonplace.

'So when does long summer end?' she asked.

'Next proper rain, whenever that comes,' the barkeep

said. 'Either that, or come the Harvest Moon; never heard of anyone being taken by the parched ones after that.'

'Parched ones?' Sulian said, raising an eyebrow, but the barkeep just looked a bit defensive.

'Well, we've got to call them something, don't we? But I don't know no one who's seen it, or them, or whatever. Not and come back to talk about it.'

'Yes, but Harvest Moon?' Kitt exclaimed. 'We're still in Hay! That's weeks away!'

The barkeep shrugged. 'That's how it is. Anyone travelling south of the river at this time of year knows to keep the journeys short, and not past the middle of the day. If you're abroad when the sun's hot and low, and your shadow's taller than you are, that's when trouble finds you.'

'Not north of the river?' Sulian asked.

'Don't know they have the same problems across the water,' the barkeep said. 'Not that I've heard of, anyway. But it's a good day and a half to the Solwynd at the best of times, and not enough places between here and there to stop safely in long summer.'

'Let's assume we don't have the time to sit around here for a moon or more,' Kitt said, 'and that we're prepared to take the risk. Which way would we go?'

The barkeep puffed out his cheeks. 'Well, you'd be fools for doing so, but you'd just take the east road out of town. That leads down to pick up the river road. Assuming you're still alive, head upriver. All told, you'd get to Derringsmoot in about three days.' He moved away, muttering under his breath and shaking his head, somewhat like a cow bothered by flies.

'The countryside *really* sucks,' Derna said. 'You don't get this sort of bullshit in cities.'

'Derna, every wall down an entire street in Sandycliff got infested with tentacles last year,' Kitt reminded her.

'So? At least you knew where they were. You just didn't walk down that street.'

'Can these "parched ones" really be worse than slydewasps?' Donal asked, in the tone of voice of someone only hoping for an honest answer to his question if it was the one he wanted.

'Why are you all looking at me?' the Swallowmage asked, after a few seconds of silence.

'You're a mage!' Pigtail Vem said. 'Don't you know stuff like this?'

'No,' Sulian said flatly, taking another pull of her beer. 'Never heard of these things, never want to meet them. *But*,' she continued, 'we only have a few days to reach Derringsmoot, so it seems sort of pointless to cross the high moors and fight off slydewasps only to then sit in a town for weeks because we're scared of what might be out there. I guess we press on.'

'Yeah,' Vem said encouragingly. 'Business is probably slow, the guy's just trying to scare up some more custom by getting us to stick around!'

Kitt nodded. 'I'm sure that's it.'

'I mean, there is another explanation for why he wants us to stick around,' Falzine Halfshade offered.

Kitt glanced over at him. 'What's that?'

'Well, we're in the countryside, after all,' Falzine said, with a sly look at Derna. 'And he never did say what the meat in this stew was…'

TWENTY-ONE

There was only one bed.

Well, in actuality there were three beds, one in each of the inn's available rooms, but there were six people in Kitt's party, and that led to troublesome sleep arithmetic. Pigtail Vem and Falzine Halfshade agreed to share one, since they'd known each other for years and were generally unbothered by each other's company. After that, it got complicated.

'So, how are we organising this?' Donal asked. He cast a sly glance at Derna and the Swallowmage. 'Will you two be sharing a room, or…?'

Kitt groaned inwardly at the option with which she was left, and was about to protest when Derna did it for her.

'I'm not being in the same bed as her,' Derna said, folding her arms and glaring at the Swallowmage. 'She snores.'

'Do not,' Sulian protested.

'As someone who's roused you out of bed many times and has heard those snores through the damned shutters, I can confirm that you do,' Derna said firmly.

'Well, I'm not being in the same bed as *her*,' the Swallowmage said, pointing at Derna, 'because she'll stab me in her sleep!'

'Fine! Then I'll share a room with Kitt!'

Donal looked uncertainly at Sulian, who burped at him and shook her head. 'Guess again, pretty boy. Ask about the hay loft.'

And that was how Kitt ended up sharing a room with Two Tongue Derna, and why there was only one bed. It was a reasonably sized bed, in fairness: a roughly carved wooden frame with a mattress stuffed with what felt like straw, and topped with blankets. Kitt sat on it in her smallclothes, staring out of the window. The sun had set, but the evening was still thick and warm with a lingering heat that hung in the air and clung to bodies. The only light now came from the inn's windows, and those of Hobden Bridge's other above-ground dwellings. Some way off, past the slightly paler expanse of the town's downslope fields, Kitt could just make out the darker mass of the woods into which the east road eventually descended and disappeared.

'That,' said Derna, coming in the door wrapped in a large towel and carrying a bundle of her clothes, 'is better.'

The inn had a bathhouse at the back, with a well-enchanted firestone to heat the water without bothering with fuel and flames. The barkeep still charged a hefty price for the luxury, but Kitt and Derna had both paid willingly. Derna especially, since she'd still been spattered with slydewasp ichor.

'So, what do you think?' Derna asked, dumping her bundle on the floor and discarding the towel to reveal only her own smallclothes beneath.

'Excuse me?' Kitt squeaked, abruptly as alarmed as if someone had pulled a knife on her. There was more of Derna visible than she'd seen since they were kids running around the streets of Duke's End, and while none of it was *exactly* scandalous – the thin straps of Derna's camisole exposed a lot of collarbone, and there was a fair bit of leg on show, but everything between was pretty well covered – the question still felt so forward that it was practically already past Kitt and accelerating towards the horizon.

'This whole "parched ones" thing,' Derna said, rubbing the towel over the mass of damp ringlets on her head. 'Reckon it's a cover for local bandits, or what?'

'Oh.' Kitt hastily readjusted her mental processes. 'I... don't know. I don't think so, actually. I wouldn't want anyone spreading rumours about monsters if I was a bandit. It'd make people less likely to wander around alone.'

'It means you're less likely to get hunted down, though,' Derna pointed out. 'If everyone's blaming a monster, they're not looking for you and your friends. But you're right, it's probably not deliberate. Still doesn't mean there are definitely monsters out there, though.'

'No,' Kitt admitted, lying back onto the bed. They were on the inn's first floor, and despite the fact some townspeople had clearly decided they preferred living underground, even the barkeep hadn't suggested that the parched ones might come into Hobden Bridge itself. Out there, beyond the boundaries of wall and door, was their supposed hunting ground when the sun sank low and the shadows lengthened. Having the window open felt like an act of minor bravery for Kitt, cocking her snook at a danger that wasn't coming to get her anyway.

'Well, if we keep the Swallowmage vaguely sober then we should be okay,' Derna said, sitting down on the other side of the mattress. 'I'm sure she can deal with anything we run into.'

'That necromancy really took it out of her,' Kitt said dubiously. 'I know it's not her thing, but still. I don't think we can rely on her for more than one big hit.' She turned her head to look at Derna, and winced when she saw a large, puckered scar peeking out between the gap in Derna's clothes, just above her right hip. 'Ouch! What was that from?'

'This one?' Derna twisted around and poked it with her finger. 'That bastard when we were fifteen. He gave me this one, too.' She tapped a shiny line that ran across her right thigh. 'And this one,' she added, twisting the other way and pointing to a mark on her left bicep. 'And...' She turned around completely, sat cross-legged on the bed facing Kitt, and pulled up the front of her top with one hand. 'This one!'

'Oh,' Kitt said, staring at a narrow, triangular scar just under Derna's breastbone. Her hand went without thinking to the healed wound in her own side. 'Wow. He got you straight on, didn't he?'

'Yeah,' Derna said, letting the cloth of her top fall again. 'Didn't exactly run me through, because the blade didn't come out the other side, but that was when he thought he'd killed me. Good job I got him in the heart right after; that's what impressed the sash so much that they dragged my bleeding arse to a healer rather than let me die in the street.' She pointed to Kitt's side. 'How's yours doing?'

'This?' Kitt pulled up the side of her top, since that seemed to be what they were doing. It was an oddly secretive feeling to be comparing scars, and strangely thrilling as well, even if Derna's had been garnered from several years of street duels – there were others dotted over her skin, although the lack of other sizeable ones was testament to her improvement as a swordswoman – and Kitt's happened when she hadn't noticed a would-be assassin until he'd shoved a knife into her side. 'I mean it's there, but I don't really feel it anymore.'

'Sulian did a good job with it.' Derna reached out and lightly ran her finger across the smooth scar tissue. 'It looks years old already.'

'It does?' Kitt asked, restraining a shiver at Derna's touch. It wasn't a bad shiver, but nor was it a good shiver, as such. It was just a shiver that she clamped down on so she didn't have to explain it, or excuse it, or apologise for it, or make Derna feel that *she* had to apologise for it. Derna's touch had been very gentle for someone whom Kitt normally thought of as stabbing things, and it had taken her a little by surprise.

'Yeah, if I hadn't known, I'd have thought you'd got it years ago,' Derna said with a smile. She swung around and stretched out, laying down on the mattress, then propped herself up on one elbow again. 'Hey, did you want to be next to the window?'

Kitt glanced sideways at it. 'I'm not bothered. Do you want this side?'

'Yeah, go on,' Derna said with a grin. 'I'd feel better if I'm between you and the parched ones.' She produced a sheathed dagger from behind her back, and had Kitt not been up against the wall then she would have fallen off the bed in surprise.

'Where you did hide—I've been looking at you since you came in the door!'

Derna stuck her tongue out and waggled both halves of it at Kitt. 'I have my ways. Come on, shift over.'

Kitt shuffled towards Derna's side of the bed, and was entirely unprepared for Derna to simply straddle her to get past with the same familiarity and lack of self-consciousness they'd had to each other's proximity when they'd been kids. There was momentary pressure on the mattress on each side of her, the lingering touch and heat of Derna's water-warmed body passing over her own, and Kitt's face was brushed by Derna's still-damp hair as their noses passed close. Then Derna was on the other side of her and settling down into the space that Kitt had been occupying a moment before.

Kitt rubbed at her mouth vigorously. 'Your hair tickled my lips, damn it.'

'Hah! Sorry.'

There was a candle on the nightstand beside her, and Kitt found her gaze caught by it. She stared into the flame for a few seconds, captivated by its endless flickering, changing shape.

'What are you thinking about?' Derna asked, from her right.

It was a soft question, and it transported Kitt back years to when they'd throw stones into the waves and talk nonsense after being chased off the dock front for getting tangled up in guy ropes, under people's feet, or both. There were many answers she could have given – about the parched ones, about why they were here, about what they should do next – but the one that came out of her mouth was a surprise even to her.

'I wish you weren't a duellist,' she said simply, and as soon as the words left her lips she cursed herself for uttering them, and braced for scorn or anger.

'Why?'

Derna didn't sound either scornful or angry. Kitt rolled over and found the Queen of the Streets looking at her with her cheek resting on one palm, and her brown eyes quite serious.

'Because it scares me,' she said honestly.

Derna bit her lip for a second. 'Why?'

Kitt really wished she'd never started this conversation, but she had summoned the beast, and so she would slay it. She took a deep breath, and tried to ignore the fact that her heart had started racing. Derna was unpredictable, after all.

'I'm scared you'll get hurt. Badly.' Kitt hesitated, then plunged on. 'I know you're really good, but someone else just has to get lucky, or decide they don't want a fair fight and get their mates involved. I know it happens. And you're a bit weird, and you're a bit scary—'

'Scary?'

'You take a knife to bed!'

Derna snorted a laugh. 'Fair point.'

'—but you're my friend,' Kitt continued quietly. That much was definitely true. She hadn't been sure about that for a few years, if she was honest with herself, because how could anyone really interpret what Derna did? But then Derna was there when it counted; she saved Kitt's life, and was here with her now, so what else could Kitt call it? 'I don't want you to change anything about yourself, but I also don't want you to get hurt.'

'You *don't* want me to change anything about myself?' Derna asked softly.

'I know how pointless it would be,' Kitt said, smiling at her. 'But also, no. You wouldn't be Derna if you changed who you were just because someone else wanted you to.'

Derna rolled onto her back and stared up at the ceiling. 'You know, I think that might be the nicest thing anyone's ever said to me.'

'Wow.' Kitt chewed that over for a few seconds. 'I'm sorry?'

'For saying something nice?'

'For never saying anything nicer.' Kitt grimaced. 'It's a mediocre compliment at best.'

'Well, I'll take it,' Derna said. The flickering candlelight made it hard for Kitt to tell, but she wasn't sure if Derna's eyes might be slightly moister than usual. The thought that Derna – Two Tongue Derna, the Duchess of Death – might be getting emotional about being told that someone didn't want her to change was so unnerving that Kitt rolled onto her back as well, to avoid having to look at her. The ceiling above them was white plaster, cracked and crazed with age but with surprisingly few cobwebs around the edges.

'I wish you didn't go divining on the moors,' Derna said, after perhaps half a minute of silence.

'Well, yes,' Kitt said, wryly. 'I think you covered that when you rounded up a bunch of mercenaries, blackmailed Mizzik, surrounded my party and threatened me into handing over that destiny I found.'

'I never threatened you!' Derna protested, rolling over to look at Kitt again.

'You did!' Kitt said, shifting to face her in turn. Only a few inches of bed separated their noses now.

'I did *not!*' Derna's expression was not one of anger, but of hurt. 'I told you I really wanted the destiny, that was all!'

'You had a whole warband with you!'

'That was to prevent Falzine and the others from making a fuss,' Derna said earnestly. 'I never threatened *you.*'

Kitt thought back. She'd been sure that Derna *had* threatened her into handing over the destiny, and had written it off as Derna's mercurial and essentially violent nature, but was that actually the case? Or had Kitt seen a bunch of armed mercenaries and jumped to a very reasonable conclusion, but not listened to the exact words Derna had spoken? Derna was a very literal person, after all.

'You know what?' Kitt said slowly. 'I'm going to believe you. You've definitely earned that. But for reference,' she added, poking Derna gently in the shoulder, 'when I find myself led into an ambush, I definitely *feel* threatened.'

'Noted,' Derna replied. 'But I wouldn't threaten you, Kitt. Not and mean it. I do hate the destinies trade, for all the reasons I've told you before, but...' She bit her lip. 'I don't want you going up on the moors, because I don't want *you* to get hurt.'

Kitt swallowed. 'Thank you.' Her own parents had said similar things to her, but it had always felt different. It sounded like over-protectiveness from them, a sense that she wasn't grown up enough to deal with dangers they didn't really comprehend, and the words had been laced with faintly disproving resignation. Derna was a street duellist. From her, it sounded like 'I know what danger is, and I don't want it to find you'.

'You're welcome,' Derna said simply. 'I owe you, anyway.'

Kitt frowned. 'For what?'

'For being my friend when we were kids,' Derna said. 'You were pretty much the only person that was nice to me, and I know I was... weird. Weird*er*, probably.'

'You weren't—' Kitt began to protest reflexively, then stopped herself. 'No, okay, you were weird. That wasn't a reason not to be nice to you, though.'

'No one else seemed to think that,' Derna said. She smiled. 'You're a good person, Kitt. Always have been.'

Kitt felt her cheeks heating. On a logical level, Two Tongue Derna declaring you to be a good person didn't seem like something that would hold a great deal of weight, but Kitt was equally aware that Derna was not the sort of person to say something like that out of politeness. If she complimented you, she damn well meant it. They held each other's gazes for a few more seconds, neither of them speaking, until Kitt lost her nerve and rolled onto her back again. Why? Had it been a staring competition or something? It felt ridiculous, but she'd done it now.

'I think I might blow the candle out,' she said. She tried to sound light and casual about it, but felt she had all the success of a butterfly made of lead.

'Yes,' Derna said, thickly. 'We should probably get some sleep.'

Kitt leaned up and puffed out the flame, then lay back down and stared at the ceiling some more, trying not to be so completely aware of exactly what distance Derna's body was from her own in this reasonably-sized-but-not-huge bed, until sleep snuck up behind her and dragged her into an alley of unconsciousness.

TWENTY-TWO

They left Hobden Bridge the next morning, with Donal still picking hay out of his clothes. The air was comparatively cool, but it felt like a lie; a brief respite while the sun caught its breath, before it noticed that people were up and about and doing again. Even the early morning here didn't have the same freshness Kitt was used to from living nearer to the sea, and she didn't relish the idea of travelling both farther inland and off the hills, down into the Solwynd's valley.

The east road out of town was more like a dirt track than anything else, and clearly would have been rather more overgrown if the dead plants that had attempted to conquer it had any rainfall to sustain them once they'd pushed above ground. As it was, they were a collection of slumped-over stringy brown stalks, and the occasional faint breath of breeze brought a dry hissing from their desiccated leaves, like the warning signal of an apathetic rattlesnake.

The road wound past fields of cracked earth in which wheat still stood defiantly, but even Kitt — for whom wheat was merely bread's semi-mythical former life — could tell that the crops were not doing well. The whole countryside felt like it was being pressed down under a hot, heavy heel, and walking through the landscape was like crawling across the surface of a cooking pan that had never really cooled, and under which the fire could be lit again at any moment.

'This isn't natural,' the Swallowmage muttered, as they trudged towards the welcoming shelter of the woodland farther down the slope. The road was taking a very shallow angle to get there, however, and their progress downhill felt painfully slow.

'It's just summer,' Vem said, with a slightly forced cheerfulness. 'It feels a bit stuffy, sure, but—'

'I wasn't opening a discussion, I was stating a fact,' Sulian said shortly, cutting him off. 'It's *not* natural. There's magic all over the place here, twisting everything up.' She stuck her tongue out as though to taste the air, pulled a face, and spat. 'Chronomancy aftereffects. Time hasn't stopped here completely, but it's getting stretched in strange ways. Can't you feel it?' She shuddered. 'That'll be why the summer feels like it lasts forever.'

Kitt shivered, despite the gradually increasing morning temperature. The notion of being trapped under a sweltering sun for an indefinite period was not one she relished. The timeless lands north of Mereport had been there for centuries, so they were an anomaly with which she had been familiar all her life, but this was something new and unpleasant.

'Did things like this exist before…?' An image of the rift flashed up in her head, with the bright flare of the Swordstar at one corner. 'You know.'

'Not that I know of,' the Swallowmage muttered. 'Just another way in which the world is falling apart.'

They finally reached the woods at about midday, by which time the shelter of the canopy of leaves was very welcome. Summer gripped hard in here, too; the grass was crisp and dry, the flowers were long dead, and even the leaves of the trees were tinged with yellow. The dappled shade cut out the sun's most punishing rays, but the trunks throttled the breeze until Kitt felt like she was walking deeper and deeper into a warm clothes closet. It was a landscape that was clinging on, one that had ceded ground to summer but had not fully surrendered to drought and death… yet.

Their first attempt at a camp came under the wide boughs of a massive gnarloak, but that fell through when Donal saw a bit of bark move and prodded it with the butt of his knife. When it unfolded into a creature about the size of his hand with comparatively long, barbed arms and a tiny humanoid face in which were set oversized, sharklike teeth, they all decided to find somewhere else. Sleeping near a dryad nest was a reliable way to lose weight, but only due to waking up finding yourself owning less skin and muscle than you used to.

Their second location was a little farther on, between a trio of beech trees and set a short way back from the road, but close enough that they could still see it. They didn't bother with a fire, since the air was warm enough anyway and the ground so dry that the slightest stray spark could have set light to half the forest. They took watches again, but without the silent threat of slydewasps only one person was needed at a time, and so Kitt rose the next morning without feeling quite as dead as she had done up on the moors.

The road still headed gently downhill, at least on average. Every now and then they crossed dry runnels on wooden bridges that should have been green and slippery with moss, or walked past hollows in which dead leaves had collected where a pond should have been. At about mid-morning, so far as Kitt could estimate with the sun mainly out of sight, they saw their first building since they'd left Hobden Bridge.

'Woodcutter's cottage?' Falzine asked, leaning on his spear. It was a small, one-storey house of vertical plank walls, with other boards forming the sloping roof. A single window faced the road, next to a simple wooden porch in which the front door was gaping open. Of any occupant, however, there was no sign.

Kitt frowned. 'Hang on.'

'Are you thinking what I'm thinking?' Derna murmured,

loosening her sidesword in its scabbard.

'If you're thinking that the door doesn't look like it's open so much as hanging off the hinges, then yes,' Kitt said grimly. It was hard to tell in the shadow of the porch, but she was fairly certain the darker opening of the doorway had the uneven edges that suggested all was not as it should be.

'Do we care?' Donal asked. Everyone looked at him, and he spread his hands defensively. 'Genuine question. We don't know who lives there, and we've got urgent business further down this road. Why should we be sticking our noses into someone else's house?'

Annoyingly, he had a point. However, Kitt shook her head.

'I just want to take a quick look,' she said firmly. 'I want to know whether it's bandits, or whether there actually is something out here with us.'

'This feels like looking for trouble we don't need,' Pigtail Vem said, scratching his head.

'Fine,' Kitt said shortly. 'I'll go and have a look by myself, and then we'll head off again!'

'I'm coming with you,' Derna said immediately, to Kitt's immense relief. No one else volunteered to approach the house with them, so Kitt drew her short sword and headed up the path that led from road to cottage, with Derna at her elbow.

'I would have taken a look even if you hadn't said you'd come,' she whispered defensively, after they'd put a few feet between them and the rest of their party.

'I know,' Derna whispered back. 'That's why I said I would.'

They took a few more cautious steps.

'So, how much of this is just morbid curiosity for you?' Derna asked, her feet crunching over dry leaves.

'Definitely less than half. Honest.'

They were halfway to the porch now, and Kitt could clearly make out the door. It had indeed come off the top hinge, and was leaning drunkenly into the cottage like a particularly untruthful market trader attempting to affect a nonchalant air.

'Well, I guess that's that settled,' Kitt said. Her stomach was starting to twist a little, but she didn't stop walking.

'Still doesn't mean it was monsters,' Derna said, although she moved to put herself slightly between Kitt and the cottage. 'It might just be shoddy workmanship.'

They got to within a few feet of the door before Kitt saw the heavy lines scored across it. There were four of them, set close together, and the pieces of what had once been a latch were laying in the middle of the doorway.

'I don't think it was shoddy workmanship,' Kitt said tightly. She became dimly aware that her right hand was hurting from the death grip in which she held her short sword, but no amount of messages from her brain about the importance of flexibility to sword fighting was able to convince her fingers to loosen their hold.

'Could have been a bear?' Derna suggested.

'Have you ever heard of a bear knocking in someone's front door?' Kitt hissed.

'Sure, what's that kid's story with the bear that breaks in and eats porridge?'

'That's not what I meant, and you know it!' Kitt snapped. 'Do you even know anything about bears?' Bears were, strangely enough, not common in Mereport, or indeed anywhere up the relatively densely populated Song valley. Kitt was vaguely aware you were supposed to pretend to be dead if you met one, and that if you weren't extremely convincing then the bear would make sure you got a lot better at it.

'No,' Derna admitted. 'Do you?'

'No! And that means that if I say it's not a bear, you don't know enough to say that it is,' Kitt said, hoping to achieve with certainty what she lacked in logic.

'Are we going back to the others without actually finding out what did this?' Derna asked, and for the briefest of moments Kitt considered stabbing her. Not hard, but definitely enough for her displeasure to be registered.

'*Fine*,' she said, swallowing against the bile rising in her throat. 'But let's do it quickly. And you're going in first.'

Derna moved ahead, her sword held ready, and edged her way around the doorframe. Kitt hung back from a moment, ready to intercept anything that might try to jump at Derna while her back was turned, then followed her in.

The interior of the cottage was a single room, with solid wooden beams comprising the framework to which the wall and ceiling planks had been nailed. The wooden theme continued with the table and single chair, the washtub, and the simple dresser on which sat a couple of tin plates and mugs, but was contrasted by the cheerful blue-dyed curtains and tablecloth, and the dark, gently buzzing heap of flies in the middle of the floor.

the

what

'Don't!' Kitt said urgently, but she was too slow. Derna had reached out and prodded the heap with the tip of her boot.

A small cloud of flies flew up, making the angry buzzing that flies make when they're rudely interrupted in the process of eating someone's face. The form beneath became briefly visible before they settled again, which was a mercy: just before they did so, Kitt caught a glimpse of dried, leathery skin stretched to breaking point over the bones of a skull, and a ragged wound on the neck that should have been wet and bloody but instead just looked like someone had given up shortly after starting to devour a chunk of jerky.

'*Shit!*'

Kitt was outside again. She didn't remember stepping outside the cottage, but on the other hand she couldn't fathom any possible way in which she would have wanted to remain inside, so all in all she was fine with this turn of events. It was about the only thing she *was* fine with, to be fair.

'Okay,' Derna said, emerging behind her. 'I'm prepared to concede that was probably not a bear.'

The expressions on the others' faces when Kitt and Derna got back to the road suggested that they could guess, at least broadly, what had been inside the cottage. Kitt simply kept walking, her lips tight.

'Well?' Sulian asked Derna, her tone that of someone who wants to hear the worst in order to get it over with.

'I don't know if the innkeeper was actually *right*,' Derna said, 'but there's something out here doing what he said it was, so I guess the details don't really matter.'

TWENTY-THREE

The morning was warm, and midday was hot, but the afternoon was interminable. There was little change in the scenery now they'd reached the forest, and no one else on the road headed in either direction. Other nondescript routes joined or forked off, but Kitt and her companions kept plodding onwards, sticking to the best-worn road and fighting for every breath against the thick, oppressive air that lurked beneath the branches.

'I think my shirt is just a part of my skin now,' Derna grumbled, plucking at one of her rolled-up sleeves and pulling the sweat-soaked fabric away from her flesh with an expression of disgust. Kitt just grunted in response. She'd opened her own shirt down to just above her belly button, but there was no breeze to make the extra ventilation worthwhile. The air felt skin-warm, blood-warm, as though she and everything around her were all in the same bowl of soup. The men had removed their shirts entirely, but even that didn't seem to have benefited them much. Donal and Vem were still sweating profusely – the sight of Donal shirtless might have sparked somewhat conflicting memories in Kitt's head, had she not been so warm that the very thought of coming into physical contact with another living being made her feel nauseous – and even Falzine's skin was glistening, although it was harder to make out on him. His unnaturally shadowed form was less obvious in the forest, even though more of his skin was on show than usual. The leaf cover above was still thick enough to cast deep pools of shadow across the path, despite the sun's strength, and Falzine Halfshade slipped from one to the next like a fish moving between clumps of waterweed, if the fish in question was far too hot and rather tired.

'How much farther until we join the river road?' Vem asked, wiping his brow somewhat ineffectually with the back of a wrist that was very nearly as sweaty.

'Don't know,' Kitt said shortly. Her feet felt like they'd swollen to twice their normal size in her boots, and she was trying not to think about anything involving distance. She let her mind linger on the notion of a river, instead: wading off the bank to dip her feet, then slipping into its cool embrace as though its waters were the finest, softest sheets on a bed, perhaps swiping her arm and throwing up a glittering, shimmering spray of water to drench Derna on the bank…

'How much longer until we can stop?' Sulian grumbled, and Kitt gritted her teeth in annoyance.

'We'll stop when it starts to get dark, just like yesterday,' she said, fighting down the instinct to demand to know why everyone was looking to her for answers. Annoying though it was, it was a lot better than the rest of her party deciding that they'd had enough of Kitt Carver's Quest To Derringsmoot, and abandoning her.

'But it's not *getting* dark!' Donal protested. 'I swear the sun hasn't moved for hours!'

Kitt turned around to argue with him, then squinted up at the sky. The sun was more of a *presence* than anything else, a white blob of heat and suffering emitting an endless scream of hate somewhere far above the treetops. The leaves made it impossible to get an exact fix on its location, but occasional shards of blinding light still stabbed down into Kitt's eye sockets as the canopy shifted ever so slightly in whatever faint breeze still existed up there. She could get an idea of where the sun was, and it was not an idea that pleased her.

'I could have sworn it was there a couple of hours ago,' she said slowly. 'Long enough that it shouldn't still be there now.'

'See?' Donal waved one hand vaguely towards the sky in weary, parboiled triumph. 'It's not moving!'

'Are you sure?' Derna asked Kitt, frowning upwards.

'Yeah,' Kitt said. Her stomach was churning now, and she was fairly sure it wasn't just from the heat. 'I don't know exactly where it should be, but it shouldn't be *there*. It's not far past where it was at noon, and noon must have been hours ago.'

'Well, that sucks,' Derna said flatly.

'I don't suppose you want to do something about… this?' Falzine asked Sulian from within a patch of deep shadow in which his upper half had nearly disappeared.

'About what?' the Swallowmage retorted grumpily. 'The sun? I told you all, it's chronomancy twisting everything up. I wouldn't risk messing around with that for all of Mereport's city treasury, even if you removed the dragon first.'

'What are we supposed to do?' Vem asked. 'Just walk on like this forever?' Even his usual good nature had evaporated, and his moustaches were slick with sweat. Kitt shuddered at the thought of that much damp hair on her lip in this heat.

'Being a mage isn't just waving your arms and solving other people's problems, you know,' Sulian snapped, rounding on Vem. 'I've never even looked twice at chronomancy, partly because I've got better things to do, and partly because it's a good way to get your head cut off. I'm certainly not going to start trying to figure it out here and now!'

'We keep walking,' Kitt announced. She held her hands up. 'I know, I know, it's going to be miserable, but what option do we have? Time was working properly earlier, and I'm going to guess that the farther away we are from the timeless lands, the less likely we are to be stuck in whatever this is. We're probably just in a weird pocket of it, like an undertow or something.'

She turned and began to trudge onwards. That was something she'd learned from her mother: the more you acted as though something was settled, the less likely other people were to think that it wasn't. Besides, in this case she was moving in the right direction, so everyone else's options were to follow her, stay in the same place and argue, or go back the way they'd come. Unsurprisingly, within a few seconds she heard the dusty thumps of footfalls and the rustle of dry leaves behind her as the rest of her party grudgingly goaded themselves into movement again.

Still the forest road went on, an apparently endless variation on a theme. Kitt settled into a warm daydream, her mind vaguely wandering along somewhere else entirely while her eyes and her feet gently guided her around potholes, over eminently trippable sticks, and past low-hanging branches in a manner that didn't let her concuss herself. She had no idea how much later it was when she became aware of an odd conversation going on inside her head.

Hey, brain, her eyes seemed to be saying. *You should take a look at this.*

But you do the looking, her brain responded. *That's what you're for. I do the thinking.*

Well, do the thinking then, her eyes insisted. *Because we don't know exactly what we're seeing, but something isn't right here. This is a bit more than a hole-in-the-road problem, is what we're saying.*

Kitt blinked and came to a halt, jerking out of her muzzy musings and paying proper attention to her surroundings for the first time in something between ten minutes and a hundred years. Her eyes had been right: something *was* wrong, or at least *different*, but it took her a few seconds to get a handle on exactly what. Everything seemed darker, the shadows deeper, and she had to blink again a few times to check that her eyes hadn't just burned themselves out from staring at a fixed point a few feet in front of her for however long it had been.

'Hey, the sun's moved!' she called, checking behind her as the pieces dropped into place. Sure enough, the sun had finally deigned to shift itself from its post-noon position at some point without her noticing, and it was now sinking into the south-west, blinking at her through a chance gap in the trees. The temperature still hovered somewhere between 'very unpleasant' and 'for fuck's sake', but there was the faintest hint in the air that some sort of slight respite might be on the way. The day now felt like they were surrounded by the still-hot walls of a bread oven, rather than being inside it with the door closed and the fire stoked high.

'Kitt,' Derna said warningly, pointing. Kitt glanced back the way they'd been heading, but there was nothing to see there except for the path, and her shadow on it.

Her shadow.

It stretched out from her feet in the early evening light, deep and dark and black, and now far taller than she was. It was a perfectly normal result of a low sun, and under normal circumstances Kitt would have thought nothing of it. She might have even disregarded the barkeep's warnings, had she and Derna not seen what *something* had done inside the woodcutter's cottage, and had they not all been trapped under the sun for this strange, drawn-out afternoon. Long summer was definitely real, here.

'What was that?' Donal said. Kitt's head snapped around in time to see him looking off into the trees to his right.

'What was what?' Derna asked, drawing her sidesword.

'I thought I heard something moving in the trees,' Donal said. 'Over there, I think.' He pointed to his left. 'Or possibly… over there?'

'That's the opposite way!' Falzine hissed. He had been using his spear as a walking staff, but now he gripped it ready in both hands. From Kitt's point of view, bare-chested and with the sun behind him, he looked like a statue carved of shadow that someone had inexplicably stuffed into a pair of trousers.

'Forests are confusing!' Donal protested.

They all stood in silence for a few moments, every ear straining to pick out a potentially hostile rustle through a heat so thick it felt like even sound couldn't be bothered to move very fast or very far. Every breath felt like a betrayal, every faint creak of leather or scrape of skin over a weapon haft a distraction. Kitt hardly dared move for fear of masking some crucial sound, but she slowly pivoted on the spot to face the way they had been walking. If nothing showed itself in the next twenty seconds, she would declare a false alarm and get them all moving again rather than stand here frozen in indecision and quite literally jumping at shadows.

If nothing shows itself in the next twenty seconds, her brain complained, with the absolutely useless level of gut-churning foresight that can sense something about to go wrong without the ability to do the slightest thing about it. *Why oh why did we think* that?

Something detached itself from the shadow of a tree trunk in front of her.

It was tall, and thin, and ragged, with stooped shoulders and crooked knees. It was humanoid, in that it had the right amount of arms and legs and heads in the right sort of places, but it had rather too much of the former; it was taller than Kitt, even with its less than upright posture, but the long, ragged-nailed fingers on its large hands trailed nearly to the ground. It also had more antlers than humans normally possessed, since three-tined stubs protruded from both sides of its skull, pushing through the long, lank hair that trailed down to its chest.

There was nothing to it but bone covered in skin, and skin that had been blasted and dried by the relentless sun of long summer, at that. Its lips were shrunken and pulled back from its jagged, chipped teeth, and its eyes had boiled or burned or rotted away completely to leave nothing but shadowed sockets. The tattered remains of ragged garments clung to its body, too short in the limbs and too generous in the chest for what was now little more than a shrink-wrapped ribcage. It looked like nothing that should exist, and like something that if it did exist, should definitely be dead.

But it did exist, and it wasn't dead, and it was moving in jerky, shuffling twitches that carried it across the ground in increments somehow too small for Kitt's self-preservation instincts to properly kick in and do anything about except watch in horror, and then suddenly it was moving *fast*.

'Down!' Sulian yelled, but Kitt's body had tensed up at exactly the wrong moment. Although every nerve screamed at her to get out of the way of whatever sorcery the Swallow-mage was planning to hurl at the creature, it also rebelled against the idea of throwing herself to the ground and becoming even more vulnerable in the face of this terrifying threat. She managed to vaguely raise her sword before something hit her from the side and dragged her into the dust; Kitt had a momentary impression of damp ringlets and Derna's hideously warm, disgustingly moist body against her own, and then her senses focused on the gangrel creature coming to a stuttering halt above her, outlined in noxious light as Sulian yelled something unintelligible.

For a moment, the parched one shuddered, apparently locked in place and pained by the Swallowmage's magic. Then it opened its mouth wider, and began to *drink*.

The glow faded, stripping off the creature's form and flowing into its mouth as though it were inhaling a luminescent fog. Kitt heard a muffled thump, and looked over desperately to see Sulian collapsing to the ground, her eyes rolling up in her head.

Falzine sprang forward with a yell and drove his spear at

the parched one's chest with all his weight behind it. The blade struck home, but it was as though he'd tried to stab a hunk of salted beef with a butter knife; the point barely pierced a finger's breadth into the creature's hide, and one long-nailed, long-fingered and just generally *long* arm came up to seize Falzine by the throat with a hand the size of a cooking pan.

'No!' Pigtail Vem yelled, hacking at the limb with his axe. Vem was a stout man, and a strong one, and his downward blow should have severed or at least broken any normal arm, but his weapon rebounded as though he'd tried to chop down an oak with one swing. The creature swatted him away with its free hand, sending him sprawling into the dust and leaves. Donal had his own blade out, but his attempt at rushing in fared no better.

'Get up!' Derna shouted, wriggling out of the straps of her pack and rising with her sidesword in hand.

Kitt rolled away from her and swung her own weapon at the parched one's wizened leg as she came up to one knee, with no more success than Vem had achieved with his attack. Derna tried slashing, but her blows had no noticeable effect either. Falzine tried to drive his spear in, but the creature simply pulled him towards its mouth, and his hands slipped down his weapon's haft without it penetrating any further. The parched one opened its jaws wider, and Kitt could *feel* the desperate, burning thirst coming from within; not the thirst of a desert, for deserts were places where rain was rare and whatever lived there had learned to adapt. This was the thirst of the cracked fields, of the dry well, of the merciless open blue sky that brought no rain and provided no shelter from the sun.

They were going to see every drop of moisture drained out of Falzine Halfshade, and there was not a thing that any of them could do about it.

'*Move!*' a new voice shouted, from the direction of the setting sun.

He came like the wind, appearing past Donal and Vem as they tried to get back to their feet, and travelling at a speed that seemed impossible. Kitt caught a momentary glimpse of a dark robe, and then *something* hit the parched one in the chest so hard that it was knocked clean backwards and off its feet. Falzine dropped from its grip, and his spear tumbled loose from where it had been precariously lodged in its chest to clatter against the dry ground.

'What manner of evil thing are you?' the new arrival asked grimly, his robes still settling around him after the speed of his arrival. He was a bald man – a *very* bald man, as bald as a man could get, with the light reflecting off the smooth skin of his head – but seemed otherwise unremarkable.

The parched one unfolded back upright, hissing like the ghost of a stream, its dead eye sockets trained on the man who had just flattened it. Its fingers twitched hungrily, and its mouth opened again.

'Don't try to fight it!' Kitt shouted. 'Everybody run!'

'Wait!' the bald man commanded. He rolled the sleeves of his robes up, exposing forearms around which looped tattoos of broken chains.

'Yeah, I think it's gonna take a bit more than that,' Derna said grimly. 'Seriously, friend, we need to—'

The underside of the man's forearms erupted. Twin shards of razor-edged blackness cut their way out through his flesh, starting just before the elbow and pivoting from the wrist. Within a second they had completed a half-circle, and two long, hiltless blades of glistening obsidian had come fully free from his body, their handles now nestled in his palms.

'Holy *shit*,' Derna said.

The parched one took a step forward, but the bald man raised his weapons and pointed them both at the creature's chest. It stopped, tilting its antlered head to one side, and Kitt got the distinct impression that those empty eyes were *studying* the man in front it.

Then it turned and ran, scuttling back into the trees as quickly as it had first rushed at them. After a few long moments, the shadows suddenly seemed a little less stretched and dark, and a faint weight of oppressiveness lifted from the back of Kitt's neck.

'Well, I'm glad they still work,' the bald man said, to no one in particular. He opened his hands and the blades swung back into place, cutting their way into his forearms once more. The skin closed up again after them with no blood, and with only the faintest straight scar line visible in the aftermath, until he pulled his sleeves down again and turned to face them.

'This road does not seem like a good place to be travelling alone,' he said, to their stunned expressions. 'Would you object to me joining your party? I'm heading for Derringsmoot.'

No one seemed inclined, or even able, to answer him. Kitt ran through a few responses – *Who are you? What are you? Why do you have knives in your arms?* – but there seemed only one sensible reply. Falzine would be dead without the newcomer's arrival, and probably the rest of them shortly afterwards.

'Thank you,' she said, shakily. 'And, sure. Do you have a name?'

The bald man smiled. 'You can call me Plainsong.'

TWENTY-FOUR

They did not go without a fire that night, despite the lingering heat, the dustiness of the ground, and the crackling leaves underfoot. Sleep was going to be hard enough to come by anyway after the nightmarish encounter with the parched one, let alone laying there in the darkness knowing that the person on watch was mainly relying on their hearing to detect such a creature reaching out for you with its long-fingered hands.

'So,' Plainsong said, as they sat around the flames and tried to convince themselves that the additional sweating was a worthwhile price to pay. 'Do any of you know what that was? I've not heard tell of anything like it, let alone encountered one before.'

He was a strange one, and no mistake. He had no hair on his head – none at all, not even eyelashes – and that was a mite unusual. He wore simple robes like a monk or a priest might wear, but Kitt couldn't see any sort of religious or devotional symbols about his person. Then there was the rather larger fact that he could summon obsidian knives out of his arms, which was… Well, Kitt had met more than a few odd folk, and heard tales of odder still, but that was a new one on her.

'The barkeep in the town we passed through a couple of days ago called it a "parched one",' she said, in answer to Plainsong's question. 'We weren't sure if they were real or a folk tale, but it looks like that question's been answered.'

'It was particularly unpleasant,' Plainsong said. He had a curiously precise way of enunciating his words. He didn't sound *posh* exactly, not like some of the toffs Kitt had done divining work for in the past. It was more like he carefully lined the syllables up in the split second before they left his lips. Everything was very measured: it was impossible to imagine him breaking into spontaneous song, for example, or partaking in quick-witted repartee.

'It seemed scared of you,' Derna said. She was sitting on the other side of the fire to Kitt, and her dark eyes had scarcely left Plainsong since they'd all sat down.

'And I am very glad that it was,' Plainsong replied, with a small smile. 'I don't know how the fight would have gone had it decided to push the issue.' He never showed his teeth when he smiled, although he definitely had them; Kitt had seen them when he spoke, and they seemed pale and fairly even, and pretty unremarkable as teeth went. He smiled, and it was friendly enough when he did so, but he never *grinned*. It was as though everything was locked away inside him, and he was either incapable or unwilling to let much come to the surface at once.

'You hit it hard enough,' Falzine Halfshade said. 'I caught it straight on with my spear and it didn't move, but you knocked it flat.' His neck and jaw still bore the scratch marks from where the parched one's ragged nails had gripped him, and he unsurprisingly seemed somewhat shaken by the encounter. Kitt had no idea how facing down a parched one stacked up against an encounter with a draksnipe, but then again, she didn't know how upbeat and chipper Falzine had been after that, either.

'Momentum,' Plainsong replied, with another of his small smiles. 'But I'm not without my own tricks, it's true.'

'Like the knives in your arms,' Derna said bluntly, which had roughly the same effect on the mood around the fire as would dropping a bag of angry flame vipers into the middle of an orgy. Kitt winced internally, although it wasn't as though Plainsong hadn't brought them out in front of them all. He surely expected someone to mention them at some point?

On the other hand, there was mentioning them, and there was mentioning them in Derna fashion.

'Yes, like those,' Plainsong said, after a few tense seconds. He didn't seem offended by Derna's statement, but there was a slight change in his manner. He looked a little sorrowful now. To Kitt, it felt as though he had been enjoying a polite fiction and was now resigned to returning to reality.

'They're *really* cool,' Derna said, either not noticing or studiously ignoring the sudden change in atmosphere. 'How did you get them? Or have you always had them?'

'Derna!' Kitt said, shocked. 'You can't just *ask* people about their… arm knives.'

Derna shrugged. 'He doesn't have to answer.'

'And he won't,' Plainsong said, levelly. 'Suffice to say that I was young, and I was foolish, and I was curious, and I made bargains that I did not properly understand. There were undoubtedly some benefits, but the true costs only became clear to me as time passed.' He looked around the fire. 'However, if I can return to my earlier question: what *is* a "parched one"? Have they always been here, or are they a recent curse on this land?'

'Sulian's got a theory,' Vem said, nudging the Swallowmage, who grunted. Whatever the parched one had done to the magic she'd thrown at it had somewhat discombobulated her, and she had been very subdued ever since.

'And you are a mage?' Plainsong asked politely.

'Of sorts,' Sulian admitted.

'I have always been curious,' Plainsong said. 'How does one find out that you are a mage?'

'Nightmares from childhood and hearing voices, in my case. It turned out they were fragments of the future, but knowing what they were didn't make them any easier to deal with.' Sulian shrugged, as though unconsciously trying to dislodge an unpleasant memory from where it wrapped around her shoulders. 'Then the usual way, I guess: accidental outbursts of power that first you hide, then you try to deny, then you accidentally incinerate your cousin and have to leave town in the dead of night at the age of thirteen with a burgeoning drinking problem and no clean underwear.'

Kitt stared at her in sick horror. Sulian had always just been *around* since she was a child, a grumbling thundercloud who'd got gradually older and greyer, respected and pitied in equal measure for her power and the things she had to do to keep her own brain from making her life unbearable. But Sulian never talked about her past, and Kitt had never asked. She wondered if her parents knew.

'I thought mages went to college,' Vem managed, considerably less jovial than usual.

'We have to live that long first,' Sulian replied, not looking at him. 'Things were… *rougher*, where I'm from.'

'And where is that?' Plainsong asked.

'I don't think it exists anymore,' Sulian muttered. 'Something else that's fallen out of the world. Can't say that I'm sorry.' She took a swig from her flask and grimaced at the fire. 'But you were asking about the parched ones. I don't know if it's a good theory, but it's *a* theory. This whole place is in the grip of some sort of chronomancy, after mages tried to fix the event that created the timeless lands. I reckon the parched ones are people who've been caught in some sort of dreadful endless summer, and have been twisted by the magic. Just another wonderful thing to lay at the feet of that nameless god who tried to kill the future.'

'He wasn't nameless,' Plainsong said quietly.

'Well, I'm sure he wasn't,' the Swallowmage said, heaving

a grumpy sigh. 'But since no one knows which one of the bastards it was—'

'It was Altrinchor.'

Plainsong's hands were folded in front of him, and sitting cross-legged in his robes with the firelight playing off the angles of his bald skull, he really *did* look like a monk. Or possibly a priest.

'Altrinchor?' Sulian echoed with a frown, her gaze sharpening properly for the first time since the parched one's attack. 'The god of chance and gamblers?'

Kitt let out a grunt of surprise. Altrinchor was hardly a major god; he had a shrine in the Temple of All Gods, on which was placed shattered dice and torn playing cards, and inscribed with the words *Better Luck Next Time*. He was a god to whom one might mutter a prayer when faced with a difficult choice or great uncertainty, in the hope that he might be listening and give circumstances a nudge in your favour, but no one Kitt knew of really *worshipped* him as such. You had to be truly desperate – or the most devout of believers, which was often the same thing – to give yourself over fully to the whims of chance.

'That is how we know him today, yes,' Plainsong said, with a slight twist to his lips that was not a smile. 'As I said, I was young and curious once, and although I was most certainly also foolish, I learned much in my travels. Before he tried to slay the future – and before the other gods punished him for doing so by making him an object of ridicule – Altrinchor was the god of fate.'

'Why would the god of fate try to kill the future?' Pigtail Vem asked.

'One would guess he did not like what he saw written there,' Plainsong said, with a shrug. 'The tale, as I heard it, was that Altrinchor knew how things must unfold. He could see the road but not the destination, insofar as we can put the understanding of the gods into words. However, the gods are reflections of us, and they mirror our fears, our hopes, and our loves. Altrinchor began to piece together what he could see of how fate unfolded, and grew to fear what was coming, although no account I ever found speculated what that was or why he feared it.' He poked the fire slightly with a stick, causing a slight flare of flame.

'Altrinchor went to Orlanva the smith-god and persuaded her to forge him the first weapon he had ever wielded,' Plainsong continued. 'He tasked his three heralds with bringing him the broken blade Sunderstorm, which was shattered when the hero Glaviyan used it to slay the Wolfdragon, and which had been buried with him. Orlanva took the sword, but even she could not bind its pieces back together using the arts of smithing alone, for nothing the Wolfdragon did could ever be undone. Only when Altrinchor sacrificed his own left arm to the flames of Orlanva's forge could the smith goddess rekindle Sunderstorm's fire. She shaped it into a star which could kill the very sky itself, because Orlanva found enough beauty in her craft that she rarely questioned for what her creations would be used.

'One-armed and injured, Altrinchor sent his heralds to delay the hosts of the other gods, and climbed to the place where his foresight suggested he must strike to kill the future he so feared. When he reached it, he swung the Swordstar Orlanva had forged, and...' Plainsong spread his hands. 'Well, the rest is somewhat better documented, I suppose. The other gods – or at least, those who took an interest in such things – discovered that killing the god of fate was no easy feat, so they waged a war on his followers and ensured no one remembered Altrinchor except as a god of coin tosses and unlikely occurrences.'

'That's a hell of a story,' the Swallowmage said, after a silence. 'Where did you hear it?'

'A long way from here, and many years ago,' Plainsong said. 'The gods' persecution was not as thorough as they would have liked, and there are still those here and there who remember the old tales. Of course,' he added, 'one can rarely be sure of the provenance of such stories, but I've seen enough to convince me that Altrinchor was once more than he is now, and that it was the other gods who brought him low. That is the truth of the matter, as I understand it.'

'You're telling me,' Derna said slowly, 'that the Swordstar used to be *Sunderstorm*? One of the most famous swords that's ever existed in the world?'

Everyone else apart from Plainsong looked at her blankly.

'Seriously?' Derna protested. 'It was the only weapon that could kill the Wolfdragon, because the lightning spirit trapped in the blade prevented the wounds it made from healing! Honestly, none of you bastards would know history if it walked up and slapped you.'

'None of us like swords as much as you do,' Kitt reminded her. Derna glowered across the fire in return.

'Kitt, you stopped me from picking up *Sunderstorm*,' she said. 'We're going back the same way, right? Because I'm definitely getting that on the way back.'

'What do you mean, she stopped you from picking it up?' Plainsong interjected, looking intently at Derna. 'You've been onto the high moors? You've *seen* the rift? The Swordstar is still there?'

'We came over the moors from Mereport,' Falzine said, before Kitt could even figure out how she might warn the others not to say anything further. 'That rift is a sight I won't forget in a hurry, that's for sure.' He smiled proudly. 'First ones to come all the way, so far as we know.'

'I've never seen the rift,' Plainsong said softly. 'That must indeed be a wondrous sight.'

'Bloody terrifying, is what it is,' Donal said, with a shudder. 'Gave me the creeps.'

'That didn't stop you from—' Vem began, then broke off as Kitt elbowed him in the ribs. To her relief, he seemed to cotton on that mentioning the destinies Donal had lifted from the moors might not be the wisest course of action in front of this stranger. Who knew what Plainsong's opinions were about destinies, or what his morals might be about robbing his new travelling companions? Self-deprecating though he might have been about his capabilities against the parched one, Kitt wouldn't fancy crossing blades with him.

'What brought you all the way across the high moors from Mereport?' Plainsong asked curiously. 'That's a dangerous journey, as I understand it.'

'It's a private matter.' Kitt smiled at him politely and cast a quick glance around the fire to ensure everyone else got the message. Someone in Mereport had tried to have her killed, after all.

'Fair enough,' Plainsong said. 'I won't pry.'

There were a few more seconds of silence, other than the fire's snaps and pops as it chewed its way merrily through dry wood.

'If I tell you, will you tell me about the arm knives?'

'*Derna!*'

TWENTY-FIVE

Derringsmoot was, Kitt supposed, a large town. It was nothing like the size of Mereport, but she was less inclined to dwell on feelings of superiority than she was just grateful to be back in civilisation.

There had been no reoccurrence of long summer, and no more visitations by the parched ones, to everyone's great relief. The weather was still uncomfortably warm, but that strange, suffocating, endless afternoon had been left behind, and they reached the river road in the late morning of the day after they met Plainsong. That brought them to the gates of Derringsmoot as the evening began to draw in, and Kitt for one felt rather more secure with the reassuring bustle of people around her, and the skyline partially obscured by buildings and roofs.

'I will leave you here,' Plainsong said, as they reached a bridge. He turned and nodded to them, as a group. 'May fate smile upon you.'

Kitt felt she should say something in return, but wasn't sure exactly what. It seemed her companions were in a similar dilemma, and so Plainsong received a reply of half a dozen broadly positive murmurs, but very few distinguishable words.

That appeared to suit him, since he gave one of his small smiles and departed without saying anything else, his bald head wending its way through the crowd.

'We're just letting him go like that?' Pigtail Vem said quietly. 'He was really useful.'

'And really creepy,' the Swallowmage said. 'There's something strange about that one, mark my words.'

'You mean apart from the arm knives?' Derna asked.

'And the fact he doesn't sweat?' Kitt added, which was something she'd noticed, and to her mind was somehow even more alarming than the arm knives.

'Yes,' Sulian said firmly. 'I'm glad he's not going to be with us anymore.'

'Me too,' Kitt said. Plainsong had been interesting, but in the same way that a large predator watched from distance was interesting. Although you might understand that it bore you no ill will, and you might marvel at its assurance and grace, part of the interest was in making sure it didn't slip out of sight and then pop up behind you. It was an interest that felt most comfortable at a safe distance. With Plainsong, Kitt was not entirely sure what that distance would be.

Just to be sure, she led her party in the opposite direction from that in which Plainsong had disappeared, and they soon found a large and rather rambling inn by the name of the Wooden Heron. This had more rooms available than the Hanging Rock and seemed to cater to lone travellers, meaning that although Kitt's lodgings were small she at least had some blessed privacy for the first time since they had all set out on this… well, 'adventure' didn't seem right. That felt like it should involve rope bridges over perilous chasms, and she couldn't bring herself to use the word 'quest' unironically, even in the privacy of her own head. 'Journey' felt rather too mundane for something that had featured giant wasps and terrifying, antler-headed creatures that dwelt in a nightmare summer caused by the aftermath of a god attempting to kill the future.

'"Foolishness",' Kitt muttered to herself. 'That about covers it.'

She tossed and turned, trying to get comfortable in her sweat-stained smallclothes on a pallet of blankets in a room with one small window that had caught the full force of the afternoon and evening sun, but she was back in a town again. The shouts, clangs, and general noise that occurred even after dark in a place like this might have disturbed someone used to more idyllic surroundings, but they were as good as a lullaby to Kitt Carver, child of Mereport. She had no tree roots in her back, no heather in her ear, and no Two Tongue Derna a mere few inches away from her, somehow being incredibly *there* even when unmoving and making no noise. She should fall asleep in minutes.

And yet for some reason, she did not.

First, her thoughts strayed back to her family and how they might be doing. They were almost certainly just chugging along as usual, since it was only Kitt who had a job that involved much in the way of danger or uncertainty. Her mum and dad would probably be losing bits at cards to Nana Carver; Annity would be in their own house with Tavid, either catching up on their reading now the kids were in bed, or possibly engaged in activities with their square-jawed husband loosely adjacent to making a third child. Kitt's mind skittered away from those thoughts but hung around in the general area, and before she knew it she was thinking about Donal.

It was frustrating, was what it was. Kitt had no need for someone to be a good person to find them attractive, or indeed for her to act on that attraction. 'You don't go to the temple for a piece of brisket', as Nana Carver would say; basically, that you shouldn't expect any one person in your life to do everything or be everything. The aggravating thing about Donal was that he'd been fine for that one night, and ever since then he'd alternated between being infuriatingly eager to please and absolutely unwilling to do anything that might actually be pleasing. Kitt had been ready to give him a chance, but there seemed nothing more to him than what she'd seen so far, and in fact possibly less. It felt like she could poke a hole through him, as though he were paper-thin.

In many ways, he was the exact opposite of Derna. Donal said all the right things, but then you found out he'd sold your conversation on to a rich stranger, or he'd run away when the slydewasps were coming for you. Derna hardly said the right things *ever*, and sometimes she ambushed you to drive a hard bargain for the destiny you'd just found, but when someone had just stabbed you, or the slydewasps were coming, Derna was there.

Derna wasn't a good person; on that the laws of both gods and humans would vehemently agree. Even if you accepted her statement that most of the people she'd killed had been in self-defence, firstly you had to ask what had happened to those that weren't covered by 'most', and secondly you had to ask why, if this remotely bothered her, she hadn't tried to make changes to her life to stop getting into so many situations where she apparently had to kill people in self-defence. Kitt was thoroughly prepared to take the side of the victim, but there was a difference between stabbing someone when they tried to slit your throat because you'd walked through the wrong part of town while wearing clothes that suggested you had a heavy coin purse, and wandering down the street yelling 'Come and have a go if you think you're hard enough!' to all and sundry. No, Two Tongue Derna was not a good person.

But she was good *to Kitt*, and that counted for quite a lot, from where Kitt was standing. Or lying down.

Kitt shifted slightly in her bed again, and from the other side of the thin panelling next to her came the faint, muffled sound of someone doing the same thing far less gently. It was Derna, in her own room. Right up against the panelling, by the sound of it, so she actually *was* just a few inches away. Just like she'd been in the bedroom of the Hanging Rock.

Only this time they both had their own window, with fewer unnatural threats likely to come creeping in, and so there was no need for Derna to clamber across Kitt to lay between it and her.

More's the pity, Kitt joked saucily to herself, but her mind didn't take the joke and move on. Instead, it insisted on replaying that second or so of contact where Derna slid across her. The pressure, the warmth of Derna's body through their respective smallclothes, the infuriating tickle of her hair on Kitt's lips…

Well, it wasn't like Kitt was doing anything *useful* right now, like going to sleep. She gave herself permission to actually think about Derna like that, just to see what happened. She remembered Derna's fingers on her scar, that gentle touch that felt so caring and so at odds with the face Derna usually presented to the world. Kitt touched her scar, felt the strangely smooth texture of it, and imagined her own fingers tracing the similar marks that adorned Derna's body. Across her thigh… above her hip… the deceptively small one, the width of the sword blade that had nearly ended her life, nestled under her breastbone…

Kitt remembered the naked hunger in Derna's eyes when she'd looked at the Swordstar and, ludicrous though the notion was of Derna feeling that way about something which wasn't a weapon, imagined it to be directed at her. Derna *was* pretty, pretty like a knife that might just skewer you through the heart if you weren't careful, and the hungry Derna in Kitt's mind's eye came closer and pressed up against Kitt's hand, which splayed out from her gentle caress of Derna's scar to encounter warm, unmarked flesh, and—

Kitt suddenly became aware of her heart, which was pounding so fast it was a miracle that Derna couldn't hear it. Derna, a mere few inches away, if that, pressed up against the panelling that separated them. Kitt wondered what she was doing, what she was thinking. What if, as a purely hypothetical extension of the previous thought experiment, Kitt were to creep out of her room, knock quietly on Derna's door, and…

And…

Kitt bit her lip.

'*Shit.*'

TWENTY-SIX

THEY MET UP for breakfast the next morning to discuss their next move – or at least, some of them did. Falzine viewed that his involvement had been to get Kitt to Derringsmoot and become one of the first people to make it clean across the high moors, and he had little interest in what she did now she was here, so the next move for him and Vem was apparently to go and look around Derringsmoot, which was the farthest from home that either of them had ever been. That left Kitt with Sulian, whose dream had apparently indicated that Kitt needed to successfully warn these people, Derna, who had attached herself to Kitt until this was over one way or another, and Donal, who had done more or less the same as Derna, but with Kitt being rather less comfortable about the whole thing.

Truth be told, Kitt wasn't massively comfortable with Derna's presence now either, which was (for once) nothing to do with Derna and everything to do with Kitt's slightly sleep-deprived revelation from the night before. She kept sneaking what she hoped were unobtrusive glances, trying to work out when her friend had got hot and, more importantly, why Kitt hadn't *noticed* until now. The problem was that was a door, once opened, apparently couldn't be closed again. Those thoughts had led to Kitt taking advantage of some blessed privacy for the first time in days, fully expecting to feel a bit ashamed about it in the cold light of morning, but no such shame had bubbled up. Instead, she found herself thinking about how soft Derna's lips looked, and how beautiful her eyes were, and finding her own eyes drawn to the shadow of Derna's cleavage where her shirt was only part-laced in the warmth of the Wooden Heron's common room.

Shame might have been shouldered aside by somewhat startled lust, but unfortunately guilt made an appearance as well. Derna seemed to have made her peace with being – in her words – really bad at being a person, but she still wanted to be liked by the people *she* liked, of which Kitt appeared to be one. How would Derna feel if she got it into her head that the only reason Kitt was spending time with her was due to physical attraction, rather than liking the admittedly rather odd person that was Derna Towbright? Kitt wouldn't have described herself as 'shallow' so much as 'cheerfully uncomplicated', but she really needed to sort through exactly what was going on in her head.

'What's the plan?' Derna asked, with what Kitt might not have felt was obnoxious enthusiasm had she actually slept well. 'Are we walking up to the front gates, or what?'

'It doesn't feel like the best idea,' Kitt said, well aware that she was low on best ideas herself. 'I don't know how likely it is that some noble family will believe what I've got to tell them.'

'It won't be them you'll have to convince first,' Sulian said. 'They won't answer their own door. You'll need to persuade a servant that you should be allowed to see the toffs.'

'Oh, great!' Kitt wailed. 'Any more obstacles, while you're at it?' It shouldn't have felt like Sulian was dropping an enormous roadblock in front of her, but the combination of anxiety, guilt, and poor sleep was like someone had wound a spring up inside her, and despair was its easiest outlet.

'But the servant won't be a toff, so they'll possibly be more likely to listen,' the Swallowmage said with a shrug. 'Besides, what's the other option? Sneak in and try to speak to Lord and Lady Whatsit without warning? That's a good way to get yourself stabbed. Again.'

Kitt ground her teeth in frustration, but the Swallowmage made a good point. Kitt's experience of dealing with the nobility was pretty much non-existent, but she was fairly sure that if someone she didn't know showed up in *her* home unannounced she'd shiv them first and ask questions later.

'Fine,' she muttered, reaching for more bacon. 'We go to the front gates and try to be convincing, or whatever.'

DERRING HALL LAY in the north of Derringsmoot, and although it was no larger or grander than some of the buildings in Mereport, it seemed to stand taller and shine brighter through dint of being the sole structure of its size in the entire town. Kitt only caught a glimpse of the roofs over the intimidating stone border wall until they reached the iron-barred gate that served as the main entrance, at which point even the impressive trees on its grounds couldn't obscure its magnificence from the street – which was almost certainly the point, Kitt thought uncharitably. However, her cogitation on the habits of the wealthy to ensure they could be marvelled at from a distance convenient to them was interrupted by the pair of guards taking an interest in her and her companions.

'The ball's not till tomorrow,' one of them said, looking the four of them over. Both guards wore stiff leather hauberks, and held halberds with the suggestion that they weren't just for show. 'What *are* you, anyway? Tumblers of some sort?'

Kitt blinked in confusion. 'Uh, no. I'm a diviner.'

To her surprise, both guards' eyebrows raised. 'Nah,' the second one said, although he studied her with renewed interest. 'What would an actual diviner be doing here?'

Of course, Kitt realised, most diviners from anywhere near Mereport went there to seek their fortune, so they would be in short supply in Derringsmoot.

'She is, though,' his companion said. She pointed at Kitt's thigh pouch. 'Those are divining rods, bet you anything.'

'Huh,' the second guard grunted. 'Guess so, then.'

'Hey, I'm a diviner too,' Donal said, tapping his own moonstruck iron. Derna rolled her eyes.

'Yes, and this is the Swallowmage,' Kitt said, gesturing to Sulian, who was leaning on Jandi and looking as unimpressed as might be expected of a mage, although that was probably at least partially because she wasn't in a tavern. Still, Kitt felt that her party could do with all the added reputation it could get, if they were going to try to talk their way inside.

'And what are you?' the first guard asked Derna.

'Trouble,' Derna replied, grinning at her in a way that Kitt was distressed to note caused a tingle of envy.

'We *really* need to speak with a member of the Grike family,' Kitt said, trying to hit that delicate balance between urgency and earnestness. 'There's something important that I need to tell them. It's kind of an emergency.'

'Have you got an appointment?' the first guard asked, in the bored tones of one who knew the answer was 'no' but also knew exactly what her job entailed and was going to do it properly, damn it all.

Kitt spread her hands. 'Emergencies don't really make appointments, folks. That's sort of what it means.'

'No one gets in unless they have an appointment, or they're important,' the first guard said. 'Convince me you're important.'

'I'm a mage, for crying out loud,' Sulian said impatiently. 'Surely that's important enough for us to be able to speak to *someone*.'

'Alright, prove you're a mage,' the second guard said.

'*Fine*,' Sulian said, shouldering her way in front of Kitt and levelling Jandi at the gates. 'Oh, you two might want to step back a bit for this.'

The guards looked at each other, then at the gates, and then at Jandi.

'Now hang on a second,' the first one said, her eyes widening in alarm, 'you can't—'

'It's your funeral,' the Swallowmage said through gritted teeth, as Jandi began to glow with an unpleasantly shimmering light. 'Well, more like a cremation—'

'Okay, fine, fine!' the second guard said hurriedly. 'You're a mage!' He looked at his companion. 'A mage saying that she needs to speak to someone as an emergency probably counts as important, right?'

'I'm convinced,' the first guard agreed, and rang a bell that hung from the gatepost next to her.

'You're not expecting anyone to hear that from here, are you?' Kitt asked, looking past them towards the hall.

'It's a sympathy bell,' the guard explained. 'I ring this, and an identical one rings in the house. It's enchanted, see?'

'And one of the gate guard jobs is to keep the little shits around here from ringing it and running off,' the second one muttered. '"Oh, it'll save work", that's what Marquin said, but he never said who it would save work *for*.'

Kitt frowned. 'Marquin? Is he the factor here?'

'You know him?' the second guard asked, his face taking on the guarded expression of one who had just uttered a mild disparagement of someone else and now realised that he knew nothing about the connections of those in front of whom he had uttered it.

'Not as such,' Kitt said. A dry, dusty voice scrabbled up in her memory, forever now linked with the glow of a lightstone and the smell of preserving agents. 'But I think we had a mutual friend.'

TWENTY-SEVEN

THEIR ESCORT TO the hall was not, as Kitt had been expecting, more guards. Or at least, not the sort of guards she'd imagined.

'Stonewardens,' the Swallowmage grunted, as two walking statues approached bearing halberds of similar design to those carried by the gate guards, albeit of greater size. The statues themselves were around seven feet tall, and for reasons that Kitt could not quite fathom, had been carved as though they were wearing full plate armour even though they were made of stone.

'Give me the bloody creeps,' the first guard confided. 'But they're useful enough, so long as you don't ask them to start thinking. You two!' she added, raising her voice. 'Escort these four visitors to the house!'

'Don't leave the path,' the second guard added to Kitt, with a laugh that was not entirely friendly. 'They won't like it if you do.'

'This has got to be some pretty powerful magic, right?' Donal asked, as the four of them began to trudge up the gravel path towards Derring Hall, with a towering stonewarden thumping along on either side of them.

'Powerful, yes. Not particularly complex,' Sulian said, eying the one closest to her. 'Stonewardens *look* impressive, but that's mainly what they're for. They can't understand any sort of complicated instruction, and they're useless as actual guards because even though they can technically see and hear things, they don't know what's suspicious and what isn't.'

'And if we *do* leave the path?' Derna asked curiously.

'One of them would likely grab you and haul you back onto it,' the Swallowmage said. 'Probably won't be too gentle with you either, so they might break a bone or two. But we could be walking up here right now talking about how we're going to kill everyone in there, and they wouldn't know what was going on.'

'Huh.' Kitt looked up at the impassive statue clomping along next to her, then down at the gravel beneath their feet. 'Are you made of path, or is the path made of you? You don't knooooow...' She drew the last word out spookily and waggled her fingers at the stonewarden, which – mercifully – took no notice of her. Derna snickered, however.

'Could *you* make a stonewarden?' Donal asked Sulian, who clucked her tongue.

'Right now? No. I'd have the juice to pull it off, but I'd need to research the enchantment. It's not that complicated, but you've still got to do it *right*.'

'What happens if you get it wrong?' Kitt asked.

The Swallowmage sighed. 'The same thing that happens every time you get magic wrong, Kitt. Pain.' She winced, and one of her eyes half-shut for a moment.

'Foretellings?' Kitt murmured. The Swallowmage nodded wordlessly, then passed Jandi to her as she fumbled for a flask. Kitt took the knowood staff somewhat hesitantly, but there was no spark between it and her fingers when they closed around it, and she did not suddenly burst into flame or experience terrifying visions. It felt just like normal, relatively smooth wood beneath her fingers, but she knew there was *something* in there. For one thing, she was fairly sure Jandi had deliberately slipped out of Sulian's grip and tripped her when she ran headlong towards the rift. Sulian also once claimed to Kitt that Jandi could levitate but didn't like to do it when anyone except her could see it, and Kitt didn't know what to do with that information at all.

'Not sure that's going to make a great first impression,' Donal said disapprovingly, as the Swallowmage took a swig of whatever liquor she had on her person today.

'I'm *trying* to make a good impression by not getting distracted by annoying voices,' Sulian said, replacing her flask without looking at him, then stretching out her hand to take Jandi back from Kitt. 'Don't make it harder for me by adding yours to the list.'

Kitt was half-surprised when the stonewardens did not take them around the side, but instead marched up the stone steps to the main doors. Clearly, a mage was not someone that even the nobility insulted by sending to the servant's entrance. The doors were opened by a girl somewhere in her teens, decked out in sober livery and a generous helping of acne, who ushered them wordlessly into a small waiting room. She backed out, closing the door behind her and leaving them standing looking at each other awkwardly.

'Sooo,' Kitt said. 'What happens—'

Another door opened on the room's far side, and an old man entered with the silent grace one might associate with a rural nobleman given to occasionally floating in through someone's bedroom window and helping himself to the contents of their veins. The impression was somewhat heightened by the sharp cheekbones, piercing blue eyes, and rather bloodless pallor, although contraindicated by the faint scent of chamomile that arrived with him.

'Good morning,' he said, his tone walking a narrow tightrope between entertaining the possibility that this was not a gross intrusion into the household's affairs, and threatening dire consequences if that turned out to be the case. 'I am Marquin.' He cast a brief, assessing eye over them all, and Kitt got the strong impression that he did not like what he saw. 'What, may I ask, is your business here?'

'Um, hello,' Kitt began, suddenly realising that she hadn't rehearsed this at all. How was she going to convince someone of a threat to this family without sounding like she was spouting nonsense? Marquin's eyes focused on her and narrowed to a scrutiny so intense she was briefly worried that he might burn a hole right through her, which did little to calm her nerves. 'My name's Kitt Carver, I'm from Mereport. We're all from Mereport, actually. Not that that matters, really. Um, so—'

'*Get out.*'

Kitt blinked. The old man's face had gone even whiter, and he stared at Kitt as though nothing else in the room existed. His mouth barely moved, but the words sliding past his teeth and lips seemed to have been expelled by his soul without it bothering to inform his body of its role in matters.

'Sir,' she said cautiously, 'if you'd just let me—'

'I said *get out!*' Marquin repeated, quivering with emotion. He raised one hand and pointed towards the door by which they'd entered. 'You will leave, *now*, or I will summon the stonewardens to remove you!'

'That seems a bit excessive,' Sulian said, stepping forward. 'Listen, I'm a mage...'

Marquin, it seemed, had no intention of listening whether he was being addressed by a mage or not. He squeezed a charm hanging from a bracelet at his wrist, and from beyond the waiting room came the bang of the main doors being thrown open by stone hands for whom appropriate care of architecture and furnishings was a concept to which they had never been introduced.

Kitt opened her mouth to protest again, but another look at Marquin's face convinced her of the futility of that approach.

The man didn't just look furious, he looked *terrified*, as though Kitt and her entire party were spectres draped in clanking chains and wearing the bloodstained faces of his closest kin.

'You know what?' she said, spreading her hands in what she hoped was a placating manner. 'Sure. Fine. We'll be off.'

'Do not return to this estate!' Marquin said, raising his voice as the stonewardens lumbered in. 'In fact, I strongly advise you to leave Derringsmoot entirely!'

'Okay, I get the picture!' Kitt snapped, as they began to file out towards the main door beneath the stone stares of the Grikes' security. The spotty doorgirl was staring at them in mute horror; it was probably the most interesting thing she'd ever seen in her job.

'Marquin? What's going on?' called a voice from above.

Kitt looked up and saw a young man roughly her own age, quite slight and not particularly tall, peering down from the grand landing that overlooked the hall. He was not dressed in the servant livery of the doorgirl, or even the unadorned but still servant-like garb worn by Marquin. His clothing was not particularly grand, but the slightly unlaced shirt and messy, faintly ginger curls combined to give a picture of someone who was not about to get shouted at for his appearance. Not a servant, in other words.

'Master Arkony, please go back to your room!' Marquin called up, sounding even more distressed than before, if that were possible. Kitt peered up at the apparent Arkony, trying to see how he reacted to that instruction, but Marquin deliberately stood directly in front of her to block her view.

'But Marquin—'

'Master Arkony, I must *insist!*'

Kitt saw nothing further: the stonewardens closed in and effectively shunted them out of the door, then began driving them down the path with a steady gait that cared nothing for what a comfortable pace would be for them, halberds held crosswise as though daring them to make an issue of it.

'Can't you do something about this?' Donal complained to the Swallowmage. 'I feel like a bloody sheep!'

'What do you want me to do?' Sulian demanded. 'Blow up the enchanted guards of the most powerful family for twenty miles around? How do you think that will go for us?' She pressed ahead, Jandi thumping into the gravel as they hurried down the path. 'This is the Grikes' town, boy! As it stands, we're just being kicked out. If we start making trouble, we'll be kicked *in*.'

They reached the gates, which were opened by the two guards they'd encountered on the way in.

'Ah,' the first one said neutrally, as they walked past. 'Didn't go quite as you planned, then?'

Kitt waited until her feet hit the road outside the gates – accurately assuming that the stonewardens would stop caring about her as soon as she was no longer on the property – and turned to give the guard a withering assessment of her manners, general conduct, and probably hairstyle. However, Donal slipped in front of her and flashed the guard a sheepish grin that Kitt recognised, *damn it*, from when he'd flirted with her in the Dubious Gecko. And fine, maybe she'd *technically* flirted with him as well, but given that she'd fallen out with him since then, she'd officially deflirted him in her brain.

'They all seem kind of on edge up there,' Donal said smoothly. 'Didn't you say there's something going on tomorrow, some sort of big event? I bet everyone's getting ready, that was probably it.'

'Yeah, we're hosting the summer ball, for Master Arkony's birthday,' the first guard said. 'Everyone knows *that*.'

'Listen to you!' the second said with a laugh. '"We're" hosting it, are we? Lady of the house now, are you?'

'Shut up, Cham.'

'Summer ball! That'll be it!' Donal said, snapping his fingers. 'Lots of stuff to organise, I guess they've no time for anything else. We'll try again in a few days when everything's calmed down a bit!' He turned away from the guards and spread his arms as though to envelop Kitt, Derna, and Sulian.

'Touch me and I stab you,' Derna said flatly.

'Just walk away,' Donal said through his teeth, doing his best to usher them without actually making physical contact. Kitt hardly liked the idea, but what else was she to do? Go back and argue with the stonewardens?

'You're planning something, and I don't like it,' Sulian said to Donal, as they all began to move off down the road.

'You don't even know what I'm planning yet,' Donal protested.

'Accurate, but irrelevant.'

'Something fishy's going on there,' Donal said. 'Kitt barely opened her mouth before that jumped-up walking stick kicked us out. He didn't even hear what she had to say. It's something personal with him.'

'How?' Kitt asked. 'How could it possibly be personal? I've never met him!'

'What if it was because you said we were from Mereport?' Sulian suggested. 'He knew that destinies merchant, or at least bought things from him.'

'He can't have been worried about that, though,' Kitt said. 'Mazen said Marquin was nice!'

'Maybe Marquin doesn't know that,' Sulian said. 'Maybe he's done something he thinks Mazen's found out about.'

'If we were intending to cause trouble, why would we show up at the front gate and announce ourselves?' Derna put in.

Kitt looked at her. 'You totally would do that, though.'

'Okay, point taken. But they don't know me, do they?'

'It doesn't matter *why* Marquin felt so threatened by us that he had to immediately call the walking statues,' Donal said, 'what matters is that he *did*. We're not going to get a fair hearing that way, so we either abandon the whole thing and go home, or we try something else.'

Sulian massaged her forehead with her hand. 'You know,

there are times when I hate having my powers of foretelling. Most of the time, actually. But *particularly* when it means I know it's somehow important that Kitt warns these people of what's coming, and so we're probably going to have to listen to whatever godawful plan you've come up with in the three seconds since we were kicked out of that house.'

'The ball tomorrow is for that kid's birthday, the one on the landing,' Donal said, as though Sulian had instead extended a polite and glowing invitation for him to expound his thoughts. 'Marquin called him "Arkony" when he was shooing us out. That means Arkony's going to be there, and probably the parents as well. If we can get into the house then, they should be nice and obvious for Kitt to speak to one of them and warn them!'

Kitt stared at him. 'That has to be the least complete plan I've ever heard. It's like you've skipped ahead to the end without bothering with the beginning and the middle.'

'There are going to be all sorts of people going in and out of that place tomorrow!' Donal said excitedly, jerking his head back in the direction of Derring Hall. 'Musicians, caterers, everything. All we'll need to do is blend in and look busy.' He thought for a moment. 'Well, Vem and Falzine are too obvious, Sulian might start yammering nonsense at any moment, and Derna's too likely to stab someone for looking at her the wrong way.'

Kitt groaned. 'So you and me, right? That's convenient.'

'It makes sense!' Donal protested. 'You get in and warn them, I watch your back and run interference until you get the chance.' He smiled at her. 'I said I wanted to help, right? This is me helping.'

'Have you done this sort of thing before?' Derna said sceptically. 'You know, sneaking into toffs' houses while everyone's busy?'

'I *may* have been hired to track down one or two items that turned out to be in rather surprising locations.'

'So you're a thief,' Kitt said. 'Why doesn't that surprise me?'

'I'm more of a middleman,' Donal said, wobbling his hand back and forth. 'I never *kept* anything, I just moved it from one place to another after I'd found it. What was I supposed to do, demand to see everyone's records so I knew who the legal owner was before I agreed to track anything?'

'You know, that's about the first thing you've said that I agree with,' Derna commented. Kitt groaned and covered her eyes with her hand in the hope that it would keep the foolishness out.

'We'd still need to find a way to blend in,' she said, when that approach didn't work. 'We don't own servant clothes, and we don't work for anyone who's going to be supplying stuff to the house!'

'You've forgotten the secret ingredient,' Donal said happily. 'Bribery!'

'Bribery with what?' Kitt demanded, as loudly as she dared while they were walking down a public street. 'I'm not exactly flush with cash right now!'

'With *these*,' Donal said, holding one of his pouches out to her. Kitt looked in, privately dreading what she was going to see.

It wasn't as bad as she'd feared.

'Okay,' she said slowly, looking at the half-dozen or so destinies clustered together. 'Okay. I'm not saying it's a *good* plan, but it's *a* plan.' She thought of the knife sliding into her side, and the fury she'd felt when the man with the wobbly face and the strange voice – whom she'd admittedly never met, but it wasn't hard to put together a mental picture when the description was so accurately vague – hadn't even waited around to see if she was dead. It didn't matter if the Grikes' factor hated all of Mereport or just her in particular for some reason that she couldn't fathom, Kitt still didn't like the idea of leaving the family unwarned about the trouble she felt sure was heading for them. And all, it seemed, over this destiny that Mazen had sold…

'Wait.' She thought of the glimpse she'd caught of the apparent Arkony, standing above them all on the landing. 'Mazen said he'd only sold the destiny recently. I'll bet you any money that it's a present for Arkony's birthday, which means *he's* going to be the target for these bastards!'

'Ugh,' Derna grunted. 'Bloody aristocracy and their bloody kids.'

'Right,' Kitt said, ignoring Derna's disgust. The whole thing took on a slightly different shade for her now she'd actually seen the person whose life was at risk. How could she give up? Anyone could die at pretty much any time for a large variety of reasons, and there was not much that could be done about that, but it was a bit different if you knew a definite scheme – well, a probable scheme – to kill a specific individual but did nothing to warn them. If she went back to Mereport now and her family asked her if the trip had been worth it, how could she answer them?

'We know the person we most need to warn, and we *kind* of have a plan for how to get inside to do that,' she said, trying to bring her focus back to the here and now. 'Now all we need is a bit of—'

Something caught at her eye and she jerked around, but there was nothing there. Just an empty street corner where her brain had been sure it had seen a bald head, and a robe…

Plainsong?

'…luck,' she finished, uncertainly.

TWENTY-EIGHT

ARKONY TURNED FIRST one way and then the other, but there was no solution to be found. No matter how he twisted, no matter how he contorted himself, he was helpless.

'Marquin,' he said with a sigh, trying to ignore his own dejected face in the gilt-framed, full-length mirror in front of which he was making such a fool of himself. 'Would you mind? I can't tie this damned cummerbund properly.'

'Of course, Master Arkony,' Marquin said agreeably, gliding forward. He rarely did anything as obtrusive as walking. According to the ancient gossip that Arkony had unearthed, Marquin had at one point been a figure of some menace in Derringsmoot, while simultaneously quickening a few pulses for those who liked their men a little gaunt and perpetually sombrely dressed. These days, the factor was more akin to a stern old uncle, whose glare was still sufficient to send children fleeing but who held little fear for adults.

At least, unless they had crossed the Grikes.

'Thank you,' Arkony muttered, as Marquin's quick fingers secured the offending clothing item at the small of his back.

'Well?' Marquin asked, with something that sounded a great deal like fondness in his voice, as he stepped away again. Arkony turned back and forth with less urgency than before, eyeing his reflection with considerable scepticism.

'I feel like I should think I look ridiculous,' he said, after a few seconds of consideration. 'Unfortunately, I'm not sure I do.'

'That is a good thing, surely?'

'I suppose,' Arkony admitted. 'I don't know if I like the idea of being someone who thinks he looks good in a suit.'

'Well, Master Arkony, it can be our little secret,' Marquin said, with a small, precise smile. 'I wouldn't dream of betraying your trust to your parents. Although,' he added, with the faintest hint of reproach, 'you should remember that this is what you were born to do.'

'What, wear a suit?' Arkony asked with a laugh. To his surprise, Marquin nodded.

'Indeed. Being a Grike means responsibility, it means living up to expectations. It isn't just about *being* the master of the lands, it is about *looking* like you are the master of the lands.'

'I'm not master of the lands yet, though,' Arkony pointed out, 'and nor will I be for a long time.' His mother was fast approaching fifty, while his father had just cleared it. 'Father's only been lord for eight years, since Grandad passed. Besides,' he added hastily, trying to head off Marquin's inevitable rebuke about it never being too early to be prepared for his responsibilities, 'I'm not seeing anyone this evening of whom I'll be master. It's all,' he deepened his voice to imitate his father's intonation, '*our* sort of people.'

'And it's their opinions that matter, Master Arkony,' Marquin said earnestly. 'It's vital for you to maintain your standing in the eyes of your peers. They will expect to see the heir of the Grike family looking smart at his birthday ball, and comfortable in his surroundings.'

'What about being polite to them?' Arkony asked, stifling a shudder at the thought. 'Friendly?' The serried ranks of interchangeable shining faces loomed in his memory from earlier social events, each nose more upturned than the last.

'To be honest, Master Arkony, that is more of an optional extra when it comes to these things. Especially when it takes place in your own house.'

'My parents' house,' Arkony corrected him swiftly.

'Now come, that's not—'

The factor was cut off by the door to Arkony's room opening, without knock or warning, to admit the head and right shoulder of Draymere, Seventh Baronet Grike, Fifth Lord of Derringsdale, and Arkony's father. He was a vaguely triangular man, broad of shoulder and comparatively narrow of waist even just into his sixth decade; somewhat at odds with Arkony's build, which was of generally straight lines up and down, and without a huge amount of Arkony between them.

'Is he ready yet?' Draymere asked without greeting or preamble, looking at Marquin after giving Arkony the briefest of glances.

'We have just secured the cummerbund, sir,' Marquin replied, with a slight bow. 'I was giving Master Arkony some last-minute coaching, as it were.' Lord Draymere was always 'sir' to Marquin, whereas Arkony was 'Master Arkony'. Sometimes, Arkony wondered if the factor was subconsciously emphasising Arkony's title simply to ensure he remembered who he was supposed to be.

'I'm also standing right here,' Arkony put in, addressing his father. Draymere's moustache twitched, but he gave his son a slightly longer glance this time, entirely unapologetic.

'Yes, and looking the part, I see. I wouldn't trust your opinion of whether you're ready, though. I know how much you hate wearing formal clothes.' He looked back at Marquin. 'The guests are arriving. Make sure he's outside the ballroom in five minutes.'

He withdrew, shutting the door behind him. There were shooting stars that would have considered Draymere Grike to be somewhat brusque.

'If this *was* my house,' Arkony said quietly, without looking at Marquin, 'my father would not enter my rooms in such a manner.'

'The opinions of your parents can be as important as those of your peers, and can be shaped in the same manner,' Marquin said with a smile. 'Now, Master Arkony; since you apparently do not hate yourself in those clothes, and since you wish your father to trust your judgement a little more, shall we proceed to the ballroom where you can make a good impression on the other families of good breeding?'

Arkony sighed. 'Very well.' He plucked at his cummerbund for a moment, trying to summon the courage to ask a question he knew very well he would be knocked back on. Marquin was the family's factor and technically was supposed to do as he was instructed, but Arkony had already learned that this was not necessarily borne out in reality.

Nonetheless…

'Marquin,' he said. 'Who were those people who came to the house yesterday? The ones you had the stonewardens remove?'

'No one you need concern yourself with, Master Arkony,' Marquin replied smoothly, just as Arkony knew he would. 'They should not have come here, and I made them aware of that fact.'

'But who were they?' Arkony pressed. He caught a flicker of something in Marquin's eyes and decided to assert himself. 'Marquin, I heard you. You were quite agitated. Who were they, why were they here, and why did you think it was so urgent to get rid of them?'

Marquin sighed, and took Arkony by the shoulders. It was a light touch, not designed to intimidate; in fact it was almost fatherly, although Arkony had little frame of reference for that. Draymere Grike was not an unkind man – to his family – but he was not given to displays of sentimentality, nor physical contact beyond a brisk handshake or, perhaps, a brief pat on the back for a job well done.

'Master Arkony,' Marquin said, almost sadly. 'We have

spoken before about the role of a factor in a noble house. I have a variety of responsibilities, which I undertake to ensure that things run smoothly. It is not necessary for the family to know the details of many of these. And some of them…'

'…it is best if we do not,' Arkony finished gloomily. He shook his head. 'You know I don't like that, Marquin.'

'Well, when you *are* master of the lands, then that is something that you may change as you see fit,' Marquin said cheerfully. 'And by the time that happens, my days in the role will long be over.'

'So those people were something we should not know about?' Arkony said, unwilling to let Marquin off without at least hearing him admit it.

'Yes, Master Arkony,' Marquin said, looking him in the eyes. 'I promise you, nothing but trouble and pain could come of them being here. It is far better for everyone, and particularly this family, for them to stay away. It is best if you forget you ever saw them.'

That was not going to be easy. Drawn by the thunder of the stonewardens entering the house, Arkony had only caught a brief glimpse of the intruders, but they had been a strange bunch. One man perhaps a few years older than Arkony, good-looking and with evenly grey hair that surely could not be natural, and three women, one older one with a staff and an expression like she was chewing a lemon, and two of about Arkony's age. One of those two, with dark curls, had worn a sidesword and carried herself with the swagger of a fighter; Gerone Plynn had the same sort of gait. The other… Why had she looked familiar? And what possible connection could Marquin have to any of them?

'So no more of this, yes?' Marquin asked, ignorant of Arkony's wheeling thoughts. 'Put this out of your mind, and go and enjoy your evening. It is all about you, after all,' he added fondly.

'Yes,' Arkony muttered, straightening his cuffs. 'All about me.'

...

THE GREAT HALL was the grand centrepiece of Derring Hall:
a huge space of hardwood floor, grown as one gigantic piece
by the combined efforts of four woodwyrders, with a stage
at the north end. It served as a dining hall when required,
although these days the family more commonly took their
meals in a smaller and more private dining room. Tonight,
however, it had been called into service once more, with table
after table lined up while the distinguished guests were served
the kitchen's finest preparations. All the servants knew the
Grike name hung in the balance, and the anxiety had spread
throughout the house like the aroma of cooked cabbage.

Now the meal was finished, the guests had been served
drinks and encouraged to wander the gardens while the tables
were cleared away and the floor swept, and the musicians set
up on the stage where Arkony and his parents had taken
their meal. Arkony never really felt comfortable eating up
there and looking down on everyone else, despite it being
his family's house. He always felt incredibly on show, even
though he should have been the one doing the observing.

He was about to be on show in a very different way.

'Master Grike?' prompted the young woman in front
of him. She was Thirelda Goodweil, of the Glass Valley
Goodweils, and apparently known informally as Thi-Thi; a
pair of syllables about which Arkony felt he might prefer to
lose the power of speech entirely than actually bring himself
to utter. Nonetheless, she was an entrancing vision in a silken
gown of beautiful forest green, subtly picked out with perfectly
matched pearls, and Thirelda herself was unassumingly
pretty. Hers was not a face that would set sculptors and artists
at each other's throats for the chance to capture her features
for posterity, but she had the sort of mild, soft-edged looks
that would probably keep their charm through exertion, grief,
bad weather, and age alike. She was one year younger than

Arkony, a couple of inches shorter, and standing directly in front of him with an expression that was shifting from slight apprehension into slight impatience.

'Of course,' Arkony managed. 'Forgive me.' He took her hand and her waist, and the musicians struck up.

Dancing had never been Arkony's favoured activity. In fact he had actively disliked it, until one day his dancing tutor and his fencing master had put their heads together and come out with a framing that made sense to him. Both required nimble footwork and balance, along with a certain amount of strength, and the ability not to lose one's grip was a definite advantage if one did not wish to see one's sword fly out of one's hand or, as in this case, one's partner slip backwards and hit the floor. The aim of both pastimes was to combine these factors to achieve the desired result; it was simply that in one you were opposed to another, and in the other you were working in partnership with them.

Despite his more recent acceptance of dancing, and his determination to be good at it, Arkony still didn't relish everyone *watching* him while he did it. However, since his parents had chosen to make their traditional summer ball coincide with his birthday since his youth, the focus was always on him. When he was younger, this meant gifts from those families who wanted to stay in his parents' good books, and that was everyone. Now he'd grown up, there was rather more focus on him actually doing stuff and being someone.

'You dance very well,' Thirelda said, so softly that he could barely hear her above the music, and without moving her lips a great deal.

'Thank you,' Arkony replied, in a similar manner. Everyone would be watching them until they were done, at which point the rest of the ball would take to the floor to start the second dance. 'I might say the same of you.'

'And yet I sense that you are not entirely here,' Thirelda continued. Her gaze didn't leave his face as they pirouetted around the floor, and it wasn't hostile, but it wasn't exactly warm. There was a hint of challenge to it.

'I was thinking that I don't know what your parents promised mine for you to get the first dance with me,' Arkony said, deciding on the spur of the moment to go for complete honesty. 'I was told that this was not up for discussion, so I apologise if you were led to believe it was my doing.'

'Well,' Thirelda said softly, her lips not moving from the slightest of smiles which was appropriate for a dancing partner, 'it was not my doing either. My parents secured me the first dance simply to deny their rivals' children the opportunity of it.'

'Ah.' Arkony twirled her around and let her fall towards the floor, catching her at just the right moment with one hand in the small of her back and the other clasping hers. 'Well then, at least we understand each other.'

'All in all,' Thirelda said, returning to upright in a swirl of silk, 'it is a good job both that I enjoy dancing, and that you are good at it, or this would be a complete waste of our time.'

'Likewise,' Arkony agreed. They twirled on, the long drilling of his lessons ensuring that he placed every foot perfectly despite his unfamiliarity with his partner, until they finally came to a halt standing next to each other, his right hand still in Thirelda's left and slightly raised, facing the musicians on the stage.

Applause broke out around them, which Arkony felt might even be genuine rather than polite, and he released Thirelda's hand to turn and bow to her, which she returned with a curtsey.

'I hope you do not consider your parents' pettiness to have caused you an entirely wasted journey,' he said softly.

Her lips twitched in a small smile infinitely more genuine than the show one she'd worn during their routine. 'Perhaps not entirely. Thank you for the dance, Master Grike.'

'You're welcome, Miss Goodweil,' Arkony said, as they withdrew from each other. His parents had not exactly been leaning hard on him to find a suitable spouse, but hints were definitely starting to be dropped now he was about to turn twenty-three. It would be expected of him to find one from amongst the 'appropriate' social circle, and so it was likely that the summer ball was playing host to his only reasonable prospects. Unless, of course, he decided to venture further afield and dip a toe into the waters of Mereport society, or that of Kir-Lu, or...

He next danced with Fontessa Harylebone (tall, angular, decisive), then Kenrin Vowfax (attempting a moustache before his lip was properly ready for it), and then Lurita hi za Chaview (probably capable of breaking Arkony's neck with one arm, but nervous in her steps to the point that he had to guide her back on course more than once, not without some difficulty). After that he found himself at least partially coincidentally next to Thirelda Goodweil again, and they danced again. She *was* pretty, and she danced well, and she also knew the other dance steps of manners and politics that the children of noble families had drummed into them, but she didn't fully agree with them. They were both smiling when they parted this time, and Arkony began to wonder whether this ball was quite as bad as he'd expected it to be.

Then, after a rest and two more dances, the musicians did not strike up again. Instead, Arkony's parents stepped out in front of the stage.

They went through the usual preamble; thanking everyone for coming (as if they had a choice, if they wished to remain relevant), hoping they enjoyed the food (as if the Grike family themselves had done more than nod through the menu suggestions of Samil, the head cook), and hoping everyone was having a good time (by which they meant had been suitably impressed). Then they got to the part that Arkony had been expecting. Not quite dreading, but definitely expecting with a certain amount of apprehension.

'Now, we would like our son to come forward,' his mother

Scintilla declared, stretching her hand out to him. Arkony made his way towards them as calmly as he could, his steps sounding loud on the wooden floor. This was inevitable, the ball being centred around his birthday as it was, but how this next part played out was anyone's guess. He had his hopes, but he also had his fears.

More flowery words. Talking about his birthday, as though anyone there was not aware of it. Vaguely hopeful statements about what a wonderful young man he had grown into, which was half emotional blackmail aimed at him to avoid disappointing his parents, and half carefully calculated sales pitch for the other parents in the room in possession of similarly aged heirs who were as yet unmarried.

'And so,' his mother concluded, 'we would like to present Arkony with his birthday gift.'

Here it came. Arkony had not been asked what he wanted. Marquin had been absent for a few weeks earlier in the year, which might have been entirely unrelated, but then again, might not have been. He never did talk about his business, unless Lord Draymere expressly involved Arkony in the conversation.

Arkony's father reached into his jacket pocket and removed a case small enough to fit into his hand. It was about the right size for a ring, but it seemed unlikely Arkony was going to be gifted his own signet, given that the Grike seal remained the purview of his parents.

'Happy birthday, son,' Draymere Grike said, handing him the box.

Arkony took it, and opened it.

It was a rough-shaped lump of colourless... something. Arkony frowned and picked it up between thumb and forefinger. Was it a gem of some sort? If so, it was uncommonly plain. Where was the sparkle? Where was the lustre?

Then it began to glow – not just reflecting light, but an actual warm, honey-coloured glow from within the thing itself. The crowd made slight noises of appreciation, and Arkony looked at his parents in wonder.

'What is it?'

Draymere snorted. 'It's a destiny, of course.'

Arkony jumped as if stung. What a fool he'd been! What else could it be, when Lord and Lady Derringsdale were framing it as an appropriately extravagant present for their only child, whose birthday was being publicly celebrated in front of everyone in their own home? Destinies cost money, and big destinies, the ones that the rich and powerful considered worth having, cost the sort of money that would make even the rich and powerful wince. Otherwise, what would be the point?

He knew what he was supposed to do. His face was supposed to light up in delight, he was supposed to thank his parents profusely, he was supposed to play his part and pretend that this was all for his benefit. And it was partly for his benefit, he had no doubt of that: his parents loved and cared for him, at least in their own way, and they wanted the best for him. One problem was that their view of what was best for Arkony was not always the same as Arkony's view of what was best for him.

The other problem was that they had given him this present here, now, in front of everyone, to drive it home into everyone's minds how good a match he was. He was going to have a grand destiny, as well as being the heir to the Grike estate and fortune. Not just a rumour, not hearsay, but in a way that everyone would witness. Could there be a better match for any eligible young noble than Arkony Grike?

He hastily replaced the destiny in the case. 'I told you,' he said firmly, staring at his parents, 'I want to make my own destiny.'

'Arkony,' his father said. There was no hint that any other words were going to follow. It was a one-word statement, and the ever-efficient Draymere Grike was able to weight it with at least a couple of sentences of meaning.

'Whatever do you mean, dear?' his mother said softly, with

the diamond-tipped smile of someone determined to flatten all obstacles to her desired outcome through sheer force of will, and stubborn refusal to acknowledge that anyone could want anything different.

'I want,' Arkony said, slightly louder, 'to make my *own* destiny. I want anything I achieve to be because *I* did it!'

The hall was quiet. Probably not quiet enough to hear exactly what he was saying, but the sense of awkwardness was palpable. It was already abundantly clear to everyone in the room that things were not going as expected, and Arkony found that emboldening. It was already too late to smile and thank his parents for this gift he didn't want and had never wanted. The social damage had been done.

'Arkony,' his mother said again, even more softly. 'Look.'

He looked down. The destiny…

…had crumbled.

Aghast, he looked at his own fingers. Had he been too forceful when he put it back? Had he unconsciously accepted the destiny anyway? But he hadn't wanted it! He'd never wanted it! And yet the destiny was dissolving into finer and finer powder, as though being blown away by an invisible wind, and now Arkony's hand was tingling, and the sensation was starting to move up his arm…

'What have you done to me?!' he demanded, throwing down the case and rounding on his parents.

'We're giving you greatness, boy,' Draymere said, and he wasn't shouting, but he wasn't keeping his voice low now, either. 'Greatness on a plate!'

'Then that doesn't say much about your opinion of my ability to achieve it on my own!' Arkony snapped. He could have stopped there; he should have stopped there. 'And it doesn't say much about *this family* that you think money is the only way it can help me get there!'

His father's face darkened into proper anger, while the flush of embarrassment that had been threatening Scintilla's cheeks was headed off at the pass by the white of genuine fury, but Arkony was beyond caring. He held up his hand. The tingling had reached his bicep now, this imposter future displacing the one he'd intended to forge for himself.

'Make it stop!'

'We can't,' his mother said, clearly unable to comprehend why he would even ask that.

'Then I think it's time I got some air,' he said, to the world in general, and turned away. He headed for his family's private entrance to the ballroom, and shut the door behind him just as the hubbub of shocked and scandalised conversation sprang up.

The drawing room was large, but it felt enclosed and stuffy. Arkony passed through it at a pace so brisk it could barely be called a walk, barrelled out into the corridor beyond, and almost collided with someone.

'I'm so—' Arkony began, then realised that although dressed in a nondescript fashion, the person to whom he was speaking was not wearing proper Grike livery. Nor was she any of the servants he knew. She was probably about his age – allowing for the somewhat weatherbeaten look and tanned skin of a person who spent most of her time outdoors – with a smattering of freckles and a jawline that looked as though it could win an argument on its own. Was she additional hired help, brought in for the ball? But then why did she look so familiar?

'You!' he exclaimed, as recognition hit him a split second later. One of the young women from the day before! She'd hidden her hair under a cap, but there could be no mistake. All of Marquin's words flooded back to him, and he panicked. What sort of pain had the factor been talking about? He didn't have his sword with him. Where was the nearest sword?

'Have you been given a destiny?' the girl demanded, staring straight at him.

'What do you—'

'Your life might be in danger; have you been given a

destiny?' she snapped, cutting him off in a manner sharp enough to be his father. She seemed genuine, and worried.

'Yes,' he said. There seemed no point in denying it. All the local nobles had just seen him take it, for crying out loud. The tingle of it passed across his chest, causing him to shudder. 'Who are you?'

'Oh bollocks,' the mystery visitor said, appearing to deflate from one kind of tension into another, then gathering herself. 'Listen, I know this seems weird, but I can explain.'

'Please do,' Arkony said, as the tingle rose up his neck and reached his jaw.

The girl opened her mouth, just as the drawing room door opened again.

'Master Arkony?' Marquin said, his tone one of concern mixed with disappointment, not that he paid attention to Arkony for more than a second. When his eyes landed on the young woman he'd had forcibly ejected from the house the day before, his eyebrows shot up towards his hairline.

'You!'

'Will people stop saying that?' the girl demanded, but her indignation was cut off as Marquin lurched across the gap separating them with a speed Arkony had never witnessed from him before, and grabbed the intruder by the front of her shirt.

'What have you said to him?' the old factor snarled, pressing her up against the wall with surprising strength. The girl was clearly startled too, but she was obviously in no mood to answer his question and grabbed at his wrists to try to prise his hands loose.

Arkony hovered, torn by uncertainty: Marquin's reaction was violent and apparently disproportionate, and Arkony's instinct was to haul him off and apologise for his conduct. On the other hand, the girl *had* clearly snuck into a house where not only she shouldn't have been, but from which she had already been forcibly removed once, and Marquin's entire life revolved around keeping Arkony's family safe. Shouldn't he be trusting the factor's judgement here?

Then the drawing room door opened *again*.

'Arkony!' Draymere Grike thundered, stepping through with Scintilla on his heels. He paused mid-stride as he took in the scene, then shot Arkony a glare, but it was placeholder anger, designed to keep his son where he was so he could be dealt with once this new problem was resolved. 'Marquin! What is going on here?'

Marquin did not reply.

This was unheard of. Arkony had never known Marquin to be hesitant. He always had an immediate and ready answer for any question from a member of the family. Now, however, the factor stood looking at his lord with his mouth open like a freshly landed fish. It was an unexpected opportunity, and Arkony took a breath to leap into it, but the intruder got there first.

'My name's Kitt Carver, and I'm a diviner from Mereport!' she said hurriedly, still grappling with Marquin's hands. 'I'm the one who found the destiny this guy bought from Mazen Rauk at Destiny Calling!'

Marquin released her and staggered backwards, his face a picture of shock. 'You… You are?'

'About a week ago, someone tried to kill me,' Kitt Carver said, ticking off fingers. 'They were also going to kill the guy they paid to find out from me who I sold that particular destiny to, and they *did* kill Mazen Rauk, and burned his shop and his records. I figured they probably didn't have good intentions towards whoever had that destiny, and I was pretty pissed off they tried to kill me, so we came over the high moors to get here first and warn you. Him,' she corrected herself, pointing at Arkony. 'Eh, you get the point.'

'Marquin?' Draymere said, his tone flat and stern.

'My lord, I cannot believe Mr Rauk would betray the confidence of his buyers,' Marquin said, glaring at Carver. 'I suspect *she* is the one at fault for his death!'

'Oi!' Carver snapped, pointing a threatening finger at him. 'I *liked* Mazen! Fine, he said you like chamomile tea! And also you bought another big destiny from him, something like twenty years ago.'

Arkony frowned. He'd not heard anything about this other destiny, and he fully expected his parents and Marquin to call her on this falsehood. However, each of them looked like they'd been poleaxed. There was clearly something going on here of which he was thoroughly ignorant, and Arkony Grike found that he'd had enough of ignorance.

'Marquin knows her,' he said into the shocked silence. The tingle had reached the top of his head and subsided now, but it hadn't left him feeling any different. He was still furious, for one thing. 'She came to the house yesterday with three others, and Marquin summoned the stonewardens to remove them. Then told me not to say anything about it,' he added deliberately, as Marquin's eyes flickered towards him in horror. 'He said that only pain could come from them being allowed into the house.'

'I don't know anything about that,' Carver said hastily. 'The pain part, that is. We did come here yesterday, and I have *no* idea why your man here was that jumpy, I've never seen him before but he definitely didn't like me, and then he grabbed me just now—'

'You disguised yourself to sneak into this house!' Marquin snapped.

'Yeah, fair, but then you started yelling at me about whether I'd told him anything, and—'

'Marquin!' Arkony's mother said, loudly and clearly. 'Do you know this gel? If so, how?'

Marquin swallowed. 'My lord, my lady, perhaps we can remove the intruder first?'

'No,' Scintilla said, narrowing her eyes. 'No, I think her presence may be crucial to this conversation. Draymere, she has your jawline.'

'I never took nothing,' Carver replied instantly.

'I mean you resemble him, you silly gel!' Arkony's mother said exasperatedly. 'Marquin, is this what you were concealing?' She turned to look at Arkony's father, hands on her hips. 'Is she some by-blow you've been hiding from me all these years?'

'You say that to *me*?' Draymere Grike retorted angrily. 'Look at her nose! Look at her ears! You could match them up to any painting from your side of the family!'

'Draymere, the gel can't be any older than Arkony,' Scintilla scoffed. 'Are you suggesting that I somehow hid a pregnancy from you, for nine months, under the same roof?' She pointed at Carver, who looked over at Arkony and mouthed *what the fuck is going on?*

I don't know, Arkony mouthed back, but his parents weren't finished yet.

'She looks more like you than Arkony does!' Draymere shouted.

'Well, she looks more like *you* than Arkony does!' his mother insisted, drawing herself up to her full height. They stared at each other for a moment, the air between them nearly flickering from the intensity of their glares.

Then, as though turned by the same kyn-made mechanism, they both swivelled slowly on the spot.

'*Marquin. Explain.*'

TWENTY-NINE

Kitt hadn't really known what to expect from sneaking into a grand house like Derring Hall, but to her simultaneous relief and irritation, Donal had turned out to be more or less correct: when places were incredibly busy, if you looked like you belonged and knew what you were doing then most people were too concerned with their own business to be bothered to challenge you. Kitt had left him on lookout and to make sure their escape route was as secure as it could be while she made her way into the family's private areas. She'd hoped against hope that she might encounter the young man she'd seen on the landing the day before, since he seemed the most likely recipient of the destiny that was causing all this trouble, and for just one moment she'd thought that luck was on her side.

Now she didn't have the faintest idea what was going on, other than her physical features were being pointed out like a beast at market, but she knew she didn't like the sound of things in the slightest. The only upsides of this very confusing conversation were firstly that she hadn't yet been stabbed or thrown out, and secondly that Marquin, the man who'd called the stonewardens on her and had also just grabbed her, had been figuratively pinned to the floor by all the displeasure that could be brought to bear by two toffs in search of answers.

'Out with it!' Lord Draymere snapped, and the old factor finally folded.

'Very well, my lord.' He straightened and looked between them all with what seemed to Kitt to be a particularly long pause at Arkony. 'Although do not blame me if none of you find the tale to your liking.

'After the birth of the Grike family's heir, I was sent to Mereport to purchase a grand destiny. My instructions were that it had to come from Mazen Rauk's boutique, since his was the premier destination at the time, and to return in time for the autumn ball. A summer storm delayed my departure from Solmouth by more than a week, since it wrecked the ship upon which I should have embarked. The replacement, when I found one, was significantly slower, and I arrived in Mereport greatly behind schedule only to discover that Rauk had only one grand destiny in stock. Its power was unquestionable, but he had not yet had it soothsayered to determine its nature. With very limited time, and given that the unsoothed nature lowered its price, I made the decision to purchase so I could fulfil my instructions.

'The journey back to Derringsmoot was similarly slower than intended, and upon my return I arranged for a soothsayer to inspect the destiny. The soothsaying was done in the nursery, with the soothsayer, myself, and the lord and lady standing around the crib.'

'We know all this,' Scintilla Grike snapped. 'How do you know the gel? That is the question we asked!'

'Forgive me, my lady, but I am providing context for those who were not there,' Marquin said, glancing between Arkony and Kitt. 'These things are relevant, I assure you.' He cleared his throat and continued his story, although it looked to Kitt as though a great weight was bowing his head further and further as he did so.

'The soothsayer touched the destiny to read its nature, and screamed. He dropped it, in fact, and began clawing at his own eyes.'

'Wow,' Kitt said, unable to stop herself. 'I've never heard of a soothy reacting like that, and believe me, I know some characters.' She became aware that three pairs of aristocratic eyes were now glaring at her, and she shut her mouth again. 'Sorry. Pretend I'm not here.'

'I *tried* to,' Marquin muttered venomously, then sighed. 'By the time the soothsayer had been… removed… and the safety of the lord, the lady, and the child were assured, we realised that we did not know exactly what had happened to the destiny. It was only then we realised that the accursed soothsayer had dropped the damned thing into the crib, and onto the child.'

'Oh, yikes,' Kitt said, biting her lip. 'Onto a baby? They've got no self-control, that'll just go straight in as soon as it makes contact with the skin! Why would you put a destiny in the same room as a baby? That's… sorry, shutting up now.'

'As you have so accurately deduced,' Marquin said, with a frustrated look in her direction, 'the terrible destiny infected the child. The lord and lady were beside themselves. I was given the strictest instructions to take the child to Mereport, the centre of the destiny trade, and find a way to remove the destiny.'

'Good luck,' Kitt snorted. 'There's no way to remove a destiny once it's taken hold, everyone in the business knows that. The best you can do is overlay it with another one, and even then it has to be much more powerful, *and* you need to be careful in case they interact—' She caught sight of Arkony's face, which was a picture of devastation with highlights of anger. 'Sorry. That was thoughtless of me.'

'Marquin *did* find a way to have it removed,' Scintilla Grike said, every word razor-edged. 'Mind your tongue, gel. You may be a diviner, but you don't know everything.'

Kitt didn't bother to hide her disdain. 'Yeah, whatever. I don't know everything, but I know destinies, that's literally my job.'

Marquin took a deep breath. 'There was no cure to be found.'

Kitt pointed triumphantly. 'See? Told you!'

'I could not return with a child cursed with an unknown destiny so bad that it had made a soothsayer literally claw his own eyes out. I would not only have failed to get the child cured, I would be bringing a plague back into the house of the family I had sworn to serve,' Marquin said, every word dropping from his lips like lead. He turned towards her. 'Nor could I overlay it with another. Destinies even more powerful were few and far between in the world, beyond the means of all but the richest. The family were counting on me, so I did the only thing I could think of.

'I found a poor Mereport family with a baby of similar age and appearance, already with one young child and struggling to make ends meet, and bribed them to swap children. Then I returned with a child who was an imposter, true, but who was not cursed with anything other than common blood. You were supposed to live out whatever days were allotted you none the wiser, and far from here. Fate, it seems, has a grim sense of humour.'

Kitt stared at him. Words flashed in her brain, jostling for position: denials, abuse, questions. She eventually settled on:

'You fucking *what?*'

Then:

'Hang on, he's a *guy!*' She pointed at Arkony, then at his speechless parents. 'Are you telling me they wouldn't notice the difference?'

Marquin smiled at her, thin and bloodless. 'Actually, Master Arkony was presumed to be a girl when he was younger. He informed the family of this misconception around the time of his eighth birthday, whereupon we engaged the services of a mage in order to ensure that he could develop as he wished.'

Kitt looked at Arkony, who gave a slight forward twitch of his head to acknowledge the truth of the factor's words. There was something there, something in his face that was bothering her, even more than every ridiculous, far-fetched thing that Marquin had come out with…

It clicked into place with a suddenness was as startling as it was unpleasant.

'Oh *shit*,' she said, as the bottom dropped out of her stomach, leaving only a hollow void. 'You look like Annity. My sibling. That's why I thought you were familiar.'

'Marquin!' Arkony's father thundered. No, not Arkony's father. Arkony didn't really resemble him, once you knew what to look for.

In terms of the nasty business of flesh and blood, Draymere Grike was *Kitt's* father.

'What is the meaning of this?' Draymere bellowed. 'Is this how you claim to serve our family?'

'Yes, my lord!' Marquin stuck out a finger to point at Kitt, despite facing his lord down. '*That* child would have brought ruin upon your house. A curse that bad could mean nothing else! Had you been blessed with a second child then perhaps I could have revealed my deception, but if you thought Arkony was your issue, and *he* thought he was your issue, and everyone else thought he was your issue, then at least the Grike family name would remain intact!'

'You had no right to keep this from us!' Scintilla shouted, but Marquin turned and faced her down as well.

'I had every right, my lady! The duty of a factor is to make the difficult decisions to protect the household, and save their lord and lady from dirtying their hands!'

Kitt was only half listening. In fact, she was leaning against the wall for support. Suddenly, things dropped into place. Nana Carver couldn't have known, surely? Not actually *known*. But the crafty old bird must have at least subconsciously realised that something was up, given the amount of times she'd joked that Kitt was too smart, or too brave, or too pretty to be her son's daughter, and why Kitt's dad could never laugh the comments off. And then there was how her parents had managed to move out of the poorholes not long after she was born and get a place in Duke's End, which wasn't exactly fancy, but was a damned sight better. They didn't like to talk about it and just made guarded comments about 'coming into some money' whenever any of their friends or family who'd been around at the time mentioned it. No one pried too closely, not even Nana Carver, despite her fondness for secrets. If someone found a way out of the poorholes, you were glad for them and left it at that.

'This wasn't a "difficult decision"!' Scintilla was half-screaming. 'You decided to *get rid of our child!*'

'Yeah?' Kitt shouted, as an explosion of roiling anger erupted in her stomach and instantly filled the void there. She pushed away from the wall. 'Stow it! If you'd bothered to go with him instead of sending him to do it himself, it wouldn't have happened! If you'd noticed that he came back *with a different kid*, you'd have found out then and there!'

'I…' Draymere Grike began angrily, then faltered. His face folded in on itself as he tried to reconcile his first impression of her as a suspicious intruder, and therefore absolutely fine to be shouted at, with the realisation that she was, in all probability, his daughter. 'Listen—'

'No!' Kitt shouted. She was the daughter of *toffs?* And not just toffs, but toffs that hadn't even cared about her enough to check whether their factor brought the same child back? The rage swelling inside her boiled up and outwards, extending her arm to point a quivering finger at his face. 'Fuck you.' She pointed at Scintilla. 'Fuck *you.*' She pointed at Marquin. '*Definitely* fuck you.' She flapped a hand awkwardly at Arkony. 'Sorry? *Bye!*'

Kitt ran for it.

THIRTY

'WAIT!' SOMEONE SHOUTED from behind her.

Kitt didn't, on the basis that once you've started running away from the people whose house you've snuck into, you probably shouldn't stop. Her mind was whirling like a drunken ballerina. Her mum and dad – as in, Farren and Lavine Carver – *sold* their child?! How could they? But they also took *her* in, and Kitt couldn't say that they'd treated her badly. They'd treated her differently to Annity, but she and Annity were different people, and she'd never felt that they'd loved Annity more; at least, not apart from the occasional way that all siblings probably felt at some point.

Selling a child was generally agreed to be a bad thing, but what about... swapping a child? Swapping a child for money? Money you could then use to improve your life, and that of the child you already had? Not to mention the person offering the money didn't seem to want *their* child, so that kid probably wasn't going to benefit from staying where they were...

It was confusing, and Kitt didn't know what to think about any of it. She felt she should hate Farren and Lavine for not telling her she was adopted, but given no one else knew either, that was sort of understandable (wait, Annity couldn't have known, could they? No, they were awful with secrets, and it would have come out when they'd argued as children. There were only two years between them, so Annity probably never noticed that their baby sister looked a little different one day). And Kitt certainly felt she *should* hate Draymere and Scintilla, but they hadn't been callous, they'd just been… careless. Besides, they were strangers, so Kitt didn't care about them enough to hate them, plus they were toffs, which meant she already had an underlying dislike for them anyway.

Somehow, all of this was freewheeling around her head while her body was focused on the more immediate aspects of keeping her upright, moving forward, and not colliding with anything inconvenient like walls or tables, which probably confirmed Kitt's theory that her body did some of its best work while her mind was elsewhere entirely. However, her headlong flight came to a clattering halt when she tried to burst through the door that led back out into the house's more public areas, and hit something on the other side.

'Shit!' Kitt yelped, as the door rebounded into her shoulder and knee hard enough to leave bruises, but not hard enough to fully stop her momentum. She tumbled through the doorway headfirst and landed face down on the carpet, then looked up to see what she'd hit.

Which, predictably, was Donal Klae.

'*Ow!*' he said, rubbing the back of his head and glaring at her. 'What the hell was that?'

'You were supposed to be *watching* my way out, not leaning against it!' Kitt snapped, pushing herself up.

'Why are we running?' Donal stretched out his free hand to her. 'Did you mess it up?'

'Oh, things are definitely messed up, but this time there's no way it's my fault,' Kitt said. She slapped his hand away irritably, just as the door cannoned open again. Donal howled and curled up around his hand as the wood smashed into his knuckles, and Kitt stumbled hastily backwards to avoid being run into by Arkony Grike.

'I said *wait!*' he puffed.

'Why?' Kitt asked, backing away from him and down the hallway. 'I don't think it's a good idea for me to stay here.'

'Yes, I feel the same way,' Arkony agreed, looking back over his shoulder.

'Right,' Kitt said, irritated. 'So, let me—' She broke off as his meaning dawned on her. 'Wait, you mean *you?*'

'Yes!' Arkony closed the door and leant against it. 'I'd just publicly humiliated my parents by being angry that they gave me a destiny without my consent, and now they've found out I'm not actually their son! This is not a conversation I intend to continue in person!'

'He can't come with us,' Donal said, cradling his hand and glaring at Arkony.

Kitt narrowed her eyes, thinking. 'If they send the stonewardens after us, can you call them off?'

'Yes,' Arkony replied instantly. 'They have to obey all members of the family. If they get conflicting instructions, they just don't do anything.'

Kitt grabbed his arm. 'He's coming with us.'

Getting out of a stately home's grounds was considerably easier than getting into them, particularly when accompanied by the heir. Arkony led them in a quick sprint through bloodrose gardens, cut left through a yewery, and led them to a small but very sturdy-looking gate in the west wall.

'I hope you brought a key,' Donal said as they pulled up in front of it. There were shouts behind them now. Kitt had no idea whether that signified a pursuit, but she didn't want to hang around and find out.

'It's a family lock,' Arkony said, approaching the gate with his hand outstretched. 'Magic attuned to the Grikes.'

'I thought you weren't their son?' Donal said dubiously.

'Family isn't just blood.' Arkony laid his hand on the

handle. Something *clicked* inside, and he hauled the gate open and ushered Kitt and Donal through. 'Come on.'

Kitt paused for a moment and reached out her hand as Arkony pulled the gate shut behind them, but then she thought better of it. There were some questions to which she did not really need the answer, no matter what that answer was.

'Great, what now?' Donal asked, pulling his hat off and running his fingers through his hair. 'We're on the run with the heir to the manor, who's incidentally wearing a suit that probably cost more than I make in a year? We're not exactly going to be inconspicuous!'

Kitt really hated it when Donal had a point, which he somehow managed with annoying regularity. 'How well-known are you in the town?' she asked Arkony.

'Reasonably,' he admitted, looking slightly shamefaced. 'At least, around the more salubrious parts.'

Kitt raised an eyebrow. 'Around the what?'

Arkony coughed in embarrassment. 'Uh, "nice".'

'Don't mind her,' Donal cut in with a grin, 'she's from Mereport. They don't have *anywhere* salubrious.'

Kitt shot him a glare, but their hasty escape would be for nothing if they were caught arguing in the street, so she grabbed both men and propelled them forwards. 'Come on. I'm sure we can find an appropriately lowbrow place where no one will know who you are.'

'Although they might knife you for your jacket,' Donal said nastily.

'Shut *up*, Donal.'

'LET ME GET this straight,' Derna said in a low voice, as they huddled together over their beers in the corner of the Wooden Heron. 'You, Kitt Carver, are actually the child of nobility?'

'Sure,' Sulian said, pointing a wobbly finger with an even more wobbly smile and one half-closed eye. 'Can't you see it in her face?' She huffed a laugh that ended in a snort, ignoring the looks the rest of them gave her. Kitt wasn't sure if it had been particularly insistent futures or just the tension of waiting that the Swallowmage had been numbing with alcohol while Kitt infiltrated Derring Hall, but whichever it was, Sulian was well on her way to losing fights with both gravity and somnolence.

'And *you*,' Derna continued, looking at Arkony, 'are Farren and Lavine's kid?'

'Apparently,' Arkony said uncomfortably. 'It's not like I remember them.' He was wrapped in a cloak despite the tavern's warm interior, mainly because he wasn't the right size for any of the clothes they had to hand, being shorter than Falzine, slighter than Donal and significantly thinner than Vem, but too large for anything owned by Kitt, Derna, or Sulian. He was also sweating. Kitt didn't think it was just because he had suddenly been introduced to Two Tongue Derna, who was unlikely to be much like anyone he'd met before, but it was probably a factor.

'Well, this is wild,' Derna said, sitting back. She looked around the table. 'What now? I was sort of assuming we'd tell the toffs, and if they believed us then they'd ensure that Bastard Man got dealt with, job's a good'un. Now we've got a new friend.'

'You've no idea what the destiny is?' Kitt asked Arkony, who shook his head miserably.

'None. I don't feel any different, I don't seem to have any compulsions to do anything new. It just feels like there's something hovering behind me which is going to grab me at *some* point, and I'm stuck here waiting for it.'

'Is that our problem, though?' Falzine asked, his voice still a bit raspy since the parched one had grabbed him by the throat. Arkony had done very well not to ask questions about Falzine's permanently shadowed visage, but Kitt could feel and understand his uneasiness. It was truly disconcerting to meet someone on whom light never had the same effect as anyone else, and Kitt felt that it was a testament to the elasticity of her brain that she'd somehow got used to it.

'Kitt, you came here to stop this guy from killing someone,' Falzine continued, after taking a long swig of his drink, 'and it looks like you've done that. Arkony knows the danger now. I think we can all be proud, and we should go home. If you're planning on taking it further, and actually trying to cause problems for this man with big resources who has no problem with killing people…' He took another mouthful of his drink, and grimaced. 'Well, I think I'm going to wish you the best of luck, and leave you to it.'

That was probably the most words Kitt had ever heard out of Falzine Halfshade at once, and she felt it was something of a shame that they arrived in the form of withdrawing his support. However, she could understand it. Falzine hadn't been stabbed by Bastard Man's thugs, nor seen Mazen Rauk and his guard lying there with their throats cut while their shop burned.

'You're drinking a lot,' Derna commented.

'It's hot,' Falzine said without looking at her. 'And I'm thirsty.' He took another mouthful.

'You're all asking the wrong questions,' the Swallowmage slurred. Kitt sighed, and nudged her in a vain attempt to get her to sit vaguely upright.

'What's the right one, then?' she asked wearily.

Sulian focused on her at the second attempt, and waved a finger somewhere off to her right. '*Why* was Kitt Carver caught up in the scrying?'

Kitt snorted. 'Because I found the destiny.'

The Swallowmage tried to tap her nose, but missed. 'That's what we thought. But that was before we knew that *you* have one, and before we knew that *you* are actually a Grike, at least in some sense.' She spread her hands, nearly knocking her drink over as she did so. 'Scrying's like a net, right? You throw it out, and you try to find things relating to what you're after, but it doesn't tell you *how* they're related. You gotta put the pieces together yourself. So if it's the destiny that you *found* that's going to be the problem for these people, for whatever reason, why didn't the scrying just bring up who's going to get it? Why did they even need to find out what the biggest destiny you sold was, and who you sold it to, and then who *Mazen* sold it to?'

'Because they would never assume a diviner was important enough to be the focus in her own right,' Arkony said slowly, then raised a hand hastily when Kitt looked at him. 'No offence, that's just… how my family would think, if they were the ones doing this.'

'Exactly!' Sulian cackled at him, causing him to jerk backwards. 'I knew something didn't add up, but I couldn't put my finger on it!'

'Oh, and you're suddenly seeing clearly now?' Derna demanded, poking the Swallowmage's tankard meaningfully.

'Look,' Sulian said, rounding on her, 'I'm perfectly capable of functioning when drunk. I healed *her* when I was drunk!'

Arkony leaned closer to Kitt in a sort of horrified awe. 'You let her heal you when she was *drunk?*'

'It was that or bleed to death,' Kitt muttered. 'Neither were my first choice, believe me.'

'Okay, let's say we go with this,' Donal said, over the burgeoning quarrel taking place beside him. 'Let's say we assume that actually, Kitt is the focus of all this that's going on, and the people who tried to kill us—'

'They never got to you, thanks to us,' Derna interrupted him smugly.

'Fine, the people who tried to kill *Kitt* just haven't realised her importance yet,' Donal continued, glaring at Derna. 'What do we do about it?'

'We need to find out what destiny Kitt got when she was a baby, I guess?' Vem said.

'Shouldn't that be easy?' Arkony asked. Kitt shook her head grimly.

'No. Soothsaying a raw destiny is fairly easy for those

that have the gift for it, but it's very hard to make out once a destiny's in a person.'

'So if the destiny wasn't known when the soothsayer dropped it on you, how do we find that out?' Derna asked. 'Has Kitt got to go back to the mansion and ask nicely if anyone thought to get that information from the soothsayer before they kicked him out of the door?'

'They wouldn't have kicked him out of the door,' Arkony said sadly. 'I heard the way Marquin said *removed*. They couldn't afford to let him live, having seen that. He could have ruined the family. I doubt he made it out of the house alive.'

They all stared glumly into their drinks for a few seconds – or at least, five of them did. Falzine appeared to have already decided that it was just a matter of time until the rest of them concluded that he was right in wanting to be shot of the whole business and return to Mereport, while Sulian was slumping sideways onto Kitt's shoulder and starting to breathe heavily.

'You know,' Donal began.

Kitt shut her eyes. 'No. Absolutely not.'

'I'm just saying—'

'*No.*'

'I'm a diviner,' Donal persisted. 'You're a diviner. We can probably find the right grave between us, even if it's an unmarked one.'

Kitt growled, but damn it all, he wasn't necessarily wrong. And if she had a curse hanging around her neck, a curse so foul it made a man claw his own eyes out when he witnessed it… Well, deep down, she wanted to know what it was. It was almost irresponsible *not* to find out. At least if she knew it, she might be able to mitigate it somehow, find a way to keep the impact on those she loved to a minimum, even if she couldn't do the same for herself.

'Is he suggesting… necromancy?' Arkony asked weakly.

'Yeah,' Kitt said with a sigh. 'Welcome to the fuckery.'

THIRTY-ONE

'Right,' Donal said, smoothing down the front of his tunic in the light of the setting sun. 'I've got my moonstrikers, I've been meditating all day, and I've been drinking a herbal tea my mother said works excellently for concentration.' He smiled at Kitt. 'We are going to *find* this grave!'

Derna nudged Kitt. 'Do you want to tell him, or shall I?'

Donal frowned. 'Tell me what?'

Kitt sighed. 'We know where the soothsayer's buried.' She tried not to notice Derna smirking beside her, but the woman smirked so *loudly.* You could hear Derna's smirk across a pitch-black room with your eyes shut. Also, Kitt's body had apparently decided that the correct response to a simple nudge from her was excited gooseflesh, which was faintly mortifying.

Donal was doing his best to ignore Derna, mainly by focusing solely on Kitt. 'How? Did you go divining without me? I said I was going to help!'

Kitt snorted. Sometimes, people forgot that divination was what you turned to when you had no other way of finding something.

'I asked.'

The soothsayer, it turned out, had been called Lerry Third-Eye, although Kitt would have been very surprised if that was what his mother had named him. Nonetheless, he had been a person of some note in the local Guild of Omens, which covered soothsayers, fortune-tellers, and others whose individual flavour of magic allowed them some kind of precognition; notable enough that when Kitt had gone in asking about a leading local soothsayer (since the Grikes would only have approached the best) who'd died or disappeared suddenly about twenty years before, it hadn't taken long before someone knew who she was talking about.

'Terrible thing, or so I heard,' the young woman at the front desk said to her earnestly. 'He'd been asked to go up to the Grikes at Derring Hall, but the poor chap never made it. Got jumped by footpads as he was going across town. Must've been some sort of vendetta against him. They clawed his eyes out, and snapped his neck clean as a whistle!'

Kitt swallowed, thinking of big, stone fingers closing around the head of a blinded soothsayer in the halls of the Grike's home, and *twisting*. It wouldn't have taken much for Marquin to move the body and leave it in an alley somewhere, and not much more to ensure that any investigation into the death came back with the answer that the family wanted. Such were the benefits of wealth.

'He's buried in Edrik's Field, the main graveyard,' Arkony said. He was fidgeting in the new clothes they'd procured for him, with his hair – so similar to Annity's, now Kitt knew what she was looking at, just with less full-on ginger colouring to it – tucked away under the cap that Kitt herself had worn the previous night.

'What's the matter with you?' Donal asked scornfully. 'Are the garments not up to m'lord's usual standards of comfort?'

'Well… no,' Arkony admitted. 'The shirt's all scratchy.'

He hadn't said anything, but Kitt guessed from his surprise when Vem came back from the tailor that these were the first clothes Arkony had worn for which he had not been measured first. They were decent enough, but they were items the tailor had already made, ready for whoever was roughly the right size and wanted them. Arkony looked slightly swamped by them, and it heightened his youthful looks.

'Hey,' Kitt said sharply to Donal. 'Stop being mean to my step-brother!'

There was a moment's confused silence.

'Your *step-brother?*' Donal repeated, looking between the two of them.

'I guess?' Kitt replied, shrugging. 'He's the son of the people who raised me, and he's Annity's brother, so what else would you call it?'

'I… Well, I suppose that makes sense,' Donal said after a second. 'Fine. I'm sorry if I've been harsh,' he added to Arkony. 'I'll go and get Sulian, make sure she's ready.' He left the taproom, heading upstairs to the Swallowmage's room.

'Got to be honest, I'm not sure how I feel about being the son of people who sold me,' Arkony admitted quietly to Kitt.

'I can understand that,' Kitt said. 'Not sure how I feel about any of this, to be honest. At least Donal might stop being an arse to you.'

'Well yeah, you've called Arkony your brother,' Derna chuckled. 'Donal doesn't think he's a threat now.'

'A *threat?*' Kitt looked at her, then groaned. 'You don't think—'

'—that Donal thought you'd agreed to let Arkony hang around because he's hot? Yeah, reckon so,' Derna said, ignoring the flush that was creeping into Arkony's cheeks.

'How could *I* think he's hot?' Kitt protested. 'No offence, Arkony, but…' She pointed at Arkony's face. 'He looks like my parents, Derna! He looks like my *sibling!*'

'This is all really weird, and I would like you both to stop now, please,' Arkony said, shutting his eyes primly – which was just as well, since it meant he missed the obscene gestures

Derna was making, and the mimed vomiting that Kitt did in return.

'What the hell have I walked into?' Sulian's voice demanded, and the Swallowmage appeared at their table with Donal in tow.

Kitt exchanged an embarrassed look with Derna. 'It's probably best you don't ask.' *Hang on*, her brain interjected suddenly, *does* Derna *think Arkony's hot…?*

'Suits me,' Sulian said with a shrug. 'Well? Are we doing this, or not?'

Kitt forced her mind back onto the matter in hand. She had to admit, the Swallowmage actually looked the part for once. She didn't have the same ostentatiousness of the society mages – the sort that worked enchantments for the high and mighty, or put together teams of treasure hunters to have serious arguments about squatter's rights with dragons – but she was clean, her clothes were clean, she'd washed her hair, and she wasn't accompanied by a haze of alcohol fumes that overpowered even the background smell of the tavern. Only the tic at the corner of her left eye suggested to the outside observer that something wasn't quite right, but it was the balancing act they were going to have to risk. Sulian being overcome by rogue foretellings in the middle of a necromantic raising would spell disaster, but that was hopefully fairly unlikely to occur at that exact moment. Her attempting the ritual while off her face, on the other hand, would almost certainly mean death for everyone concerned.

'Yes,' Kitt said, fighting back the memory of Mazen's dry un-voice, and the nagging sensation deep in her gut telling her that she didn't want to hear the words of this soothsayer, that she didn't want to learn what fate had in store for her, and she should just run away, and hide, and pretend she knew nothing about a cursed destiny. 'We're doing this. Let's go.'

...

'Everyone assumes that necromancy is best done at night,' the Swallowmage said, as their little group strode through Derringsmoot's streets towards Edrik's Field. 'And they're correct. Do you know why that is?'

Kitt recognised the signs of nerves in Sulian's question, but since her own stomach was jumping around like a frog that had trodden on a nail, she was more than happy to engage with a distraction. 'Is it something to do with spirits not liking the sun?'

'Good guess, but no,' Sulian said. 'Anyone else?'

'Honestly, I want to know as little about this as possible,' Falzine Halfshade said. He and Vem were tagging along, ostensibly to provide protection and a lookout, but Kitt couldn't help but think it was mainly because they were nosy about exactly how much trouble she was in. She hoped there was concern for her mixed in as well – after all, she'd had a good working relationship with them both for a couple of years now – but she wasn't going to kid herself that it wasn't mainly to work out if they ever felt safe going up on to the moors with her again.

'I think I know.'

That voice came from a dark alley past which they were walking, and all of them turned as one and placed hands on weapons. Kitt's pulse thundered into her ears, hammering so fast she could barely count the different beats.

'Who's there?' she demanded, in a credibly steady voice. 'Show yourself!'

The shadows parted, and disgorged a bald man in a plain robe. His hands were spread as though to reassure them that he held no weapon, but Kitt knew that was little reassurance when his blades lay hidden in his forearms.

'Plainsong?'

'It is because no one is particularly comfortable with necromancy,' Plainsong said, addressing Sulian calmly and as though he didn't have half a dozen anxious people facing him down and ready to draw their weapons. 'Given that, it is better to do it at night, when there are fewer people around to see it. It has no effect on the power or quality of the spells themselves.'

Sulian huffed, and leant on Jandi. 'Alright, smartarse.'

'You must have very good hearing,' Falzine said suspiciously.

'As a matter of fact, I do,' Plainsong said agreeably. 'It is good to see you all again. I am sorry if I startled you.'

'Not wishing to sound distrusting,' Kitt said levelly, 'but would you care to share why you were waiting in an alley for us to pass by? And don't pretend you were there for any other reason, because I'm not buying it.'

Plainsong studied her for a moment, and Kitt's throat dried. There was some sort of power there, and not just whatever it was that allowed him to pull obsidian blades out of his own flesh. It wasn't power like the Swallowmage's, either. It was different, in some way Kitt didn't have the words or the experience to verbalise. Whatever it was, it was the sort of power that made you wonder if it was wise to attract its full attention.

Plainsong smiled one of his little smiles that showed no teeth. 'I hope you will not take this the wrong way, but I am really here to see *him*.' He clasped his hands at his waist, and nodded in the direction of Arkony.

'Me?' Arkony asked, taking a half-step back that put him further behind the imposing bulk of Pigtail Vem.

Kitt flexed her fingers around the hilt of her short sword. 'You never did tell us why you were coming to Derringsmoot.'

'And you never shared your intentions with me, either,' Plainsong agreed. 'There are people with whom I was formerly associated who were *very* interested in the heir to the Grike family. They are coming here now, as it happens.'

Kitt swallowed. '*Formerly* associated?'

Plainsong's eyes went flat and hard, and his voice, when it emerged from his mouth, was razor-edged. 'Indeed. They had me bound to their will, but they were not suitably dutiful with maintaining their hold over me.'

'The broken chains,' the Swallowmage said. 'On your arms. I did think those looked like shattered compulsion enchantments.' Kitt stared at her, along with the others, and Sulian glared back. 'What? It was his business, not ours, and he *had* just saved us.'

Plainsong nodded. 'You were correct.' He pulled down the neckline of his robe to show a similarly shattered chain tattoo encircling the base of his throat. 'Their control over my free will and my weapons has been broken. Sadly, some elements of my self remain constrained for now, but the longer I am free of their influence, the more likely it is that those enchantments too will degrade, and I will be my own man again.' He took a deep breath, and sighed. 'I should probably have run and hidden a long way from where I knew they would be heading, but I had to see for myself what it was about which they were so desperate that they would take me out into the world and risk releasing me from my bondage. Tell me,' he said gently, smiling at Arkony. 'Have you accepted a destiny lately?'

'Not *accepted*, as such,' Arkony said hesitantly. 'It just sort of… happened.'

'Ah.' Plainsong nodded sorrowfully. 'That is unfortunate, if predictable. No foretelling is guaranteed to be accurate, of course, but my former captors have considerable resources, and they were extremely sure of their findings.'

'And just to check,' Kitt said carefully. 'What were they planning to do with Arkony once they got here?'

'Oh, kill him, of course,' Plainsong said, as cheerfully as though he was discussing a tea party.

'And you're quite sure that they don't have control over you?' Derna asked suspiciously.

'If they did, I would not be here now,' Plainsong said. 'They would not risk me ranging so far afield. I am – I *was* – a weapon of last resort.' His smile this time was a sorrowful one. 'But now, I must do what I should have done before, and make myself scarce. No good comes from tempting fate, as I know better than most, but may fate smile on you all.' He fixed his eyes on Arkony for a moment, just before he turned back toward the alley. 'Especially you.'

'Wait!' Kitt said. Plainsong halted and looked back at her. 'Who were your captors? Who's behind this all? Who tried to kill me, who—' she pointed at Arkony, 'wants to kill *him?*'

Plainsong opened his mouth, then closed it again with a rueful expression. 'My apologies, Miss Carver. They can no longer bind my will to theirs, or my weapons into my flesh, but secrets are always the last to be released. I can give you no names or locations, and I dare not guide you to them myself in case they ensnare me again. In any case, to do so would be no favour to you. All I can advise you is to *be careful.*'

This time he was gone, without another word.

'Careful,' Derna said. 'Right. Careful. That's us.'

THIRTY-TWO

THE GRAVEYARD WAS a fairly standard design, intended to accommodate anyone whose beliefs dictated that their mortal remains were placed into the ground, with the unspoken but definite subtext that they shouldn't get up and start walking around again, thank you very much. The lock on the gates proved to be only a brief barrier to Donal, who pulled out a pair of slim tools and had it open in a matter of seconds.

'No one ever thanks you for picking a lock,' Donal remarked, as they quickly filed in past him.

'It always makes them uncomfortable about what else you might use it for,' Kitt informed him. Gods above, but she was glad she'd rented that room at the Dubious Gecko instead of taking him back to her place. He could have let himself back in and swiped anything he wanted.

Donal snorted, and swung the gate shut again. 'Oh, so *I* pick locks and that's bad, but Derna *stabs people* and everyone's just fine with that?'

'Apparently,' Derna said with a grin, and sauntered off in search of the grave.

The search would have been quicker had their party been able to use any sort of light, but the whole point of sneaking into a graveyard after dark, the Swallowmage reminded them, was so no one saw them doing things they were almost certainly not meant to be doing – especially when two of them had broken into the local lord and lady's party, and one of them was said lord and lady's runaway son. Or ex-son, or imposter son, or—

'Yeah, yeah, we get the picture,' Arkony sighed.

The resting place of Lerry Third-Eye wasn't hard to find, as such – it was sitting in plain view – it just took a while, since the cemetery was not a small place. Pigtail Vem found it, predictably enough, given he could read inscriptions from the path whereas the rest of them had to pick their way up to each marker and then try to make out the script. It was quite a nice headstone, Kitt thought, as one does when one is trying not to think too hard about what one is about to do: the edges had been carved to look like scrollwork.

'You'd have thought they'd have added something like "He didn't see this coming",' Derna said casually, as they clustered around it.

Kitt elbowed her in the ribs. 'Shut *up.*'

It occurred to her that a couple of weeks ago she would never have dared do such a thing, for fear of losing her arm. Now, however, it felt a bit like she and Derna were back to how they had been as girls, albeit with a new, tingling undercurrent located somewhere in Kitt's stomach. And sure, Derna was *weird*, and unpredictable in occasionally sharp and terminal ways, but those sharp and terminal ways seemed to be aimed at protecting Kitt rather than endangering her. Perhaps, so far as Derna was concerned, things had never changed between them. Perhaps it was only Kitt who'd assumed they had.

Sulian stomped and huffed her way to the head of the grave, Jandi thudding into the ground with every other step. She lowered herself into a sitting position, cracked her neck, and sighed. 'Alright, let's get this over with.'

'Has she done this before?' Arkony asked quietly, as the Swallowmage began to mumble.

'Once, that I know of,' Kitt whispered back. Arkony's eyebrows rose in horror.

'Only once?'

'The first time's the hardest,' Kitt said. She looked back at Sulian, who was starting to sweat. 'Probably,' she added.

The difference, of course, was twofold. With Mazen Rauk, the Swallowmage had been dealing with a spirit that had left the world of the living mere hours before. Kitt wasn't sure how time worked in the realms of the dead and was in no hurry to find out firsthand, but she sincerely hoped that it was a little less rigid than in the world of the living, or she suspected she was going to get extremely bored when she eventually ended up there. Nonetheless, there had to be *some* similarities, and Lerry Third-Eye had been severed from his mortal remains for upwards of twenty years.

In addition, Lerry's body was somewhere below the topsoil, and very probably rather more decayed than it had been, instead of present and fresh for Sulian to very carefully not lay her hands on. It might seem like a minor difference, given the Swallowmage had never actually touched Mazen either, but Kitt knew enough about magery to know that small variations could produce massively different outcomes. With a less familiar shell to connect to, and a longer time away in the first place, it was going to take more effort to bring the shade of Lerry Third-Eye back for a conversation.

'We're going to have to keep this brief and to the point,' Kitt said, trying to modulate her voice so that the others could hear her, but without disturbing Sulian's concentration.

'Are you sure you want to be the one to talk to it?' Donal asked, reaching out to lay his fingers on her forearm. 'If it's going to be too much—'

'No!' Kitt snapped, snatching her arm away. 'I mean, yes, I *am* sure I want to be the one to talk to it.'

That was a lie, but she was damned certain she didn't want anyone else to address the spirit and ask questions about the destiny that might or might not be residing in her, and at the very top of the list of the people she didn't want to be doing it was Donal Klae. She had a sudden urge to tell him to piss off and never come back, which to be honest was not the first time, but the problem was that he kept being *useful*. Lock picking, finagling entry to private parties of the nobility, even the necromancy suggestions; he was sort of awful, but highly practical. Honestly, given his face and his arms – and maybe certain other areas of his anatomy – and the ways in which he'd repeatedly helped out, Kitt might well have already forgiven him for making a bad call when in need of some money, had he not also repeatedly just been a bit of a creep. That perhaps said something about her that she needed to consider more closely, but—

Pale blue light crackled and sparked over the Swallowmage's hands, casting sudden and strange shadows across all of their faces, then Sulian plunged her fingers into the grass.

For a moment, nothing happened. Kitt sat there with the rest of them, every muscle tense as she waited for the Swallowmage's signal. Then something changed, and Kitt had the distinct feeling that something was *beneath* her. A presence, a spirit; call it what you will, it was down there in the dirt, sharing space with the worms.

'Who'zat?'

The voice was hoarse, and slurred as though with sleep or drink. It sounded like the man at the end of the bar in a tavern, giving his opinions on the trouble with kids today, or foreigners, or what are they going to do about this bloody weather, I'd like to know? The sort of man who spoke as he saw, and couldn't understand how anyone could take offence to the *truth*, unless it was someone else's truth with which he didn't agree, in which case the speaker needed to learn about *respect*, and probably *patriotism*. There was always one: the man whom the bar staff don't remove because he's just irritating, not actually a *nuisance*, and bar staff always have something else that needs doing; and whom no one else takes issue with because they assume that since he hasn't already been removed, he must be best mates with all the bar staff.

Kitt grimaced. She was stalling herself with her own thoughts, and this conversation was going to be difficult enough without picturing the dead soothsayer as Florid Fyll from the Dockworker's Arms, with his face like someone had overinflated a baby's head and left it in the sun for a week. She got a grip on herself – and Derna's hand, she realised a moment later – and took a deep breath. The Swallowmage nodded, an action which seemed to take far more effort than it should have done to simply move a few neck muscles.

'*Who'zere? Wotcha want?*'

'Lerry Third-Eye?' Kitt asked cautiously. She'd known it was Mazen, in the chamber beneath the morgue. She had no idea whether the right person had been buried in this grave, and it made sense to check that part first, so the Swallowmage could cut the contact and save her strength if they'd been led astray.

'*Yeah, that's… me?*' Lerry sounded uncertain for a moment, but then his voice hardened and strengthened with surety. '*That's me.*'

'I want to ask about the most recent destiny you read,' Kitt said carefully. She needed to avoid mentioning the Grikes if at all possible. They had almost certainly killed Lerry Third-Eye, and drawing the spirit's mind towards them would lead everyone into places they had no desire to go. 'I'm told it wasn't a pleasant one. I need to know what it was.'

'*The most recent one?*' Lerry's spirit grumbled. '*That was… Oh, bugger me sideways, that one?*' It should not have been possible for a spirit to sound unwell, but he did.

'Yes,' Kitt said, her throat tighter than the very finest corset. 'I just need to know what it was, and then I promise you can forget about it.'

'*Those bloody posh idiots,*' Lerry said, with a distaste that

Kitt found herself sharing. '*They were going to give it to the baby! They were going to end us all!*'

Kitt's heart nearly stopped.

'They were *what?* What was it?' She wet her lips and tried again. 'What was the destiny, Lerry?'

'*It was the future,*' said the ghost of Lerry Third-Eye, in a hollow tone that Kitt knew had nothing to do with him being a ghost. '*The kid was going to destroy the futures. Everyone's future.*'

'No,' Kitt heard her lips say immediately, while her brain took its hands off the wheel and went for a short walk, whistling idly in an attempt not to think about what it had just heard. Unfortunately that just left the spirit's words echoing around her head with nothing to soften the blow, nothing to apply the brakes of reason. *How can I destroy the future?* Kitt thought desperately. *I don't feel like someone who would destroy the future! But would I know, if this was my destiny since before I could remember?*

'No, that can't be right,' she stammered, trying not to look at the others and how they must be looking at her; yet simultaneously desperate to look at the others, to find out how they were looking at her. 'You, you must have got it wrong, or—'

The problem with the man at the end of the bar in a tavern was that they could be completely oblivious to things such as reasonable speaking volumes, personal space, or appropriate conversational topics, but would abruptly and without warning tune in very intuitively to signs of weakness.

'*What's the matter?*' Lerry Third-Eye asked, and it was not a question laden with sympathy. Kitt could practically hear the proto-sneer laced into it, just waiting for an excuse to burst forth into the world. '*This one personal for you, is it?*'

'No!' Kitt said, the instinctive response to being confronted with an ugly truth by someone you didn't know but already didn't like.

'**LIAR,**' Lerry Third-Eye said with delight, in a voice like cracking granite.

You don't ask the spirit a question until I tell you to go ahead

'Oh shit,' Kitt said, bile rising in her throat, as the Swallowmage's head snapped backwards, her face contorted into a rictus of pain.

You don't keep addressing it if I tell you to stop

'Kitt?' Derna asked urgently, dragging her fingers out of Kitt's death grip in order to take hold of her sidesword.

You do not ask about the death of its body, where it is now, or what it's experiencing

'Get back,' Kitt said. Her voice sounded hopeless and small to her own ears. 'Get back!'

and you never

One hand burst up through the grass, sending soil and roots flying. It was not a human hand, and it had never been a human hand. It was too long, and it was too wide, and it had too many fingers with too many joints, and it crackled with a greasy, pale blue light that reflected strangely off the whorled, grey skin that covered those fingers.

ever

Another followed.

lie to it

The ground heaved upwards, and *something* shouldered its way out. This was not a reanimated corpse. This was something else, something that had broken through the walls between the worlds, simply because Kitt Carver had been careless, and reckless, and hadn't remembered the rules of necromancy. Its limbs were long and sinewy, jagged with exposed spurs of what might have been bone or might have been stone at the elbow and shoulder and knee, its back was massive but hunched, and where the head should be sat nothing but a howling vortex of swirling darkness and strangled fire.

It turned to look at her with eyes that did not exist, and smiled with a mouth she could not see.

'HELLO, KITT,' said the demon.

THIRTY-THREE

KITT SCREAMED. IT seemed the thing to do, in the moment.

The demon was big, far bigger than any human, maybe even bigger than a snow troll, with long arms and shorter legs so it moved on its knuckles. There was a slight flickering insubstantiality about it, as though its body couldn't quite decide exactly what size or shape it was supposed to be, but the soft ground of the graveyard still showed the impression of its weight. Regardless, it was far too big to fight with a sword, which didn't stop Two Tongue Derna.

'Kitt, get out of here!' Derna yelled, slashing at the thing with her sidesword. She caught it on one long forearm as it stretched the limb out to take a step, and her blade pierced whatever served the thing as skin, but the demon did little more than jerk a little, then swatted at her with one stone-knuckled hand with enough force to shatter her ribs had Derna not rolled beneath it at the last moment. The demon growled and raised its hand, fingers clenched into a fist to smash downwards in a blow that Derna could not avoid, and Kitt's stomach contracted like a slug in an oven.

'Hey!' she yelled, throwing a displaced clod of earth at it. 'Over here!'

The earth did nothing, but the demon's attention snapped back to Kitt, and Derna scrambled backwards out of range. Of course, that left Kitt as the centre of its attention again.

Then Falzine came at it from behind with his spear, yelling in the way one does when bravery is short and has to be replaced by volume. A tail that Kitt hadn't seen came up and wrapped around his neck, without the demon even turning towards him.

Vem yelled in rage and hacked at the appendage with his axe, but he was too late: there was an audible *crack*, and Falzine collapsed. The demon came on, its long limbs carrying it across the ground far faster than Kitt could have run away, even had she been able to get her body properly under her control instead of stumbling backwards while staring in terror. The vortex of the demon's head was mesmerising, sucking her in and promising eternity. It reached out towards her, and she could do nothing to avoid it.

Then the Swallowmage was there.

Sulian simply threw force at the demon, snapping its arm out and away from Kitt, and staggering it. The spell, or hypnotism, or whatever it was broke, and Kitt hastily backed off, finally remembering to draw her short sword.

The Swallowmage's greying hair rose upwards with the power coursing through her body, and Jandi was floating and spinning through the air of its own accord in front of her. Strands of light erupted from the knowood staff like gossamer, streaming out to envelop the demon, which snarled in rage.

'Kitt, why are you still here?' Sulian said tightly, as her hands began to weave through the air in a counterpoint to Jandi's motions. This was mage magic, pure and powerful, and far beyond Kitt's minor gift for divining.

'IT DOESN'T MATTER WHERE SHE GOES,' the demon snarled, swiping ineffectually at the magic enveloping it. 'I CAN FOLLOW HER SPOOR WHEREVER SHE RUNS!'

'That's disgusting,' the Swallowmage said flatly, and

brought both of her hands together, clenched into fists. The cloud of glowing threads all pulled taut at once, wrapping the demon up and binding its limbs to its body. 'Kitt, *run!* Derna, get back, if you even *touch* it with that sword then I swear to all the gods—'

'I'm not touching anything!' Derna shouted, holding her weapon ready but, for once, not actually using it. Donal had his own sword out and was, Kitt was relieved to see, shepherding Arkony behind him. The demon roared, but despite the sudden outbreak of sweat on the Swallowmage's brow, her hastily woven web appeared to be holding it. Quite what she intended to do with it next was beyond Kitt's ability to guess, but so long as no one did anything foolish…

Pigtail Vem, weeping in rage and shock and grief, swung his axe with both hands at the demon's back.

The impact ran through the bindings instantly; they blackened and faded, and fell away as though a single knot had been severed. The Swallowmage's knees buckled, and Jandi clattered to the ground.

The demon reared back upright with a roar and brought one clenched fist down on the man who had inadvertently freed it. Vem had no time to get out of the way. Kitt caught the briefest glimpse of his tear-tracked face staring upwards in the disappearing light of the magic he had just destroyed, and then the blow landed with the force of a starstone falling to earth.

Sulian made it up onto one knee, snatched Jandi, and launched a scorching beam of fire at the demon, but it was ready for her magic this time. It caught the blast on the palm of a huge, cupped hand, and redirected it towards Derna, Donal, and Arkony. The trio scrambled out of the way, but a line of flame sprang up where the Swallowmage's reflected magic kissed the long, dry grass. Then the demon vomited darkness in return.

Sulian only just managed to make it up to her feet before

the deluge struck, but she was already spinning Jandi through the air. A protective half-dome of magical force shimmered into existence, and the demon's energy rebounded off and flowed around it like a wave breaking over a boulder. The Swallowmage staggered, though, and didn't hit back as the demon prowled closer.

'Why bother, little drunkard?' it growled, as the flames licked higher and spread wider behind it. 'The girl is mine now, and by letting me take her you will save all of your futures. The spirit spoke only the truth.'

'Kitt, in my right belt pouch there's a bracelet of woven leather,' Sulian said, without looking away from the demon. 'Tie a strand of your own hair around it, then put it on. It's a concealment charm that will keep you hidden from this thing.'

'You just had that ready?' Kitt demanded, doing as she was bid while trying not to get in the way of anything Sulian might be about to do. Pressed up close as she was, she could smell fresh sweat and old alcohol on the mage's skin.

'What do you think I was doing in my room all day?' the Swallowmage asked. 'I knew this might go sideways, so I tried to prepare for it.' She huffed out a breath; her protective shield was starting to flicker. 'Put it on, and *get away*. If this bastard could take me easily then it wouldn't bother talking to me, but I don't know how much of a head start I can give you.'

'Not enough,' the demon said mockingly, as Kitt's fingers closed around a narrow strip of woven leather strands. She hastily pulled it out, then fumbled at her head. She found her own hair in places it shouldn't be all the time, why was it so hard to get at a single strand now…?

The demon sprang. The Swallowmage yelled in anger and fear and effort, and her protective shield inverted, closing in around the demon like a prison. The demon snarled, and lashed out with one talon-tipped hand. The shield flexed for a moment, then popped and vanished as though it was no more substantial than a soap bubble. Sulian flung up another desperate magical barrier, but the demon battered first it and then her aside just as Kitt finished tying a knot in the hair she'd just managed to yank out, which by the sensation had taken a small chunk of her scalp with it.

'THE CHARM MEANS I CAN'T TRACK YOU,' the demon said, with malicious glee. 'IT DOESN'T PREVENT ME FROM SEEING YOU WHEN YOU'RE RIGHT IN FRONT OF ME. TIME TO GO, KITT CARVER.' It drew back one hand, ready to claw her apart, rend her soul, or possibly just flatten her like it had done to Vem. Kitt stared up at it with her short sword raised, determined to at least take a swing at this thing while it killed her, and whatever was passing for thoughts deep inside the churning sea of fear within her wondering whether maybe, given the prophecy, this wasn't actually for the best after all.

The demon…

…hesitated.

And then Plainsong stood between her and it.

He was bare-chested, his robe flung to one side and leaving him in nothing but simple trousers gathered at the waist by a belt of rope. His blades were already out and in his hands, but it wasn't those that caught Kitt's eye. It was the tattoos, *all* the tattoos, chain after chain after chain that stretched around his throat, around his torso, and around his arms. Most were broken; only two that stretched diagonally across his back, from each shoulder to the opposite hip, remained intact. Every one a constraint put on him by the people who had set this entire thing into motion in the first place, and nearly all of them no longer effective.

'WHAT IS ONE OF *YOU* DOING HERE?' the demon growled, and its voice was no longer amused or contemptuous.

'Making a mistake,' Plainsong said. 'I should be long gone by now, but I find that I have a nose for trouble, and *you*,' he pointed one of his blades at the demon, 'reek of it so strongly that I could sense you before you even emerged.'

'**WHAT IS THE GIRL TO YOU?**' the demon demanded, its fingers clenching into fists and then unclenching again.

'Nothing,' Plainsong said calmly, and with such utter certainty that Kitt felt like she'd just been punched in the chest, because in the delivery of that word she truly understood that her life meant nothing, *literally* nothing, to Plainsong. 'But I owe one of your kind for the lives of a village, many years ago now, and you will do for my retribution as well as any other.'

'**A VILLAGE? AND WHAT DID THEY MEAN TO ONE LIKE YOU?**' the demon snarled. It was knuckling back and forth, pacing like a caged predator, but nothing truly held it in place save for fear of the being in front of it.

'Nothing,' Plainsong repeated. The increasing light of the growing grass fire reflected off the smooth lines of his skull, and the sculpted curves of his shoulders and arms, making him look almost like a statue. 'But I was blamed, and punished. And now I will take my revenge.'

He raised both of his blades and charged. The demon snarled and vomited darkness once more, engulfing both it and Plainsong, and then Kitt. Then its snarls changed pitch, and Kitt saw a line of black fire that did nothing to illuminate the darkness she found herself in, but which she somehow *knew* was an obsidian blade slashing across demonic hide.

'Kitt?'

She stiffened in terror, but it was not the demon's voice.

'Kitt!'

It was Derna. Kitt relaxed for a moment, insofar as she was able when caught in a cloud of stygian darkness while, somewhere not far away, a demon and something in the shape of a man did battle. Then she rapidly unrelaxed again, because that was the voice of Two Tongue Derna Towbright, the Queen of the Streets, Mereport's premiere duellist, and the person in all the world whom Kitt was most confident would always do what she thought was right, and damn anyone else's opinions, or indeed the consequences. Two Tongue Derna, who had just learned – from the mouth of a spirit that hadn't lied – that Kitt was destined to destroy the future.

If destinies weren't fireproof, then they certainly weren't Dernaproof.

Kitt turned. She couldn't see anything. The night had been dark enough anyway, given darkness was one of the predispositions of night, but the demon's exhalations meant even the light of the fire was dimmed. However, she could hear the demon's snarls and the clashes of blades against its skin, and she could tell in what direction Derna was calling her from, and she could stumble away from them both with her short sword clutched in one hand and the other outstretched to prevent her from blundering into a gravestone.

She, Kitt Carver, was a danger to the world, and everyone in it. There was one very obvious answer to that, but it wasn't one that Kitt wanted to explore, so she continued stumbling and sobbing until she broke clear of the demon's darkness and could see the cemetery wall, and then she ran for it as fast as she could. If the demon got past Plainsong, maybe it would follow her and leave her friends in peace. If it didn't, maybe distance could help Kitt keep her curse from claiming those closest to her, at least for a while.

Behind her, she heard a roar of rage and the splintering of stone as something heavy was thrown bodily into a statue. Perhaps she wasn't destined to destroy the future, as such.

Perhaps she'd already started.

THIRTY-FOUR

Tommas made his way up onto deck as soon as he heard the shouting. Once he got there, it did not take him long to work out what the commotion was about.

The *Spirit of Liberty* had made fairly good time up the river, which was still navigable this far up its course even for a sea-going vessel like theirs, and they were now approaching Derringsmoot. Or at least, what was left of it.

'What in the name of all the gods happened here?' Tommas breathed in horror as the town came into view. A couple of thick, ugly streams of smoke rose into the sky above the trees that lined the riverbank just downstream, and a more general haze fogged the air. It was primarily the sharp scent of woodsmoke, but laced here and there with the tang of other, less pleasant elements.

'I suspect I know,' Carl Whyteaves said, his voice taut. The factor was chewing his lip as he gazed ahead towards Derringsmoot. 'I suspect you do, as well.'

Tommas stared at him. 'You don't mean... *him?*' He looked back at the town, which was sliding gradually closer as the *Spirit of Liberty* approached. Some buildings had flames licking at them, others looked like entire chunks of wall had been knocked out or through, and in general the whole place seemed unlikely to meet even the very loosest building standards code.

'Did you think I was exaggerating?' Carl asked sourly. He stretched out a hand, indicating the devastation ahead of them. 'This is what he is capable of. This is what he *revels* in. The consequences for this will be severe, but I still have a job to do.'

'The consequences *will* be severe?' Tommas demanded. 'What, for you? You're going to get hauled over the coals by your superiors because your private disaster wrecked an entire town?' He shoved Carl in the chest, uncaring of how the factor would take it. 'I would say the consequences are *already* pretty fucking severe!'

'Don't try to take the moral high ground with me,' Carl snapped. 'As an assassin, you hardly have a leg to stand on.'

'Individuals!' Tommas replied indignantly. '*Individuals*, of specific note or importance! The work is clinical, not haphazard. Not multiple buildings destroyed, fires set, and lives lost simply because something got *out of control!*'

'Do you think that makes it any better for your victim's loved ones?' Carl asked. 'Honestly, I'd like to know.'

'Of course not,' Tommas sighed. 'Besides, it's not as though I chose this path,' he added, bitterly. 'That damned destiny—'

'Yes, yes, the destiny that cursed you to have bloodstained hands,' Carl said dismissively. 'Tell me, did you even consider work as a butcher, for example?'

Tommas swallowed. 'The meaning was clear that—'

'Or a surgeon, perhaps?' Carl added, as though Tommas hadn't spoken. 'I would imagine that would have sated it.' He clapped Tommas on the shoulder. 'But enough of this. The asset was here recently. Since he has visited his wrath upon this town, the least we can hope for is that he happened to remove our target while he was at it. Our course of action will be to restrain the asset and learn what has happened. If he did not complete our mission, our ability to restrain him should give us access to the local nobility, which will enable you to fulfil your purpose as *clinically* as you wish.'

'You want us to restrain the thing that did *this?*' Tommas replied, incredulous. They were coming up on the docks now, where a body floated in the water. Tommas was not by nature averse to dead bodies, since he was in the business of creating them, but he recoiled when he saw that the face and chest had been gouged open by what looked like enormous claws.

'I don't *want* us to, I *require* us to,' Carl said primly. Only the tightness of his eyes gave any indication as to his true feelings on the matter. 'We have everything prepared. There is no reason why it should not work.'

'Remind me,' Tommas said. 'How did he escape from your control in the first place? Oh yes, you don't know.' He shuddered. Tommas hated magic, at least of anything more than the very simplest kind. A person's natural abilities were one thing, but taking the raw stuff out of the air and using it to weave spells and enchantments was quite another. The more complicated you made it, the more potential there was for something to go wrong, and Tommas hated variables over which he had no control.

And yet here he was, about to try his hand at trapping something capable of demolishing half a town. Partly, make no mistake, because it *had* demolished half a town, and the notion of leaving something like that running around free was not one that sat well with him, despite his professional relationship with death. The other part was because while he didn't completely trust that Carl had been telling the truth about *the asset* – Tommas realised he'd got out of the habit of even thinking the name – wanting vengeance on him for simply being associated with those who had done the original enslavement, it did not, on balance, feel like the sort of thing he wanted to leave to chance any more than he had to. Unreliable though magic was, Carl or his associates had clearly been able to perform the binding at some point in the past, which made it a more likely tool for saving Tommas's skin than a stammered attempt at explanation if and when a hooded shadow loomed over him.

'Fine,' he muttered, as their ship pulled in towards a mooring designed for craft smaller than their own, but which had the advantage of not being on fire. 'Let's get this over with.'

THE TOWN WAS not exactly deserted, but that almost made it worse. Entire chunks had been torn out of buildings, roofing tiles were shattered and scattered across cracked cobbles, and although various smouldering sites showed that some fires had been put out, some still blazed. Normally – if anything about this situation had been normal – people would have been out fighting the fire, and trying to repair that which had been damaged. However, although Tommas heard the clack of a window shutter closing, or the thump of a door being pulled shut, no one was doing *anything*.

They're not convinced it's over, whatever it was, he realised. *Some have fled, and the rest are sheltering as though it's a storm passing through.*

His own party might not have been likely to inspire confidence, he had to admit. There were nine of them, all told: Tommas; Carl; a brother and sister called Jarroll and Jerima, the mages whose duty it had been to maintain the enchantments from which Plainsong had managed to escape, and who had been working furiously to rectify their error; and five hands from the ship, who moved and dressed with the air of people whose job it was to sometimes do unpleasant things but not be particularly memorable while doing so. If Tommas had lived here, he might well have shut himself away from this group of dangerous-looking people who had apparently decided to take a stroll through the ruins of a town.

'Remember,' Carl said, the strain audible in his voice, 'keep your eyes open. He could be anywhere, and I mean *anywhere*.'

Tommas found himself looking up at the roofs, tensed and waiting for a bald head to appear, staring down at them. He abruptly wondered if this was how his targets felt… only that was ridiculous, of course, since unless he had been very unlucky, his targets did not know he was actively seeking to usher them into the next plane of existence until the last moment. This was more like hunting a dangerous wild animal, uncertain of whether your cage was strong enough to hold it, and aware that it might, at any point, be able to get the drop on you.

Tommas took a quick look around, and snorted to himself. In fact, that was exactly what they were doing.

They reached the main square, and Tommas grabbed at Carl's arm. 'Wait, you want us to go out there? Into the open?'

'You're thinking like an assassin,' Carl said. He was smiling, but Tommas could tell it was a paper-thin mask over a bubbling cauldron of anxiety. He would have mocked the other man, were he not in the same state.

'You're thinking about lines of sight, and ambushes from distance with projectile weapons,' Carl continued. 'That is not the asset's way. We are in far more danger in close quarters, where he can come upon us unexpectedly. In the open, we have a better chance of seeing him approach.'

'And how much advantage does that give us?' Tommas demanded.

'Very little,' Carl said with a shrug. 'However, I am reasonably confident that my death at his hands will be faster and less painful than the alternative, should my superiors see fit to deprive me of my life.' He smiled, a thing of broken glass and poison. 'So let's get to it, shall we?'

He strode out across the flagstones towards what had once been an ornamental fountain, and which was now a smashed wreck of carved stone leaking water in a continuous dark, glistening sheet across the ground. The rest followed him, and

Tommas was left with the option of joining them, or staying in a place where, by all accounts, he was more vulnerable to attack from the being they hunted.

In the end, the calculus of survival made his decision for him. Whether he considered Plainsong to be a predator, or a sentient being intent on revenge and inflicting suffering, the most likely occurrence was for the isolated member of the group to be attacked first. If he was with the rest, at least he might have a chance to flee and get lost in the confusion once it all went to shit.

Tommas gritted his teeth and hurried after them, with one hand in his pocket clutching the exceedingly flimsy defence that lay within.

'Fan out,' Carl instructed, as they reached the fountain. 'I want a pair of eyes looking in every direction. Shout as soon as you see him.' He took one breath, took another, then raised his voice. '*Plainsong!*'

'What happened to "he comes when called"?' Tommas demanded. He was facing back the way they had come, and although he desperately wanted to look around and see if a bald figure had appeared from anywhere else, he didn't dare turn away.

'That's the idea,' Carl said, his voice tense. 'Plainsong!'

'There!' someone shouted – it was Jerima, Tommas realised as he turned – and sure enough, there he was.

What was left of him.

Plainsong was, broadly speaking, in one piece; he still had all his limbs, his head was still attached, and so on. However, that was the limit of what could be said before adjectives such as 'battered', 'bloodied' and 'bruised' crowded in, snarling and eager as wolves at a carcass.

His robe was gone entirely. He limped, his right leg dragging slightly as he moved, and the simple, loose trousers he wore had been torn away below the knee on that same leg to reveal flesh opened down to what would have been bone, if bone had gleamed black instead of white. There was no more than a square inch of continuous skin on his torso that was not damaged or discoloured in some way, whether that was from bruising, abrasion, what looked like at least one burn on his left pectoral, or marks that appeared to have come from the same claws that had sliced open the corpse Tommas had seen in the river.

'Gods' mercy,' Tommas breathed. 'What *happened?*'

'Look around you,' Carl said. 'I think it's clear what happened.'

'No, look at *him!*' Tommas snapped back, pointing at the figure making its laboured way towards them. 'Do you think he sustained those injuries fighting against *townspeople?*'

Plainsong smiled, without showing his teeth. 'You should see the other guy.'

Tommas was very suddenly and very definitely aware that he absolutely did not want to see the 'other guy', whoever or whatever it was.

'I don't think we need to see anything,' Carl announced. His voice was a hollow drum, loud but unconvincing. 'You've given into your basest natures once more, haven't you, creature?'

'There was a demon here, you pathetic fool,' Plainsong said, with enough contempt in his voice to float a sizeable ship.

'A demon?' Tommas echoed, risking a glance around. If one of those things had somehow got loose, that would explain the damage. 'And you fought it?'

'Fought it,' Plainsong agreed, with a note of utter tiredness in his voice. 'Couldn't kill it. Drove it off, though.'

Tommas made a decision.

'No.' He stepped away from the group, and kept walking until there were a good twenty paces between them. 'Enough, Carl. You had me believing he was responsible for this!'

'He is,' Carl said, his eyes locked on Plainsong. 'Don't be fooled into thinking that he cares about life, Tommas. He's a killer, far purer than you will ever be.'

'You know nothing about me, little man,' Plainsong snarled, and he was dangerous again, despite the wounds and the weariness. 'If I am a killer, it is only the use to which I was put by you, and others before you. But I'll grant you this,' he added, still approaching. 'Yes, I will be killing again today. I'm going to slit all of your throats and leave you for your superiors to find, should they ever care enough to come looking.' He flexed his fingers. He was close, now, closer than they ever should have let him get, and to Tommas's horror blades of black stone cut their way out of his forearms and rotated around until the handles nestled into the palms of his hands. 'If any gods will listen to your prayers, you may wish to say them.'

'Tommas, *now!*' Carl shouted.

Plainsong's head snapped around, and those dark eyes burned into Tommas, seeming to see right through him, and through the fabric of his clothes into his pocket, where his hand still clutched the thing that Jerroll had given him before they'd even disembarked: the faint, flimsy protection that Tommas had just decided he wasn't going to use, but now Plainsong was looking at him, and *seeing* him, and he knew there was no explanation he could give in time which would convince this being of his change of heart—

Tommas Underwyne was only human, but he was an assassin. He was gifted with sharp reflexes that he had trained, and excellent hand-eye coordination that might or might not have been a result of a subtle magical talent. Plainsong was something other than human, with glistening black bones and blades that emerged from his flesh, but he was tired and wounded. On any other day, he might have been able to dodge what Tommas threw at him. Today, however, he simply swatted it away with the flat of one of his knives, but that was his mistake.

The tiny, enchanted chain had found its target, and it slithered down the blade and first onto Plainsong's flesh, and then *into* it.

Plainsong roared in anger and anguish, but there was no escape. The chain branded itself onto him, reforging the broken enchantments. Then Carl, Jerroll, and Jerima threw their own chains that wrapped around his body like sentient, strangling ivy, and the process accelerated: the blades snapped back in, Plainsong's arms fell to his sides, and Plainsong himself fell to his knees. The fury in his face faded, replaced by the calm expression Tommas had first seen on the deck of the *Spirit of Liberty* – with the impression that there was something underneath, something that viewed you possibly with contempt and possibly as prey, but locked away far enough inside that it could do nothing except rage behind the eyeballs.

'Ha,' Carl Whyteaves said, breathlessly. Then, 'Ha!' he shouted triumphantly, staggering in a small circle with the loose-limbed gait of someone for whom adrenaline had come to collect its ruinous interest. He looked over at Tommas and spread his arms wide. 'Well *done!* I never knew an assassin could be such a good actor!'

Tommas glanced from him to the kneeling Plainsong, now bound in place once more by enchantments that were invisible except as the freshly minted chain tattoos that crawled across his abused flesh. Principles were of little use to Tommas now. Even if Plainsong broke free, he would not forget who first ensnared him. The only logical course was to go along with Carl's assumptions.

'Of course,' Tommas said, adopting a smug smile as he crossed the flagstones back to the others. 'I am a man of hidden talents.'

'Very well, then.' Carl looked around as though testing the wind. 'We still have someone to kill. Let's not waste any more time.'

THIRTY-FIVE

Carl was good at his job, Tommas had to give him that.

Regardless of Plainsong's version of events, the townspeople seemed to consider him just as responsible for the destruction visited upon their home as whatever demon he had battled. The deserted streets had been an illusion; someone somewhere had clearly been keeping an eye on what took place in the square, and it was not long before Tommas and his companions were surrounded by well-wishers, all eager to hail the heroes who had subdued the half of their problems that had stuck around. Plainsong's shackles were back at full strength, and he was unable to do more than trudge along mutely while calls for his head echoed around them. Carl managed to assure the locals of nebulously worded 'justice', and had Plainsong bundled back to their ship while he grifted the goodwill into an introduction to the Grike family.

The local nobility had sent their two stonewardens out in a surprisingly public-spirited attempt to quell the chaos, and had been rewarded with them both smashed into bits, which said something about the capabilities of the beings involved. Now Carl and Tommas sat in the Grikes' drawing room, drinking chamomile tea served by a nervous and rather spotty young woman, and sitting opposite a couple whose faces were as stony as those of their destroyed guardians.

'Apologies for the hospitality,' Draymere Grike said, in a tone that had never met an apology in its life. 'We recently lost our factor.'

'I'm sorry to hear that,' Carl said, stirring his tea and setting the spoon down delicately. 'An accident?'

'His services were no longer required,' Scintilla said, carefully enough that Tommas paid close attention to the words that weren't spoken. If the Grikes' former factor had departed their employ upright and still breathing then he, Tommas Underwyne, was a left-handed ham sandwich.

'A risk of the profession. I do hope it was not linked to the disappearance of your son,' Carl said. Tommas stiffened, and he was not the only one. The Grikes already had an air of cautious impatience that made it clear they were only granting this audience because Carl's role in supposedly saving the town made it difficult for them not to, and now they both visibly soured even further. Carl, however, sipped his tea as though nothing were amiss. 'The townsfolk mentioned it on our way here. You have my sympathies, of course.'

'Of course,' Lord Draymere echoed. His fingers twitched, and Tommas – ever alert for threats – noticed the bracelet on his wrist that would very likely allow him to summon the stonewardens, had they not both been turned into a sort of free-form rockery. Scintilla was watching Carl like a hawk, clearly wondering exactly who they had invited into their home. Too late now, though; as Tommas knew well, once Carl Whyteaves had a grip on you, it was very hard to extricate yourself. Especially if your main security had been smashed.

'I wonder if we might be of some assistance,' Carl continued, smooth as a buttered snake. 'My colleagues and I have a variety of skills at our disposal, as we demonstrated earlier. We would be only too happy to assist in tracking down a wayward heir.'

'For a price, I take it?' Scintilla asked acidly.

'Unfortunately, the way of the world is that good service rarely comes for free,' Carl replied, with mock sadness. Tommas had to admit Carl was doing a very good job of playing the mercenary. The way of the world was that people – especially nobles – rarely *trusted* anything that came for free, unless they'd threatened or influenced someone to get it. Carl offering to find their son without charge, having already dealt with a town-destroying threat, would be too suspicious. Using that feat to bargain his way into a collecting a reward from worried parents was reprehensible, but entirely in keeping with the sort of behaviour they would expect.

'I would not, of course, expect any fee until such time as your son is returned to you,' Carl added. He let his gaze linger for a moment, as though inviting them to consider what the variety of skills at his command might do if any agreement was not honoured. Indeed, Tommas reflected, perhaps just introducing the question of what that variety of skills might do if an agreement was not *made*. A missing heir was a dangerous thing, prone to ransom demands or coerced marriage.

Draymere sniffed sharply, and glanced at his wife. 'So long as that is understood. We would of course be prepared to pay a fair price to have our child back.'

Tommas sipped his tea quietly. A fair price? Interesting. They were hardly desperate, then. Both Grikes had a hard-nosed air about them, in different ways, but Tommas would have expected them to be more eager, given their only child was missing. Instead they seemed somewhat guarded. Yes, there was definitely something else going on here.

'First things first,' Carl said with a smile, as though this was not a conversation about the life of a missing young person, with an undercurrent of intimidation. 'Do you know what prompted your son to disappear?'

Scintilla swallowed. 'It was an argument over his birthday gift.'

'I see.' Carl nodded as though this was unremarkable, but his eyes were intense. 'What was that?'

'A destiny,' Draymere said gruffly. 'He didn't want it. Seemed offended. Then… he ran away.'

Oh, that was a lie. Tommas didn't need magic to smell that one, it was written all over the duke's face. Or at least, there was a lot more there than Draymere was letting on.

'He was offended?' Carl asked sharply, then moderated his tone a little. 'I mean, that's not a common reaction. Especially since I imagine it was expensive, given your resources.'

'He wanted to make his own destiny,' Scintilla said, and there was the faintest hint of pride at the corners of her voice, although definitely mixed in with frustration, and sorrow, and a fair amount of anger.

'What manner of destiny was it?' Carl said. The Grikes looked at him, and he smiled. 'If we know the nature of it, that might give us a hint of where to start.'

'It was a good one,' Scintilla said defensively. 'The bearer was going to reach the stars, was the official reading. There's obviously some poetic licence there, since soothsayers can rarely be *exact*, but it was a strong one, and positive.'

'He took it,' Draymere said shortly. 'Accepted it without meaning to, apparently. He shouted, we argued, he ran. End of story.'

'Not quite,' Scintilla put in quietly. Everyone's attention shifted to her, and Tommas took another sip of his tea. Scintilla had the air of someone who had made what was, for her, a momentous decision. This should be interesting.

'There was a gel with Arkony, when he ran,' Scintilla said. 'They may still be together. If not, she might at least know where he is. I would also be very interested in speaking further with her, if you were able to bring her back, and I would be prepared to add a small additional fee for that purpose.'

'Scintilla…' Draymere began, but his wife raised a hand to quiet him.

'Shush, Draymere. I want to talk to her, that's all. And unharmed,' she added meaningfully, looking first at Carl and then at Tommas, even though he had been introduced by Carl as 'my associate' with no mention of his particular talents.

Carl smiled. 'Any lead is useful. Do you have a name and description?'

'I mean…' Scintilla's face was suddenly a mask of uncertainty, and she glanced desperately at Draymere. 'I suppose she was…'

'Fair-skinned,' Draymere provided.

'We didn't get a good look at her hair,' Scintilla added, 'she was wearing a hat.'

'Fairly unremarkable-looking, really,' Draymere said slowly, watching his wife's face, and seeming slightly relieved when Scintilla nodded.

'Yes, yes. Fairly unremarkable. No real distinguishing features that I can recall. Um, she was from Mereport. Had a Mereport accent.'

Tommas frowned, and leant forwards. 'Mereport?' he repeated, his first contribution to the conversation.

'She's a little out of her way,' Carl said, shooting him a glance. 'Did you catch a name?'

'Yes,' Scintilla said, nodding. 'I don't know if she was telling the truth, of course, but she gave her name as Kitt Carver.'

'Kitt Carver?'

'Be quiet, Tommas.'

Tommas had no intention of being quiet. 'Kitt *fucking* Carver?!'

'I said, *be quiet!*' Carl snapped. 'I need to think!'

They were making their way back along the river path towards the docks, having thrashed out a hasty agreement with the Grikes for the return of their son, and an additional fee for the procurement of one Kitt Carver, native of Mereport. Carl had perhaps settled for slightly less than his mercenary act should have accepted, but that was no longer their primary concern.

'No, Carl, you don't need to think!' Tommas said. 'The time for you to *think* was back in Mereport, before you hired a bunch of local amateurs to kill people who would not have the faintest idea what we were about, had you not drawn their attention to it in the most obvious way possible!'

'What's past is past,' Carl said, waving a hand dismissively, as though those four words could erase everything that had come before. 'But why the Carver girl? And why is she *here*? We covered our tracks!'

'You obviously didn't cover them well enough,' Tommas said acidly. 'And leave the "we" out of it, will you? I had nothing to do with your *exceptionally bad* plan, and I told you my opinion of it as soon as I learned of it.' He stomped on for a few seconds, then something else occurred to him. 'More importantly than why is she here, *how* is she here? How did she get here at least two days before us?'

'She would have had to come clean over the high moors,' Carl said absent-mindedly.

'And she's a diviner,' Tommas said, his gut twisting at the thought. The sheer notion of going into a place where you could potentially be trapped forever by a misstep, accident, or faulty enchantment gave him the chills. 'So she's more likely than many to be willing to attempt it, although I've never heard of anyone doing it before. But that still leaves us with "why".'

'And don't forget the Grike boy,' Carl said. 'He took the destiny and ran.'

Tommas sighed. 'I'm not forgetting him. At least let me handle it when we catch up with him, rather than indulging another of your improvisations.'

'I have always been very clear that you are here to do that

part of the job,' Carl said, his tone somewhat tetchy. 'But the Carver girl… She was the one who appeared in the scryings.'

'Wait,' Tommas said, coming to a halt. '*Carver* was the one in the scryings? Not Grike?'

'Scryings are notoriously fickle,' Carl replied defensively. 'Just because Carver appeared doesn't mean she's central, merely relevant. That was why it was decided to focus on her clients, and track down the most powerful destiny she found. The price of the one the Grikes bought made it clear it was potent. It seemed the obvious candidate.'

'You fool,' Tommas sighed. 'She's a *diviner!* You tracked the most powerful destiny she's ever *sold*, not necessarily the most powerful one she ever *found!* She might have kept it for herself! It might have been an accident!'

Carl looked at him dubiously. 'But… just a diviner? That seems unlikely.'

'As unlikely as her working out what your plan was, crossing the high moors ahead of us to reach our target, and apparently warning him with sufficient eloquence for him to abandon his home and make himself scarce?' Tommas demanded. 'Family quarrel aside, there's something else at work here. Something's driving that girl, Carl. Granted, you tried to have a knife put in her, but even so.'

Carl chewed his lip, thinking. Then he exhaled in the manner of a man who has come to an unpleasant conclusion.

'The asset. He was here yesterday, which was the day after Grike disappeared. The asset knew the name of our target.'

Tommas groaned. 'You think he had something to do with it?'

Carl spun around, heading towards the ship again. 'I *think* I'm going to need the twins to loosen the bonds on his tongue, and we're going to need to ask him some *very* specific questions.'

It did not take long for them to reach the *Spirit of Freedom*, but Tommas put a hand on Carl's shoulder as he was about to set foot on the docks. 'Wait.'

'What?'

'There's someone waiting for us,' Tommas said, nodding in the direction of their ship. It was a man in his late twenties, perhaps; tall and broad enough to be notable, but not so much that he would particularly stand out from a crowd. He did not look like he had been enjoying the best of times, judging by his weary expression and stained clothing, but that was hardly surprising in a town torn up by nightmare creatures.

'Oh, for pity's sake,' Carl growled. 'It's Klae, the other diviner, the one I bribed to get the information from Carver. What's *he* doing here?'

'Didn't you try to have him killed as well?' Tommas suggested mildly, looking around as though he had simply paused to admire the view, while he was actually checking lines of sight. They were in the open, but there were also comparatively few places where an archer could conceal themselves to take a shot. If Klae was a decoy designed to get them to pause, his associates would have to be superlatively skilled to take advantage of it.

'Well, now you get to demonstrate your talents,' Carl grumbled. Tommas snorted.

'I'm not walking up to a man on a jetty and knifing him in the ribs, that's footpad work. Besides, we will immediately lose our local goodwill if any of us are seen casually killing a man and dropping him into the river. And what's to say that he even knows who we are? Oh wait!' he added, before Carl could respond. 'That's right! You brought him to the ship to speak with him! What an excellent idea that was.'

'We can't just wait here for him to get bored,' Carl said, glowering.

'Then walk up to him and ask him his business,' Tommas suggested. 'If he attempts to kill you I suppose we could justify me intervening, but we really should not make ourselves look like the instigators of any unpleasantness.'

'I think you overestimate how much interest I have in the goodwill of this town,' Carl muttered.

'And I think *you* overestimate how likely things are to just work out for you if you continue to act as you please without considering the consequences,' Tommas said, exasperated. 'Don't walk up and shove him in the chest, that's all I'm asking.'

'I will expect your involvement at the first sign of trouble,' Carl said coldly, and began to stalk towards the *Spirit of Freedom* and the figure standing next to it.

The man looked up as they approached and placed one hand on the scabbard of his short sword, to hold it in place if a draw became necessary, but he refrained from laying the other on the grip.

'Can I help you?' Carl asked, as they came within easy speaking distance.

'I believe we made a deal in Mereport,' Klae said, trying not to look nervous and almost succeeding. 'I distinctly remember this ship, and you look like you're in charge of it.'

Carl snorted. 'We made a deal, and you got paid for it. I'd ask you why you're here, but I'm not really interested. Good day.'

Klae took a step forward. 'Well, you see, I'm here to talk about what's happened since then.'

Tommas sighed and surreptitiously loosened a concealed knife in its sheath. The fellow clearly wasn't buying that Carl hadn't paid thugs to murder him after the conclusion of their deal, so it looked like other measures were in order.

That was the problem with destinies. One way or another, they always took their due.

ONE

WEEK

LATER

THIRTY-SIX

Solmouth was a pale imitation of Mereport. It was smaller, drabber, and poorer – which was only to be expected, given it was not the thriving hub of the destinies trade. It did, however, smell the same. Fish smelled like fish everywhere, and the only difference in Solmouth was that because it was smaller, a greater percentage of its area got to experience the odour.

Nonetheless, it was still a thriving port city, and a thriving port city had plenty of opportunity for people to lose things, and when people lost things, they more often than not wanted to find them again. That meant work for diviners, and that meant work for Kitt Carver, formerly of Mereport, and now just trying to keep her head down and avoid notice, avoid demons, and preferably avoid thinking too much.

'You're certain it's in there?' the client asked, eyeing the warehouse. He was a well-dressed man in his forties named Forva, his hair starting to thin in the middle and grey at the sides.

'I've been around it twice,' Kitt said, tapping her moonstruck iron rods in their pouch on her thigh. 'I'm as certain as I can be.' It had taken her half the night to find this place, but Forva was paying good money to track down his wife's missing ring, so Kitt considered it a worthy trade for gritty eyes in the morning. 'Honestly, I'm not sure why it would have turned up here, but I'd stake my life that it's in there somewhere.'

She handed him back his own ring, the one she'd used as a focus. Set in the middle of it was an emerald, apparently one half of an original whole stone, the other half of which resided in the ring she sought. Stones had little knowledge of whether they were whole or half, of course, unless they were magical in their own right. Kitt's magic simply tapped into the connections that people attributed to things; the things that might not have any objective truth, so far as that went, but which everyone assumed were accurate anyway.

Like 'family'.

Kitt pulled her mind away from that line of thought. It wasn't one she wanted to explore, but what options did she have for getting back to her… well, to those who had raised her? Run back up into the land of long summer, and risk coming face to face with another parched one? Then head back over the high moors with no companions, no one to help her if one of her remaining chronocharms failed unexpectedly, and no one to watch while she slept? Even if she believed the theory that slydewasps only went after those trying to harvest destinies, was she prepared to trust her life to it?

The only other ways home were around the coast, through paths she didn't know, and areas largely deserted thanks to the looming presence of the timeless lands; or via ship, and she didn't have enough money to buy passage on any vessel she would trust to get her there. That was what she was doing here, in Solmouth. She was earning money to buy passage on a ship.

She definitely wasn't hiding.

'I'll take that bet,' Forva said, and Kitt blinked her way back into the now.

'Sorry, what?'

'Your stake.' He put finger and thumb to his mouth and whistled, and the shadows in the street disgorged nearly a dozen shapes that turned out to be the sort of solid-bodied folk who looked like they would have no problem with bending joints in ways there were not supposed to bend, or shove sharp objects into bodies with little regard for the other person's wishes on the matter.

'Oh bollocks,' Kitt said wearily.

She should have been scared, but honestly, at this point she was just disappointed in herself. She pulled out her short sword and made a grab for Forva, intending to buy a way out via her weapon pricking his ribs, but a spark of fierce light dropped down in front of her face and caused her to shy backwards.

'Thank you, Ferruk,' her client said, taking a couple of steps backwards.

'No problem, boss,' a voice replied. Kitt blinked, her eyes adjusting to the light, and found that it was the glowing end of a wand wielded by a wellyn and pointed directly at her face.

'Can you do anything else with that?' Kitt asked nastily. 'Or just make pretty lights?' She'd lost her opportunity, now. The thugs had closed in, and she would never get to Forva in time.

'Try me,' the wellyn called Ferruk said, flicking her wand and causing motes of light to drizzle from its tip. Kitt ached to swat her out of the air, but that was probably a foolish plan. Quite apart from any retribution she might garner from the rest of this apparent gang, the wellyn was almost certainly a gutter mage, and very unwise to tangle with. A full mage like Sulian would far outstrip Ferruk in terms of both power and ability – while sober, anyway – but gutter mages tended to have mastered a small amount of skills to which their talents were particularly suited. In the case of ones who ran with gangs it usually involved either violence or healing, and while Kitt tried not to judge by appearances, Ferruk didn't look like the healing type.

'Put the sword away, and no one needs to get hurt,' one of the others said. It was a tall kyn, with what seemed like an excessive amount of knives belted around his waist. Kyns' fur meant they rarely needed clothes to keep warm and usually only wore simple loincloths, so their belts – used to carry pouches or, in this case, weapons – were their main form of personal ornamentation, and were often embroidered or decorated to indicate their lineage. This one's was plain leather; perhaps he didn't want to be connected to his family name while doing… whatever it was they were going to be doing.

'I'm starting to get the feeling this is about more than just a lost ring,' Kitt said, sheathing her sword.

'I'm not so concerned about the ring as the finger it's on,' Forva said. He smiled at her. 'Don't worry. So long as the ring's in there, you'll get your money. However,' he added, 'I'm going to need to bring you inside to make sure we can find her if she hides herself away somewhere.'

'Hides?' Kitt's stomach sank. 'What, your wife ran away from you? And you used me to find her?'

'Probably thought she could use the ring to buy her way out of town,' the man spat. 'The ring *I* gave her! Well, she never was very smart. So either she's in there, or the person she paid with it is. Either way, I'll have her before long.' He pointed. 'You two, cover the back. Gra'al, bring the diviner. Everyone else, with me.'

The kyn reached out for Kitt's left wrist, and she snatched it away without thinking. Everyone else closed in around her, and she was suddenly at the centre of a small circle that was both unimpressed and well-armed.

'Don't make this harder than it has to be,' Gra'al said. Kitt had heard that tone of voice before, from people who did not particularly want to use violence but were absolutely prepared to do so if necessary. She gritted her teeth, and held her right arm out.

'Fine. But this arm.'

Gra'al the kyn studied her for a moment, then shrugged and took her right wrist instead. Everyone waited, and when he didn't burst into flame or collapse they began to fan out towards the warehouse.

'You're right-handed?' Gra'al asked. He had a knife out in his free hand. 'Sword's on your left hip.'

'Yes, right-handed,' Kitt confirmed, making sure she kept up with him. This had the potential to go very badly, but now she was mired in this mess she had no intention of trying to get out until she was fairly certain she would succeed.

'Just asking, because most people would want to keep their strongest hand free,' Gra'al continued conversationally. 'I know I would.'

'Ferruk,' the leader said. 'The doors, if you please.'

'Most people don't have a bracelet on their left wrist that's the only thing keeping a demon from hunting them down and killing them,' Kitt said quietly to Gra'al. 'Plus anyone that gets between it and me. I didn't want you to pull it off by mistake.'

'Huh,' Gra'al grunted. 'Well, it sounds like you've had an interesting life.'

Ferruk trained her wand on the large wooden doors with a malicious grin, and waved it. A bolt of light shot out, and the doors blew in like they'd been kicked by a god.

'Honestly, up until a couple of weeks ago, my life was pretty standard,' Kitt said, noting in passing that she'd made the right call in not taking a swing at Ferruk. 'Then someone stabbed me, and it's all gone to shit since.'

'You're looking good for someone who was stabbed,' Gra'al commented.

The thugs and their leader plunged in through the door and the kyn followed, towing Kitt behind him. She wondered how well she could draw her sword with her left hand, and whether she would be able to get it into any sort of position to menace Gra'al before he took that wicked-looking knife to her. She decided it was probably unlikely. Besides, the damage was done now, in terms of leading the bastard in charge to his runaway wife, so Kitt might as well hang around, grit her teeth, and accept the money he'd still insisted she was due.

'Yeah, well, there was a mage,' she said, waving her free hand in a vain attempt to waft away the dust and wood splinters through which they were walking.

'There usually is, with humans,' Gra'al said. 'Must be nice, knowing someone can sort you out if you get badly hurt.'

'Amelia!' bellowed Forva. They must have busted into some sort of shipping warehouse, since they were surrounded by crates, with the booms of manually operated pulley cranes looming overhead. 'I know you're in here! You weren't even smart enough to take the ring off!'

There was a moment's silence. Then something tinkled across the wooden floor. The gang boss bent down to pick it up, and Kitt's senses tingled. Her moonstrikers were in their pouch, but she was still tuned in to the object of her search, and that was it.

'And you weren't even smart enough to wonder why I didn't!' a female voice shouted back from somewhere in the darkness.

'This is an ambush, right?' Kitt said to Gra'al.

'Sounds like it.' Gra'al sighed. 'I really hate this job sometimes.'

'So why do it?'

The darkness around them erupted into shouts, immediately followed by armed figures. Kitt threw herself flat on instinct, and the kyn's grip on her wrist hauled him down with her just as a throwing axe *thunked* into the crate where his chest had been. Someone came screaming out of the gloom brandishing a hatchet, but Gra'al released Kitt's wrist to grab the axe wielder's before he could take a swing, then punched him repeatedly in the face with his knife hand until he went limp.

'Gambling debts,' the kyn explained, throwing one long arm out to ensure Kitt stayed behind him. 'I owe Forva a *lot* of money.'

The gang boss himself came back into view, staggering and tripping onto his back. He was pursued by a woman with a long, dark braid and dressed in clothes of a similar quality to his own – Amelia, if Kitt was any judge – who threw herself on top of him and began stabbing him in the chest, screaming with rage and catharsis.

'Ohhh,' Gra'al said, grimacing. 'He's not getting up from that.'

Kitt swallowed, trying not to focus on how Amelia's teeth gleamed in the dim light as she frenziedly drove her knife into her husband again and again.

'Would you say your gambling debts are cleared now?'

'I don't think he'll be coming to collect,' Gra'al agreed.

'Fancy getting out of here?'

The kyn nodded, wincing as Amelia threw her head back and let out something that was half scream, half peal of terrifying laughter. 'Yeah, that sounds good.'

They ran for it, heading for the main doors and doing their best to remain unnoticed, or at least like a lesser priority for violence than anyone else in the vicinity. They'd almost made it when Ferruk dropped down in front of them with her wand glowing and an expression that could have soured milk before it left the cow.

'Gra'al!' she snarled, levelling her wand. 'You traitor! Get back and fight!'

'Forva's dead!' Gra'al protested. 'We should just—'

Ferruk didn't bother to wait for him to finish; she simply blasted him. The same bolt of light that had smashed in the warehouse doors and left only splintered ruins struck Gra'al square in his furred chest…

…and disappeared, its power absorbed by magic's usual refusal to acknowledge the kyn's existence. Gra'al looked down at himself as though expecting to see a smoking hole in his torso, then back up at Ferruk. He bared his fangs.

'Oh shit,' Ferruk managed, before Gra'al grabbed her by the throat and slammed her against the floor several times, then turned around and hurled her back into the fight.

Kitt was already moving, clearing the warehouse and ducking out of line of fire of the doors as soon as possible, just in case Ferruk recovered enough to unleash something at her. Gra'al appeared a moment later, sheathing his knife and adjusting his belt.

'I've wanted to do that for a while,' he confided with a sly smile, then winced again as there was a loud crash from inside, and someone started screaming. 'Best not hang around, though.'

'No,' Kitt agreed, and they set off down the street with the brisk air of people who had nothing whatsoever to do with whatever was happening behind them and, quite frankly, thought the entire thing was a disgrace.

'Are you okay?' Gra'al asked, after they'd turned a corner.

'Uh, yeah,' Kitt said, checking herself over hurriedly. 'Not a scratch.'

'I meant… You've just been in a fight, saw someone die quite messily,' Gra'al continued. 'Some people don't deal well with that sort of thing.'

'To be honest, I've seen people get eaten by slydewasps,' Kitt said. 'You know, there one moment, then…' She reached out with her hand and rapidly closed it into a fist. 'Wham! Just kicking feet disappearing down a throat.'

'Oh.' Gra'al looked quite unwell. 'That sounds… bad.'

'And I've liked every single one of them more than I liked Forva,' Kitt continued, 'even the ones I barely knew. And a week ago, that demon I mentioned killed two guys I'd probably consider friends. So yeah, just now wasn't exactly *nice*, but overall I've seen worse, so I guess I'm good.' She laughed awkwardly. 'Or at least, no worse than I already was.'

'Good, good,' Gra'al said, nodding. 'Look, this is a bit awkward, I know, but I feel I at least owe you a drink.'

Kitt looked at him. 'You think?'

'Yeah, I mean you're not getting paid for the job you've just done, whereas I've just had a whole load of debt cleared off from me, so…' Gra'al tailed off. 'Wait, was that sarcasm?'

'Mmm-hmm.' Kitt nodded vigorously. 'Also, what's this "*a* drink" bullshit?'

Gra'al snorted. 'Fine. I've not got that much on me, but I'm paying until it runs out.'

Kitt from a few weeks ago would probably have thought twice about going drinking with someone who had just hauled her into a fight, albeit under duress himself, but Kitt from a few weeks ago had seen significantly less shit than Kitt from now had, and had a far lower need for alcohol.

'Now you're talking,' she said, slapping the kyn on the shoulder. 'Today sucked; let's make sure tomorrow starts even worse.'

'So,' Kitt said, putting her drink down slightly faster than she'd intended. 'It must be nice to know, to *know*, that magic is not going to fuck you up.' Her eyes went wide at the thought. 'I know you can't get healed, but c'mon! She blasted you like you were a pair of doors and it just went *fssssshh!*' She waggled her fingers in what she thought was an excellent likeness of the spell disintegrating as it struck Gra'al's chest.

'I mean, *sort of?*' the kyn replied. He held one finger up. 'But, y'know how magic doesn't always work, or so I've been told?' He waited for Kitt's nod, then continued. 'Well, sometimes the not working on kyn doesn't always work, either. It's *magic*. It's *weird*. My uncle, he got hexed and it took his leg clean off.' He chopped his hand down onto the limb in question. 'Right there, right at the hip. *Why?*'

'I dunno,' Kitt admitted.

'I dunno either!' Gra'al said, stabbing the table with his finger. 'He didn't know! No one knows. You can be walking around, a kyn doing his own thing, you think that whatever else happens at least you're not gonna lose a leg to some gutter mage with a grudge, and then *bam*! You're hopping.'

'Wow.' Kitt took another swig of her drink. 'Yeah.'

'And then there's the fact that *really*, being immune to magic isn't actually all people reckon,' Gra'al continued, warming to his subject with the enthusiasm of someone three drinks in and accelerating. 'Yeah, if someone zaps me, maybe it goes *fsssssshh*! But if someone magics, like, a crate into the air and drops it on me, I'm still gonna get flattened. If someone magics a sphere of water around me, I'm still gonna drown. I dunno what happens if a chronomancer does time stuff to me, but is time a *thing*? Like water? Cos I reckon that might still work. I know we can't walk into the timeless lands, we get stuck just like anyone...'. He paused. 'You okay?'

'Yeah,' Kitt said, staring into her drink. 'Just... What about destinies? Are they magic? Can you be affected by them?'

'Magic? Don't think they are,' Gra'al said. 'And yeah, we have destinies, course we do! Like, the future was a thing, wasn't it? And then that god—'

'Altrinchor,' Kitt said, her brain coughing the name up and then looking rather surprised that it had managed to do so.

'Altrinchor?' Gra'al's furry brow furrowed. 'Isn't he the gamblers' god?'

'Someone told me it was him who killed the future,' Kitt said, but Plainsong was another lane her memory didn't want to venture down. 'Sorry, you were saying.'

'Right, so, the future was a thing, and then a god smashed it,' Gra'al said. 'All the little bits are still *the future*, right? Just all messed up and broken. And the world's been weird since, or so they reckon.'

'I know a mage who thinks it's all getting worse,' Kitt said miserably, but she didn't want to think about the Swallowmage either, or what might have happened after she ran away from the demon.

'The whole thing's a mess, if you ask me,' Gra'al said. 'I've seen people killed over destinies, right? They're actual *things*, things that you can touch and hold and steal, not just invisible and flapping about in the air until they find whoever they're meant for, or however it used to work.'

'Yeah, well,' Kitt said, drawing an absent-minded circle with one finger in a puddle of spilled beer. 'Maybe it won't be around for long.'

'Hope not!' Gra'al said enthusiastically. Kitt looked up at him in shock.

'You what?'

'I hope it's not around!' Gra'al repeated. 'I hope someone comes along and smashes the future *again*. Smashes it *so hard* that all the little futures get mashed up into, I dunno, *paste* or something, and then you could, like, *splooge* it all back together into one big thing, like it should be.' He sat back, with the confident air of someone who had solved a problem. 'Yeah, that'd do it.'

Kitt stared at him open-mouthed, while her brain tried to process what he'd just said. It sounded like nonsense, but…

but…

…but what if it *wasn't?* Kitt's brain was broadly aware that this was a somewhat anticlimactic way of ending that sentence, but it was also very specifically aware that it was three pints deep into something that came out of a cask painted black, so quite frankly she was lucky it was retaining even this much coherence.

'Hey,' Gra'al said, peering over her shoulder. 'Are those friends of yours?'

Kitt heard running footsteps, and then something crashed into her from the side and knocked her clear off her stool and onto the floor.

THIRTY-SEVEN

Kitt panicked; her assailant had their arms wrapped around her so tightly that she could barely move, and her short sword was trapped underneath her. She thrashed, trying to—

'Kitt!'

The sound of her name being spoken with such excitement cut through the haze of fear and alcohol sufficiently for Kitt to stop struggling for a moment. She craned her neck round in an attempt to work out what was going on, and found her body released and her head being pulled into a quick, light kiss of pure joy. When the other person pulled back Kitt finally got a chance to focus on the warm brown eyes, the freckles, the dark ringlets, and a delighted smile, all about a foot away from her face.

'H-hi Derna,' she managed. Conflicting emotions flailed around inside her, trying to gain purchase: fear, because Kitt had been half-convinced that Derna would knife her next time she saw her in the interests of the world in general; relief, because given that evidence so far suggested Derna wasn't interested in knifing her, this meant that Kitt had a *friend*, an actual *friend* here in Solmouth with her; anger, because Derna had tackled her onto the floor without warning; and a roiling undercurrent of lust, because she was a bit tipsy and it had been a good couple of weeks – or more accurately, a very bad couple of weeks – since she'd been intimate with anyone in any way, and she was on her back with Derna *right there* above her, close enough for their breath to intermingle and, apparently, not opposed to kissing Kitt under at least some circumstances. All these feelings collided and effectively cancelled each other out, leaving Kitt blinking and unmoving, waiting for any part of her brain to prompt her with what she should do next.

'You know,' Two Tongue Derna said, rocking back up onto her haunches and looking slightly hurt, 'I was expecting a bit more enthusiasm than that.'

'She did run away from us,' Arkony said, coming into view past Derna's shoulder. He looked tired. Kitt supposed he wasn't used to the sort of travelling that would have brought him here, let alone fighting with demons. Honestly, it was amazing he'd stuck around…

Kitt's brain, well aware that it was drifting off course, tried to refocus. She struggled up into a sitting position, but Derna had already pushed herself off the floor and sat, looking a little hurt, on a stool to the left of where Kitt had been before her unexpected hug assault.

'Of course she ran, I told her to,' the Swallowmage said, her steps counterpointed by the wooden *thunk* of Jandi on the floor. Sulian looked tired too, but this was less the weary, woe-is-me sort that appeared to be afflicting Arkony, and more the sort that could no longer be bothered to take the time to go around obstacles if going straight through was at all feasible, or even just more satisfying.

'But what are you all doing here?' Kitt asked. She grabbed the table to pull herself up, and righted her stool. 'Not that it's not good to see you, I mean.'

'We wanted to find you,' Derna said slowly, and not without some concern. 'Have you hit your head, or something?'

'How did you know I'd be here?' Kitt asked, worry clenching at her stomach. If *they* could track her…

'We didn't, but Solmouth would be the place to get a ship back to Mereport, and once we got here we asked around for diviners fitting your description,' Sulian said, dropping into a chair with the air of someone who, if it broke under her, would probably just sit in the wreckage.

'Who's your friend?' Derna asked. 'Nice knives, by the way.'

'Cheers,' Gra'al said, raising his mug in salute. He didn't seem particularly startled by this turn of events, but Kitt had already realised that Gra'al seemed to take pretty much everything in his stride.

'Oh, right,' Kitt said, and waved her hand back and forth. 'Gra'al, this is Two Tongue Derna, Sulian the Swallowmage, and…' she saw Arkony hastily shaking his head, and quickly changed tack. 'And, er… Look, he doesn't want to use his real name and I can't think of one, so, sorry. Everyone, this is Gra'al. He sort of kidnapped me for a short while earlier, but everything's okay now and he's buying me drinks. Seriously, Derna, it's okay,' she added, grabbing Derna's forearm as she went for her sword. 'There were reasons, and we're good.'

'If you're sure,' Derna said, glaring as many daggers at Gra'al as he had sheathed on his belt. Then she glanced down at Kitt's hand on her arm, and Kitt hastily withdrew it, her fears of stabbing abruptly resurfacing. This seemed to be the wrong thing to do, though, since Derna bit her lip and looked away.

'Call me, uh, Travin,' Arkony said to Gra'al, finally taking a stool of his own. He grinned sheepishly at Kitt. 'You're right, it *is* hard to think of a name.'

'Now we're past the pleasantries,' the Swallowmage said, and reached out her hand. 'Kitt. You've still got the bracelet?'

'Yup.' Kitt held it out for inspection. 'I'm just hoping the hair doesn't come loose or break or something. Would that stop it from working?'

'Probably,' Sulian admitted, checking the leather with her

thumbs, 'but we can do something a bit more permanent.' She eyed Gra'al. 'I'm too tired to be subtle. Does he know?'

'I told him. Dunno if he believed me.'

'The anti-demon bracelet?' Gra'al asked. He raised his eyebrows, although these were somewhat less prominent on a kyn. 'I'm not saying I *didn't* believe you. I just figured it wasn't worth taking the risk, since that was, y'know, a really weirdly specific excuse for me not to hold your left arm.'

'This would have been during the kidnapping, right?' Derna asked dangerously. Kitt sighed, and grabbed Derna's shoulder to keep her in her seat.

'Yes, but he *listened*, and like I said, *we're fine now.*' Fighting down some misgivings about it, she kept one hand on Derna's shoulder while she threw back the last of her drink, then set her mug down. 'Okay folks, seriously. I'm cursed, and there's a demon after me. *Why are you here?*'

'Because you're our friend,' Derna said immediately. She reached up and patted Kitt's hand companionably with her own. 'Well, my friend, anyway. I don't know if Sulian thinks of you more as some sort of foster kid.'

'Stow it, Derna,' Sulian snapped. She slumped forward onto the table and buried her head in her folded forearms. 'How have I been in a tavern for this long and I don't have a drink yet? You're all bastards.'

'I'm basically here because I have absolutely no clue what else to do,' Arkony admitted.

'Yeah, sorry about that,' Kitt muttered, not looking at him.

'If you hadn't turned up, I might be dead,' Arkony said with a shrug. 'Plus at least I know the truth now. I'll take this as a trade-off, it's just… I told my parents I wanted to make my own destiny, but I hadn't really planned on that meaning losing everything I had first.' He sighed. 'I guess that'll teach me to be careful what I wish for.'

'Anyway, if you're going to destroy the future then it doesn't really matter if we're near you or not, right?' Derna said cheerfully to Kitt. 'Maybe you'll do it when you're really old, and the rest of us are dead anyway. *Or,*' she added, as Sulian looked up to glare at her, 'maybe you don't do it at all, because destinies aren't definite.'

'Kitt, you of all people should know that destinies don't always work out as people expect,' Sulian said, with what Kitt felt was a very obvious attempt to be encouraging in the face of adversity. 'That's why good soothsayers earn so much.'

Gra'al looked back and forth between them. 'Wow. The most interesting thing I've done recently is throw a wellyn at my old boss's wife-turned-murderer, and here you all are talking about destinies and demons and stone knows what else.' He checked his money pouch, then looked meaningfully at Kitt. 'I know I said that drinks are on me, but are your friends up for getting rounds in too, or…?'

'I'm in,' Arkony said, getting up. 'Give me a hand?'

He and Gra'al headed for the bar, and Kitt looked querulously at the other two.

'He's still experiencing the simple joy of buying things from people himself, instead of having servants do it for him,' Derna said simply. 'Suits me; costs me less.'

Something that had been tickling at the back of Kitt's mind finally flourished into a conscious thought. 'Where's Donal? Did the demon get him?'

'No,' Derna muttered. 'He just fucked off, talking shit about how he didn't want to come looking for you if you were cursed, and that we were all fools.'

Kitt bit her lip, and tried not to feel hurt. Donal was far from her favourite person, but he'd not been all bad, and had actually been helpful on more than one occasion. She probably wouldn't have got in to speak to Arkony without him, and now she was left wondering whether his reaction hadn't actually been the most sensible out of them all. After all, it seemed that she *was* cursed, and the rest probably *were* fools for coming to find her.

'How did you get here?' Sulian asked Kitt, trying to change the subject. 'Catch a boat downstream?'

'Found a rowboat and took it,' Kitt admitted. Pretty much anyone who grew up in Mereport knew how to handle a small boat, and there were no waves in a river. 'I don't know if demons can swim, but I thought I'd stay on the channel anyway. And then I figured that if I made it here, and it followed me, there might be people here who could deal with it. But what *happened?*' she asked, leaning closer. 'With the demon and… you know.' Just thinking about Plainsong made her brain water. How had she ever thought he might be human? The way he'd faced the demon down and talked quite calmly about lives that meant nothing to him, then attacked it with those strange, strange blades of his…

'Can't tell you,' the Swallowmage said with a sigh. 'We ran. It was that or get flattened by those two bastards. They levelled half of the graveyard, then started on the town. I never thought it would be possible to dislike someone so much who's saved me from two different hideous monsters,' she added, bitterly.

'So the demon might be dead?' Kitt asked. She didn't dare hope for it, partly because it might not be, and partly because if it was then that meant Plainsong was even more terrifying than she already thought, and presumably still out there somewhere.

'Maybe,' Sulian said. 'Wouldn't bet on it, though. It's probably just lurking around causing trouble and swearing in demon about the fact it can't find you.' She smiled wearily. 'And it won't; I do good work.'

'But that's just another problem I've caused,' Kitt said miserably. 'Every bit of damage it does or life it takes is on *my* head.' She buried her face in her hands and rubbed at her eyes, as all the worries she'd spent the last week trying to forget kicked in the doors of her head and began to party. 'What if the demon is what destroys the future?'

'It won't get to that,' Sulian protested. 'Sooner or later it'll run afoul of something like a mage alliance, or the sharp end of someone else's destiny. Or maybe it'll stray too close to a dragon's lair,' she added, with malicious glee. 'Demons and dragons do *not* like each other.'

Kitt tried to take some comfort from the Swallowmage's words, but no matter how she spun it to herself, no matter what possible solutions were presented to her, she couldn't see any way of looking at things other than: Kitt Carver had fucked up, and the only positives left to her now were ways in which that fuckup might not hurt quite as many people as otherwise.

'Are there no other options?' she asked. 'We just have to hope that something more powerful takes it down?'

'I mean, you *could* go looking for some ancient, enchanted weapon that would give you the power to slay it,' the Swallowmage said, pinching the bridge of her nose. 'But honestly, the odds of finding one are pretty low, or every bastard would be at it. You can't even make new ones, these days; everyone starts asking questions like "what do you need that for?", and then before you know it you've got the Society for the Liberation of Bound Spirits going trebuchet and crawling up your arse demanding to see your workings.'

Kitt and Derna looked at each other, than at Sulian. Kitt cleared her throat.

'Did you try to enchant—'

'A fork!' the Swallowmage snapped. 'I tried to enchant a *fork*, thirty years ago. Why? Because I thought it would be funny to have an eating utensil that could cut through armour like it was paper! Did I think about what that would mean for plates? No, but I never got there because someone told the damned SLBS about it and they shut me down. Am I still angry about it?' She thumped the table and glared at them. 'Yes!'

'O-kay,' Derna said carefully. 'Uh, bringing us back to the

topic of how Kitt's worried about the demon she unleashed destroying the world…'

'We can't kill it,' the Swallowmage said with finality. 'I can make a more resilient enchantment to keep Kitt hidden from it, but everything else is out of our hands now. All the known demon-killing weapons are in the possession of the sort of people who don't go lending them out, no matter how nicely you ask, and if you tell them about a demon you've released they'll probably kill *you* just to make sure you don't do it again.'

'Who's killing demons?' Gra'al asked, returning with mugs of drink, and flanked by Arkony.

'*No one* is killing demons,' Sulian said. She took the proffered tankard from Arkony and swigged from it aggressively, as though the beer within had personally insulted her, then set it down again. 'It's like I was telling these two; we can't get our hands on anything that would do the job, and we can't make something new because that would give us a whole new set of problems with people coming after us, *plus* it's just so damned hard to do, anyway.' She sighed. 'Seriously, that bloody rift didn't just screw up time, it screwed up *everything*. The books say magic used to be…' She blinked rapidly a few times. 'Used to…'

'Is she okay?' Gra'al asked, peering dubiously at the Swallowmage. 'She's only had a couple of mouthfuls.'

Kitt had seen these signs before. 'Foretelling!' she announced, getting to her feet and backing away. 'Give her some room.'

'*Black wings*,' Sulian intoned, staring through the floor. '*Black wings unfold and the world – NO! Three times round the spire, chasing a corpse's breath… the world rises or the heavens fall… clear blue skies crack open and reaches through… cinnamon… cinnamon cinnamon CINNAMON!*'

She vomited. Kitt had got out of range, and Derna and Arkony had wisely imitated her. Gra'al, however, was simply sitting on his stool and watching the Swallowmage with fascination, and so it was the kyn who received the full force of her gastric expulsion.

'What the hell?!' Gra'al wailed, recoiling far too late. Sulian slumped, and Arkony caught her before she hit the floor.

'She'll be fine in a minute,' Kitt told Arkony, who was wide-eyed and shaking.

'How can she be fine?' he demanded. 'She just started yelling nonsense, then threw up!'

'You've not met many drunk people, have you?' Kitt said, clapping him on the shoulder. 'Don't worry, she does this sometimes even when she's sober, it's just the foretellings.' She turned to Gra'al, and winced. 'I did warn you.'

'Yeah, yeah,' the kyn muttered, trying to shake some of the chunkier parts of vomit off his left arm. 'Oh, this is disgusting. This is the only reason to wear clothes.'

'Just take a dip in the harbour,' Derna suggested.

'The harbour?' Gra'al demanded. 'You serious? You got any idea what the salt would do to my fur if I let it dry?' He got to his feet. 'Hey, beer friend. Travin, right? Mind coming outside with me? There's a pump there, and I could do with a hand to wash this off.'

Arkony, still supporting Sulian, glanced helplessly at Kitt. 'I...'

'Go on, we've got her,' Kitt said. Arkony somewhat gratefully let her take the Swallowmage's weight and hurried off after Gra'al, and Kitt immediately folded Sulian forwards so her head rested on her arms on the table again.

'We're probably going to get kicked out of here in a moment,' Derna said, eyeing the spattered vomit on the floor and table.

'Yeah, probably,' Kitt agreed. The silence stretched awkwardly, and her brain nudged her mouth to do something, *anything* about the utter mess they'd both made of Derna's reappearance. 'Look, I—'

'Fuck!' Sulian shouted, jerking upright in her chair and nearly losing her balance. She grimaced, and grabbed her tankard to take a swig. 'Oh, foretelling vomit is the worst-tasting vomit, I swear.' She blinked and looked around. 'Where are the other two?'

'You got Gra'al,' Kitt told her. 'He's outside with Arkony.'

'Whoops,' Sulian muttered, and took another swig. 'Did I say anything that made sense?'

'Not really,' Derna said. 'So, about that demon.'

'Let it *go*, Derna!' Kitt said desperately. She grabbed Derna's hands and held them in hers. 'Look, I understand that you're trying to help, and I appreciate it, I really do. But you heard Sulian: there's nothing we can do.'

'But there is!' Derna said, her eyes bright. The Swallowmage groaned.

'This is either going to be a bad idea, as in it won't work, or an absolutely downright *terrible* idea,' she said, twisting around in her chair, 'as in, there's just enough chance of it working that we get ourselves killed attempting it.' She sighed, and squared her shoulders. 'Alright, out with it.'

'You said the odds of finding an ancient, enchanted weapon are pretty low,' Derna began.

'Yes, obviously,' Sulian replied. 'Professional treasure hunters have cleaned out every ruin and abandoned palace, of which there are considerably fewer than stories would have you believe, I might add.'

'But that's just it,' Derna said eagerly. 'We know where one is!'

Kitt's brow wrinkled. 'What do you—'

'We know where to find,' Derna said, grinning ear to ear, 'the weapon that *killed the fucking future*.'

THIRTY-EIGHT

'Well,' Sulian said after a couple of moments. 'Wow. We've actually found something worse than "absolutely downright terrible". I feel I should be impressed.'

'What?' Derna demanded. 'It's sitting right there! We saw it!'

'Yes,' Kitt admitted, while her mind backed away slightly from the implications of what Derna was suggesting. 'We saw the actual weapon of a god, still stuck in the sky. Derna, I've seen a demon claw its way into our plane of existence and tell me how it wants to kill me, and I'm *still* not sure I found that scarier than the Swordstar.'

'You might have found it scary,' Derna said with a sniff. '*I* just found it exciting.'

'That doesn't help!'

'Girls, I think we need to continue this discussion outside,' the Swallowmage said, rising to her feet and jerking her head. Kitt followed her gaze and saw the burly tavern owner heading towards them with an expression speaking volumes about her opinions on the redecoration of her establishment through the medium of stomach contents.

'Point taken,' Kitt said miserably, and hurried out past the other patrons and into the square outside, where Gra'al was washing in the thin stream of water that Arkony coaxed out of the pump. The kyn saw them approaching and shook his arm thoroughly, then began to squeeze the water out. Summer still had the land in its grip; even this late, and next to the sea, Solmouth was warm enough that Kitt imagined he would be dry before too long.

'I know you think I'm just after it because it's a weapon, but think about it,' Derna was saying. 'Have you got a better idea?'

'I think pretty much every other idea in the history of ideas is a better idea,' Sulian said sharply. 'Pulling my own toenails out with my teeth sounds like a better idea! It would be easier, less painful, and less likely to make the world an even worse place than it already is.'

'What are you talking about?' Gra'al asked curiously.

'We're going to get a weapon to kill the demon that's hunting Kitt,' Derna said, as casually as though she were suggesting popping to the market to pick up a couple of fish for dinner.

'Cool,' Gra'al said. Then he frowned. 'Hey, why are you all out here?'

'We got kicked out because *someone* threw up,' Derna said, glowering at the Swallowmage.

'Well, excuse me!' Sulian said, rounding on Derna. 'You think I *want* these damned things in my head? You think I want to see fragments of possible futures? The world is broken, and the pieces are ending up *inside my skull!*'

'I had most of a pint in there!' Gra'al said indignantly, staring towards the tavern with the air of one unjustly wronged.

'So do something about it!' Derna said, ignoring the kyn and placing her hands on her hips to stare the Swallowmage down. 'Help us go back and get the Swordstar so we can kill the demon, and then at least the world will be that little bit better than it is now!'

'You can't just bring that sort of thing into the world and think it will make things *better!*' Sulian shouted. 'Look what it did before! And even if just touching it doesn't kill you, and even if you can use it to kill the demon, what are you going to do with it after that? You're going to be in the middle of about five wars at once, because everyone, and I mean *everyone*, is going to be coming after you to try to get it for themselves!' She jabbed Derna in the chest. 'I'm not talking a couple of brigands at a time, I'm talking actual armies, all of them hunting you!'

'Maybe I'm fine with that!' Derna shouted back. She threw her arms wide. 'You tell me, Sulian: who's going to miss me?'

'*SHUT UP!*' Kitt screamed.

They both turned to stare at her; she was sure of that much, at least. The square was illuminated by pools of light from lamps, but through the blurring effect of the tears welling treacherously up in her eyes, Kitt couldn't make out expressions.

'I fucked up,' she said miserably. 'I lied to the spirit and I summoned the demon, and now Falzine and Vem are dead, and gods know who else. And that would be enough, wouldn't it?' she continued, with a hollow laugh. 'That would be enough shit for one person, but I'm also cursed to destroy the future, apparently. And I ran away to begin with to get away from the demon, but I never wanted you to find me!' She swiped at her eyes and tried to ignore the look on Derna's face.

'You're all meant to be somewhere else,' she said firmly, through a choked throat. 'We don't have any sort of realistic plan, we don't have anything that can help. So just *go away*, and if I fuck up again and the demon finds me, or, or I start to actually end the world or something, you won't be between it and me. That's all I'm after, at this point.'

'Kitt—' Derna began.

'No, Derna!' Kitt interrupted her. 'Let the damned Swordstar be! I don't want you risking everything just for me.

You want to know who'd miss you? *I'd* miss you!' Emotions whirled up inside, fighting against each other for prominence, and Kitt found herself shoving Derna away. 'So let me miss you! Let me wonder how you're doing, and hope you're doing okay, rather than knowing you ruined your life doing something for me that never had a chance of working!'

'Kitt,' Sulian said softly. 'We're not going anywhere.'

Kitt hesitated, teetering between the desire to attack them all, to literally drive them away from her, and to collapse into Sulian's arms and start sobbing as though the Swallowmage was her mother. But even Kitt's mother wasn't her mother, not really. One candidate took her as a part exchange on a deal to make sure Annity was fed, and the other never noticed Kitt had been replaced. Kitt couldn't have sought comfort from either of them, knowing what she did now, but at least there was the notion that one or other of them might have some duty towards her; some expectation to at least bear witness to her misery and despair. Sulian was neither of them, and she had her own problems to deal with. She didn't need Kitt's as well.

'Fine,' Kitt said, swallowing. 'If you're not going anywhere, I will.'

She turned and ran, until she was lost in Solmouth's streets and the shouts from behind her faded into nothing.

SOLMOUTH HAD JUST one bridge over the Solwynd, a gigantic arch of stone with no visible joints that looked as though it had been carved from one immense rock, wide enough for a pair of two-horse wagons to pass each other in opposite directions with space to spare, and tall enough for all but the very mightiest ships to slip beneath it on their way up and down the river. It was apparently the work of a mage who had been showing off, which seemed to Kitt to be the source of a great deal of the world's wonders and woes in roughly equal measure. Mages being who they were, he had formed the carved balustrades in such a way that when the sun set the holes in them cast shadows across the bridge's surface of a suggestive or even obscene nature. Various Solmouth rulers had attempted to cover the bridge's sides at one point or another and, the general public being who *they* were, had usually found their efforts quickly removed.

Kitt was leaning on the western side of the bridge and staring downriver towards the distant blackness of the ocean, which was all but invisible save for the occasional faint sparkle of moonlight on a wave crest. She was aware in a sort of general sense that being alone on the bridge at night was an open invitation to be stabbed, have her pockets rifled, and possibly be tipped over the side into the river, but Kitt was at the point where the prospect summoned up nothing more than a bleak acceptance. She'd come to Solmouth in a sort of daze, trying to hold on to something familiar in the aftershock of events in Derringsmoot. She found a port city, she set about earning money through divining, and lied to herself that she was simply trying to get back to Mereport, as though… what? That being back in the city she considered home would magically make everything better? That it would keep her safe from a demon that knew the scent of her soul, and could track her anywhere should she lose the tenuous protection of the Swallowmage's bracelet? That it would somehow change the destiny with which she'd been cursed as a child?

Destinies weren't fireproof, as everyone with an ounce of sense knew. However, destines were incredibly difficult to actually *thwart*. One way or another, the shards of the future tended to twist events to their own designs.

Kitt had never considered herself to be particularly fatalistic. She'd always approached life with a vaguely good-natured optimism, and the belief that if she looked out for herself and tried to be at least relatively sensible then she could have some measure of control over what happened to her.

She'd never been tempted by the destinies she'd found, but had that been her? Or was it her own destiny at work, letting her subconscious know that no matter what she did, no other destiny would be able to take hold of her now? She was going to *destroy everyone's future*. Had her entire life to this point simply been acted out in service of that end, with her own free will nothing more than an illusion?

She became aware of footsteps approaching. Not the soft and subtle tread of someone trying to hide their approach, or the hurried gait of someone out late and trying to get past this person of unknown temperament staring blankly into the night, but the simple *one-two one-two* of someone who knew where they were going and had no reason to believe that anything would prevent them getting there.

The footsteps stopped next to her, and someone leant their forearms on the balustrade, a foot or so away from her own.

'Hi, Derna,' Kitt said quietly.

'Thanks for running away,' Derna said, her tone unexpectedly containing no sarcasm at all.

Kitt's brow furrowed in surprise. She looked to her right and found Derna staring westwards too, not at her.

'Excuse me?'

'At Derringsmoot,' Derna said. 'I get it. Sort of, anyway. You ran away because you were scared, and I don't blame you. But if the demon was going to do anything, it was going to follow you, and that would take it away from us. Also, you distracted it when it was about to smash me. So, thanks. You were looking out for us.'

'I was mainly just scared,' Kitt said, honestly.

'Well, you were looking out for us, even if you didn't exactly mean to,' Derna said with a shrug, still gazing downriver. 'That's good enough for me.'

Kitt grimaced. 'Is this some sort of weird way of persuading me that my actions have good consequences even if I don't intend them to?'

'No,' Derna admitted. Her mouth quirked into a grin. 'Sounds like a solid argument to me, though.' Kitt snorted derisively, and Derna finally glanced at her. 'That, not so much.'

'How did you find me, anyway?'

'When you were upset when we were kids, you'd always go to that little bridge down at the bottom of Bell Street and watch the stream under it,' Derna said. 'I figured there's only one bridge here, but the theory might still hold.'

Kitt snorted again, more gently this time. 'As I recall, that was where *you* used to go when *you* were upset.'

Derna shrugged. 'It was a good bridge. Plus, sometimes it had you there.'

Kitt laughed softly. 'Are you saying you used to sneak out to see me?'

'Are you saying you didn't?'

Kitt's cheeks heated, and she looked away. Then she bit her lip. 'Fine, I did. And maybe sometimes I'd pretend to be more upset about something than I was, because then you'd give me a hug.'

'That's more honesty than I was expecting,' Derna said slowly, from behind her right shoulder. 'Thanks, Kitt.'

'Yeah well,' Kitt muttered. 'If I'm going to end the world then maybe I won't be embarrassed about it for too long.'

'You know, you could have just asked for a hug.'

'But then you might not have hugged me, and then I'd have been upset for real,' Kitt said. Her lips were trembling, and it felt as though all her bones had become glass.

'This is some weird normal person thing, isn't it?' Derna said. 'You can almost always have a hug, if you want one.'

'Almost always?' Kitt said, inspecting the stone beneath her fingers as though it contained the truth of the universe.

'Well, yeah. Not if I'm sick, or you're sick. Or if I'm really sweaty, because that would be disgusting. And if I've got a broken rib or something then you'd have to be gentle. But basically, almost always.'

'Ah.' Kitt swallowed. 'Okay.'

There were a few moments of near silence, broken only by the faint, never-changing, always-changing noise of the river beneath them.

'Kitt?'

'Yeah?'

'Do you want a hug?'

Kitt managed to nod, and then Derna's arms were around her, and Kitt was clinging to Derna as though she was life itself. Derna squeezed, and that faint pressure was all that was needed to burst the dam; Kitt started crying, the tears leaking down over her cheeks and dripping off her chin onto Derna's shoulder.

Someone who wasn't Derna might have said encouraging things like 'there, there', or 'everything will be okay', and then Kitt might have actually bitten them, because everything *wasn't* going to be okay, and that was the *point*. Derna said nothing. She just held on until the tears gradually stopped coming.

'I've made your shoulder all wet,' Kitt muttered, after somewhere between thirty seconds and two hours.

'Doesn't matter,' Derna said, her mouth still level with the back of Kitt's jawbone. 'Sulian threw up on someone earlier, this is way better.'

Kitt's laugh was a sniffly laugh, because her face was damp and her nose was snotty, but it was still a laugh, and it did something to shift a little of the weight that hung around her neck. She pulled back from the hug slightly, keeping her right hand on Derna's shoulder while wiping at her eyes and her nose with her left sleeve. 'Sorry.'

'Don't worry about it,' Derna said. She hadn't let go, and Kitt was in no hurry to make her. 'I'm not sure what other use I can be, but I can do hugs.'

'Hugs are good,' Kitt said. She felt emptier now, but it was a quiet sort of empty. Some of the pressure had been released, and although it didn't change anything about her actual situation, she'd take feeling a bit shaky over the permanent tension. 'You know, I wish we hadn't drifted apart after we were kids. I think that was my fault, and I'm sorry.'

'Don't worry about it,' Derna said, smiling. 'I was pretty insufferable. All I cared about was swords and fencing at that point. I'd have been an awful friend.'

'Doesn't matter,' Kitt said firmly. 'I just got scared of who you were, and that's on me. You've *never* been an awful friend, and I wish I'd realised that sooner.'

To Kitt's astonishment, Derna looked embarrassed. 'I'm sorry about earlier,' she said. 'That was sort of an awful friend thing, putting pressure on you like that. If I see a problem, I want to solve it. I was just trying to be useful, but it doesn't always work that way.'

'I know,' Kitt sighed. 'It's just… I guess I wanted to live quietly. Keep my head down, and not do anything interesting or important. Hope that if no one noticed me, maybe I could avoid ruining everything for everyone. And then you show up, and you have this idea which is the biggest thing anyone's done in centuries, and it's exactly the sort of thing which could go so wrong that it might literally end the world.' She laughed again, and felt the slight tug of mania at the edges. 'Which is an absolutely ridiculous thing to be saying about something involving *me*, but it feels true.'

Derna pursed her lips. 'The way I look at it, your destiny might be inevitable, or it might not. If it is, then nothing we do or don't do is going to change it. If it isn't, we should probably give stopping it our best shot, right? And if the demon's going to bring about the end of the world, let's try killing the bastard.' She smiled, slightly brittle. 'Hugs and killing things, that's me.'

'But what if the demon is just my problem, because I fucked up?' Kitt asked miserably. 'And what if by trying to stop *that*, we end the world?'

Derna sighed. 'This might be the weirdest thing I'll ever say, but: sometimes you just have to figure out who the people are in your life that you're willing to gamble the world for.'

Kitt stared at her with her mouth open. She was dimly aware of the concept of words, but had about as much chance of snaring them into some kind of order as a fish did of tap-dancing its way up a mountain.

'*But*,' Derna added, after a second, 'it's your future, and I'm not going to force you into anything. And if you want, I'll leave—'

'No,' Kitt said, instantly. 'No, stay. Please.' She realised that she'd unconsciously gripped both of Derna's shoulders, and relaxed her grip a little.

'Okay,' Derna said. She smiled gently, and Kitt found herself returning it.

'You know,' Kitt said, with a rueful chuckle. 'When you tackled me off my stool in the tavern, I wondered if you'd come to kill me—'

'You wondered *what?*' Derna said sharply, pulling away. 'Why would you think that?'

Kitt swallowed, trying to ignore the sudden sensation that the bridge was cracking beneath her. 'You *always* do what you think is right. It doesn't matter what the consequences will be, or how many people are standing against you. It's kind of terrifying,' she admitted, 'but I guess it's also one of the things I love about you. I just thought that maybe, given what we know, you'd figure that killing me would be one way to save the world.'

'Let me make this clear,' Derna said, and now there were tears in *her* eyes. 'The only time I would even *think* that killing you would be the right thing to do would be if you were actually asking me to do it, do you understand?' She bit her lip. 'Would you kill *me?* If you thought it might save the world?'

'No,' Kitt said instantly. 'I'd try to find another way.'

'Why?'

Derna had always sat in Kitt's mind as quite large; not because of her stature, but simply down to her personality. She took up a lot of the available space, with edges sharp enough that everyone with any sense gave her a bit more room, just in case. Now, caught in a pool of lamplight, she looked almost small.

Kitt took a deep breath.

'Because even if the world carried on, it wouldn't be as good without you in it,' she managed.

Derna swallowed visibly. Then she stepped closer again, almost hesitantly, and reached up to very delicately tuck a strand of Kitt's hair behind her ear. The tip of her finger brushed against the side of Kitt's scalp as she did so, and left a line of tingling fire on Kitt's skin in its wake.

'I know what *I* think the right thing to do now is,' Derna said softly. She trailed her finger down behind Kitt's ear and along her jawline. 'Especially since the world might end at some point. But if you tell me that it's not the right thing, I'll listen.'

Kitt's heart was beating so fast it felt like it might fly clean out of her ribcage, but she barely had the awareness to register that. Instead, she found her own hand rising up, almost of its own accord, to slip in through the mass of Derna's dark ringlets and nestle next to her head. Derna leaned into Kitt's touch slightly, but she didn't blink her warm brown eyes, or look away. Kitt had always liked Derna's eyes, and now she was starting to fall into them, along with those lips that were ever so slightly parted...

'Fuck it,' whispered Kitt Carver, and kissed her.

THIRTY-NINE

Kitt wasn't sure exactly how much later they pulled apart, but it was long enough that her skin felt on fire. Her breath hitched slightly as she breathed in.

'You okay?' Derna asked gently.

'Just terrified,' Kitt murmured. One of Derna's eyebrows quirked upwards slightly, and she hastened to explain. 'I never kissed someone who *meant* something before. You know; you meet someone, you have fun, it doesn't really come to anything and you go your separate ways. No real stakes, nothing to lose. And also,' she added, winding a strand of Derna's hair around her finger, 'I'm sort of kicking myself that I didn't try this years ago.'

'Yeah, me too,' Derna agreed. She smiled. 'But hey, at least we tried it now, right?'

Kitt nodded. A tiny golden seed had sprouted in her chest, a faint spark of light. It wasn't much against the dark hollow of background misery that still threatened to swallow her down if she thought about it for too long or too hard, but it was something. Someone knew the truth and didn't blame her; someone who had heard the nature of the destiny that wormed its way under Kitt's skin when she was a child, and had seen her release a demon into the world through sheer carelessness, still thought she was worth something. Kitt had always been a big believer in the idea that self-worth was more important than the opinions of others, but by all the gods it was nice to have some backup when her own mind failed her on that front.

'I would love to find somewhere that isn't a bridge where we could continue this conversation,' Derna said ruefully, 'but we should probably get back to the others first, before the Swallowmage starts knocking buildings down to find us.'

Kitt nodded. 'Okay, fine.' She prodded Derna in the ribs. 'I've got a room. It's tiny, and it's not worth what I've been paying for it, but it's a room.'

'Well, I *don't* have a room, on account of only just having arrived here,' Derna said, her eyes mischievous, 'so if you're offering me a place to sleep then it would be foolish of me to refuse, right?'

'Definitely foolish,' Kitt agreed, with a smile. 'Maybe even rude.'

'It's settled, then. But we really should find Sulian first, or she will actually skin us.'

By the time they got back to the square in which Kitt had left the others, it became clear exactly how close Sulian was to skinning someone. Gra'al and Arkony were sitting on the raised bricks around the pump pool and apparently passing the time by playing a game that involved flipping one of the kyn's many knives and catching it again without losing your fingers, since it appeared that Gra'al could and would easily make friends with pretty much anyone. The Swallowmage, on the other hand, was standing with her arms folded and glowering in the direction Kitt had gone, while Jandi bobbed nervously behind her.

'*There* you are!' Sulian exclaimed, as soon as Kitt came back into view. She snatched Jandi out of the air and hurried over, her face a picture of aggravated concern. 'Are you okay?'

'Yes,' Kitt said, more or less honestly. It was fairly true that she was not, in fact, okay, but she was definitely more okay than she had been when she'd fled the square, which was the question Sulian was actually asking.

'Hmm.' The Swallowmage inspected her for a moment, for all the world as if Kitt was her daughter and she was trying to work out if she'd come home drunk. Then her gaze jumped to Derna, and back to Kitt, and her eyes narrowed. 'Wait a minute, have you two *kissed?*'

Kitt's mouth dropped open in shock. She looked at Derna, who appeared similarly gobsmacked.

'About bloody time,' Sulian continued testily, without waiting for an answer, and wrenching the footing out from beneath Kitt again before she'd had time to confirm, deny, fake incomprehension, or even regain her mental balance. 'Oh, don't look at me like that,' she said to Kitt, who wasn't aware that she was looking at anyone like anything. 'I might be a drunk, but I've got eyes and ears, and a brain that works at least half the time. Which appears to be more than can be said for you two.'

'Are you done?' Derna said, putting her hands on her hips.

'I suppose,' Sulian sighed. 'And I'm also *knackered*. It's well past a sensible person's bedtime. It's a good thing the Mages' Guildhouse will put me up.' She eyed them both. 'I'll sort Arkony out as well, shall I? Guild rules say I can have a guest. And then in the morning, maybe we can talk sensibly about what we're going to do next.'

'Bright and early, then!' Derna shouted after her as the Swallowmage stomped away, Jandi thudding into the ground with every second step. Sulian flipped her a middle finger without looking around.

The night involved more kissing, not to mention quite a bit of giggling, but also some tears. Kitt tried to reassure Derna that it wasn't anything to do with her, or at least not in a bad way; it was just that she finally felt safe enough to actually *feel* something. She cried for the deaths of Vem and Falzine, and she cried for the fact that the misplaced care, or love, or greed, or ambition – or all of them – of her birth parents had cursed her with a destiny that might see her destroy the world. And then she kissed Derna some more, since there seemed to be a lot of time to make up for on that front, which was a sentiment with which Derna apparently vehemently agreed, and then…

Well, whether or not they went through with Derna's honestly quite ludicrous plan, the fact that knowing someone was willing to stand by her no matter how bad things got felt like a massive weight had been lifted from Kitt's shoulders. And she was in bed with that person, a person still as attractive to her now as she had been a week ago when Kitt had first had that startling realisation, so it seemed like that was going to stick and hadn't been some sort of brief hallucination. And Derna was very clear that she found Kitt attractive too, and so while Kitt would have been quite happy to drift off to sleep nestling into Derna's hair and simply feeling more at peace than she had done for quite some time, when Derna's kisses got a little more insistent, Kitt was certainly not going to complain.

When Derna's mouth broke away from hers, Kitt had a moment of terror that she'd done something wrong, or that Derna had suddenly thought better of it. Then Derna's kisses tracked down the side of her neck to her shoulder, and Kitt's worry melted away. Her fingers picked out the harder, smooth scars as they tracked across the soft skin of Derna's body, until she had a hand resting on the curve of Derna's hip. Meanwhile, one of Derna's hands had slipped up under Kitt's top, and Kitt gasped faintly in pleasure as those sword-calloused fingers brushed across her breast.

'Kitt?'

'Yes?'

'Are you sure you want this?' Derna asked quietly. 'Right now?'

'You're asking me this when your hand's on my tit?' Kitt whispered back, trying not to giggle. It should have been awkward, and with anyone but Derna, maybe it would have been. Maybe with Derna, either everything was awkward, or nothing was.

'Bad at being a person, remember?' Derna said. Her face was mere inches away, and her expression was soft, but serious. 'I need to know, so I need to ask.'

For answer, Kitt eased Derna over onto her back, and hovered above her for a moment. 'You're not bad at being a person. But you know what I'm *good* at?'

'What?'

'Divining.' Kitt ducked down to kiss her again, then slid her hand around from Derna's hip to the front of Derna's body, her fingers sliding under Derna's waistband and questing downwards as she did so. 'I wonder what I might find…'

FORTY

Kɪᴛᴛ's sᴛᴀʏ ɪɴ Solmouth so far might have been mired in misery and beer, but she was still a diviner, and one thing she was always capable of finding was a good breakfast. Arianne's was near the waterfront, with rickety tables and handfuls of flowers shoved into blue-glazed, somewhat asymmetric earthenware that were probably meant to be vases, and a smell of grease so strong you could practically surf on it. It was the favoured haunt of dockers, but once they'd cleared out there was space for Kitt, Derna, Sulian, Arkony and, to Kitt's surprise, Gra'al.

'What's he doing here?' Derna demanded of Sulian, who shrugged, and pointed in the direction of Arkony.

'Gra'al seemed nice,' Arkony said, slightly defensively. 'And when I was talking to him last night, he said he wouldn't mind coming with us.'

'He kidnapped Kitt,' Derna said, her tone making it quite clear what she thought about that. Kitt, who'd always been firm with herself that she would never get into a relationship with someone who started fights on her behalf, had the abrupt realisation that that ship had well and truly sailed. On the other hand, Derna had started fights on Kitt's behalf even when they'd just been friends; and for that matter, when Kitt hadn't been entirely sure *what* they were.

'And the kidnapping is sort of why I want to come with you,' Gra'al said calmly. Given how many knives he had on his person, Kitt was glad he didn't take offence easily. 'I did that because my old boss was holding my gambling debts over my head, but now his wife's *probably* taken his racket over, which means I'm either going to be very unpopular for working for him, or she might find the evidence of the debts and use that to make me work for her. Or both.' He speared a fried mushroom with yet another knife, and popped it into his mouth. 'So getting out of town sounds like a good plan, and I'm sure you all said something about killing a demon, which is definitely a goal I can get behind. My uncle was killed by a demon.'

'I thought you said your uncle lost a leg to a hex?' Kitt asked.

'I have a lot of uncles,' the kyn replied, chewing.

'You know what?' Kitt said. 'Fine. You can come. You didn't have to get me out of there yesterday, or buy me drinks afterwards, so we're cool.' She looked at Derna, expecting an argument, but Derna just shrugged.

'It's your destiny, Kitt, so it's your call. If you think he can help, bring him,' she said. Kitt wondered about thanking her, decided that might sound patronising, and settled for a squeezing Derna's hand instead. Sulian saw, and rolled her eyes.

'You're not still thinking of going after the Swordstar, are you?' the Swallowmage said, her tone indicating that she suspected she already knew the answer to her question. Her breakfast had mainly arrived in a tankard. 'It's ridiculous. Kitt, tell her.'

'I think Derna has a point,' Kitt said, quietly. 'No, seriously Sulian, she does. I don't know how much we can do about… me.' She gestured vaguely at herself. 'But maybe we can do something about the demon, and if we can, then we should. It will come for me if I take the bracelet off, right?'

'Yes,' the Swallowmage said immediately. 'And *fast*. Demons don't treat space and distance like we do; travel to them is more about connection, and desire, and hatred. If it senses you, you won't get much warning.'

'Why hasn't anyone tried to use that for travelling long distances?' Gra'al asked, curiously.

'Oh, they have.' Sulian shuddered. 'Mistakes were made.'

'As in they did it wrong?'

'As in they tried it at all.'

'*Anyway*,' Kitt cut in. 'If I take the bracelet off, the demon will come. Which is awful, and scary, but it means that at least we can use that to trap it if we're ready for it.'

'We won't be ready for it,' Sulian said. 'But, whatever. Maybe we'll kill a demon and find some way to make sure no one comes after us for having the Swordstar in the first place. But just to be clear, you are *not* taking the bracelet off until we've worked out if we can even get the Swordstar out of… whatever it is it's actually stuck into. Okay?'

'Sounds sensible,' Kitt agreed, although something was nagging at the back of her mind. However, every time she tried to focus on it, it slipped away and got lost in the nebulous mist of other worries she was wrestling with at any given time.

'I have a question,' Derna said, helping herself to bacon. 'Kitt's going because the demon is her problem. I'm going because it's Kitt's problem. Gra'al's coming because facing demons is preferable to facing crime bosses, apparently, and Sulian is coming because she's a shameless do-gooder who just pretends to be grumpy.'

The Swallowmage said nothing, but the weight of her glare could have pulped fruit. Derna ignored her and pointed her fork at Arkony. 'My question is, why are *you* coming?'

Arkony looked awkward. 'Well, I did want to make my own destiny. Defeating a demon is definitely a worthy thing to attempt, and that thing was pure evil, but I'd still rather face it again than my parents. And… you seem to know what you're doing?'

Sulian burst out laughing. 'Not even the gods know what *we're* doing!'

'Fine, maybe not in the larger sense,' Arkony admitted defiantly, 'but you're good people with good intentions, and that's something worthwhile.'

'A lot of damage has been done by good intentions,' the Swallowmage muttered.

'Oh, give *over!*' Derna protested. 'You're even worse than usual this morning. Is the hangover that bad? I didn't think you drank much last night!'

'I didn't,' Sulian said, into her tankard. 'I think that's the problem.'

'You just need to take this one thing at a time,' Gra'al said. 'Killing the demon is step one, right?'

'Oh, there are a lot of steps before we get to that,' Sulian said.

'Fine, okay, but that's the first *goal*,' Gra'al amended. 'That's a good thing to do anyway. Then, if we manage that, who's to say that we *can't* stop Kitt's awful destiny?'

'I'm really not trying to be the killjoy here, but it's just not that easy,' the Swallowmage said sadly. 'Destines are very powerful, especially the big ones. No matter what you throw at the future, it always bounces back.'

'That's it,' Kitt said slowly, as the pieces dropped into place. Everyone at the table looked at her curiously, which seemed like a reasonable enough reaction.

'What's what?' Derna asked.

'I think it makes sense,' Kitt said, speaking carefully in case the somewhat fragile construction her brain had put together fell apart if she jostled it too vigorously. 'The gods, and the destinies, and the Swordstar… Derna, Sunderstorm killed the Wolfdragon, right?'

'Yeah,' Derna said slowly. 'The enchantment on the blade prevented it from healing. It was the only weapon that could do it.'

Kitt clasped her hands together, pressed her index fingers to her lips, and took a deep breath. The simple act of speaking the words wouldn't change anything material, but it *would* determine whether or not the faint, flickering embers of hope in her chest were allowed to flare into something bigger or be stomped into cold nothingness by the booted feet of Logic and Reason.

At least, insofar as Logic and Reason held any sway here. This was magic, after all.

'We heard the story of how Altrinchor tried to kill the future,' she said, trying to keep her voice level, as though that would help her theory fit together. 'He had to sacrifice his arm – and okay, he was the god of fate, so maybe he needed a part of himself to make the weapon affect the future, right?'

The Swallowmage nodded slowly. 'It's feasible.'

'What if he needed Sunderstorm precisely because of the enchantment?' Kitt asked. 'What if he needed that specific blade *because* the future is so good at healing itself? And it was the only way he could strike it a blow that would last.'

Sulian spread her hands. 'Again, this is beyond my area of expertise, but I'm not prepared to rule it out. What's your point?'

'My point,' Kitt said, finally allowing herself to get just the smallest bit excited, 'is that the Swordstar is *still there*. It's literally stuck into, like you said, whatever it is it's actually stuck into.' She took another deep breath. 'What if it's still preventing the future from healing? And what happens if we – if *I* – take it out?'

The Swallowmage opened her mouth to reply, then tilted her head to one side. '*Fuck*.'

'If that means the future can heal itself, then all the little shards of it, all the destinies, get...' Kitt waved her hands helplessly, and ended up pointing at Gra'al. 'They get smashed into one. Gra'al put it like that last night, right before you arrived. But if the destinies become one big thing again, not divided up, then there are no more *futures*, plural. I've destroyed them. All there is left is *one* future, *the* future.'

'I was down with this plan anyway,' Derna said. 'Since it was, you know, my plan. But if we think it might go even better than expected, that's just a bonus.'

'It's… a possibility,' Sulian admitted slowly. 'There's just enough sense in that. And gods know I *want* it to be true.' She took a swig of her drink, then picked up a piece of toast and eyed it dubiously. 'It still leaves us with the problem of what we're going to do with the Swordstar, but—'

'But nothing!' Derna interrupted, eyes alight. 'We'll use it to kill the demon, like we planned! But are you listening to what we're talking about? If Kitt's right then we could heal the damned world! Who *cares* what happens after that?'

The Swallowmage stared at her for a moment, then snorted and shook her head. 'You know what? Fine. Fine. We finish breakfast, and then…' She raised her tankard in a wry salute. 'Let's go and save the world.'

'You see?' Arkony said with a grin. 'You *definitely* know what you're doing.'

FORTY-ONE

Arkony hadn't met many people who scared him. Marquin had always been kind, although had shown occasional flashes of the man he'd needed to be when acting as the family's factor. Gerone Plynn was an amiable dandy, but there was no doubt he could still be deadly, despite his advancing years; it was his manner, not lack of skill, that made him unthreatening. Both of Arkony's parents – as he continued to think of them, since they'd certainly fulfilled the role, albeit unwittingly – had scared him at times, but that was the fear most children had of their parents' disapproval. That had turned into the fear of his parents' considerable resources being turned against him instead of supporting him, rather than a dread of Draymere Grike himself appearing with a weapon in his hand. Now, however, Arkony found himself travelling up an increasingly disused road towards the timeless lands with no fewer than three people who, if he stopped to think about it, would normally have scared him witless.

The most obvious was the Swallowmage, stumping along with her strange staff in her hand. She was a mage, which by definition meant she had an enormous amount of power.

She also appeared to live on the perpetual knife-edge of being just drunk enough to keep the voices somewhat at bay, without being so drunk she lost control. That was certainly not a balancing act Arkony envied, and was definitely a background concern when being attempted by someone who could turn you inside out with only moderate effort, and whose default presentation was that of someone who might be very tempted to do just that if you annoyed her.

Then there was Gra'al. As a large furred and fanged creature with an enormous amount of knives, Gra'al *should* have been terrifying. The gobel-kyn had their own hierarchies that did not intersect and only rarely interacted with those of human nobility, so Arkony had never met a kyn socially, or even antisocially. However, much like Gerone Plynn – albeit in a very different way – Gra'al's temperament meant Arkony felt a lot safer around him than he would have predicted when he'd first seen the kyn sitting on a stool in a pub in Solmouth.

Kitt Carver wasn't scary. The demon that was after her was scary, and the notion that she might end the world was definitely cause for concern, but Kitt herself seemed nice and down-to-earth, albeit somewhat understandably frayed around the edges. Arkony kept snatching glances at her, catching the blended features of his parents in her face, except he didn't look too often because now, Kitt was often walking along holding hands with Derna.

And unlike Kitt, Two Tongue Derna was *terrifying*.

Arkony had never met someone with their tongue split before, which had startled him immediately, and things only got worse from there. Had Derna not been so insistent on finding Kitt, Arkony was fairly sure she would have tried to fight the demon that had wrecked half the graveyard in its brawl with whatever in all the hells that Plainsong person had been.

More than that, though, to someone who'd been brought up surrounded by the invisible balances of etiquette and class, Derna was terrifying in that she so obviously gave not a single shit about any of it. 'Fear of consequences,' had been Marquin's answer when the young Arkony had asked him why people obeyed his parents even if they didn't agree with them. In Two Tongue Derna, Arkony caught a glimpse of what life might be like if *no one* had fear of consequences, and it was not a world in which he wanted to live.

'Have you ever been this way before?' Arkony asked Gra'al somewhat hesitantly, as they walked. They'd made a start out of Solmouth in the mid-morning, and the road was climbing with the sort of gentle but insistent incline that barely seemed noticeable in the moment, but which his calves were really starting to notice now they'd been going for a while.

'Nope,' Gra'al said cheerily. 'I'm from further north. In fact, this is the farthest from home I've ever been.' He took another step. 'Well, now *this* is. And now... you get the point, I suppose. You?'

'I'd been down to Solmouth before, and upriver as well,' Arkony said. 'And you know, to society parties, things like that—'

'Oh, I *do* know,' Gra'al said, completely deadpan. 'Very much the social butterfly, me. Well, more of a furry moth, I suppose. Sorry, you were saying.'

'...It's just, I've never been up into the hills,' Arkony said, keeping his voice low. The other three were a short way ahead of them, and he didn't want to be overheard admitting his doubts. 'Not these ones. There have been rumours of travellers going missing in the late summer. Like, now. I just wondered if you'd heard much about that.'

'Never paid much attention to it, to be honest,' Gra'al said. 'I've not been in Solmouth that long, but no one comes up this way much so far as I know. There's nothing up here except for a few small farms and then the timeless lands, I think, so I can't see why there'd be many travellers anyway.'

'That and long summer, and the parched ones,' Sulian said, dropping back a couple of steps.

'The what?' Arkony asked, his chagrin at being overheard rapidly overtaken by concern at what the Swallowmage had just said, neither of which sounded particularly promising when delivered from beneath her semi-permanent scowl.

'The parched ones,' Sulian repeated, matter-of-fact. 'It's some after-effect of chronomancy. We met one on the way to Derringsmoot. Horrible, dried-up creature. Nearly killed Falzine, and drank my magic like it was water.'

Arkony gaped at her. 'It did *what?*'

Gra'al squinted at the Swallowmage. 'Don't take this the wrong way…'

'*Don't* suggest that I was drunk at the time!'

'Wouldn't dream of it,' Gra'al replied, grinning the fanged grin of a gobel-kyn who had very little to fear from mages.

'How did you kill it?' Arkony asked, and the Swallowmage gave a snort of disdain.

'Kill it? Hah! We did no such thing. I'd passed out by this point, but that was when our, ah, *bald travelling companion* joined us, and he apparently scared it away.'

'Bald travelling companion?' Gra'al asked, raising a brow.

'You mean Plai—' Arkony began, but was cut off by Sulian's hiss of warning.

'Don't say his name.' The mage licked her lips nervously. 'I don't know who or what he was, but some names have power, and that's the one he gave us. I'd prefer to never run into him again, assuming he survived the demon.' She shook her head. 'Anyway, I should be able to sense once we get back into long summer. When we do, we'll need to only travel in the mornings, and in the evenings once the heat of the day breaks.'

'What?' Gra'al asked. 'I mean, speaking as someone covered in fur, I'm fine with not moving on a summer afternoon, but… why?'

'To avoid the parched ones, of course,' Sulian said, fixing the kyn with a glare. 'They come in the afternoon, when the shadows are long.' She accelerated again, stomping off ahead after Kitt and Derna.

Gra'al leant down to Arkony and lowered his voice. 'So there are strange dried-up monsters that nearly killed someone, that got driven off after she passed out?' He grunted. 'I'm not saying that she got drunk and imagined the whole thing, but…'

'We could check with Kitt,' Arkony suggested. 'Or Derna,' he added, with somewhat less enthusiasm.

'It'll be hard to speak to either of them without Sulian overhearing, and I'm certainly not going to interrupt them if they sneak off together, if you get my meaning,' the kyn said. 'And even I know better than to actively question a mage's version of events in front of them, immunity to magic or not.' He clapped Arkony on the back. 'I'm sure it'll be fine.'

THE FIRST DAY was, indeed, fine. They pushed on despite the heat, and the river of sweat that trickled down Arkony's back, and made it to a village called Oakscroft by nightfall. There was a somewhat ramshackle inn, which continued Arkony's run of not finding a comfortable bed since he'd left home, and further impressed upon him the need to find a way of making money. He'd managed to sell the clothes he'd been wearing at his birthday ball once they'd left Derringsmoot, but the proceeds of that weren't going to last forever.

Running away from his family had seemed like a very good idea in the moment, but the long selection of sweaty, increasingly uncomfortable moments since then were causing him to ponder things more carefully. He *was* the Grike heir, after all, unless his parents wanted the public embarrassment of disinheriting him, along with the risk of it coming out that they hadn't even noticed their own child being swapped beneath their noses.

'You really think we can fix the future?' he asked Kitt on the second day. They were pressing on in the hope of reaching the next village that they'd been directed to out of Oakscroft, but so far the track had led them to nothing but apparently endless tree trunks on either side, and the hot, stifling air of a woodland on a still summer's day.

'Honestly, I have no idea,' Kitt said, with a slightly uncomfortable laugh. 'I certainly hope so.' She cast a sideways glance at him. 'Are you hoping it'll get rid of that one you got given, if we manage it?'

'Well, I'm also interested in making sure the people who might want to kill me don't have a reason to any more,' Arkony admitted. 'Right now they're still going to think it's me they want, and the only way they wouldn't is if they realise it's actually *you*, which doesn't sound like a good idea either. If you fix the future instead of destroying it, hopefully they'll leave us both alone?'

'I still reckon we'll need to kill them at some point,' Derna said, from Kitt's other side. Kitt looked at her in exasperation, judging by what Arkony caught of her expression as she turned away from him, but Derna just shrugged. 'What? I know I suggest it a lot as a solution, but given how eager they were to kill *anyone* involved in their little scheme in Mereport, I'd be surprised if they were willing to let it go just like—'

'Shut up, Derna,' Sulian said sharply.

'I'm just saying—'

'I said, shut *up*,' the Swallowmage snapped, coming to a halt. 'Look.' She pointed at their shadows, which were stretching out across the path and disappearing into the undergrowth to the east.

'Fuck,' Derna said with feeling, drawing her sword. 'What time is it? I didn't even think it was past noon!'

'Should we go back?' Kitt asked. Sulian shook her head.

'We've been walking for hours already. Our best hope is that the next village is close, and we can reach it before...'

A rustling in the bushes made her tail off, and the entire party whirled around. Arkony really missed his sidesword, about which he was sure Derna would have had something uncomplimentary to say, but it would have soothed his nerves just a little. Unfortunately, one didn't really dance while wearing a blade, and he'd not had time to grab it from the house during their hurried exit.

The parched one stepped out onto the path. Arkony didn't need to ask anyone for clarity. Just looking at this hideous, sun-blasted thing was enough for him to know exactly what it was.

'Well, I'll be,' Gra'al muttered. He drew two long knives, paused for a second, handed one to Arkony without looking, then drew a third to replace it.

'Hold on,' Sulian said, planting Jandi in the dust of the path and raising one hand. 'I've got this.'

'Sulian…' Kitt said apprehensively, and Arkony remembered the Swallowmage talking about how the creature had 'drunk' her magic, but Sulian grunted and twitched her fingers in a very precise manner, and… Well, Arkony didn't quite know *what* emerged from her hand, except that it made the air look wobbly for a moment, and flew down the path to strike the parched one in the chest, which flew backwards into the long shadows of the undergrowth as though it had been struck by a runaway cart.

'Fool me once, arsehole,' Sulian said with a satisfied snort, leaning on her staff.

The woods around them erupted in shrieks.

Dry shrieks, desiccated shrieks: air expulsed through throats that should have been too dry to make a noise, but from which tortured sounds emerged nonetheless. Arkony froze, every instinct telling him to run away immediately countermanded by the fact his ears couldn't determine where away *was*.

Half a dozen new shapes lurched out from between the trees ahead of them, legs crooked, knuckles of oversized hands hanging low, jaws lolling open to expose tongues like baked leather. Parched *ones*, plural.

'Oh *hells* no,' Gra'al said.

'Run!' Kitt yelled.

Her shout cut the invisible strings of tension that had held them all in place. Arkony turned and ran, terrified but simultaneously grateful that no one had uttered brave words about standing their ground and fighting. Regardless of whatever adjustments the Swallowmage had made to her magic, the parched ones didn't look like things normal people could *fight*. They were the sort of things you ran from, or they killed you, which was why it made no sense when Gra'al suddenly slowed ahead of him.

'Follow me!' the kyn shouted, and plunged off the track on the side that sloped downwards towards, eventually, the Solwynd. Arkony hesitated for a moment, caught in an agony of indecision, then followed him. Running away was better than standing still, but it wasn't exactly a *plan*, and at least Gra'al sounded like he might have a purpose for what he was doing.

Arkony immediately questioned his decision as soon as his feet hit the slope. It was steep, the soil dry and dusty, and littered with dead leaves that had succumbed to the drought and fallen from the branches above, all of which added up to footing more treacherous than a dealer in a back-alley game of three-card pike. Any attempt to stop would see his feet come to a halt while the rest of him carried gamely on its way over and past them, and turn a barely controlled gallop into an utterly uncontrolled and neck-breaking tumble, so he prayed to any gods that might be listening and carried on running, although his prayers manifested themselves as:

'Ohgodsohgodsoh*god*sohgodsoh*gods*—'

A tree trunk loomed up in his path. Arkony took the split-second decision to aim for it instead of risking his precarious balance even further by trying to veer around it, and crashed into it arms first.

'*—argh!*'

The bark tore at the skin of his forearms, and the impact

knocked the wind from him, but it halted his momentum. He spun around to check back up the slope, and saw that the other three had followed Gra'al as well, each in their own fashion. As a diviner of the high moors, Kitt surely had plenty of experience fleeing from over uncertain footing from things trying to eat her, while Derna's swordswoman's balance presumably benefited her here too. Meanwhile, although Sulian was both older and less fit than anyone else in their party, the mage had the aid of her strange staff, which seemed to be lurching around to keep her upright while Sulian clung on grimly with both hands as she ran.

And behind them came the parched ones. They shambled crosswise on all fours, legs swinging out first and then arms following to take the next step, and they were moving *fast*, and they were still shrieking those horrible dry screams.

Arkony spun off the tree trunk and ran. Either he would get away, or he'd fall and break his neck, and hopefully be dead by the time the parched ones caught him. He aimed from tree to tree, grabbing onto a branch or colliding with a trunk for a moment, just enough to slow himself and keep his momentum from running away with him, before launching himself off again. He ran until his ankles felt like they'd been jolted apart and his knees felt like they were going to shatter and fly out of his legs if he took one more giant, flying step, and then he ran some more anyway, because what other option did he have, with the shrieks of his pursuers in his ears?

'Over here!' a voice shouted, just as the ground started to level out.

Arkony desperately steered himself to where Gra'al stood by a face of exposed rock near what had presumably once been a pool of water, but was now nothing more than a dry, cracked hollow.

'Come on, come on…' the kyn was muttering, banging along the rock with the pommel of one of his knives. Arkony staggered over to him on unsteady legs, his own borrowed knife still in his hand, but with barely enough breath left to raise his arm, let alone stab anything with it.

'What in the hells are you doing?' Derna shouted, as she and Kitt stumbled to an unsteady halt next to them.

'There!' Gra'al said, as something knocked hollow under his knife. He pressed something in his other hand to the rock face, then replaced it in one of his many belt pouches.

'I said—' Derna began, but stopped as the rock began to grind open on what had to surely be hidden kyn mechanisms.

'Inside!' Gra'al barked, ushering them past him. 'Sulian! Here!'

'I'm coming!' the Swallowmage panted. Arkony needed no further encouragement: he darted under the kyn's outstretched arm and through the opening into a cool tunnel of stone. He would have kept running, legs and lungs be damned, but the spread of light from the entrance didn't stretch very far, and beyond that was nothing but blackness. Kitt and Derna piled in behind him, then the staggering Sulian, and finally Gra'al himself. The kyn did something to the rock, and it started to grind shut again.

'That had better hold them!' Derna snapped. She had her sword up, clearly not trusting to the door's speed, its sturdiness, or both.

'It will,' Gra'al said, with a confidence that Arkony envied. He could hear the shrieks of the parched ones now, closing in, but the kyn stood, apparently unconcerned, in the doorway as the gap through which light poured got narrower and narrower. Sulian hauled herself upright and raised a hand, just as Arkony heard the rushing footsteps approaching them—

—and the door closed smoothly, leaving not a ray of light bleeding through from outside. Arkony jumped as something thumped on the rock, but the impact was faint and distant. It sounded twice more, then stopped.

'What,' Sulian managed between heavy breaths, 'is this?'

'Kyn tunnel,' Gra'al replied, his voice moving past Arkony

as he spoke. 'You have roads, we have tunnels. I saw the pool from the road on the way up, and thought there might be an entrance here.'

'You *thought* there *might* be an entrance here?' Derna echoed incredulously.

'We tend to put them next to bodies of standing water, and it seemed like a better plan than "run screaming",' Gra'al said mildly. Arkony heard a faint slithering noise, which he presumed was the kyn sheathing his knife, and became acutely aware that they were standing in the pitch dark with several drawn blades.

'Where does it go?' Kitt asked.

'No idea, but it's not out there, and that has to be better, right?' Gra'al said. 'I'm sure we'll find a route to Hobden Bridge somewhere: that's a kyn town, after all. I have an uncle there, although I've not seen him in a while. Follow me, and I'll look for a waymarker.' The very faintest padding noise indicated the kyn's feet receding.

'I don't suppose you have any lights in these places?' Arkony asked, somewhat tremulously. Gra'al footsteps stopped, and Arkony heard the kyn tut.

'Honestly, you people are never satisfied...'

FORTY-TWO

Kitt had never seen a gobel-kyn town before, and Hobden Bridge, Gra'al assured her when they got there, was as typical a specimen as any.

It turned out that he had been pulling their fur, as he put it: apparently no kyn travelled without at least one light source in one of their myriad of pouches, since although they needed far less to see by than humans or wellyn, navigating in pitch dark by touch and sound alone was, as Gra'al also put it, a pain in the arse. Kitt had hoped for one of the kyn's famous automated lanterns, but to her disappointment Gra'al had pulled out a single lightstone like anyone in Mereport might have used.

'Why didn't you mention there were tunnels going to Hobden Bridge?' Kitt had asked, but the kyn had just shrugged.

'Because there's no tunnel route direct from Solmouth, the geology's wrong. I know humans think we have tunnels that go everywhere, but honestly, compared to walking around on the surface, digging tunnels is a *lot* of work. It works best if you're expanding a pre-existing cave system. Also, I didn't know those *things* were real, and humans don't tend to like long journeys in the dark, so it didn't seem worth suggesting.'

He wasn't wrong about the dark. Kitt had thought the timeless lands were bad enough, but at least it was *outside*. The kyn tunnel was cool, and dry, and smooth enough underfoot to avoid tripping hazards without being so slick that getting your footing was difficult, but after a while, travelling through them felt like getting strangled by time. A notion started to creep into her head that they were too late, that the world had finally fallen apart while they'd dawdled, and now these tunnels didn't connect to anything else, and they would just end up going round and round forever.

Then Gra'al had taken a short branching passage, fiddled with the rockface, and something ground open to reveal the cool, faint light of nighttime.

'If anyone has business to take care of, now's the time,' the kyn had said. 'I'll get hauled up in front of a council if I let a group of humans piss or shit in a tunnel. But stay close. If those things are only around when the sun's up then we should be fine, but better safe than sorry.'

And so they'd progressed, over a timescale of which Kitt couldn't be sure but which involved two sleeps on the tunnel floor where she cuddled deliciously close to Derna but didn't dare do anything more than a soft goodnight kiss, given their surroundings reflected and magnified any sound. Finally, their route intersected with a larger tunnel with lanterns interspersed along the ceiling – not as frequently as Kitt would have liked, but it was better than the constantly bobbing light from the stone in Gra'al's hand. The lanterns seemed to indicate they were approaching a settlement of some sort, and before long the rock walls around them opened up and out to reveal the kyn town of Hobden Bridge.

'You know,' Derna said quietly, 'for a species that doesn't need much light, they use it well.'

Hobden Bridge was certainly not bright, but for an enlarged cave system, it was almost ethereal. Crystals reflected, refracted, and dispersed light everywhere, creating a gloomy, glittering world that cast many faint shadows from all angles. In amongst this were terraces of dwelling-fronts, with doors just like you'd find in a human town, and even windows to let in what light there was.

There were shops, too. Kitt could hear the clang of a smith's hammer at work, and smell odours that were nearly but not quite food-like, traditional gobel-kyn sustenance mainly coming as it did from cultures of subterranean fungus mixed with whatever could easily be hunted or gathered within easy reach of a tunnel entrance. That was one reason why kyn liked living near humans, who were much better sources of things like meat, cheese, and bread, all of which kyn tended to appreciate; in return, humans found their subterranean neighbours useful for their ability to bring up water from deep underground. Kitt saw a communal pump, and noted the pipes running up the cavern wall to disappear into the ceiling, presumably to supply the Hobden's Bridge above ground.

There were a few kyn moving here and there about their business, most of whom gave their party an appraising once-over, but said nothing. There were also a few humans – Kitt remembered the barkeep talking about those who'd decided that living with the kyn was better than risking the parched ones, and she couldn't say she blamed them – who were rather pale, those of them whose skin lent itself to such things, but otherwise seemed hale and healthy.

'No wellyn,' Kitt commented, as they passed through. Hobden Bridge's undertown was considerably larger than the human village above, and it would be unusual for there to be no wellyn at all in a human settlement of a similar scale.

'Yeah, it turns out that creatures that can fly tend to be quite claustrophobic, as a rule,' Gra'al said, running the pads of his fingers over what Kitt presumed was a waymarker in the kyn's touch-script, and taking the lane – or tunnel – down which it appeared to direct him. 'Can't blame them, you wouldn't get me up into one of their tree cities easily.' He shuddered, sending ripples across his fur. 'Anyway, this way.'

Unlike the other tunnel entrances and exits they'd encountered, the link between the undertown and uppertown of Hobden Bridge was a far more official-looking affair, being a long stairwell with double doors at each end that were thick and sturdy, but left open. Kitt squinted at what felt like blinding light from ahead, after two or more days underground. The temperature was rising as well, and actually stepping out from the covered entrance into afternoon heat felt like someone had grabbed the sun from out of the sky to hold it in front of her face.

'Ugh,' Gra'al muttered, visibly wilting. 'I haven't missed this.'

In fact, nothing seemed to have changed around Hobden Bridge's uppertown; despite the ongoing drought, the fields looked no worse than before, although they certainly looked no better. It was as though the land was being kept permanently on the edge, a drawn-out death where time had no meaning except as the medium through which suffering occurred.

'You said this was a result of the… rift thing?' Arkony asked Kitt.

'That was Sulian's theory,' Kitt said. She nodded in the direction of the Swallowmage, who was leaning on her staff and squinting at the sky as though debating whether or not she could hex the sun. 'That, or chronomancers who tried to fix the timeless lands.'

She touched the chronocharms in her belt pouches, to reassure herself they were still there. She wasn't prepared to gamble she would have enough to get back across the moors to Mereport, but there would be no problem with getting back to the rift, and the Swordstar. After that…

Well, after that she just had to pull a god's weapon out from the sky and hope that fixed everything. Simple. Not necessarily *likely*, perhaps, but simple.

'How are you feeling?' Derna asked quietly, squeezing Kitt's hand. She smiled. 'Ready to save the world?'

'No,' Kitt admitted quietly. 'Can you even feel ready for something like that? But I'll give it a shot.'

'You'll do great,' Derna said. She pointed at the Hanging Rock, which squatted just across the village square in the inviting manner of a sun-soaked inn with beer inside it. 'And then, we'll—'

'Hold up!' Sulian raised her hand and straightened.

'What is it?' Kitt asked, her hand going to her sword hilt, and praying to any god who might listen that whatever the Swallowmage had noticed wasn't a parched one. It was only just past noon, they were inside a town now, and although the air was hot, it didn't have the heavy, choking feel of when they'd encountered those nightmarish creatures.

'I'm not sure,' Sulian admitted. 'It felt like magic, but everything's so weird here anyway I can't be—'

A glittering bolt of scarlet energy arced out of the shadowed doorway of the Hanging Rock and splattered against the hasty half-dome of protective energy that the Swallowmage conjured in the split second before it reached them. Dribbles of sorcerous fire splashed off and fell to the ground, where they smouldered into nothingness.

'Nope, right the first time,' Sulian said tightly. 'Who in all the hells are *these* clowns?'

'Swallowmage!' a man shouted, emerging from the inn. He was just good-looking enough for it to be noticeable without being remarkable, and had dressed himself in a similar style, apart from the several noticeably golden rings that adorned his fingers. He had curtains of brown hair and a smug smile that would probably not have been half as wide had he not been flanked by a pair of what had to be mages, unless this wiry man and woman – siblings, Kitt presumed, from the similarity of their look – had found a fun and easy way to make the air shimmer around their hands. Behind these three came a small group of soberly dressed thugs, all armed.

And behind *them*…

'Donal?' Kitt gasped in shock, which was quickly replaced by blazing fury. '*Donal Klae!*'

'Donal, you'd best have a good reason for being in the same place as whoever this lot are!' Sulian shouted.

'If I can have everyone's attention, please?' the smug smiling man said, clearly irritated that the conversation had got away from him. 'Swallowmage, you are known to my employers and I, and we have no issue with you. Likewise with Two Tongue Derna, Queen of the Streets of Mereport. And…' He squinted. 'I'm afraid I don't know you there with the fur, sir, but that means you are similarly exempt from the current quarrel.'

'"With the fur"?' Gra'al repeated, and drew two of his most wicked-looking knives. 'Mate, you just *started* a quarrel.'

'I need two people, and two people only,' the smug man continued. 'Kitt Carver of Mereport, and Arkony Grike of Derringsmoot. The rest of you are of no interest to us and can go about your business. If you try to interfere with us conducting ours, however,' he continued, 'then you will receive no mercy from us.'

'Your pet magelings just tried to suckerpunch us!' Sulian shouted. The smug man shrugged.

'And no harm was done. The only sure way to avoid a fight would have been to take you all out before you knew we were here, so since that failed, I've decided to try reason. You can step aside, and this doesn't have to get messy.'

'Donal,' Kitt said, as realisation dawned. 'Are these… Is that the guy who tried to have us killed?' Donal's shrug was all the answer she needed. 'My expectations for you were low, but—'

'Can I stab him yet?' Derna demanded, drawing her sword.

'You're going to *destroy the world*, Kitt!' Donal shouted back. He spread his hands. 'I'm sorry, but what was I supposed to do? I found Carl and told him you'd probably try to get back to Mereport over the moors. I don't expect you to understand this, but it really is for the best!'

'No, you fool, it's not!' Derna yelled. 'She's not going to destroy the world, she's going to *save* it!'

'Yes!' Kitt said, latching on to this. 'Listen… Carl, was it? Yes, there was a destiny, but the wording was messed up. The soothsayer said I was going to destroy the *futures*, but what if that means that I'm actually destroying all the destinies, and healing the actual future?' She smiled, much as it galled her to do so with this man, and hoped her argument sounded more convincing to him than it did to her.

Apparently it did not, because Carl laughed.

'I know!'

Kitt blinked. 'Wait, what?'

'We know what the destiny means!' Carl called mockingly. 'The scrying showed us! Yes, heal the future, destroy the destinies, what a wonderful plan. *Except* that means that all the destinies currently in play, and all those that have been gathered, will become worthless! They will cease to exist!' He placed his hands on his chest. 'And the people I represent – very wealthy, very *successful* people – will be without the very things on which they spent so much money to ensure their continued prominence, and that of their children!'

Kitt stared at him. '*What?*'

'It's very simple,' Carl said with a sigh. 'If someone heals the future, then it's going to ruin *everything*. Great dynasties could tumble, religions may fail, the whole works. Naturally, they are not keen for this to happen. Hence, since it seems it *was* you that the destiny found, I have to kill you – and the young Grike as well, just to make sure.'

'You know the world is dying, right?' Sulian demanded. '*They* know the world is dying?'

Carl shrugged. 'Is it going to actually *die* within the next fifty years or so, though? Probably not. That's a risk they're willing to take. Besides,' he added, 'some religions actually think the end of the world is a good thing. So really, you see where I'm coming from here.'

'No,' Kitt said coldly. 'No, I do not.'

'Well, I can't say I'm surprised, but I am disappointed,' Carl said. 'Very well. If the rest of you won't step aside—'

'Excuse me!'

Kitt jumped, as a nondescript man in dark clothing rose up from behind a stone wall to their left. How had he got there? Was he one of the locals?

'Tommas?' Carl asked, clearly both surprised and angry. 'What are you *doing*? You whine all this time about me not letting you kill anyone, and then when I'm supposed to be distracting them so you can...' He waved one hand in Kitt's direction.

'I have a question,' said the man apparently called Tommas. 'You seem to be implying that if the Carver girl succeeds in whatever she's destined to do, then all destinies, including those active right now, will become void. That would include those which are generally regarded to be curses, is that correct?'

Kitt's eyes were drawn back towards Carl.

Who swallowed nervously.

'Well then,' Tommas said, drawing a throwing knife. 'You hadn't told me that.'

'I've had enough of this!' Carl snapped, in the tones of someone who was used to the world obeying his instructions, but who had just seen a glimpse of what it would be like if that didn't happen, and didn't like it one bit. 'Jerroll! Jerima! Take them down!'

The sibling mages stepped forward, but the Swallowmage shrugged out of her pack and spread her arms.

'Alright then, magelings,' she said, as her hair began to rise of its own accord. 'I don't believe we've been properly introduced. I'm Sulian, and this is my friend Jandi!'

She cast her knowood staff into the air, just in time for

it to spin of its own accord and deflect an incoming bolt of magical lightning. Then the Swallowmage yelled, and spread her arms, and the same wave of force that had knocked Derna off her feet outside Sulian's house back in Mereport swept out and flattened everyone in front of her.

The mages rolled back up to their feet almost immediately and linked hands. Whatever they did shunted aside Sulian's next attack, which veered off and flattened an outhouse, but Jandi cut through the loop of crackling light they cast at the Swallowmage before it could find its target. Tommas threw a knife, but Carl managed to duck out of the way behind one of his thugs, and the whole group of them began to push forward with knives and clubs held ready despite the exchange of magical energies going on around them.

Kitt knew their type. You saw them around the docks sometimes on ships that put in; hard-faced killers without much temper to speak of, but who looked at you with eyes permanently calculating whether it benefited them more for you to be alive or dead. She drew her sword, but Derna shoved her backwards.

'Kitt, get out of here!' Derna snapped, as Tommas vaulted over the wall behind which he'd been hiding with a long knife in each hand, and moved to intercept his former allies. 'Head for the rift, and take Arkony!'

Kitt opened her mouth to argue, but closed it again almost immediately. She felt bad about running away again, but fighting was not her strength, and Arkony looked terrified, so she grabbed him and headed for the town's northern edge as fast as she could. She caught a brief glimpse of an old man peering out of his front door to see what all the disturbance was, and rapidly thinking better of it.

'Stop her!' Carl shouted from behind her. 'Stop them both, damn it!'

Kitt grinned, looking back. Gra'al, Tommas, and Derna had moved to intercept the thugs; she saw Derna sway away from a club swing as though she'd always known it was coming, then press forward with a flurry of slashes that had her opponent desperately back-pedalling. Carl stood in front of the inn, fists clenched and visibly furious, but powerless.

Then he fumbled with something on his wrist and pulled it away. It glinted in the sunlight; a fine chain of some sort?

'*Plainsong!*' Carl yelled, and Kitt's blood went cold as a hooded figure emerged from the Hanging Rock. If Plainsong was back under the control of their enemies…

Carl pointed towards her. 'Kill them.'

Kitt's mind whirled. She couldn't fight Plainsong. She couldn't outrun Plainsong – not even over the half mile it would take her to reach the timeless lands. She certainly couldn't hide from him now he'd seen her.

'Kitt?' Arkony said, tugging on her arm. Oh yes, she should be running, pointless though that would be. The Swallowmage was busy with Carl's pet mages, and Kitt had no idea whether Sulian's magic would be of any use against Plainsong anyway. No one could help her. No one could stand against him.

Except maybe…

She bit her lip, but there was nothing for it. Plainsong was gliding forward now, deceptively fast. His black blades sliced out from his arms, opening his sleeves on their way, and she made her decision.

'This is a very bad idea,' she told Arkony, 'and I'm sorry.'

She ripped at her own wrist and pulled away the woven leather cords around which a single strand of her own hair was tied.

The air changed, almost instantly. The dry heat of Hobden Bridge's long summer was replaced with an oppressive malice, and in the middle of the street, a mere few yards in front of Carl and just behind Plainsong, a massive hand covered in whorled, grey skin burst upwards from the ground.

The demon shouldered its way into the light, somehow even more terrifying now than it had been at night, sniffing around with a snout that didn't exist. Plainsong stopped and half-turned, the cowl of his hood letting just enough light fall on his face for Kitt to glimpse the faintest, subdued hint of recognition and anger.

'Plainsong!' Carl shrieked, now in mortal terror for his own life. 'Kill it! *Kill it!*'

For a moment, Plainsong's mouth opened. Kitt saw his dark eyes fix on her and *felt* the truth he wanted to divulge: the demon was coming for her, and all he had to do was get out of the way and it would do their job for them. But the compulsions laid on him to obey were too strong, and he turned his back to her as the demon reared up, claws at the ready.

'YOU!' the demon snarled, the fire-laced vortex of its head somehow focusing on Plainsong. Well, maybe it wouldn't have come straight for her after all.

'Can we run now?' Arkony asked desperately, as the two beings that sought Kitt's blood charged at each other.

'Yes!' Kitt said, suiting actions to words. She had no idea how much time her ruse would buy her.

She just had to hope it would be enough.

FORTY-THREE

'PUT THIS ON!' Kitt said, fumbling in her pouch as they approached the edge of the last field, somewhere beyond which lay the border into the timeless lands. Her fingers closed around a spare chronocharm – her only spare, now – and she passed it to Arkony. 'Keep it around your neck, or you'll become trapped in time.'

'Can they follow us in there?' Arkony gasped breathlessly, looking back at Hobden Bridge as a mighty roar rang out. A cloud of dust flew up, and part of a roof came down.

'I don't know,' Kitt admitted, her chest tight with fear. Humans couldn't, not without chronocharms that were only readily available in Mereport, and Donal probably had a couple of spares at most. Plainsong and the demon, though, were another matter entirely. Kitt had no idea if they would be bound by the same restrictions, and she wasn't prepared to chance it.

'Wasn't the plan to not let the demon know where you were until we knew we could get the Swordstar?' Arkony asked, as they clambered awkwardly over the dry stone wall of the final field.

'The plan was also not to get butchered before we even

reached it!' Kitt retorted. 'Trust me, this is actually the better option. You're wearing the chronocharm?' Arkony patted his shirt, and Kitt nodded. 'Okay, we should be crossing over any moment. The main thing to do is not freak out.'

She took three more steps, and then the world changed.

Gone was the bright sunshine, the heat of summer, and the distant – although not distant enough – sounds of fighting, magical battle, and Plainsong and the demon tearing chunks out of each other and the town. In their place was the pre-dawn darkness of the sky, and the endless silence of the high moors.

'Wow,' Arkony said, appearing at Kitt's side and gaping in wonder. 'It's… beautiful.'

'Trust me, it gets old fast,' Kitt told him. She pulled her moonstruck iron divining rods out. 'We haven't gone in where we came out last time, so I just need to get a fix…'

'A fix on what?'

'The rift,' Kitt said, trying not to let him put her off. 'Well, more accurately, all the destinies that have collected around– Oh, *there* we go!' She felt the pull in her bones, it was so strong; her moonstrikers swivelled so fast and so hard that she would have risked friction burns if she'd been gripping them tightly. 'This way!'

She didn't even need to keep the rods out. Now she was tuned into it, the pull of the destinies was strong enough that she could follow it like a hound on a trail, and she did just that. It was almost like magnetism; a couple of times she had to make herself take the easier but longer route around a ridge of land, rather than scrambling over rocks on her hands and knees.

'What's that light?' Arkony asked from behind her. He'd kept up with her pace over the rough ground, but now it sounded like he was starting to wonder whether that had been a good idea after all.

'That's the rift,' Kitt said. Her stomach was clenching as

the reality of what she was about to attempt began to worm its way through her body. She was going to try to draw the Swordstar; the weapon that had wounded the future, and had sent the world into a slow, drawn-out death spiral. What was more, this hadn't gone according to plan. She couldn't take her time, couldn't work herself up to it, couldn't think better of it at the last moment.

There was a demon on her trail now, and unless she laid her hands on a weapon that could kill it then it was going to kill her. Unless, of course, it was somehow killed by Plainsong, in which case *he* was going to kill her.

'No pressure, then,' Kitt muttered, rounding the last outcrop and bringing the rift into sight.

It was still ethereally beautiful, still so strange, and still so very *wrong*. The sky was not supposed to have a rent cut through it, even a sky as still and unnaturally never-changing as this one. It was as though someone had carved the likeness of giant faces into a great mountainside: intimidatingly impressive, and breathtaking in its own way, but very definitely not supposed to be there.

'Oh my,' Arkony managed. 'That's… that's it?'

'You were expecting something bigger?' Kitt asked, sliding down a small scree slope and starting through the heather. 'Careful now, it's easy to twist your ankle up here.'

A bellow split the air.

'**Kitt Carver!**'

'Okay, fuck careful,' Kitt squeaked, and lurched forward with Arkony panting alongside her. The demon was here! It was here, in the timeless lands! It wasn't as though she could have hidden up here for long before becoming a frozen statue, but maybe that would have been better than whatever torments the demon had in store for her.

Despite the vague logic of Derna's plan, and Kitt's hopeful reassessment of her destiny, deep down Kitt was still terrified of this moment. Why would she not be? She, a regular human with nothing going for her other than a small amount of very specific magic, a destiny of somewhat dubious provenance, and a relatively resilient personality, was going to try to touch, draw, and indeed wield the weapon of a god. That was ludicrous. It was nonsensical. It was also the only thing that gave her even the remotest chance of survival.

Saving the world could wait. Right now, Kitt just needed the Swordstar.

'Please work, please work, please work,' she muttered desperately as she stumbled to a halt next to the rift. She tried to block out everything else: the strange light, the thumping, clawing sounds of the demon racing over the high moors towards her, the trepidation over what pulling the Swordstar out might mean, and the bone-wrenching fear of what *not* pulling it out would mean. When every choice was bad, you picked the one that looked the least worst, and you went for it.

The Swordstar was right there, chest height above the ground, a blazing ball of light. Kitt hesitated, despite the rapidly approaching noise of the demon. How was she even supposed to hold it? What if she touched it and just… disintegrated?

Well, that might still be preferable to the demon's claws.

She reached out before she could completely lose her nerve, and grabbed at the light. For a moment her hand passed through glowing nothingness, and her heart sank. Then her fingers snagged on something within; a grip, a pommel. She grabbed it, and she began to burn.

Not literally, or at least not visibly. No flames ran up her arm, but her blood felt like it was boiling in her veins. Kitt screamed, grabbed her right wrist with her left hand, and pulled as hard as she could. Even this pain would be worth it, so long as she could just get the damned… thing… free…

But it wouldn't budge. And now the demon was here, lumbering over the outcropping that Kitt had skirted, its claws biting into the rock and its invisible mouth almost singing her name in a voice like rubble.

'KITT CARVER,' the demon growled with satisfaction, as though naming its favourite dessert. 'KITT CARVER…'

Kitt screamed, and let go of the Swordstar. The pain fled immediately, and her hands were unburned, but the weapon simply would not come loose. She had nothing except the short sword at her side, and she might as well have faced an avalanche with a teaspoon for all the good that was going to do her.

'Arkony,' she whispered. 'Run. It doesn't want you.' She swallowed. 'And if you see my parents, tell them I'm sorry.' She glanced sideways at the rift. It was beautiful, after all. Would whatever lay beyond be worse than what was approaching, all towering menace and savage claws?

'No,' Arkony said.

Kitt blinked at him, wondering how he'd heard her thoughts and on what grounds he had an opinion, but immediately realised that he was replying to her words instead.

'Don't be a fool!' she hissed. The demon was nearly on them now, but it wasn't hurrying. It knew she had nowhere to run.

'I said I wanted to make my own destiny,' Arkony said, his lip and voice both trembling, but his body remaining upright nonetheless. 'And I will.'

He grabbed the Swordstar.

He screamed too, of course. Kitt wrapped her arms around him, trying to pull him away from it, trying to get him moving with a shove in the hope that once his legs started carrying him away from the demon then common sense would keep him moving.

'Come on, you bloody fool!' she yelled into his shoulder blades. 'You've got your whole future ahead of you!'

Arkony came backwards, still screaming.

And the Swordstar came with him.

Kitt twisted aside desperately as they both stumbled and fell, and the blazing weapon thudded down into the heather, casting strange lights and shadows as it half-disappeared between the stems. The demon, now a mere twenty yards or so away, stopped in its tracks.

'WHAT…?' it growled, sounding unsure for the first time. It didn't sound scared, just… puzzled. As though it had no idea how what it had just witnessed could have occurred. Then it chuckled, a sound like hail on a slate roof, and loped forwards before rearing up with a snarl, one taloned hand sweeping down to obliterate Kitt where she lay.

Kitt scrambled to her knees, grabbed the Swordstar, and swung it.

It was nearly weightless. The raging pain of holding it almost threw her aim off, but the demon's hand was not much smaller than her, and the arm was as thick as a young tree, so accuracy was not hugely important. The Swordstar's edge, wherever *that* was inside the blazing ball of light, met the demon's wrist.

And sheared right through it.

The demon howled in pain and rage, whipping its newly truncated arm back with a steaming, glowing stump where its hand had been a moment before; a hand that now lay writhing in the heather, its clawed fingers still twitching in some sort of infernal reflex. Kitt had no time to think further about it. She gripped the Swordstar, screamed through the pain that wracked her body, and charged.

The demon didn't seem to know what to do. Even its battles with Plainsong had not seen it mutilated in such a way. It began to swat at her with its remaining hand, thought better of it at the last moment, then tried to turn to flee.

It was too slow. Kitt rammed the Swordstar into its side, piercing its skin and driving the weapon deep into its core.

The demon screamed, a sound like a fault opening in the world's crust, and the vortex of its head span faster and faster. It knocked Kitt away with its hand, and she felt one of her ribs crack at even that casual contact, but the pain was almost a blessed relief compared to holding the Swordstar. The demon clawed at the weapon's hilt, the tiny piece of brightness that still protruded from its body, but pulled its hand away as its fingers began to blacken like burned parchment. Darkness was spreading over its body from the wound now, the progress clearly visible in the fierce light thrown out by the Swordstar. No matter how it thrashed, its flesh continued to char.

Kitt got up to her knees and flipped it a middle finger. The demon howled once more, in rage as well as pain, and then it collapsed. Within a few moments its entire body began to crumble into ash, like the powdery logs at the base of a long burned-out fire.

'Kitt!' Arkony shouted. 'Kitt, you did it! You did it!'

Kitt screamed in pain as he slammed into her with a hug. 'Arrgh! Get off, get off!'

'Sorry!'

'That's okay,' Kitt said through a grimace, gingerly pushing herself up again. Up until a few weeks ago she would have said that the pain in her rib felt like she was being stabbed, but having had a far more personal experience of that since then, she was aware of the inaccuracy. It was painful enough, but overall she would take the trade-off. 'Besides, I didn't do it. *You* did it.'

'You killed the demon!' Arkony said. He looked over in awe at where the Swordstar still stood proud within whatever passed for a corpse when demons were concerned. 'That's… amazing.'

'I honestly could have happily gone my whole life without doing that,' Kitt admitted. 'But under the circumstances…'

'What about the future?' Arkony asked, looking around as though expecting to see the permanent night of the timeless lands dissolving. 'Did it work? Did you heal it?'

'I don't know,' Kitt admitted. 'Maybe it takes some time to have an effect.' She swallowed. 'Or, I guess, maybe it doesn't work like that after all.'

'*Miss Carver!*'

'Oh fuck, what now?' Kitt groaned, but she already knew. She knew that voice. And sure enough, rounding the rocky outcrop and dragging a familiar, curly-haired figure by the neck, came the last being she wanted to see.

Plainsong.

FORTY-FOUR

'STAY BEHIND ME,' Kitt said to Arkony, taking a couple of steps towards the demon's body. 'He *does* want you as well.' She raised her voice, grimacing at the flash of pain from her rib. 'Alright, you bastard! You can see what I've done to the demon! Put Derna down, and no one has to get hurt!'

'Unfortunately, I cannot do that!' Plainsong replied. He had Derna's neck trapped in the crook of his left elbow and was dragging her along in front of him. He was not much larger than her, no bigger than an average man, but the difference in strength was obvious, and Kitt's breath caught at the notion that a single twist could break her girlfriend's neck. 'Your friend is a dangerous fighter. It's a good thing she didn't have the Swordstar. Had she possessed a weapon that could have hurt me, I might not be here now! You can appreciate that I don't want her to get her hands on it.'

'So why bring her at all?' Kitt demanded desperately. She flexed her fingers, her entire body clenching up at the thought of subjecting herself to the Swordstar's pain again, but unwilling to face Plainsong down without a weapon. Especially not one he had just admitted could hurt him.

'She was already on her way to you,' Plainsong said, still

approaching at a steady pace, albeit with a slight limp. The demon hadn't killed him before it came hunting Kitt, but it had torn rents into his flesh. 'She saw the demon leave, and broke away from the fight to come and assist you. I just overtook her, and thought she might be useful. You have some tenderness towards her, do you not?'

Kitt eyed him. 'What business is that of yours?'

That was too close. She'd seen how quickly he could move: she grabbed the Swordstar and staggered backwards, holding it up in front of her as her entire body reignited. She was dimly aware of Arkony hovering behind her, but most of her focus was on Plainsong.

Plainsong, and Derna, still struggling uselessly against his grip even though he could have killed her with a simple twist of his arm. Kitt swallowed, and tried to put the image out of her mind. Focus on anything rather than that, even on the pain wracking her body.

'You are aware by now that the compulsions on me have been renewed,' Plainsong said, speaking of his own slavery as calmly as someone might discuss the weather. 'I cannot act in any way that is contrary to the wishes of my masters.' A brief flicker crossed his face, visible only thanks to the Swordstar's light, at that final word, but then it was gone.

'And your masters want you to kill us?' Kitt said, through gritted teeth.

'Indeed.' Plainsong nodded. 'I know what that weapon can do. Were I to fall to it, my masters' wishes would be left unfulfilled, and so I cannot risk it. Hence I have Derna, to ensure your compliance.'

'Kitt!' Derna choked out. 'Don't listen to this arsehole! You killed a demon, you can take him!'

Plainsong flexed his right wrist, and the familiar blade slid out of his flesh to pivot around into his hand again. He took another step closer. 'If you do then she will die before you get near me, and then I will almost certainly kill you in any case, wounded though I am. Throw the Swordstar away from yourself and the rift, Kitt Carver, or keep holding it long enough for it to kill you before you even get around to making a decision. Or, if you must, attack me, and then all three of you will die, instead of just two. My masters can accept no other outcome.'

Kitt swallowed. She could no longer suppress a grimace. Every nerve of her body was being consumed by fire, just like the demon had been. She had no doubt Plainsong was telling the truth. This was the weapon of a god; even holding it would be fatal for a human like her. Discarding it would mean her and Arkony's death when Plainsong attacked, but Derna would live. Plainsong had no reason to kill her.

'Take! The swing!' Derna shouted as best she could, struggling and kicking. Her eyes met Kitt's. 'For fuck's sake, do it! We've ridden our luck this far!'

Two Tongue Derna, Queen of the Streets. Champion duellist of Mereport, who'd taken her life into her hands more times than Kitt could count. If anyone knew when they were ready to face death, it was Derna.

'If we go,' Derna ground out, 'we go together. Right?'

Kitt's vision began to blur with tears. They burned as well.

'Right,' she whispered. She took a deep breath.

'Wait!' Arkony shouted, placing himself in front of her.

'Arkony, what the—'

'Give us the options again!' Arkony said, pointing at Plainsong. 'Quickly!'

'She throws the sword away from herself and the rift, and I kill you both; she holds onto it long enough for it to kill her, and then I kill you as well; or she attacks me, and I kill all three of you,' Plainsong said calmly. Calmly, but… something else? Kitt tried to blink away the tears. Was that…

…eagerness?

'And your masters will accept no other outcome?' Arkony demanded.

'My masters will accept no other outcome,' Plainsong agreed.

Arkony nodded, then turned to look at Kitt. She met his eyes in pained incomprehension for a moment.

Then she understood. Plainsong was bound by the enchantments, so he couldn't tell them anything that went against his hated masters' wishes, but he could omit things. And just because Plainsong's masters wouldn't accept any other outcome, that didn't mean there were none to be had.

Plainsong realised she'd understood in the moment it happened, and the enchantments took over. His face twisted by warring emotions, he shoved Derna away and snapped out his other blade, then surged forward, faster than any human could move.

Kitt swung the Swordstar. Too soon for the point of it to connect with Plainsong, despite the speed of his movement. However, at the far reach of the swing, she let go.

Into the rift.

The Swordstar sailed through the rippling curtain of light. There was a flash, as bright as the death of a sun, and in its aftermath there came

sunlight

and breeze

and sound.

Not just the sound of Kitt's pained wheezes. Not just the sound of Arkony's breathing, or the groan of Derna as she hit the ground, or the roar emerging from Plainsong's throat as he came for her with both knives aimed at her throat—

And stopped, the points of his blades just grazing her skin. Kitt stumbled backwards and sat down, crying out as her cracked rib jarred again, but Plainsong simply held his position, arms extended and trembling as though fighting himself.

Then he relaxed, and the blades slid back into his arms, and he breathed.

'Yes?' Arkony looked around in delight. 'Yes!' He spread his arms and laughed up at the newly blue sky. 'Take that, logic tutors! Who can't reason his way out of a paper bag *now*, you bastards!?'

'Kitt!'

Derna came scrambling across the heather – the heather that was now lit by the sun, and from beneath which the destinies had all disappeared – relief and joy warring on her face.

'Careful,' Plainsong said, stepping away. 'She is hurt. It was not my doing,' he added, as Derna whirled towards him. 'I suspect the demon.'

'You're not compelled any longer?' Kitt asked him, rising unsteadily back to her feet.

'No,' Plainsong said, and he smiled, showing a full set of even teeth. 'You have healed the world, Kitt Carver. Destinies have dissolved, and many things that have been in place for centuries have changed.' He inhaled, as though drawing the world into his lungs. 'I am glad you were able to understand me.'

'Understand what?' Derna asked suspiciously.

'Even within compulsion, certain choices can be made,' Plainsong said. 'I could not tell Kitt how to heal the world, and therefore break the compulsion placed upon me. But I *could* tell her what my masters desired, in the form of making demands of her, and hope she would pick up on what I did not say: the one course of action open to her that my masters could not accept.'

'So are you… back to normal, now?' Kitt asked tentatively.

'Yes,' Plainsong said. He began to pull away what remained of his robe, to reveal skin upon which the chain tattoos were dissolving. He stretched, and twisted his neck to look down at his back. 'Ah, even these have gone. Marvellous.'

And then mighty wings of obsidian erupted from his skin.

Kitt screamed, as one of the razor-edged fans of feathers nearly took her nose off. Plainsong turned, a ferocious joy written on his face.

'I fear that "normal" for me is not what you envisaged, Kitt Carver,' he said, and now he was human only in form. His body, his skin, his eyes; they could all pass individually, but there was no disguising the energy that ran within him. 'I was once a man, but as I said, I was young, and I was foolish, and I was curious, and I made bargains the nature of which I did not properly understand.'

'So what are you?' Kitt managed.

'You recall I told you that Altrinchor sent his three heralds to delay the emissaries of the other gods?'

Kitt nodded speechlessly. Plainsong leant closer to her, his lip curling back.

'He did not tell us the nature of his plan, or we would not have obeyed him. Now my former master has been humbled and reduced, and I have spent centuries in the service of insects who enslaved me. No more masters for me, I think. I will find Altrinchor, or whatever shell is left of him, and I will kill him.

'But first,' he continued, snapping his blades out once more, 'there are others more deserving of my attentions. Or at least... closer.'

He leaped upwards, and his mighty pinions spread and beat, and he soared away northwards. Back towards Hobden Bridge.

'Did... did we just release a murderous angel on the world?' Arkony asked.

Kitt grimaced. 'Come on. We've got to get back to Sulian and Gra'al.'

THEY COULDN'T GET there ahead of Plainsong, of course. They saw the faint speck of him descend, and once they'd got past the last rise of the ground before the land sloped down into the fields of Hobden Bridge, they could see the town itself.

'This is so weird,' Kitt said as she struggled on, trying to ignore the pain in her side. 'That should all be night.'

'Only a diviner would think it's weird to be able to see out of the high moors,' Derna said beside her, but there was no life in her humour. They were still some way short of the first fields when a tiny shape rose into the air once more and, wings beating like the wrath of the sky itself, headed east. They crouched in place until he was out of sight, unwilling to risk attracting his attention. Then they pressed on at the best pace Kitt could manage, sweating under the sun. It was some way past noon now, but whatever might have happened to the twisted time of long summer, they were still into the hottest part of a summer's afternoon, and a cracked rib was not a good travelling companion.

'Who's that?' Arkony said, pointing. 'Coming this way?'

Kitt squinted, wiping moisture from her forehead before it dripped into her eyes.

'Are there two of them?'

'Yes,' Derna said, a smile breaking out on her face. 'And one has a floating staff.'

They moved slower after that, and it was not too long before the figures coming up from the town became recognisable as one gobel-kyn, somewhat bedraggled but still carrying an impressive amount of knives, and one human, puffing and panting but doggedly keeping up. Kitt finally gave up, and sat down on the ground.

'This is so no one hugs me!' she called out, as Gra'al and the Swallowmage approached. 'I think I've got a cracked rib!'

'You did it!' Sulian shouted back, and it was not a question. She looked exhausted but delighted, practically radiant. 'Kitt, they're gone! The destinies, the voices; they're all gone!' She whooped with delight and twirled in an exhausted circle. 'I've not been alone in my own head since I was a kid! Is this what you lot feel like *all the time?*'

'Are you hurt?' Derna asked.

Gra'al pointed to his shoulder. 'Ow.' He pointed to his thigh. 'Ow.' He pointed to his head. 'Ow.' He grinned. 'But

I'll live. Kyn hide is tougher than human hide, plus the fur helps, so it wasn't the knives that were the issue so much as the clubs. I'm going to be sleeping gingerly for a week or two.'

'What happened?' Kitt asked. Sulian shrugged.

'Me and the mages were having it out, and they were good, but I fight dirty. I managed to stun a couple of the thugs, and Gra'al and that other guy – Tommas – were taking care of the rest. Then suddenly I just… felt it. It was a like a fog lifting. It affected Tommas, too: he shouted something about becoming a baker, put another one down with a throwing knife, and ran. And then *he* arrived.'

'Killed them all,' Gra'al said, matter-of-factly. 'It wasn't pretty, but it was fairly quick. Although he took his time a little with Carl.'

Kitt bit her lip. 'Donal?' He was an absolute arse, but he probably hadn't deserved *that*.

Sulian shook her head. 'I saw him run as soon as the demon appeared, and he didn't come back. He's probably fine other than being, you know, him. But what happened up *there?*' she added, pointing towards the moors. 'I know it worked, I can feel that much, even the time here isn't twisted up any more, but what *happened?* Did you just,' she made a tugging motion. 'You know, pull the Swordstar out?'

'Second question,' Gra'al added, raising a finger. 'What happened to the demon?'

'Arkony pulled the Swordstar out,' Kitt said, slapping him companionably on the thigh from her seat on the ground. 'I killed the demon with it, and—'

'And you are *so* cool for that, by the way,' Derna cut in, grinning widely. 'If I didn't have a crush on you before, I definitely would have now. I also might hate you a bit because I'm never going to be that cool, but mainly I'm just in awe.'

'And then she threw the Swordstar into the rift,' Arkony said. 'That's what healed the future.'

'And removed all the compulsions on Plainsong,' Kitt said.

'It turns out that he was actually a herald of Altrinchor, and he is *majorly* pissed off about this whole thing. I think he's got a bunch of anger to work out. Thankfully, that doesn't seem to include us.'

'He was a *what?*' Sulian repeated incredulously. She stared up at the sky. 'I was wondering about the wings, but still. That's pretty amazing. And, um, terrifying.'

'*But*,' Kitt said, determined not to let the moment slip away, 'we did it! We healed the world! We fixed the rift, we made the future whole again!' She let loose a disbelieving laugh, then winced as her side complained. 'Ow! But seriously, can you believe it? *Us?*'

'No,' Derna said slowly. 'No, I cannot. And I think it's best we don't go shouting about it, because there are going to be a *lot* of people who will be very angry about what we've just done.'

Kitt bit her lip. 'The entire destinies trade in Mereport, for one.'

'Probably most of the toffs in Highmarket and Temple Cross, too,' Derna added. 'And the churches.'

'Quite a few mages,' Sulian agreed.

'Pretty much everyone my parents know,' Arkony put in. 'And I don't know if we'll get blamed for what happened in Derringsmoot, but I don't want to chance it.'

'I don't think Hobden Bridge will be pleased with us for what happened to their town, either, and then there's everyone that Carl guy was working for,' Gra'al finished. 'Well. That is a lot of new enemies to make in one day. In fact, I'm confident that's a personal record.'

They stood – or in Kitt's case, sat – in silence for a few moments.

'Did we *tell* anyone what we were trying to do?' Kitt asked.

'Don't think so,' said Derna.

Arkony shook his head. 'Nope.'

'I suppose we might have been overheard when we were

having breakfast in Solmouth,' Gra'al offered. 'We weren't exactly whispering.'

'And I guess anyone above ground in Hobden Bridge will have heard what Carl was shouting,' the Swallowmage said. 'So we probably have to count them as possibilities.' She grimaced. 'More than I'd like, but fewer than it could be. It's a good thing we're not particularly distinctive.'

'You mean apart from the fact that Carl shouted everyone's names apart from his?' Derna pointed out, looking at Gra'al.

The kyn grimaced, showing his fangs. 'Ooh. Yeah. That's rough.'

'Right, so Hobden Bridge probably don't want us,' Arkony said, ticking off on his fingers. 'Solmouth is a bit iffy since people *might* have overheard us, and also Gra'al has gambling debts there anyway. There's no way I'm going back to Derringsmoot right now.'

As one, they turned to look at the moors.

'I mean, we don't know of anyone who wants us dead in Mereport,' Kitt said. 'Not that *knows* they want us dead, anyway.'

'Yet,' Derna added, but she was smiling.

'I've always wanted to see it,' Arkony said. 'Although I guess I have, I was just… too young to remember.'

'And all my stuff's there,' the Swallowmage grunted. She sighed. 'Well, we've probably got enough food and water, especially since Gra'al was good enough to grab your packs.'

'I will not be making a habit of carrying everything,' the kyn said firmly.

'What about the slydewasps?' Kitt asked. Sulian flapped her hand.

'Don't worry, they'll have gone. They can't exist in normal time.'

'Are you sure?'

'Probably.' The Swallowmage stretched out her hand, and Jandi thudded into it with a meaty smack. 'Let's find out.'

Kitt prised herself up off the ground, and gingerly accepted her pack from Gra'al. 'Ow. Ow.'

'You want healing?' Sulian asked.

'No thanks,' Kitt said quickly. 'Not after last time. I think I'll just have to gut this one out.'

Derna kissed her on the cheek, and smiled. 'Well done for saving the world, Kitt.'

Kitt grinned back at her, then kissed her on the lips in reply. 'Thanks. I couldn't have done it without you.' She took a deep breath. 'Okay. Let's find out what a saved world looks like.'

And so they set off into the afternoon sun, four humans and a kyn: far from the largest force in the world, or the smartest, or the deadliest, or even the most close-knit. Prone to squabbling, getting sidetracked, obsessing over minor details and, in at least one case, drinking more than was strictly good for them. Individually, largely unremarkable, or at least no more than mildly remarkable, and yet through chance, luck, sheer bloody-mindedness, or even – whisper it – fate, capable of accomplishing something amazing.

'You know, I have an uncle in Mereport…'

AUTHOR'S NOTE

Some readers may be asking 'What happened to the slydewasps?', but this is not the correct question. The correct question is 'How can we dismantle unjust systems that concentrate resources into the hands of those who already have them, which thereby limits the opportunities of those who do not?'.

Nonetheless, for those who were wondering, the answer is: nothing happened to the slydewasps. They kept on doing slydewasp things, it's just that with time no longer so majorly damaged, it was not so easy for people to exist in the same place as them. However, I say 'easy' for a reason.

There has been much speculation as to why we have not been visited by time-travellers from the future. Theories range from it never being possible; to it becoming possible but if you try it then Jean-Claude Van Damme kills you;* to suggesting that we *have* been visited by time-travellers, but they have followed appropriate rules to ensure that we remained unaware of their true nature. In fact, none of these things are true. With the correct equipment, and a suitable understanding of the laws of the universe, it is entirely possible to slip between the seconds and travel through time.

The problem is what is waiting for you, striped and winged and eerily silent, when you do.

* If you live in a future where they've remade *Timecop* then a) insert appropriate actor name here, and b) I'm very sorry.

ACKNOWLEDGEMENTS

When the time comes to write acknowledgements I always then remember that I really should have been keeping track of these things as I went, since my brain has the retentive powers of a sieve made of spaghetti. However, I will do my best.

Firstly, Sir Terry Pratchett. I never met or communicated with him in any way, but the Bromeliad Trilogy was a firm favourite of mine as a child, and when I discovered the Discworld in my high school library I never looked back. *This Is Where The Future Bleeds* isn't a deliberate homage, but it turns out that when I just write what I feel like as opposed to trying to stay within specific genre boundaries, my brain veers into what I consider "Pratchett mode". I make no claim to be as good, but it's a fun way to write, and hopefully fun for others to read.

I must also thank George Sandison at Titan for seeing the potential in this book, and Elora Hartway for prodding it into its final form; Bahar Kutluk and the rest of the team for the stellar publicity work; Natasha MacKenzie for the absolutely stellar cover, because *dang*; and anyone else at Titan who has had any sort of input, influence, or improvement.

I must thank Stewart Hotston for information about swords and for feedback in general; Jane Torbeck for being the perennial rubber duck helping me untangle writing threads, with the advantage of (unlike most rubber ducks) also offering helpful advice; Luke Scull and Laura Dodd; all the regular convention crew, too many to name, for continuing to make the SFF community something I want to participate in; the Scriptorium Recaf Station for their tolerance and support, particularly of my adventures while un-agented; and Laura Bennett at the Liverpool Literary Agency, who ended that agent-less time and helped get *Future* over the finish line. And Katryn, without whose photography of Zathras *The Dubious Gecko* would likely have had a different name. To anyone else I should have included: my apologies, it's not personal, and I assure you I'll be very embarrassed when I remember.

Finally, my wife Janine, who in one sense had no direct impact on this book, but in another sense is key to it. The author of a book is (for better or for worse) the only person who can write it, and you can't spend over half your life with someone without it having a huge influence on who you are. So thank you, for so many things, but including this.

ABOUT THE AUTHOR

Mike Brooks is the author of The God-King Chronicles epic fantasy series (*The Black Coast, The Splinter King* and *The Godbreaker*); the Keiko series of grimy space-opera novels (*Dark Run, Dark Sky* and *Dark Deeds*); and various works for Games Workshop's Black Library imprint, including *Brutal Kunnin, Alpharius: Head of the Hydra*, and *The Lion: Son of the Forest*. He was born in Ipswich, Suffolk, and moved to Nottingham to go to university when he was eighteen, where he still lives with his wife, cats, and snakes. He worked in the homelessness sector for fifteen years before going full-time as an author, plays guitar and sings in a punk band, and DJs wherever anyone will tolerate him. He is queer, and partially deaf (no, that occurred naturally, and a long time before the punk band).

For more fantastic fiction, author events,
exclusive excerpts, competitions, limited editions and more

VISIT OUR WEBSITE
titanbooks.com

LIKE US ON FACEBOOK
facebook.com/titanbooks

FOLLOW US ON TWITTER AND INSTAGRAM
@TitanBooks

EMAIL US
readerfeedback@titanemail.com